The Scourge of the
KAISERBIRD

Translated from the original Afrikaans novel
"Die Keiservoël oor Namaland"

Koos Marais

ISBN: 978-0-994-69131-6

With thanks to the Cordis Trust
Cover photograph - Johan Grobbelaar
Page layout and type-setting: Janet von Kleist
Blog: https://kaiserbird.com

Published by Kwarts Publishers
Centurion, South Africa

www.kwartspublishers.co.za

Although many improbable events are embedded in this narrative, like skeletons buried in the Namib Desert, the irony is that they are all based on facts that are stranger than fiction.

ORIENTATION

BASED ON HISTORICAL FACTS

I n 1939 the greatest tragedy of the Twentieth Century, the Nazi Holocaust, took place, but the seeds for the genocide perpetrated at Auschwitz, Buchenwald, Dachau, and all the other death camps were sown thirty-three years earlier on the freezing rocks of a small island in the harbour of Lüderitz, then known as Lüderitzbucht, in the south of German South-West Africa, today Namibia.

The Namas of Namibia, descendants of the Khoi-Khoin, were the first inhabitants of the south of this arid land. Hendrik Witbooi, the legendary soldier and warrior, led the Nama soldiers – first under the German flag against the Hereros in the north, and then, following the Herero genocide on the Waterberg Mountain and in the Omaheke Desert, against the Germans.

In 1906, when the Namas were fighting the German Schutztruppe, the Luchtensteins, an immigrant family, arrived at Lüderitzbucht harbour. They departed by ox wagon to a new home two hundred miles into the interior. Ahead waited the hot, treacherous sands of the Namib Desert, the thirst, heat, cold, raging wind, wild animals and the enemy. A Nama commando led by Cornelius Fredericks, son-in-law of Hendrik Witbooi, captured them but Cornelius personally intervened to set them free again, only to fall victim himself to the German soldiers. A bond of friendship developed between the young Ernst Luchtenstein and the captive Nama captain, Cornelius Fredericks.

Thousands of Namas ended up as prisoners of war on Shark Island where cruel experiments and murders were committed at the behest of a doctor who shipped the body parts to the Kaiser Wilhelm Institute in Berlin.

Ernst started a new life, learnt about the culture of the Nama people and met the attractive orphan, Regina. The First World War separated them but he escaped from a prisoner-of-war train and hid in the Karas Mountains until fate intervened to bring them together and lead them to Namaland's greatest secret.

PROLOGUE

Many centuries ago the Khoi-Khoin, the first people, who were livestock farmers, and the Khoi-San, Bushman roaming hunters, migrated to the south, away from the water-rich interior of Africa in search of land and freedom from black domination. Many years later these Khoi-Khoin watched as three sailing ships unloaded a considerable number of white people on the beach of a bay beneath a flat-topped mountain that resembled a table. Some of these Khoi-Khoin farmers, the Namas, later fled north again, this time to escape the white domination that came with the sailing ships. They settled in the hinterland of Namaland, across the Gariep River.

The nineteenth century saw the arrival of German missionaries, the businessman Adolph Lüderitz, steamships laden with immigrants, Schutztruppe, and later, war in Namaland.

In 1906 the German scientist, Dr Eugen Fischer, sponsored by a Swiss pharmaceutical company, travelled to the then German South-West Africa to do research. He collected human research material, the body parts of Nama and Herero prisoners of war held on Shark Island in Lüderitzbucht (today Lüderitz). To this day the Kaiser Wilhelm Institute in Berlin still preserves skulls and other body parts. Dr Fischer found the Namas to be an "inferior race".

Seventeen years later a young corporal, Adolf Hitler, who was found guilty of high treason, read Dr Fischer's book, Principles of Human Heredity and Racial Hygiene, in the jail in Landsberg, Germany. This inspired him to write Mein Kampf. After his release from prison, he and Fischer met frequently. In 1938 Fischer published Racial Origin and the Racial History of the Hebrews. The following year Hitler appointed Dr Fischer to head up the Third Reich's racial hygiene programme at Auschwitz. He believed Fischer would find a solution to "the Jewish problem".

Part One of this book depicts, in alternate chapters, the trials of the immigrant Luchtenstein family and the history of the Nama nation, specifically the !Aman from Bethanien, between 1883 and 1906.

Contents

PART THREE

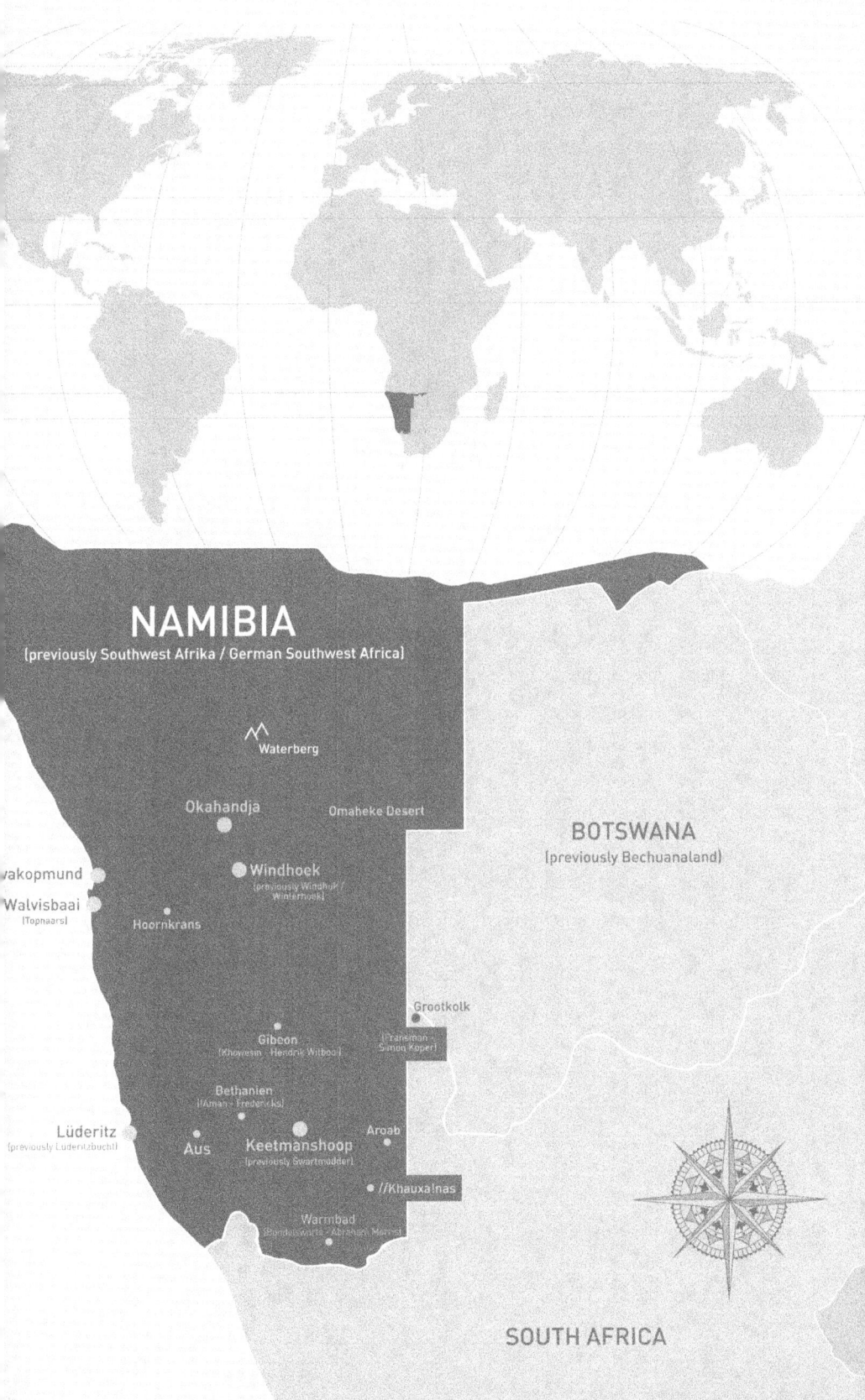

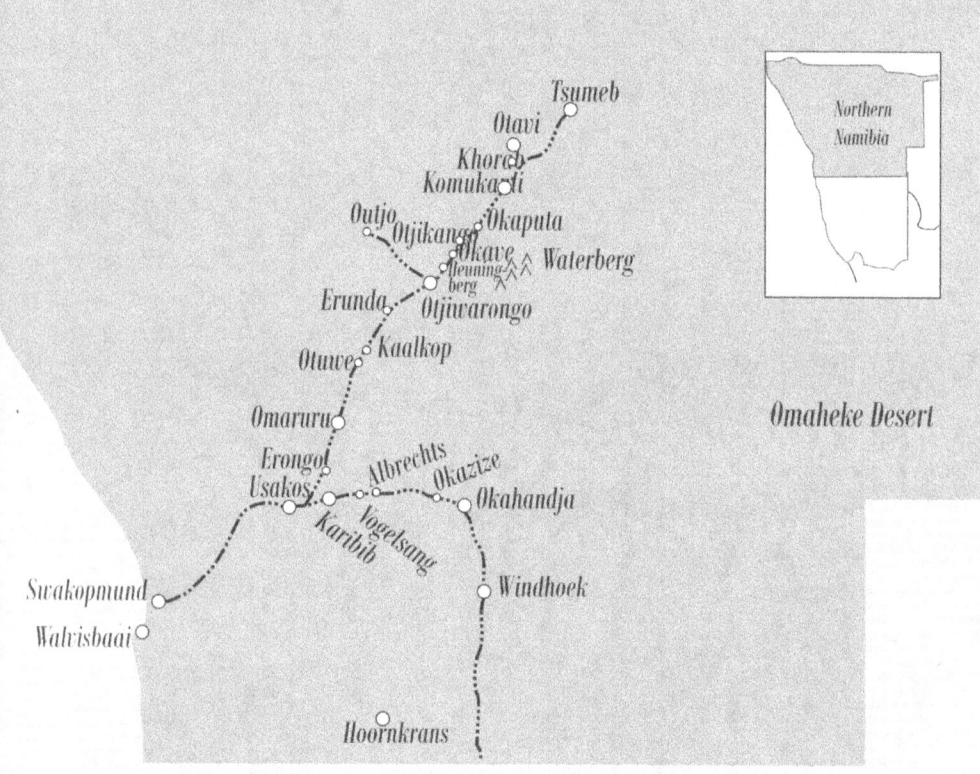

The north of Namibia

After the surrender of the German soldiers at Khorab in 1915 they were taken to the concentration camp at Aus in the south, but Ernst Luchtenstein had other plans. The old place names are omitted on this map.

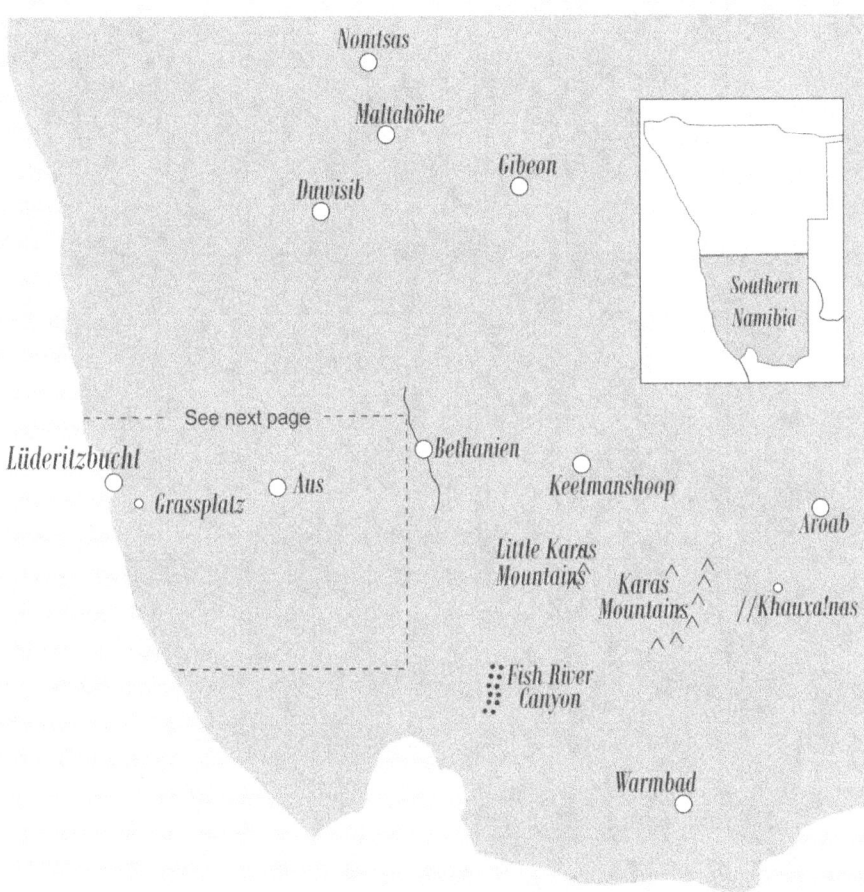

The south of Namibia

This area was previously known as Namaland. A few important place names are shown. //Khauxa!nas does in fact exist but does not appear on any other map.

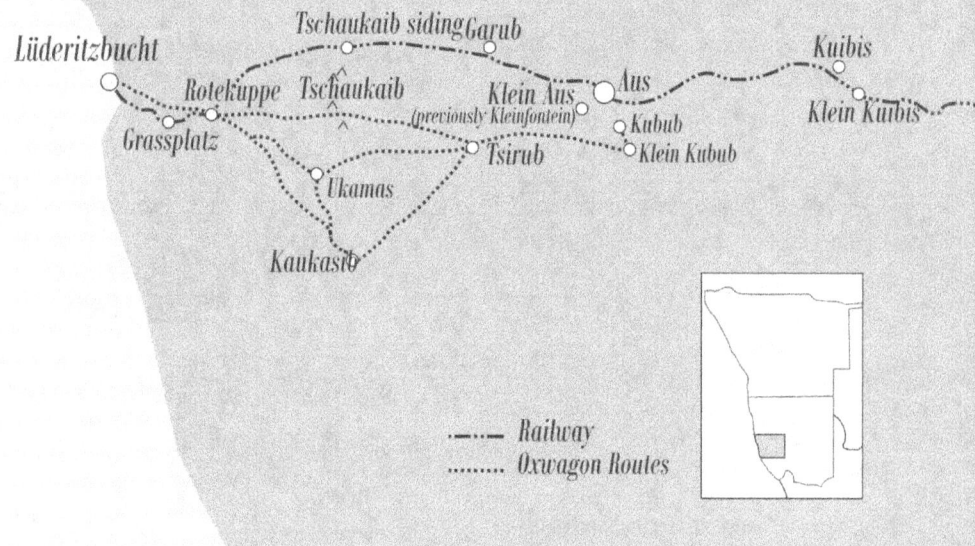

Map of the ox wagon routes between Lüderitzbucht and Aus. The selection of the route was based on the availability of water, mainly at Tschaukaib, Ukamas and Kaukasib.

THE KAISERBIRD SETTLES DOWN

27 March 1906

Lüderitzbucht with Shark Island in the background.

The gusts of an icy wind snaking across his back made Ernst Luchtenstein shiver. The fine hairs on his thin forearms stood upright in the last glow of the afternoon sun.

With his chin in his hands and his elbows resting on the starboard railings of the Gertrud Woermann's foredeck, Ernst's slight body swayed with the movement of the cumbersome steamship. He was fourteen years of age, with many questions on his young mind. He stared at the strange island in the bay in front of him – the bay known as Lüderitzbucht. The island was covered with hundreds of small circular shelters, like a rash on a diseased person's body. Short, slight, copper-coloured figures were crawling into and out of the shelters. Were they real human beings?

Now and then the cold wind carried a nauseating stench from the island towards the ship, making the German boy hold his nose in disgust. Surely real people could not smell like that, he thought to himself. And did real people stay in such shelters? Or were these perhaps cages, like the ones in Hamburg's zoo?

Ernst let go of his nose and sniffed the air again, hesitated and then inhaled more deeply so that the stench lingered deep in his throat, causing his stomach to churn. It reminded him of the dead rats he always had to remove from the attic in his parents' house and dispose of on the rubbish dump.

The steamship carried him, his mother Therese and his six-year-old sister Charlotte to a pioneering life in German South-West Africa. Tomorrow they would occupy this new homeland where his father, Joseph Luchtenstein, had been working as a *transportryer*[1] for the past three years, and was now awaiting his family's arrival.

Questions whirled around in Ernst's mind. Who would he be from tomorrow morning onwards? German? Jew? German South-West Afrikaner? African? He would ask his father, when they saw each other the next day.

His glance fell on a shiny patch of oil on the water directly below him. The shaky image of his reflection seemed to mimic his uncertainties and doubts. Questions shrieked and swooped around him like the seagulls among the ships in the bay. It occurred to him that at least these seagulls knew who they were.

During the voyage Ernst had mostly lounged around on deck, high above the sea and the beckoning horizon, daydreaming of the adventures that lay ahead. Little Charlotte, minus a couple of teeth, and with her thick blonde hair in braids, was never far away from her mother. She told her rag doll and teddy bear about all the wild animals they would be seeing.

For the past four days the ship had been battling against a ferocious south-easter along the coast of German South-West Africa. All Ernst could see on land was sand, sand and more sand. Everywhere the same; beaches bleached white like freshly laundered sheets on a clothes-line. Empty, white, dead. He knew nothing could exist there. Only white sand, nothing else.

Once they passed a larger bay with quite a number of docked ships, but the captain steered towards the deep sea because the bay belonged

---

1   *Transportryer* (singular), *transportryers* (plural): generic term for the men involved with operating an ox wagon trek and transporting goods, including drivers and *touleiers*.

to the English king. That was the only variation in the endless, boring stretches of sandy beach.

At last, after an exhausting and monotonous three weeks at sea, they were lying at anchor in the cold, purple-orange dusk of Lüderitzbucht.

Two dozen other German families were on board the Gertrud Woermann in search of a better life in the colony of the Kaiser.

Also on board was a group of German *Schutztruppe*[2] with their horses.

Ernst knew these were battle-hardened men bearing the stamp of the Kaiser's great power, the sharp edge of his sword, and the assurance of each and every German subject's right to the land in the new colony.

Dr Eugen Fischer, stern-looking and skinny, with a grey goatee, grey eyes and grey features, travelled alone. He spoke to nobody except the captain. He wrote a lot, but slammed the blue cover of his writing pad shut when anyone approached. Passengers shared their thoughts about the strange man. Some said he was a scientist like Darwin. Others thought he was a special envoy of the Kaiser. Children peeped around corners at the severe-looking doctor, but fled if he directed his cold frown towards them.

Eventually they reached the small bay and anchored just inside the harbour mouth. A ship's officer immediately rowed ashore to arrange for the huge process of disembarkation that would take place the following day. Now, at dusk, the sailors declared it too dangerous for the ship to enter the harbour and navigate between other ships, boats and anchor cables. So they had to wait until the next day.

On the port side, the dark, brown-speckled island appeared strange and different from anything Ernst had ever seen in his life. The hundreds of figures, bundled together on this rocky hump in the bay and constantly moving, looked like the carcass of a primeval animal covered with crawling flies.

To starboard, a whaling ship floated a couple of hundred meters away in an oily mess streaked with blood and entrails. Further away three other ships lay at anchor. From the beach the long, narrow, wooden pier pointed towards the deep sea like a bony finger. Ernst knew they would all walk on that pier to the land of this new country the next day.

On the beach Ernst noticed a few dwellings, horses, a strange wagon pulled by a span of oxen, and some people wandering around. Perhaps one of them was his father waiting for them.

---

2   *Schutztruppe*: German. Literally "protecting troops."

2

1883 Namaland

The residence of Josef Fredericks at Bethanien

Cornelius and Hans, Nama shepherd boys, lazed under the scanty shade of a shepherd's tree. The sheep stood head to head, drowsy from the quiet, dry heat hanging over the grazing-veld.

Cornelius peered out from underneath his floppy hat at the tattered shoes on his feet. Father could have asked the uncle fellow a long time ago to make him a new pair, he grumbled to himself. He was an adult - well, almost, but he still had to run around in patched clothes looking like someone out of the Bible. The young girls laughed at him, he knew that. He often had to tie the tops of his shoes to the soles with steenbok *riempies*[3] but yesterday the mongrel got hold of his last piece of steenbok

---

3   *Riempies*: Diminutive form of riem, (singular) or rieme, (plural), leather thongs used as binding or stitching material.

hide and chewed it up. And how long would it take for him to get his hands on another steenbok?

He reflected on the many hours he had spent stalking with a slingshot and a stone, the traps and snares he set, only to return home empty-handed every day. He remembered the stories of the firesticks the white man used. The missionary, Pastor Bam, became annoyed when the children nagged him about these things.

"Instruments of the devil, those things! We will not speak of them. Come now, get on with your work!" he scolded them in Sunday school class when they asked him about the firesticks or the firewater that !Xam, the wrinkled old Bushman, had told them about.

Old !Xam knew all about fire. He was terrified of the firesticks because the white people in the Colony had used them to hurl balls of fire at his people over the top of a mountain until everybody except him, was dead. The white people used these firesticks to hunt and to make war. They were very clever and had made all the other people of the world their slaves through those firesticks of theirs.

!Xam also knew about the firewater. Old !Xam loved the firewater, he told them. The firewater was much like *kougoed*[4], only far better. When a man drank firewater he became strong and smart. It was very different from the *kougoed* they picked from shrubs on the mountain. No, the firewater was something else. It was the Dutchman's thing and it made one happy. Now, old !Xam only talked about it, because there was none of this wonderful firewater in Namaland. Pastor Bam was glad that it was so. He didn't like firewater at all.

Cornelius was puzzled. Why did !Xam like the firewater, while the German missionary did not? Both were intelligent people. In the veld old !Xam was the most skilful of all. Pastor Bam might be able to read the Bible and his other books, but old !Xam could read the veld.

"See here, Cornelius," he would say, "*klipbok's*[5] mate is hiding their new-born. Now he walks by himself. See here where he left his droppings to confuse the hyena. So that the hyena would not catch the little one."

Yes, old !Xam knew all about fire. He taught the children how to make a fire with sticks like the old people used to do; how to select a proper piece of acacia wood and a raisin bush branch, cut them correctly, and roll the tip of the one piece of wood in a small hole in the other, until a

---

4   *Kougoed*: edible plant with stimulating effects.

5   *Klipbok*: Nama-Afrikaans for *klipspringer,* a small rock–hopping antelope.

wisp of smoke appeared. Then, little by little, they had to add some fine pieces of grass till a small flame began to burn.

It was Cornelius's great dream to get his hands on a firestick one day. He would not kill people, only antelope, particularly steenbok for their hide from which to cut *riempies*. But also a kudu. Then he could make his own shoes, all by himself. Yes, one day when he was grown up; if only he could get his own firestick.

Cornelius's stomach rumbled from hunger. Lately they had to let the sheep graze further away because it was late autumn and the edible veld plants were becoming scarce.

The sun was rising later now and the vegetation around Bethanien was in a poor state. The *koekemakranka, agorkies* and *snotterbelle* and the other special veld foods were getting more and more scarce. Here and there a *suuruitjie*[6] or two were found, but mostly they returned to their shelters at dusk with empty stomachs.

Last week they were fortunate to find a lone tortoise. Cornelius pierced the tortoise's neck with a long white thorn from the sweet thorn tree and then slit its throat. They cut up the meat and kindled a fire as they had been taught by old !Xam. They skewered the pieces of flesh on a small green branch and cooked it by rotating it in the flames. They knew only too well not to divulge any of this to the *taras*[7], their mothers. Tortoise meat was excellent food, and if the *taras* were to find out that they came across such good fortune without bringing it home, they would certainly be in trouble. They hid the shell to present it later to the mothers as if it were a lucky find. Such a shell became the container for !*uros*[8], the treasured perfume of the *taras*.

"Cornelius, what men do I now see over there on the dune?"

Startled, Cornelius turned his head and quickly sat up. Both he and Hans screwed up their eyes at the two human figures approaching, an ox at their side. West. Towards the desert. To the north was Gibeon, to the south Kubub, and east was Swartmodder. Everyone knew that was where people, and trouble, came from but in the west lay only desert

---

6   *Koekemakranka, agorkies, snotterbelle, suuruitjie*: Edible plants eaten by the Namas.

7   *Taras*: Nama word for older women, mothers, used with respect.

8   !*uros*: Tortoise shell filled with a mixture of natural products, the Nama equivalent of perfume. The word is also used for the initiation school or kraal of young Nama maidens.

where Cain lay buried. Nobody lived in the desert except for the few people who stayed with the guano gatherer at the water's edge. The place with the odd name. What was it again? Ankra or Angra, something like that. But what would these two now be doing here if they were from the Angra place?

They stood up and wiped the sand and grit off their behinds while watching the two strangers approach. They were Namas, older than themselves, with their faces covered in white dust. The skin of the emaciated ox with its wide horns was also powdered white with dust. Its head hung down low. On its back were three empty leather water containers. It looked as though there might still be a little bit of water left in one of them. On top of the bags was a longish canvas bag with something inside.

"Good afternoon, uncle. Afternoon, uncle," they greeted, raising their floppy hats politely.

"Afternoon, boys. How far is Bethanien still? We have been on the move for the past three days already."

"No, it's not too far. We come from there. Come, you can walk with us."

The boys whistled to get the sheep moving.

"Are you uncles from the sea, from the guano gatherer's camp?" asked Cornelius.

"Yes, that's right, son. We work for Mr Radford. He sent us to Bethanien to fetch horses for the men on the ship. They want to come and talk to the captain. Captain Fredericks."

"That's my father, uncle. My father is Captain !Korebeb//Naixab, Josef Fredericks of Bethanien," said Cornelius proudly.

"Now then, take us to him," the one stranger replied.

Josef Fredericks stood at the front door of a humble stone building, his official residence. He squinted and raised his chin.

"Good afternoon, Captain. I am Lukas and this is my brother Petrus. We are from Angra Pequena. Mr Radford sent us."

"Good afternoon, or perhaps I should say good evening," Josef greeted the men. "Why has he sent you so far?"

Lukas explained how the large ship had entered the bay. Three Germans rowed ashore in a small boat and without wasting any time began to speak with Radford, talking and drinking until late into the night. At sunrise the next morning, the three of them started walking eastwards into the desert with Radford arguing and protesting that they were going to die from thirst, but they just said they were in a hurry to finish their business. They would see Radford again in a week's time.

Radford shook his head and crawled back into his hut. Two days later the same three white men, burnt red by the sun, stumbled back and fell down next to Radford's hut.

"Water…water!" they begged, and that was all they could say for over an hour.

Radford revived them. The next day he instructed two of his guano gatherers, Lukas and Petrus, to prepare to travel to Bethanien and to request Captain Fredericks to send a horse patrol to come and collect the Germans.

Radford planned the expedition carefully. He gave orders that a supply of water from the ship be provided along the desert track. It took Lukas and Petrus three full days to carry the water in leather pouches on the back of their pack ox, deep into the desert, bury it and cover the sites with rocks.

They rested at Angra Pequena for a day and began the trek at dusk. All they could take with them was more water, a little seal meat and a gift for the important captain.

"Now what makes those white men think that I will give them my horses?" protested Josef.

"Petrus, fetch that gift for the captain," Lukas ordered his younger brother.

Petrus loosened the canvas bag from the back of the ox.

"The German, the big *baas*[9], sent this, Captain. He said there were many more."

Josef Fredericks held a firestick for the first time in his life. He felt the old battle blood rise in his veins. All he saw was the firestick. He knew about the power of these firesticks, because his forebears who moved from the Colony brought old muskets with them, but this one was different. This one he did not know. This was new.

"Keep your hands off it, Cornelius! It's not a toy!" Josef snapped at his son, barely thirteen years old. Cornelius was fingering and examining the weapon from all sides. He noticed a small package lying to one side on the canvas.

"The bullets?" he asked.

"Indeed, Captain," the two visitors confirmed.

"Can I open it, please, Father?" Cornelius begged.

---

9   *Baas*: Boss, Afrikaans term for boss, loaded with racial overtones, now considered archaic, patriarchal and politically incorrect.

"No, wait. These things are dangerous," said Josef, turning the small parcel over and over in his hands. He reflected on the meaning of this unexpected gift. He, Josef Fredericks, had long been enthralled by the power these firesticks could give but the man of God, Pastor Bam, had often warned him against them.

"Captain Fredericks, my friend, forget about these instruments of death. Those who live by them, will die by them. A Christian has no need to kill."

"Father, please, may I?" pleaded Cornelius, hopping first on one foot, then the other, all around the group.

"Wait, child. Give me your knife."

Josef sat down on the *riempiesbank*[10] on the stoep. He levered the tip of the knife carefully between the layers of brown paper and wiggled loose the glue surrounding the five cartridges, each one as thick as a man's thumb. He removed one of them and turned it around in his hands, The cartridge cases were made of paper, the rear end of copper, and the point of the bullet was blue lead.

Suddenly Pastor Bam stood in front of him.

"What is going on here, Captain?"

An embarrassed Josef looked up and tried to explain.

"Captain, I have said this before and I will say it again. These are instruments of war and death and will one day mean the end of your country and its people."

Red in the face, the missionary turned around. His black boots crunched on the narrow path as he marched off to his church.

To Josef's mind, this firestick was even more beautiful than the pocket watch Captain Moses Witbooi had received as a gift from the missionaries. In the whole of Namaland it was only Witbooi, Simon Koper and Jakob Morenga who had firesticks like the whites, but none were as beautiful as this one. He did not know how to load the cartridges or how to shoot with the firestick, but he was not going to let on to the bystanders that he didn't know.

"Lukas, what do the Germans want? Is it only the horses? Or what?" he asked, biting his lip and frowning deeply.

"No, my Captain. They did not say. They only told us to tell Captain that they had another two hundred of these rifles on their ship. And that

---

10   *Riempiesbank*: lounge couch made from wood and leather thongs.

Captain should send six horses to fetch them. They had tried to travel on foot, but they nearly died of thirst, Captain."

That evening !Koreb//Naixab, Josef Fredericks of Bethanien was deep in thought. He was the leader of the !Aman, the Namas of Bethanien. The Namas were Khoi-Khoin, real people, the first people of the land of the Southern Cross. They were here first, had been here forever, long before both the whites and the blacks. But they always had to flee, flee from the invaders. He did not want to flee any longer. This was their land, Namaland, their stronghold.

"Daniël, my son, you are my successor and you must now listen to me very carefully. The Germans must be fetched, there at Angra Pequena. You are the captain of this trek. Have old !Xam come here. He knows the best road to travel," Josef instructed, the following morning.

He ordered his men to prepare six pack-oxen and six horses for the journey. Together with Daniël he planned the expedition in minute detail. They gathered all available waterbags and ostrich eggshells together. That same day the first three oxen and two men travelled sixty miles west to Klein Kubub. The following day, a further three oxen, six horses, two of Josef's best men and the guano gatherer's two workers stood ready to depart. Cornelius, cap in hand, approached his father cautiously, while his older brother looked on, nose in the air.

"Father? Father, can I go too? Please, Father?" he begged.

After a couple of minutes' protestations, particularly from Sara Fredericks's side, Josef Fredericks relented.

"All right, my son. But you have to listen to your brother and to old !Xam, do you hear?"

"Wait, my child. Over my dead body will I allow you to leave without a proper *karmenaadjie*,"[11] said Sara.

Sniffling, Sara filled a *//hob*[12] with food. There were a couple of *aslêers*[13] left over from the night before, also *!narra*[14]-bread from the larder, and lastly a tin of biltong.

---

11   *karmenaadjie*: Nama-Afrikaans word for a gift of food for the road.

12   *//hob*: Nama word for a bag made from an animal skin by dissecting the carcass without major cuts.

13   *aslêers:* Afrikaans word for a bread baked directly on the ash from an open fire.

14   *!narra:* edible desert fruit, also used to make bread.

"Josef, how can you do this to my child?" she complained, but Cornelius could not keep still from excitement.

"!Xam, now you listen to me, otherwise I will personally feed you to the hyenas," warned Josef for the last time.

Two years previously Josef had saved the old Bushman from certain death. His family had abandoned the frail old man in the veld to die, as was their custom, and moved away. Josef came upon him and for two days fed !Xam goat's milk and *suurpap*,[15] until he opened his eyes again. Since then !Xam saw himself as Josef's property, his slave.

Josef found it interesting that somewhere in the distant past there must have been a family connection between the civilized Namas and !Xam's wild predecessors, the Khoi-San, the robbers. There were so many similarities between the 'clicks' and the 'clacks' of their languages and the stories they told, but the Namas were increasingly speaking the language of the Boers.

Josef wanted !Xam to teach Cornelius about the ways of the veld and the animals before it was too late. He himself had already grown too old and weak. He knew that it was important for his sons, Daniël and Cornelius, to be trained for the day that he was no longer able to work.

He regarded !Xam almost as a dog or animal. The Bushmen were like animals, even the whites thought so, but !Xam these days tended more and more to act like a real human, a Khoi-Khoi and not a Khoi-San. His two years at Bethanien had taught him to behave like a real person.

"!Xam, you go wherever Cornelius goes. Do not let him out of your sight. You look after him well, do you hear?"

"I hear, my Great One. I will watch over him."

"Now listen carefully. This is what you men will do. This evening you have to be at Klein Kuibis. Tomorrow evening at Klein Kubub. There you stay over so that the animals can rest and drink water. Then you trek into the desert with the oxen, full water bags and ostrich shells. !Xam will show you where to bury the water. Then you return to Kubub for more water, taking it even deeper into the desert, towards Ukamas. Cornelius must stay at Klein Kubub until the water arrangements are complete. Only when the water has been properly stored may he accompany you into the desert. You are not to remain in the desert for longer than three days. If there is no water at Ukamas or Tschaukaib or in the Kaukasib,

---

15   *Suurpap*: porridge with clover leaves added.

you turn around and come home. The Germans must then take care of themselves. Then everything will be over. Do you understand me?"

"We understand very well, Captain, very well," they all answered together.

"Well then. When you meet the Germans from the ship, you first have to get more water and take it into the desert. !Xam, that is your job. I don't know the area around Angra so well, but I do know there is no water there. You have to take water from the ship with you into the desert. In a week from today, another team will leave Bethanien for Kubub, with fresh oxen and horses. They will meet up with you at Ukamas with water and food for your journey back. Do you understand?"

"Yes, Captain" they chorused.

Josef Frederick sighed. He had to get those firesticks, come what may. Times were changing, and if he did not change as well, then time would pass him by. It was like winter. He had to have those firesticks the same way as a man had to have a *karos*[16] in the winter. Without a *karos* a man did not sleep well. Moses Witbooi and Simon Koper got their *karosses* long ago, but two hundred firesticks? No. Even the great Moses Witbooi would swop half his flock of sheep for two hundred firesticks, this he knew. These were new times and one had to adapt to survive. Just the other day some of Witbooi's people were here, saying that the Hereros also had firesticks now. It was only a matter of time before they and their cattle stopped at his front door. What would he do without a firestick?

Cornelius took leave of his parents. The trek disappeared in a cloud of dust accompanied by a noisy horde of high-spirited children and yapping dogs. The men were on horseback while old !Xam went on foot, proud and upright, with all his earthly possessions, and the three pack-oxen.

---

16   *Karos*: heavy blanket, sometimes made from animal skin.

3

28 March 1906
Therese and Charlotte go ashore

The wooden jetty at Lüderitzbucht, with workers
unloading a precious cargo of water barrels.

The morning mist hung like a grey curtain over Lüderitzbucht, and also
lay heavily on the mind of the captain. He frowned. He had to disembark
the Gertrud Woermann that morning. One hundred and thirty-eight
passengers, with their baggage, had to clamber down the rope ladders into
the rowing boats down below. He also had to get the horses ashore safely.

The main deck teemed with sailors and passengers. Officers were
barking commands, children were running around, laughing and shouting, tripping over the luggage, while five rowing boats bobbed up and
down at a distance, waiting for their precious cargo.

The captain, splendid in his stiff, high collar, tie and black coat with
gold braid on the sleeves, felt the wind tug at his trousers. Again he

frowned. The beach and the jetty were hardly visible through the blanket of grey mist. If an anchor rope should snap, the ship would run onto the rocks in seconds. Why had a proper quay not been erected yet? This was a German colony, after all. In Germany such pathetic ineptitude would not be tolerated. The passengers would simply not understand if they had to stay on board for another one or two days.

"All hands on deck! Prepare to sail!" the captain commanded.

The ship's officer relayed the command. Sailors scurried into position.

"Lift anchor! Full power! Steer to port!" The first officer repeated the captain's words to the crew who carried them out with skill.

The Gertrud Woermann steamed deeper into the bay with the rowing boats following behind.

"Reduce power! Twenty degrees to port! Reduce power! Ten degrees to port!"

The huge ship approached the small, brown, speckled island where an amazing sight loomed through the mist. Thousands of men, women and children, copper-brown in colour and small in stature, dressed in sacks and rags, crept out of their low, tortoiseshell-like dwellings, and wandered aimlessly around the island. They did not appear to be interested in the ship steaming past them, hardly looking at it.

"Forty degrees to port! Stand by, anchors!" Ernst heard.

The huge ship turned sharply to port. All the passengers moved across to the starboard side to stare at the land, but two passengers' eyes remained fixed on the island.

Suddenly the two passengers became aware of a strange sight: directly below them the water was churning and seething. Then, in a patch of sunlight, they saw the flash of a round eye and the vicious teeth of a reptile, fish or some other creature.

"What was that?" asked Ernst.

They glanced at each other in surprise for a second or two, before Dr Fischer jerked his head away, turned around and strode off.

The thick mist still shrouded the area between the ship and the land. The five rowing boats bobbed up and down in the water nearby, waiting.

"Cut power! Anchors! Man the gangways!" commanded the captain.

Slowly the large ship came to rest alongside the speckled island.

"Rowing boats!"

The non-commissioned officers at the gangways shouted commands to the sailors waiting below in the rowing boats a few yards away from the great steamship. The sailors rowed the small boats to their respective positions opposite the gangways. From the deck, rope ladders were thrown down from the gangways, only to flap like flags in the wind above the bobbing boats and hands trying to grab hold of them.

With the huge Gertrud Woermann rocking on the swell, the crew in the rowing boats pushed and tugged at the rope ladders so as to not let go of them or let them smash against the bow. More rope was thrown down to secure the rowing boats to the ship. In every boat a sailor had to keep pushing an oar between the two vessels to keep a safe distance between them.

Two sailors clambered down into one of the boats. Two trunks were handed to them by mates clinging like finches to the rope ladder. Then Dr Fischer followed. The two sailors rowed him ashore to the rickety wooden wharf in silence.

Only when Fischer's boat was some distance away, did the action resume.

"Women and children under ten, first. One piece of baggage per lady," commanded the captain.

Therese, dressed in her finest blue silk dress with the white cotton collar and small round blue hat, hugged Ernst tightly against her. She kissed him quickly.

"Be good and listen to the captain. See you ashore."

"Don't be concerned, *Mutti*. I will make sure that all our baggage makes it aboard. Say '*Hallo!*' to *Vater*. I will soon be with you. But please just be careful, *Mutti*."

With Charlotte's hand tightly clenched in her left hand, Therese approached the gangway.

"Let us take her, Madam," the sailor said, stretching his arms out to Charlotte. In one movement he swung her over the gangway and down into the waiting hands of another sailor, half way down the rope ladder. He, in turn, handed her swiftly to another pair of hands below him. Within seconds little Charlotte was settled in the bobbing rowboat. Therese followed. She embraced her little girl while staring anxiously up at Ernst waving down to them. When the boats had been filled with the other women and children, the sailors pushed away from the danger of the massive ship and started rowing, into the teeth of the wind.

The curtain of mist gave way before the wind so that the people ashore became recognisable. Therese's eyes searched for her husband's face. She had last seen him three years before when she said farewell to him on the dock at Hamburg, and was afraid that she would not recognise him now.

She was afraid of this new country with its barbarians and wild animals. She also feared for her children's safety, their future and their lives. She pressed her lips together tightly while peering at the people on land who were growing steadily larger as the boat drew nearer.

What would it be like to have a husband again? To feel his hands, to recognise his smell, to hear his voice again? Do I still love him? Does he love me? And the children? she wondered.

The small jetty was now only a few yards away and with another two oarstrokes the rowing boat thudded against it. A sailor jumped up onto the jetty and tied the boat firmly to the wooden pole. When Therese looked up again, there was her husband, Joseph Luchtenstein, standing before her. She drew her breath in sharply.

"My darling, Joseph, my husband! It has been so long."

"Welcome to Africa, Therese. Hand me your case."

He gave her a quick kiss. She smelt the strange, sour smell of his breath.

Therese followed her husband, dressed in his black coat, wild beard and dirty, tousled hair. Her one bag in his hand, they walked along the jetty. With Charlotte on her hip, she had to jog to keep up, but after seventeen days at sea, the firmness of land underfoot on the boardwalk felt unfamiliar.

"Therese, is Ernst still on the ship?"

Joseph did not wait for her response.

"Johannes!" he bellowed. "Come here! Start loading the wagon".

A skinny youngster with a coppery complexion, wispy beard, frizzy hair, wide nostrils and narrow, green-brown eyes ran across the sand towards Joseph.

"Sure my *baas*, where is the *kleinbaas* then, my *baas*?"

"He will be here later, he is still on the ship."

"Hello, Johannes. You are Johannes, aren't you? I am Mrs Luchtenstein," Therese introduced herself to the shy, copper-brown boy in German, the only language she knew.

"Good afternoon, Madam. Pleased to meet you," Johannes replied in perfect German.

Therese was surprised.

"Joseph, the boy speaks German! My dear husband, it's been so long. I missed you so much. And you?"

"Mmm, what was that? I'm sorry. My lovely wife. Yes. Yes. Yes. It was difficult. It was a long time, difficult but good. You will see."

"Joseph, do you still love me?"

"Of course! Of course, my wife. Yes, I love you. This is our new fatherland. Forever. I am going to build a large house for us. You will see. When will Ernst be here?"

"Joseph, here is Charlotte, your daughter. She doesn't actually know you. She was only three when you left."

The little girl clung to her mother.

"Come here, little one, come to your father," he tried.

He put his arms out to her, but she clung even more tightly to her mother's hand. Joseph picked her up and held her above his head. She shut her eyes tightly. Then he unexpectedly put her down and walked to the water to enquire why his son and the baggage had not yet arrived on land.

Therese stared after him, speechless.

May 1883
Adolph Lüderitz purchases Angra Pequena

Heinrich Vogelsang (left) with his two co-workers,
Francke and Wagner, before their mission to buy
Angra Pequena on behalf of Adolph Lüderitz.

Cornelius's heart pounded with excitement This was his greatest adventure. He was on his way to the sea. And, at the end of his journey, there was a real firestick waiting for him, the symbol and instrument of power. His life was on track. Now he was a man, a man about to get his own firestick. Pastor Bam hated firesticks, probably because he believed all power belonged to God.

Cornelius dismounted from his horse as soon as they were out of sight of the townsfolk. The men knew they had to spare the horses. They rode for two hours, dismounted and for the next two hours walked beside their horses. The section to Kubub was easy, with many springs to water man and beast, but from Kubub to Angra Pequena only a little brackish water might surface out of the desert at Ukamas, the Kaukasib and Tschaukaib. According to !Xam it all depended on whether Keinaus, Great Snake of Namaland, was at peace with the people. The old Bushman mumbled that he would cut fresh buchu[17] leaves near Kubub to scatter onto the water at Ukamas and the other places to ensure peace, otherwise they would have problems.

Cornelius did not understand how Great Snake could simultaneously be at Bethanien and Klein Kubub as well as at Ukamas, Tschaukaib and Kaukasib. The old people's tales were difficult to understand. Perhaps they spoke nonsense, but he dared not express such an opinion to old !Xam. The old man would be very angry. One day old !Xam told him that Great Snake could fly: he saw it with his own eyes. A great wind arose and swept around in circles. It came to a stop above their watering hole, turning and turning; then, as if commanded to do so, swirled away. Thereafter the watering hole was left bone dry. All this, !Xam declared, had been caused by the girls who, against all the rules of decency and to the displeasure of Great Snake, had gone swimming in the watering hole the previous day. Cornelius silently hoped that nobody had played in the water at Ukamas.

The veld was verdant, with hills and ridges in the distance and *blou-dak, knietjiesgras* and *litjiesgras*[18] nodding cheerfully in the light north wind. This sight soothed the eyes and hearts of the Namas. This was their world. They, the *!Aman* of Bethanien, were part of the Oorlams[19] people who had moved out of the Cape Colony, away from the white people, the Boers and the English, with their firesticks. Some Namas elected to remain behind on the far side of the Gariep River, deeper into Namaqualand, the place of the Nama, but their people, the real Oorlams, chose to bid farewell to the land of the white people forever, taking their

---

17   *Buchu*: plant with multiple medicinal and some alleged magical purposes.

18   *Bloudak, knietjiesgras* and *litjiesgras*: Grass species of Namaland.

19   *Oorlams*: Afrikaans word for Nama people who had accepted the Dutch way of life, implying cleverness.

livestock and horses with them. They crossed the river to establish a new, free Namaland. When they first arrived, the land was empty, with only small, occasional groups of Bushmen traversing the land. They erected their *!haru-oms*[20] and put deep roots down into the earth.

Recently, more and more people were travelling to Namaland. Radford, the guano collector at Angra, and the German missionaries were the first to come. Now there was talk that the Hereros from the north wanted to come and scout the *!Aman's* land. And then there were also the new ship-people waiting at Angra Pequena. What did all of them want to come and do in this country?

As far as they travelled they saw herds of oryx, ostrich, springbok, and now and then a klipspringer or steenbok. Once they even saw a herd of giraffe and another time a herd of eland. The game was tame and Cornelius was already daydreaming of what he would do with the new firestick he was going to get from his father. Also, he would never have to wear tattered shoes on his feet again. Mother would be able to cook *!kom*[21] every day. Nowadays she could only put that delicious food in front of them three or four times a year, but once he had his fire stick, they would eat it every day.

On the way old !Xam taught Cornelius about the veld and the plants. About the *kougoed* that made your head feel good, and the sweet *koe-kemakranka*, the *snotterbelle, taaibos, soutslaai, bergpruim, veldpatat, kambro, ghaap, borrelgom* and *slymstok.* Cornelius learnt which plants worked for headaches, toothache, colds, and also for a broken heart.

That evening they slept beside a spring with clear, sweet water, but old !Xam made sure that they did not make their fire too close to the water.

"To maintain peace with Keinaus," he said.

No one was keen to prepare a meal and they made a small fire and ate from the *//hob* leather bag. The animals grazed nearby.

"Old !Xam, how long have the Bushmen been here in Namaland?" Cornelius asked while scratching in the coals with a stick.

The crinkled old face on the squatting body turned and looked up at the stars.

---

20   *!haru-oms*: circular Nama dwellings made from reed mats fitted over wooden slats, suitable for taking down and erecting in another place.

21   *!kom*: typical Nama dish of finely cooked venison or mutton.

"From long before time, long, long ago, from eternity. The Bushman were the first people of this place, but we walked together, my people and your father's people. Us and you."

"Tell me, old !Xam. Please? About those times. Where do we come from?"

The old Bushman swayed slowly on his heels and turned towards Cornelius.

"Our people have always gone together. From there at the top, from the place of plentiful water. We came together, but alone, each of us."

"How do you mean together, but also alone, old !Xam?"

!Xam sighed.

"We are Khoi people, you and I, Cornelius. We are the same – my people and your father's people, but you are the people of things, and we are the people of the veld, of the world."

"How do you mean, old !Xam? What things are you talking about?"

"Your people want to own everything, sheep and horses and money and homes and pretty things from the Colony. Our people, the Bushmen, we only want life. We are content. Everything belongs to us. Everything. We have all that we need. We are like the larks. We live here, here in the veld, on the rocks and the dunes. Yes, you are different. You look for a nest like the Dutchmen and the honeybirds, a place where you can stay and farm. And like the Dutchmen and the honeybirds, you take over the other man's nest, lay your eggs there and so multiply. In the Cape Colony the Dutchmen took over the nests of your people, the Namas. But we Bushmen, we are the people of the veld, larks. We do not need another man's nest. We do not live in nests because our nest is the veld. We live everywhere," old !Xam explained, spreading his arms out in front of him.

Before falling asleep, Cornelius thought about how privileged he was to be a real person, a Khoi-Khoi, and not a Khoi-San like old !Xam.

At dawn the next morning, they trekked further. In the late afternoon they arrived at Klein Kubub with its shining spring-water pool. Here they met up with the team who had gone ahead of them, and who reported that they had on that day already taken one load of water into the desert.

Klein Kubub's grazing was lush. Four *kraals*, each consisting of a number of *!haru-oms* with areas separated by screens of branches where the *taras* cooked, were home to offshoots of Hendrik Hendricks's *//Hawoben* Namas. They all asked about the purpose of their trip, but the *!Aman* from Bethanien told them that they were on their way to Angra to mail Pastor Bam's letters.

Every day for the next four days they trekked into the desert to bury the skin bags and ostrich eggshells filled with water from the spring. In the late afternoon, man and beast returned to Klein Kubub, tired, thirsty and hungry, only to do it all over again the next day. !Xam had to lead every expedition because only he could find the hidden water again.

Cornelius was not permitted to accompany them. He whiled away the time by playing with the //Hawoben children and hunting in the hills and valleys of Klein Kubub. One day he killed a fat *dassie*[22] with his slingshot, providing a tasty meal for the footsore *!Aman* menfolk.

On the day of the great march, with a nightjar's continual warning call ringing through the early morning darkness, the last of the water bags were loaded onto the backs of the oxen. Nobody spoke as they trekked over the rise into the throat of the naked Namib Desert, which lay grinning before them. They had to cross this desert within three days, perhaps four. If not, they would die because their water would not last beyond that. They had sufficient water to reach Ukamas, but they needed to retain some reserves in case Ukamas and Tschaukaib were dry. It all depended on whether there was peace in Great Snake's head, according to old !Xam.

They reached the first water point at midday. Every man, including Cornelius, drank only what could be scooped up in their hands. Each ox and horse was allowed only a hatful of water before the trek moved on again. They reached the second water point after dark and applied the same rationing system. The older folk warned Cornelius not to eat biltong until they were sure of their water supply. Biltong would worsen his thirst.

The next evening they arrived at Ukamas. Everyone talked and laughed loudly for, right in the centre of the rock circle, shone the pool of water. The animals were going mad with thirst because they had smelt the water from a long distance away, but old !Xam refused to let them drink until he had gone closer with his buchu leaves "to preserve the peace". The Namas, and even Cornelius, thought the old Bushman was soft in the head. What snake could live in this little pool of water? Stooping, the old man stepped closer, muttering, with his buchu and witchcraft bones. He carried out his age-old ritual before allowing the animals to get closer. They sniffed and tasted the brackish water, lifted their heads and walked away before their thirst compelled them to return and take deep draughts of the water.

---

22   *Dassie*: Afrikaans word for rock hyrax.

The next day they moved on with a few bags of water from Ukamas. They spent another thirsty night in the desert.

Late the next morning the mighty ocean greeted the bewildered people of the Bethanien veld. Cornelius could not believe his eyes. How could there be such a lot of water in one place? Lukas and Petrus told him that this water was more salty than that at Ukamas. Why did the Almighty think it right to make so much bad water?

Far out at sea, Cornelius saw what looked like a huge wagon. The ship, Lukas explained, that had brought the people with the white skins.

"Why does that thing remain on top of the water and not simply sink?" asked Cornelius. Old !Xam reckoned that they must have a lot of buchu on that wagon.

Cornelius also noted the small islands, splashed white by the guano of thousands of rowdy birds. It must be their droppings that made the water so salty, he thought. The island closest to them drew his attention.

"That is Shark Island," said Lukas. "Some people have actually seen Great Snake in Shark Island's waters."

Cornelius felt a cold shiver run down his back.

They moved on, guided by Radford's two workers, to the low building on the beach with the corrugated iron walls and iron roof. At the front door two huge white bones protruded from the sand in a graceful, welcoming arch.

"Whale ribs," said Lukas in passing.

Cornelius was still contemplating Jonah inside the stomach of the big fish when three white people with sunburnt faces emerged from the house. He immediately knew them to be the Germans.

"Where is Captain Fredericks?" asked one abruptly.

Cornelius remained in the background while Daniel was doing the explaining. Why were these white people so arrogant?

Later the Englishman, Mr Radford, arrived in his rowing boat laden with guano. Cornelius did not see any buchu, and wondered if it was hidden under the manure.

"When can we leave for Bethanien?" one of the Germans asked. The Namas did not understand this restlessness. They took pains to explain that they first had to take water to store in the desert.

Mr Radford had to row to the big ship to collect water. Nowhere was buchu to be seen. The little bird of doubt about the old people's tales whirled round and round in Cornelius's head.

These Germans had different manners from the *!Aman* of Bethanien. One of them, *Herr* Vogelsang, who was the leader of the three, spoke volubly and rapidly, but did not listen when Lukas, Petrus or Daniel wanted to explain. And not once did he look Cornelius in the eye.

It took a full five days to transport the skin bags, seal bladders and eggshells, all filled with water, into the desert and to hide them for the return trip.

The group set out on their journey again, eastwards into the desert against a light wind. Cornelius preferred old !Xam's company. He glanced furtively at the three stony-faced men on horseback in their smart clothes, their faces already red from the Namaland sun. Cornelius did not see any sign of firesticks.

Without warning, a furious east wind came up. No one spoke again. For the next two days they struggled against it, hats pulled down low over their faces, peppered by the stinging desert sand. Both man and beast were totally exhausted by the time they reached the circle of rocks around the pool of water at Ukamas.

When old !Xam tried to move forward, the German pushed past him on his large horse. Cornelius looked closely at the Bushman's face, but saw no sign of hatred or anger. Whilst everyone unpacked, Cornelius watched old !Xam disappear quietly behind a sand dune.

The party rested for a full day next to the spring. A smaller group went on ahead with a few bags and eggshells filled with water. On the fifth day they met up with *!Aman* people coming in the opposite direction, carrying more food and water.

One week after leaving Angra Pequena, the travellers arrived at Klein Kubub, and two days later at Bethanien. Three weeks had passed since they had left the small missionary town. Joseph Fredericks had had prior information about their arrival from his scouts. He wore his black suit for the occasion.

"Welcome to Bethanien, gentlemen. Captain Josef Fredericks is my name," he greeted the visitors.

Cornelius and Daniel greeted their father.

Sara rushed out of the house. "My children, my children!"

Josef looked all over, but saw no large bags that might contain firesticks. He restrained his curiosity and politely invited the visitors inside. Soon afterwards Pastor Bam also arrived, but he was not over-friendly to the visitors.

"Mr Vogelsang," Josef Fredericks said, "I wish to thank you very much for the gift you sent me."

"No need to thank me, Captain. There are still plenty on the ship. We need to talk. Just let me know when you are ready to do so. In the meanwhile, here is a gift to you from the Kaiser."

Heinrich Vogelsang handed him a bottle wrapped in brown paper.

Josef insisted on convening a full church council meeting for the following day.

Just after eight o'clock that evening Pastor Bam again knocked on the door of the Fredericks's house. Cornelius opened the door.

"Come in, Pastor. You are most welcome. Please be seated," Josef welcomed his visitor and spiritual leader.

"Captain Fredericks. I am deeply disturbed about this visit of my fellow German and his two friends. It cannot hold any good for you and your people. *Herr* Vogelsang told me they are the agents of a rich man from Bremen and that they want to buy land from you – that they want to buy the bay, Angra Pequena, from you."

Fredericks laughed. "But Pastor, what do we Namas want with that little piece of dry desert? There is not even a small spring or a bit of grazing there. There is nothing there at all. Why would we want to hang on to that useless little scrap of ground?"

Cornelius, on his bed behind the blanket curtain, listened to the adults' conversation.

"Captain, you will find out one day, one day when it is too late, that a bay is like a road. Without a bay people cannot reach you. They cannot do anything if they cannot get to you. The one who owns the bay, owns Namaland, Captain."

Josef took out the bottle of brown liquor Vogelsang had given to him.

"How about it, Pastor? My throat is dry from all the talking."

"*Ach so*, Captain. This also? The juice of the devil. Pour a little then, just a small one."

Long after Pastor Bam had departed – somewhat unsteadily – to his rectory later that night, Josef Fredericks sat and considered the role he would play in the future of this country. He wondered if he should enter into an agreement with Moses Witbooi. But Witbooi was such a quarrelsome man. Why did he always have to be at war? If it was not with the Bondels, then it was with the Hereros. He saw a threat behind every camel thorn tree. But then, with two hundred firesticks, he, Fredericks, would be a force to be reckoned with and Witbooi would surely join the *!Aman* team.

The sun was already two hands high when the church council members sat in straight rows in the small church in their black suits, for all the world looking like a flock of crows.

A little late, as became a man of his stature, Captain Josef Fredericks of Bethanien, !Koreb//Naixab of the *!Aman,* strutted down the aisle between the two groups of men. Behind him came Heinrich Vogelsang and his two compatriots. At the front of the church stood the pedal organ, the Holy Communion table and four chairs. The four men took their seats. Behind them, against the wall above a humble pulpit, Martin Luther's eyes looked down on them sternly from inside his picture frame. The rest of the congregation sat in the pews behind the venerable church council.

"Brothers," Josef began solemnly.

Pastor Bam entered and all the brothers fell silent while the missionary slowly took his place behind the pulpit.

"Welcome, Pastor. We were just wondering where you were," said Fredericks.

Pastor Bam nodded stiffly.

"Brothers, I welcome you to this important occasion which will pave the way for the *!Aman's* progress."

Captain Fredericks spoke and spoke. At every window the young children crowded like geckoes with their noses pressed against the window panes. Eventually Vogelsang was asked to address the gathering. He spoke about the mighty German Kaiser's special envoy, Mr Lüderitz – an important man.

"I am here today to discuss business, friends. On my ship in Angra Pequena are two hundred rifles. Real German rifles like the one I sent Captain Fredericks. For those two hundred rifles and for another hundred pounds, Mr Lüderitz is prepared to take that dry little bay which does not even have a drop of fresh water or any grazing, off your shoulders. Oh yes, and with another five miles or so of land around it."

A commotion rose from the meeting. All the men in their black suits spoke at the same time.

"Silence brothers, quiet! Let him finish!" commanded Fredericks.

Vogelsang continued and talked and talked until Fredericks's head started nodding. The children were called to serve refreshments. They brought in cool spring water in ostrich eggshells, but the overseas guests drank from the old-fashioned English crystal glasses the *smous*[23] from the Colony had brought Sara Fredericks.

---

23 *Smous:* travelling vendor.

Eventually Josef Fredericks announced they would break for lunch. Outside under the giant fig tree, the *taras* had laid a long table with white starched linen for twelve people. The *taras* carried dishes of delicious smelling Nama food to the table. The overseas guests' mouths watered. They had not seen fresh food like this for months. First the *taras* brought a shallow dish containing strange, brownish vegetables. The aroma was familiar. Surely it can't be, thought Vogelsang. Truffles? Here in the desert? He recalled the aromatic dishes in the Amsterdam cafés, prepared from the expensive fungus imported from France.

"Excuse me, Captain, what's in this food?" he asked.

"Oh, that's the last of this year's *!nabbas*,[24] Mr Vogelsang. Please have some more."

The *taras* then placed a round clay pot in front of each of the twelve men. The overseas visitors coughed and spluttered when, upon lifting the lids, they were confronted by sheeps' heads grinning up at them. The Namas laughed at the expressions on their guests' faces. Later the *taras* brought in dishes filled with *!kom*, tender mutton, and sheep's tripe with *veldkool, surings and prei*.[25] In the middle of the table they put three large round loaves of potbread.

When the last of the food was consumed, Vogelsang excused himself and returned with a brown bottle. He poured generous tots for Fredericks and his headmen. The Namas' eyes froze as if Great Snake was staring at them, but Captain Fredericks raised his glass and knocked the liquid back. The others followed him. They all laughed uproariously.

Late that afternoon, with the last rays of the sun shining into the little church, !Korebeb//Naixab drew a cross on a piece of paper. When they got outside, one of the Germans raised a flag with the black and red colours of the crimson-breasted shrike, the Kaiserbird,[26] on a branch of the camel thorn tree.

That evening Josef Fredericks retired to bed early, but tossed and turned all night long. Inside his head Great Snake hissed but he did not understand its language. Eventually he saw the reptile with the shiny stone on its head rise up and fly over Namaland. Away, to the east.

24   *!nabbas*: Kalahari truffles, similar to European truffles.

25   *Veldkool, surings, prei*: edible plants.

26   *Kaiserbird*: literal translation of *"keiservoël"*, colloquial Nama-Afrikaans term for the crimson-breasted shrike, a bird with the colours, red and black, of the then German flag. Synonym for *"keiservoël"* is *"Duitse vlag,"* German flag.

5

28 March 1906
Ernst in the cold water of Lüderitzbucht

A large shark caught in Lüderitzbucht.

Ernst, unable to contain his excitement, waited for his turn next to the gangplank. The wind was picking up with every passing minute, lifting the swells higher and higher so that the rowing boats heaved to and fro and up and down. The sailors hung onto the ropes and pushed with their oars to keep the two vessels close together, but sufficiently apart to prevent the boats from being smashed against the bow of the large ship. They passed the Luchtensteins' travel baggage as well as Therese's trousseau chest down to the rowing boat. Last of all, Ernst had to climb down into it.

Three huge successive swells lifted and dropped the little rowing boat which strained at the ropes and the ladder anchoring it to the Gertrud Woermann. Down below in the boat, passengers fell over one another and baggage was strewn all over the tiny vessel.

In one movement Ernst swung himself down the rope ladder. His free foot searched for the next rung of the ladder. Twice he stepped wildly in the wind, felt and found the rung and stepped further down, his other foot kicking around as it searched again for the next rung. As the rope ladder tautened, Ernst saw his chance, but another swell pushed the rowing boat upwards like a whale surfacing so that the rope ladder went slack again and nearly swung Ernst against the bow of the ship. Then the swell sank down again, sucking the rowing boat deep into the trough and tightening the rope ladder. Ernst clung to the rough rope chafing and cutting into his hands. The salt spray stung his eyes. It felt as if a monster was trying to pull his body apart. Fear paralysed him so that he could think of nothing else except to keep holding onto the rope ladder. Again he felt for the next rung with his foot. He heard the officer above and the sailors below shouting instructions.

Again and again the swells and troughs came, increasing in size every time, and still Ernst was swinging back and forth from the rope ladder. The sailors battled to control the ropes and rope ladder, at the same time using the oars to stop the rowing boat from smashing against the ship's hull. Another swell picked up the boat and immediately let it fall as if the earth was collapsing. The trough sucked the boat further away from the ship so that the tension of the ropes caused the little boat to tilt at a dangerous angle.

"Let go of the ropes!" yelled the seaman in charge of the rowing boat. The two sailors released their hold on the ropes and rope ladder.

Ernst swung on the rope ladder and hit the side of the ship with such force that he blacked out momentarily. He fell into the churning water. It was dark and the salt water stung his eyes, but he swam furiously until his lungs began to burn. When he broke surface for air, he saw the shadow of the ship towering over him with the brown-speckled island a distance away.

"Swim away from the ship! Away!" Ernst heard the shouting as if from far away. With his last bit of strength he swam in the direction of the island, away from the danger the large ship presented.

"Where is he? Where is he?" shouted the sailors on the rowing boat before they spotted him swimming towards the island. They rowed with their oars splashing and churning up foam in a desperate and uncoordinated effort to reach the floundering boy.

Then they saw the sharp grey fin slicing through the water towards Ernst. The sailors went berserk. One threw the anchor rope at the grey creature followed by a small suitcase belonging to one of the passengers. The shark swung around and yanked the anchor rope with such force that the boat listed wildly.

"Swim! Swim! Don't stop! Swim!" the sailors shouted, all the time rowing madly. They kept on shouting and hitting the surface of the water with their oars to distract the shark.

Ernst's strength began to fade. The rowing boat was about three yards behind him. He could see the rocks on the island, when he felt a massive blow to his side. A dark curtain sank down over him.

On the island a group of the copper-brown people, Nama prisoners from the Shark Island concentration camp, were watching the drama in silence. At first they only saw the rowing boat and the swimming youngster, but soon they also saw the fin.

"Great Snake is chasing him!" one of them shouted.

"Great Snake is going to take him!" yelled a frightened brown woman.

She plunged into the seething water and searched under the surface. She got hold of the boy's face, then his hair, and started dragging his limp body towards the shore. Two other women waded into the water to help take the weight. The first woman slipped on the sharp rocks beneath the water. When she raised her head, the water directly behind her boiled. The huge grey shark propelled the front half of its body right out of the water, revealing its white belly, as the copper-brown people on the island watched.

While the two women continued trying to drag Ernst's cold body towards the rocks to safety, the Namas and the sailors on the boat saw the first woman being pulled violently beneath the water and disappearing from sight.

The fin of the huge shark turned swiftly towards the deep sea, the body of the Nama woman clenched in its jaws and a stream of red bubbles following in its wake.

6

Lüderitz steals Namaland

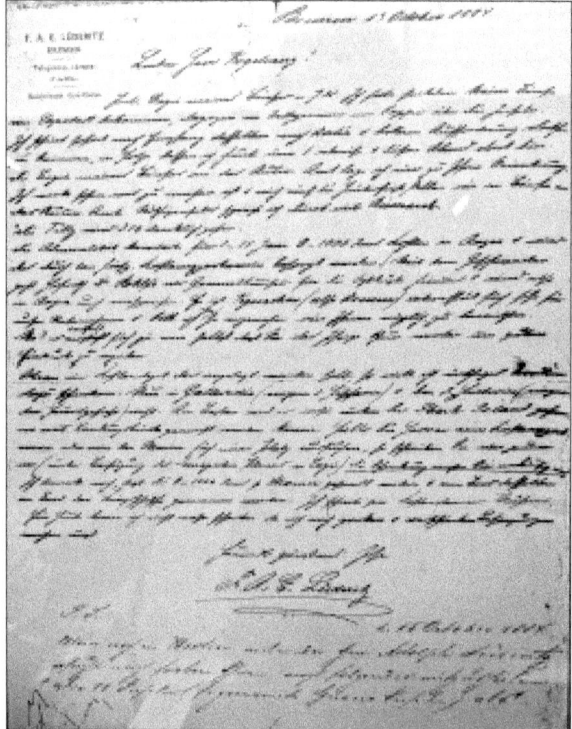

Adolph Lüderitz wrote to Heinrich Vogelsang and instructed him to keep the !Aman Namas in ignorance of the fraudulent transaction.

In the time it took the *!Aman* to make three return trips to transport all the rifles to Bethanien, the world of the desert had made its nest in Cornelius's soul – just like a dune lark.

Between Ukamas and Tsirub they found two more secret watering holes, but at the end of winter both had dried up.

Cornelius learnt that the desert was not a place of death but rather, in its own unique way, a source of life. Not like the grasslands between Kubub and Bethanien which had an abundance of water, but still, in its own different way, a place which sustained the people and animals that loved and respected it. It was a beautiful place, a place where God Himself spent forty days, without being concerned about food and or sheep. He lived in the desert with the dune lark and with the *horingsman*[27], the springbok and the oryx, the *spekvreter*[28] and the *skaapwagtervoëltjie,*[29] and also the eland, the hyaena and the *sonkykergeitjie.*[30] Children of the desert, all of them.

With the rifles delivered, the !Aman of Bethanien resumed their usual life, but every night Cornelius would take his new rifle from behind his mattress. He would rub the stock with the palm of his hand until it gleamed, while his mind roamed far away. He turned the five rounds with their paper cartridges over and over in his hands, painfully aware that he had only five shots. He simply had to get more of these rounds. He mastered the loading and unloading of the rounds into and out of the magazine. One of these fine days he would shoot a kudu or a gemsbok, or even an eland.

With his first four attempts, he pulled the trigger with the barrel of the rifle just pointed in the general direction of the antelope. On each occasion the antelope galloped away unharmed, and disappeared over the horizon. He finally realized that to succeed he needed to take careful aim, as he did with his catapult.

He now had only a single cartridge left, with no idea of how to get hold of any more. But he still had one opportunity to shoot something. His appeals to his father were met with a stern glare.

"You must shoot better, Cornelius."

---

27 *Horingsman*: Nama-Afrikaans word for sidewinder snake, literally meaning 'man with horn'.

28 *Spekvreter*: Afrikaans term for the chat, *Cercomela* species of birds, literally translated as "eater of lard."

29 *Skaapwagter/skaapwagtervoëltjie*: Afrikaans term for the wheatear, *Oenanthe* species of birds, literally translated to shepherd/shepherd bird.

30 *Sonkykergeitjie*: sungazing gecko.

One of the Namas accidentally shot and killed his own brother on the day he got his rifle. Pastor Bam's face was red with fury. After the funeral he reproached Josef Fredericks.

"There you are, Captain. I warned you and I will say it again: if you live by the sword, you will die by the sword."

All the other Namas fiddled and played with their new rifles, conscious of the new status the firearms conferred on them, but soon problems arose. From the onset the shortage of cartridges was an issue. Josef Fredericks berated himself for not negotiating a better deal. A rifle without rounds was worth less than a broken ostrich eggshell. That was the reason why the muzzle-loaders the old people had brought from the Cape Colony turned into rusted ornaments. Josef Fredericks frowned more and more, because his people were complaining that the rifles would no longer shoot. The things were faulty and there was no one to fix them. Did the Germans cheat him? Each time he saw a Kaiserbird in the camel thorn tree in front of his house, he cursed the pest.

One day Moses Witbooi, leader of the *Khowesin*[31], his son Hendrik and six men on horseback stood before Bethanien's captain. They had heard about the transaction and the rifles.

"No man, Captain Fredericks. Looks to me the Germans sold you *penswater*[32] for onion soup. These rifles are Dreyse needle guns. They give more trouble than a horny billy goat," Witbooi declared.

Josef Fredericks stared at his hands and clenched his teeth. He would murder the Germans if he got his hands on them, he thought.

Hendrik took his rifle from his horse's back, stating that the German army no longer used Dreyse rifles, because all their soldiers now fought with Mausers. Like this one. The Mauser carried eight cartridges, not five only, like the Dreyse. Also, the Mauser cartridges were not made of paper, but of real copper. Josef Fredericks's eyes widened when he took the Mauser in his hands. So, the Germans did cheat him with these antiquated Dreyse rifles.

One afternoon Cornelius went for a walk with his Dreyse and his last cartridge. He crossed a ridge and froze at the sight of a kudu bull. He quickly sat down and pulled his soft hat down over his eyes. The blue-grey spirit of the bush glided from the shade of a shepherd's tree to the

---

31 *Khowesin*: Nama clan of Gibeon, under the leadership of the Witbooi dynasty.

32 *Penswater*: Fluid from a slaughtered animal's rumen.

sweet green leaves of the buffalo thorn tree, unaware of the young hunter, with his dry mouth, watching.

Cornelius lay down flat on the stony ground. He was afraid to even look at the massive animal. This was his best chance up till now. He had wasted the first four rounds. This was his last round. Who knew where and when he would be able to get more? Over the drumming in his ears, he could hear the kudu entwining its huge spiral horns around a branch in the buffalo thorn tree. Then the branch snapped. Cornelius turned his head slowly. He peered at the spectre from under his hat, but the kudu was too intent on the lush green leaves to notice the human figure lying down flat in the dust.

Cornelius felt his heart pounding and shallow breaths rasping in his throat. Today he had the opportunity to become a man, or he could once again taste the shame of defeat, like the bitter fruit of the wild fig. He must shoot this kudu bull. His hands refused to move, to aim the rifle at the animal's body. He had slaughtered many sheep. He knew where the heart and lungs were. He did not want this bull to escape. It had to die on the spot. He decided to aim at the huge, blue-grey neck.

The bull raised its heavy head. It's over, Cornelius thought. The grey giant had heard something. But the bull looked away from Cornelius, silently twitching his big ears back and forth. Cornelius hardly dared to breathe. He did not even feel the hot sun on his back. A fresh light breeze startled him. Oh no, thought Cornelius, not that. Please let the wind hold, he prayed. He repositioned the rifle for a better aim, waiting for the kudu to turn its head. He prayed that the kudu would not flee. When it moved forward so that its neck was exposed, he was going to send his last bullet on its way.

The kudu stiffened. He jerked his huge head around. He stared straight at the funny little brown man in the dust. Too late. Cornelius pulled the trigger. The huge animal's hindquarters sank to the ground first and then he fell with a loud thud. Cornelius did not move. He had not even felt the recoil. Or heard the shot. He stayed down for a while, staring at the grey colossus. Then he slowly got up. He prayed for the animal not to jump up and gallop away. Crouching, he circled it, looking for any sign of life. He threw a small stone at the animal. No reaction. Only when he touched the kudu's eyelid and nothing happened, did he know that he had indeed shot it dead.

Today he had come of age. Today he had become a man. No longer was he just a snotty-nosed little shepherd. Now he was one of the adults!

He could not carry the kudu by himself, and Bethanien was far. What about those damned jackals? If he left his kudu untended, these sheep robbers would certainly eat it all. He placed branches of the buffalo-thorn tree over the carcass. Then he placed a few large rocks on top of the branches followed by more branches on top. An hour later he marched into Bethanien. He took no notice of the kids playing in the dust with their clay oxen, calling out to him. Cornelius walked straight home.

"Cornelius, my child, I am so proud of you!" Sara exclaimed when she heard of his triumph. She dried her hands on her apron, wanting to embrace him, but Cornelius was not in the mood for childish hugs and embraces today.

"Where is Father? It is getting late and we must cut up the kudu before nightfall."

Almost the whole town followed Josef Fredericks's two-wheel ox cart, laughing and singing. Cornelius led the procession. His father had already promised to try and get more cartridges from the Germans. Better still, he was going to get a real Mauser rifle, not this cheap Dreyse stuff.

The crescent moon had moved a great distance across the sky by the time they had the kudu quartered and hung high up in the wild fig tree. Cornelius himself washed and spread out the skin before salting it in the storeroom behind the house.

The following morning the Fredericks family ate kudu liver with a thick dark sauce. Josef wiped out the last scraps and sauce with a slice of pot bread. Life in Bethanien was good.

Heinrich Vogelsang and his entourage visited Bethanien again, this time without an escort and on horseback. The !Aman were surprised that the Germans could find their way by themselves. They had learnt fast, thought Josef.

"Captain Fredericks, Mr Lüderitz sent me again. He sends his greetings as well as the best wishes of the Kaiser. Mr Lüderitz will visit you personally soon."

Josef regarded the German with suspicion.

"Yes, Mr Vogelsang. What is it you want this time and why should I allow myself to be cheated again with a load of outdated needle rifles?"

Vogelsang jerked his head up.

"What do you mean, Captain?"

"You know very well what I mean, Mr Vogelsang. These rifles that you so generously sold to me are only good for making a fire. And the rounds of ammunition were far too few."

Josef Fredericks's eyes remained fixed on the bottle in the brown paper in Vogelsang's hand.

"I will confer with Pastor Bam tonight. Perhaps we can discuss the matter with you further tomorrow."

Vogelsang was worried. His boss, Mr Lüderitz, from Bremen, wanted more land and already Captain Fredericks was being difficult over the first transaction. He handed over the bottle.

The following morning Vogelsang spoke eloquently and at length. With the aid of a compass and a map he indicated to Josef Fredericks exactly where Mr Lüderitz's new border would reach to. However, on the proposed contract there was a word not known to the *!Aman*: 'geographic'[33] mile. They only knew an English mile. But, a mile is a mile, not so?

After the signing of the agreement, Vogelsang handed Josef five hundred pounds and within one month Josef received sixty real Mauser M71 rifles, the new type that carried eight rounds in its magazine, as well as two thousand rounds of ammunition from Angra Pequena. All the German wanted was a further twenty miles of sand all along the sea – a total of twenty-five miles of useless land along the coast. The German's ruler had indicated on the map the precise position of the border. Surely this was much better than the first transaction, reasoned Josef, satisfied with the deal.

Nowadays *!kom* appeared on the !Aman's menu often, even though they had to walk a bit further to find springbok and oryx.

Adolph Lüderitz wrote to Heinrich Vogelsang:

"Because the contract states 25 geographic miles into the interior, we should also refer to it as such. Let Josef Fredericks believe for now that it is 25 English miles."

"Captain Fredericks, I warned you about these people," barked Pastor Bam at him. "Now you have a problem."

He threw a German newspaper down on the couch next to Josef and folded his arms. Josef looked up.

"What is it now, Pastor?"

The pastor picked up the newspaper and started to read:

---

33   Geographic mile: One geographic mile as was used in Germany equals 4,6 English mile or 7,4 kilometer.

"German businessman purchases land in South-West Africa. The young businessman from Bremen who recently also spent time in Mexico, *Herr* Adolph Lüderitz, acquired the coastal area north of the Cape Colony in a bargain deal three months ago. He purchased a strip of twenty-five geographic miles from the captain of the area, one Josef Fredericks, for a payment of seven hundred rifles and six hundred British pounds."

Pastor Bam indicated the area with his finger on the map next to the article.

"Here you are, Bethanien. Here is Kubub and there is Angra. Only 20 geographic miles, 100 ordinary miles from here. Captain, I am sorry to say this, but now you are a tenant on your own property. Do you understand? A geographic mile is not the same as an English mile. One geographic mile is nearly five English miles! You have lost all your grazing as well as the land at Kubub and Klein Kubub, your best land and all your springs. For a few rifles and a few pounds. Ask Ruben. He arrived from Kubub this morning. The Germans are already building dams at Kleinfontein, and they are paying your people with liquor and tobacco. What's more, at Kuibis there is already a store. This is the beginning of the end for Namaland, Captain."

It took Fredericks a few minutes before he began to understand. His mouth went dry and his jaws clenched tightly together.

"The deceiver. I will murder him."

Pastor Bam turned around, and walked away slowly while Fredericks stared before him. The newspaper was on the floor. The wind picked up one corner of the front page, but then it fell back again.

That entire night Josef Fredericks tossed and turned on his bed, plagued by visions of the Kaiserbird and Great Snake.

7

28 March 1906
The Luchtensteins reunited

The harbour at Lüderitzbucht.

On the island a group of soldiers rushed to the circle of Nama women surrounding the unconscious German boy.

"What's going on here? Trouble again?" barked the sergeant.

"No, Sir. This young man came swimming towards the shore with a small boat behind him. Then Great Snake also came behind and we got him out before Great Snake could get hold of him. But Liesbet is gone, Sir, Great Snake took her, in his place… sir."

The sergeant knelt beside Ernst. He pressed with all his strength on Ernst's chest and water streamed from his mouth. He then gave him a hard blow on the chest. Ernst's eyes fluttered and opened. He gave a choking cough and more slimy seawater ran from the corner of his mouth. He saw a circle of people hovering over him.

"OK. Away with you, rubbish!" ordered one soldier. He hit the by-standers out of the way with the butt of his rifle. "We will take over here, get away, all of you!" The Namas slunk off, their faces downcast. Two soldiers lifted the young boy onto a stretcher and carried him off to the hospital.

Why were they struggling? What was taking them so long? They should have been here a long time ago. Joseph Luchtenstein paced up and down alongside the beach. No one there was aware of the near tragedy taking place a short distance away.

"Come sit here with me, Joseph. We have been apart for such a long time," pleaded Therese.

"Therese," was all that he could get out as he sat down next to her.

"Joseph. Tell me. How are you? Are you well? Are you happy? And your work? Do you like it?"

Joseph gazed at his hands, without noticing the thick, black dirt caked under his fingernails. He sighed and looked into Therese's eyes.

"Therese, my darling. I am sorry. I am a little confused. It has been three long years, but German South-West has been good to me. It is a good country, but a harsh one."

Therese relaxed her shoulders. She smiled.

"My husband, as long as you are happy. That's all that matters."

"Therese, what is happiness? I work and the sun shines every day. One of these days I will get a farm. That is happiness. A farm in Africa. I will never have to work in a factory in Germany again. Ever."

"And us? Your family? What about us? Do you still love us?"

"Yes, I love you all, you and the children. I am going to build a house and we will be together forever. Happy. We will be the first real people in this beautiful country."

Joseph jumped up again.

"There they are now. At last."

The rowing boat approached. Therese walked closer. With another couple of strokes, the sailors manoeuvred the boat next to the jetty.

"What took you so long? Where is the baggage? Is everything here? Where is my son?" demanded Joseph.

One of the sailors walked towards Therese.

"Madam, the young boy, Ernst. He is your son, not so?"

Therese's stomach churned.

"Yes, yes, yes. But what? Why do you ask? Where is he?"

"Sir, Madam, there has been an accident. The boy fell into the sea, almost drowned and a shark nearly took him."

"What are you saying? What do you mean?" asked Therese, an icy-cold hand closing round her throat.

"Madam, I think he survived. He swam to the beach, to that island over there," he replied and gestured towards Shark Island. "We followed him in the rowing boat and saw him being dragged ashore by a couple of women."

The world was spinning and inside his head something was whistling like the wind around a corner. Ernst tried to open his eyes, but his eyelids felt as though they were glued together. He heard voices, as if from a distance. "*Aber er ist doch nur ein Jude…*".[34]

Then everything grew dark again. He felt somebody tugging at him and again he tried to open his eyes but the sharp glare of lights stabbed like thorns. A head moved in front of the lights and Ernst squinted at the face. Dr Fischer! What was he doing here?

Ernst could not move. Slowly he breathed in, hesitated and then breathed again more deeply. The air reached deep down into his throat and the sharp smell of formalin stung his nose.

Suddenly, whatever was restraining his arms released them. Immediately he rubbed his eyes, and saw that he was in a strange room. Against the wall were rows of bottles containing strange-looking pieces of fleshy material. To him they looked like the pictures in his school books of human or animal brains. To one side lay two skulls. He tried to sit up, but felt something, no, someone, pushing him down again. He felt a burning sensation in his arm. He looked down and saw a needle being withdrawn from it. A drop of blood oozed out of the vein, then another and another, till it formed a little trickle. Then a drop fell on the white sheet on which he lay. The drop spread across the fabric and slowly expanded. Darkness settled over him once more.

When he woke, everything around him looked different. He was in a different room, and the doctor had gone. There were no bottles or skulls. Had he just been dreaming? "*Aber er ist doch nur ein Jude…*". I am a Jew,

---

34   *Aber er ist doch nur ein Jude*: But he is only a Jew.

only a Jew, someone had said, but who? The questions whirled around in his befuddled brain. Was that all?

On the beach a soldier arrived on foot. He called to the people all around.

"Who are the parents of Ernst? Where are Ernst's parents?" Therese heard the soldier and ran towards him.

"It's me. I am his mother, Where is my child?" she asked, clenching her fists.

"He is with us, Madam, in hospital. He is fine. Come with me, please. I will take you to him."

As Therese, Charlotte and Joseph walked with the soldier, he told them briefly what had happened. They came to a gate and noticed a narrow causeway connecting the island to the mainland. They waited while the huge gate was unlocked. The road led to another high gate. The sides of the road were secured with a high barbed wire fence, patrolled everywhere by guards with Mausers and German shepherd dogs on leashes. Above the gate, grey steel letters proclaimed the words: '*Wissenschaft ist Weisheit*'.[35]

The guard took them to a small office where they had to sit on two upright visitors' chairs. Charlotte sat on Therese's lap.

After about three-quarters of an hour, Ernst came through the door. He was dressed in an over-large German uniform and on his head a soldier's hat with the brim turned up on one side sat crookedly on his head. Behind him was a young, blonde officer, smiling broadly.

"*Herr* Luchtenstein? Your son nearly became food for the sharks, but here he is, hale and hearty. Our doctor just wanted to ensure that everything was in order with him before he could go."

Ernst hugged his mother tightly. She pressed him close to her.

"My son, my son, my son…" she murmured.

Joseph stood up, looking at the floor.

"Thank you, Lieutenant. Thank you for all your assistance. I regret all the trouble we have caused you. May we leave now?"

"But of course, *Herr* Luchtenstein. You are welcome. Have a good day. Stay away from the sea, do you hear Ernst?"

"Goodbye Sir. Thank you very much," mumbled Ernst, slowly letting his mother go.

He turned to Joseph, raised his hat and held out his hand.

---

35 *Wissenschaft ist Weisheit*: Science is wisdom.

"Good day, *Vater*," he whispered, biting his lip.

"Yes, son. You had us worried with your fun and games."

Joseph tousled his son's hair with a rough hand.

At the door on the way out, Ernst turned around and looked back, into the eyes of Dr Fischer. In his hands he held a glass bottle. He jerked the bottle away and hurried away down the passage.

What had happened here? What was going on here? Why did that voice say "*... nur ein Jude...*"?

Dazed by the events of the morning and the smell of dead rats and chemicals, he passed through the steel gate onto firm ground and straight into the blinding light of German South-West Africa.

8

1885-1893
Cornelius meets Magdalena Witbooi

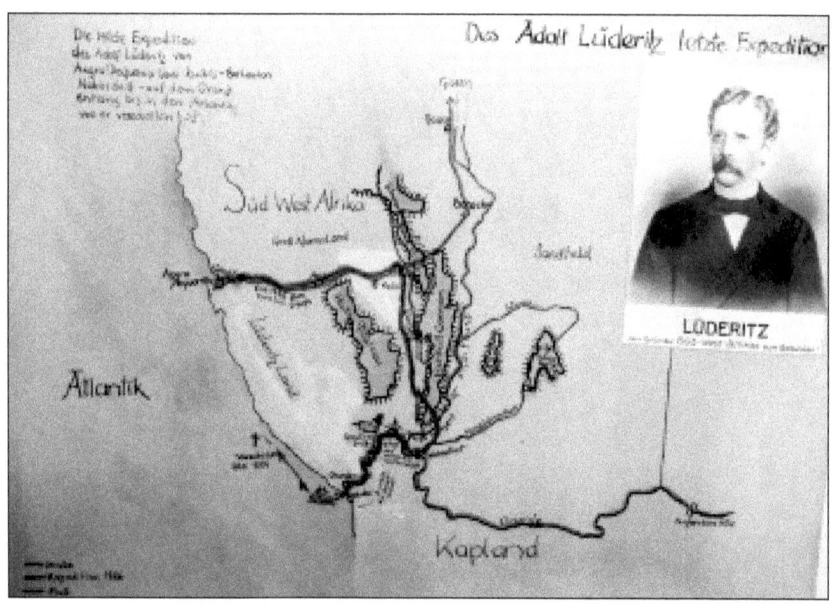

A map showing the last journey undertaken by Adolph
Lüderitz. (His name is misspelt on the map.)

Joseph Fredericks chewed his lower lip, his forehead furrowed with worry. The black danger from the north, the Hereros, troubled him.

Hendrik Witbooi, who had now succeeded his father Moses as captain of the *Khowesin,* had made it known that he wanted to see Josef. These days Josef did not like the idea of spending the whole day in the saddle, but Hendrik Witbooi was forever talking and fighting, looking for trouble behind every shepherd's tree despite the fact that the !Aman's sheep grazed as always and the springs were flowing abundantly.

The Germans didn't seem to be so bad. He was at peace with them. They were very clever people, those Germans. Perhaps they would still bring prosperity to Namaland, Fredericks told his son, Cornelius.

It was convenient to send Cornelius to Daniel at Kuibis to fetch a small brown bottle. It helped such a lot for nagging gout and rheumatism. Previously the nearest shop was in the Colony. Now Daniel worked for the German in his shop at Kuibis.

He would go and see what Witbooi wanted to discuss with him, and hear what he had to say about the political situation. But he would only sleep over one night. He knew that Witbooi was intolerant of firewater.

Late in the afternoon Josef, Cornelius and the rest of their horse commando called a halt at Witbooi's settlement at Gibeon. Hendrik Witbooi was there to greet them, dressed in a suit and wide-brimmed hat.

"Welcome to Gibeon, Captain Fredericks."

Witbooi led his guests to the centre of the residential area, dotted with //haru oms arranged in small circles, each circle with a fireplace and cooking screen. To one side there was a separate screen of tree branches forming a kraal, the !uros,[36] from which a number of hokmeisies[37] peeped surreptitiously. The two captains deliberated under the stars of Namaland, while the young men stood around idly, hands in pockets, sneaking looks – always in the direction of the !uros.

Witbooi told Fredericks that he was led by God to move northwards. Nothing would stop him from doing so. Witbooi was deeply unsettled by Fredericks's transaction and the stupid actions of Jonker Afrikaner.

"First you sell the !Aman's land and then Jonker Afrikaner sells off Winterhoek as well. And for one hundred pounds only. The first thing the Germans did was to change the name to Windhuk. This is what I am now trying to stop. I cannot remain at Gibeon, Captain Fredericks. The world around here is too small and the grazing scarce. My people need more land, but you went and flogged your inheritance for a pot of lentil soup – gone, Captain. Just like Esau."

---

36   !uros: Here the word is used as a synonym for the initiation school or kraal of young Nama maidens.

37   Hokmeisies: girls of pubescent age undergoing initiation rites.

Fredericks's ears burned but he remained silent. Witbooi's words pierced him like thorns.

"I ask you, Captain, on whose side are you? On the side of the Germans or the side of Hendrik Witbooi? On the side of the white people or your own people, the Namas, the descendants of the Khoi-Khoin? You know very well that our ancestors, the people of our blood were here first, here and in the Colony and everywhere south of the great river up in Africa. What are you choosing, Fredericks?"

Josef stared down at his feet for a long time. His mind dwelt on the brown bottle of firewater still in his saddlebag.

"How do you mean, Captain? But of course we are the *!Aman*, the *Khowesin's* friends. Our mothers and fathers, the Oorlams, crossed the Gariep River together, into Namaland. We are all Oorlams people, one and the same. We come out of the same kraal, captain Witbooi. For now and forever."

Witbooi stared at the man with the watery eyes in front of him, the leader of the *!Aman*, Josef Fredericks.

Cornelius sauntered past the *!uros* kraal where the girls were. One caught his eye, but he was not permitted to speak to them. This was the *!uros* time of the girls. They had to remain in this kraal until the *taras* had finished instructing them and they had learnt about the ways of a woman. And of the things about Great Snake, Keinaus. From now on they may not play in the water and they may not do this and they may not do that, otherwise the monster with the great, shiny star on its head would be waiting at the drinking place and would do all kinds of things with them. What things? wondered Cornelius, whilst drawing lines and circles in the sand with a sweet thorn twig.

If they behaved well and could keep the peace, the girls were allowed to take a man and have children, even become a *taras*. To wear many beads and put on *!uros* powder, prepare food, make clothes and take charge of the *//haru oms* household. A *taras* was her husband's strength, the pride of the clan and the family's leader. It was she who built the *//haru oms*, served the food and disciplined and pampered the children. It was the husband's work to herd the sheep and horses. And to ensure that strangers did not take over the land.

Cornelius had to find out the name of the one with the small hands and the large, friendly mouth. He liked her, but got a fright when he heard she was Captain Witbooi's youngest child, Magdalena.

They had hardly returned to Bethanien, when Hendrik Witbooi and his people moved off, northwards, towards Hoornkrans.

"I wonder why he didn't tell me he was going to leave Gibeon?" wondered Josef Fredericks aloud.

"Have they all left, Father?" Cornelius asked with a heavy heart.

"No, the *smous* said that about a hundred people stayed behind at Gibeon."

Cornelius wondered if he would ever see the beautiful Magdalena again.

Bethanien was in a state of frenzied activity. They had an important guest, and a doctor at that, Dr Gustav Nachtigall. Pastor Bam said that he was a good man, better than that sly Vogelsang with his crooked stories. Josef hoped that the doctor had brought medicine with him. Especially for the gout and the rheumatism.

All the important men of Bethanien, dressed in their black suits, sweated in the pews. Today the matter of Lüderitz and Vogelsang would be discussed in the presence of the doctor, particularly that nonsense that had appeared in the newspaper. And this thing about the geographic mile. What on earth was that? The Oorlams were educated people and they only knew one type of mile and that was the Englishman's mile. No, today he was going to be told whose land this was. Bethanien-Aus-Kuibis-Kubub. This was *!Aman* land, nothing more and nothing less. The German, that Lüderitz fellow, purchased Angra Pequena as far as Hotnot's Bay plus twenty miles – twenty English miles – into the desert.

It was a solemn occasion. Dr Nachtigall was that kind of man. Tall, erect, grey-haired, with eyes that showed he listened and a mouth that smiled easily. One felt as if one had known him for a long time. From his black briefcase he took out the map and the agreement Vogelsang and Josef Fredericks had signed.

Captain Fredericks showed him the map in the German newspaper. He gave the doctor the true version of events. About the miles and so on, of the measuring stick and how Mr Vogelsang had used it on the map to indicate the land he had wanted to purchase. In between they all smoked and drank water, but the doctor would not smoke.

When they had finished deliberating, the doctor stood up and looked at the men before him.

"Friends, friends, what you have told me here today is an enormous injustice. This is not the way of the German nation and the great Kaiser."

Pastor Bam's face relaxed.

"I will be returning to Germany today, but I am now going to correct this injustice, right in front of your eyes."

He took his black pen from his jacket and drew two thick lines through the word 'geographical' and above it he wrote the word 'English'.

Captain Josef Fredericks wondered why Hendrik Witbooi was so embittered. Any intelligent person could see that these Germans were the Namas' salvation. Only Hendrik Witbooi thought differently. Just like his father, he looked for an enemy behind every shepherd's tree.

Later that night Josef Fredericks felt the heat of the brown liquid soothe the pain in his rheumatic muscles and gout in his toes. Open-mouthed and with a grin on his face, he fell asleep.

The *!Aman* continued their quiet existence with their sheep, horses and Mausers. In the north the *Khowesin* formed a buffer against the blacks and in the south there were only the strange Germans with their shops and a few animals.

"Captain, Captain!"

Two dust-covered shepherds came running up and shouting, mongrels chasing behind them. The *taras* looked out over the half-opened stable doors. Only the rich had stable doors. The poor had to look out from the low doors of their *//haru oms*.

What could this be? Another hyena amongst the sheep? Josef was mildly- annoyed at the commotion.

"Yes, why are you carrying on so?"

"Captain, there are Germans on the way. Four of them. They are from Angra. There are four of them, Captain, and the leader says his name is *Herr* Loetrits, Captain. He says he is looking for Captain, Captain. Immediately, Captain."

Josef rubbed his chin. Loetrits? Loetrits? Oh, yes, of course. That sly Vogelsang's boss, Lüderitz. That same Vogelsang who tried to steal his land. What did he want here now? Was the geographical mile business and all that not closed? After all, the doctor had set it down in writing.

While the four Germans rested in a *//haru oms*, the children inspected all the goods on the Germans' ox wagon. Pans, shovels, sieves, bottles, paper and books, but the strangest of all was a longish canvas thing. Cornelius was proud to announce that he knew what it was. He had seen one just like it in Angra Pequena. It was a boat, a folding sailboat, a type of wagon on which you could ride on the sea if you had plenty of buchu. The children wondered what the gentleman was going to do around here with a wagon which rode on water. The Konkiep River had flowed three, no, four years ago, and then it only lasted for a week.

Again the church was filled with men in black suits. Mr Lüderitz and his three subordinates sat in front, sweating. Tobacco and water were brought out.

Herr Lüderitz fidgeted. Captain Fredericks initiated the proceedings.

"*Herr* Lüderitz, your agent, Vogelsang, was here to discuss land that you wanted to buy with those rubbish rifles, remember, those useless, old-fashioned things?"

Herr Lüderitz went red, swallowed and cleared his throat.

"Have some water, *Herr* Lüderitz. Pass on the kettle over here, man," Fredericks ordered.

"Well, *Herr* Lüderitz, we were very unhappy about that whole business, but the good doctor, Dr Nachtigall, came here to rectify it. Right here, at this very same table, he sat here and, before our eyes, with his black pen deleted that word which we did not know, the geographic mile. Right here, in the presence of us all."

Fredericks looked up and cast his gaze over the group of Nama men in their black suits. They all nodded, whispered and agreed while the four visitors adjusted their collars, coughed and fidgeted.

"Captain Fredericks," began Lüderitz, "then you are probably not aware that Dr Nachtigall never arrived back in Germany? That he passed away on board ship? We don't know what you are talking about, Captain."

A deep darkness overcame Josef Fredericks. It felt as if he was floating, but like an overfed vulture. He felt as though the anger would throttle him and two spears were piercing his back. He stared at Lüderitz. Then he hissed, spittle flying from his mouth: "*Herr* Lüderitz, the curse of the Namas rests on you! You will never see your home again. Keinaus will punish you!"

Pastor Bam jumped up, but Fredericks strode through the gathering, his jacket flapping behind him, into the street in front of his home. He went straight to the drawer where the brown bottle was hidden under his extra white shirt. All he saw before him were Hendrik Witbooi's eyes.

Dumbfounded, the four strangers departed, without bidding farewell to anyone. Nobody spoke. The people of Bethanien came out only as the riders passed them and rode off into the blazing sun. The ox wagon followed the men on horseback with one German who had taken the *leiriem.*[38] Their Nama *touleier*[39] no longer wanted any part in this expedition because of the curse of !Korebeb//Naixab, Captain Josef Fredericks of Bethanien. One had to be careful of Keinaus when the captain spoke.

A few weeks later, at the mouth of the Gariep River, Lüderitz and one of his assistants hoisted a sail on his boat, but never reached civilization again. Angra Pequena's name was changed to Lüderitzbucht in memory of the cursed and now missing businessman.

The other Germans farmed successfully at Kubub. Josef Fredericks yielded once again. He sold Nomtsas, far to the north, to the Germans as well.

Josef Fredericks's hands shook as he folded Captain Hendrik Witbooi's letter reacting to the Nomtsas agreement. He knew that the clouds of war were gathering in Namaland. He would have to send Cornelius to Witbooi at Hoornkrans to placate him. Perhaps Cornelius could, on the quiet, get Witbooi's daughter to work on keeping the peace. Cornelius must tell him that the *!Aman* would help fight the Hereros. Then Witbooi would stop complaining about the Germans.

Cornelius capered with joy, showing off like a springbok *pronking*[40] around in the veld. First he made himself a pair of new kudu *velskoens.*[41] Then he rushed off to Kuibis to buy a new waistcoat and hat at the German's shop. He asked the shopkeeper to write in the debtors' book. He would settle the amount at the end of the month when he brought in the ostrich skins and feathers.

The road to Hoornkrans meandered through lonely valleys, hills, cliffs and mountains, but water and grazing were available everywhere. Game was plentiful and Cornelius could not understand why so much hatred and acrimony simmered beneath the surface of this harsh land. Surely there was enough land for all. The closer he got to Hoornkrans, the more apprehensive he became. Hendrik Witbooi could be difficult.

---

38 *Leiriem:* Leather thong connecting the heads of the two front oxen in a team drawing an ox wagon. It is held by the *touleier*, usually a younger worker, leading in front.

39 *Touleier:* Worker with the responsibility of holding the *leiriem*, the thong connecting the leading pair of oxen's heads in the team drawing an ox wagon.

40 *Pronking:* peculiar trotting action of springbok showing streak of erect, white fur on its back.

41 *Velskoen/s:* shoe/s made from kudu skin.

Witbooi's guard appeared like a francolin in the undergrowth, as if from nowhere, and reined in his horse in front of Cornelius and his commando.

"Halt. Do you come in peace?" His rifle was at the ready.

"Now what did you scare us like that for?" Cornelius shouted, his hands in the air and his firearm in his right hand.

The guard rode with them along the mountain track which wound around rocky ridges, higher and higher. At last they reached the top and the small village with its new whitewashed church building, a few stone cottages and hundreds of neat //haru oms. The aroma of smoke and meat hung over the village. Everywhere children were running and laughing while the taras bent over their fires, pots and kettles behind the screens of branches.

The visitors stopped in front of the largest house, with its two square glass windows and a neat thatched roof.

The short, dignified man who appeared at the door caused a disturbance amongst the people. Cornelius recalled him from their previous visits to Gibeon, but could not remember whether this man had made such an impression upon him then. Today, here in his mountain fortress, Cornelius felt as if the man was cloaked in a karos of power extending over all of Namaland.

Hendrik Witbooi walked to the group of visitors who waited for him like a bunch of naughty children. To a man, they all removed their hats. Witbooi touched the brim of his hat and extended his hand to Cornelius.

"Good afternoon, Cornelius. How is your father and his people, son? I am glad to see you are not also working in the German's shop like your brother."

Cornelius was relieved that the big man remembered his name. Witbooi greeted each of the visitors and gave instructions that the horses be tended to first. He showed them where to set up camp, and left again.

Later Captain Hendrik Witbooi, or 'Kort' as he was respectfully called by his people, sent word that he was available for talks with the !Aman delegation.

A cool evening breeze wafted over Hoornkrans and its inhabitants. Above them, stars winked in the heavens and a quarter moon peered down. The sheep, mules and horses were quiet in their kraals. Everywhere the taras were producing magical aromas from food taken from Namaland's abundant veld-kitchen. Somewhere the strange sounds of a violin were heard playing a sad melody.

Cornelius's heart pounded wildly when he saw the slender girl with the wide mouth. He saw how Magdalena kept herself busy at the front door and windows of her famous father's house. Around her neck hung a single beaded necklace. So, she had not married yet, but he was not sure. He had to know for certain.

"What brought you to Hoornkrans, Cornelius? Did your father send you to see if there was still any land he could flog to the Germans? Or did he send you to see if the *Khowesin* were keeping the blacks in check so that he could continue living his comfortable life in Bethanien?"

Embarrassed, Cornelius stared at the ground.

"No, Captain. My father is not in good health. He shares your concerns about politics, and he has great respect for you. He wants to help wherever he can, Captain."

The group of *!Aman* had to endure an awkward silence from the short man.

"Good. Here is my message to your father. Not one inch of Namaland must ever again be ceded to a German. Not a single scrap of ground. All over the world the white people of Europe are busy extending their kingdoms, especially here in Africa. Up till now our people of Africa have lived here, fighting one another over grazing and water, but the new enemy is the white man. The English, the French and the Portuguese are gambling for our land. Now the Germans have joined them. Just the other day there was a meeting in Berlin where they made the rules for their game. There they decided who gets what. There they decided who is getting the land of the Namas, who is getting the land of the Basothos, who is getting the land of the Matabeles and who is getting the land of the Shangaans. Every inch of Africa was shared out the way a *taras* dishes up *suurvye*. That's how they divided up Africa's land there in Berlin, the Hoornkrans of the Germans.

"Our ancestors, the Khoi-Khoin, moved from the north hundreds of years ago when they were no better than the sly Bushmen, the San, to get away from the barbaric black robbers and murderers. Our ancestors were the first people to set foot here in the south. They settled everywhere on this side and also the other side of the Gariep River, with their sheep, long before any Dutchman or black man had trodden here.

"But later came the Dutchmen of Europe. They multiplied and became many, like the stars in the sky. They behaved like the honeybird. They danced in our land like the honeybird in front of the Kaiserbird's nest until we became angry and stood up to them and fought back. We had to fight and flee from our land just as the Kaiserbird has to leave its nest to go and fight, enabling the pest of a honeybird to lay its eggs in the Kaiserbird's nest. The Dutchmen did exactly that with our land. They laid their eggs on our land and we became their slaves and had to look after their sheep. Eventually our ancestors moved away from the Colony to escape the Englishman's whip and the Boer's halters and yokes.

"We had no choice. But later, as God willed it here in Namaland, we had our own land again, without Boer, Englishman or blacks. We were the first people, the Khoi-Khoin of this land. We were rid of the deceit of the honeybird.

"Up till the present the sand of the Namib and the Gariep River in the south have protected us, but now your father's greed has given the Germans a way to get at us. That bay that they now call Lüderitzbucht in honour of the thief to whom Josef Fredericks, !Korebeb-Naixab of Bethanien, sold it, has now become the gateway through which the Germans invade Namaland. Up to now they had to come through Walvis Bay, but that is the bay of the English, too far away from the heart of Namaland. Now, more than ever, Namaland needs a strong leader. The !Gami#nun of Abraham Morris and Morenga have to defend the south and in the east is the Kalahari and the might of Simon Koper's !Kharakhoen, but the great danger comes from that bay your father sold, Cornelius. You are the people who will have to be the barrier when the Germans' ships start dropping anchor. You are the man. You, Cornelius Fredericks of Bethanien. You stand between Namaland's heart and Germany."

Cornelius was stunned. His body felt paralysed and his eyes hardened. Everybody was staring at him and his throat became dry. He had never heard of Berlin and he hardly knew names like Portugal and Shangaan, but the captain was spewing them out like the names of Bethanien's birds and animals. He had never in his whole life seen such a clever person. Not even Pastor Bam or the Germans from Angra or that Englishman Radford were as clever as this short, dynamic man, Captain Hendrik Witbooi. He decided there and then: for this man he would fight with his life. For him he would also die, if necessary.

"Captain, your wish is my command. I will fight for Namaland, no matter the cost," was all Cornelius could utter.

Just before they left the following morning, Cornelius walked over to Witbooi's house to say goodbye. He had not yet seen Magdalena properly, let alone talked to her. He could not return home like this. He had to see her first.

And then the miracle happened. While he was taking leave of the captain, the slender girl with the wide mouth appeared in the doorway. Her father stepped aside and looked at his daughter. In her hand was a bag made of animal skin. She walked up to Cornelius. His mouth hung open and his tongue felt like the bark of a dead camel thorn tree. She was the most beautiful thing he had ever seen. She was so different to everything and everyone else. Her eyes were large and wide, quite unlike the narrow eyes of her friends. Her neck was slim and she moved with the grace of an oryx.

She handed Cornelius the bag and looked at her father.

"Something to eat and drink on the way back. This is my daughter, Magdalena. She says she knows you," he said.

Witbooi lifted his chin slightly, observing the two young people through narrowed eyes. He sensed that something was going on between the two young people and he liked the idea.

On the way home Cornelius whistled and sang aloud, *"Kai tseb ge ne steba. Ne kuri //aeb ge !gai //aeba. Hoagu !gai-ai ta ge satsa ra /nam. !Khu khoe ta a."*[42] His friends made fun of the young lover.

It was a beautiful evening at Hoornkrans. The livestock were settled in the kraal for the night. Small cooking fires were burning everywhere. The evening breeze carried the aroma of *!kom*, tripe and leg of mutton. Someone was playing a *settees*[43] on the violin in competition with a choir of croaking frogs. A cackling laugh hinted that a brown bottle or two had found its way into the little village in the mountains.

In the Witbooi home as well, peace reigned. No visitors or meetings or politics tonight. Hendrik could do as he pleased. He read the newspaper. From the trunk under his bed he took out the *Cape Times* that Esterhuizen, the *transportryer*, had left for him at Maltahöhe.

On the front page was an article about a new ballet performance, *The Nutcracker*, by the Russian, Peter Ilyich Tchaikovsky, which had been performed for the first time on two successive nights in both Europe and Russia. He found it strange that one person could be so talented and creative.

---

42   *Kai tseb ge ne steba. Ne kuri //aeb ge !gai //aeba. Hoagu !gai-ai ta ge satsa ra / nam. !Khu khoe ta a: Nama song:* Today is a festival. The season is beautiful. I love you above all. I am now rich.

43   *Settees:* Slow traditional dance music, possibly of German or English origin.

In the distance the happy *settees* changed to the melancholic melody of Psalm 42. The frog choir fell silent. He read of a man who hated Jews and who had been elected to the German Reichstag. Hendrik wondered how such a thing could happen in a civilized country. This man, one Ahlwardt, declared that the Jews were inferior people and that they had no right to exist!

"One should not speak like that about God's chosen people," mumbled Hendrik, disturbed. He read of the trouble in the surly old Dutchman, Paul Kruger's *Zuid-Afrikaansche Republiek*. So many foreigners who were after gold had invaded the Republic that his own Boer people were almost in the minority in their own country. Now the foreigners wanted the vote as well. One of these days it would be the same here in Namaland where the Germans are swarming in like grasshoppers. They do not want the vote; they want the country, that's what, Witbooi thought angrily. Fortunately there is no gold here. He entered a couple of lines in his diary and went to bed.

The *Schutztruppe* under Major Curt von Francois waited until the *Khowesin* were asleep.

"Fire! All men fire!" came the command from behind the rocks.

Immediately all hell broke loose. Germans were charging and shooting everywhere. The Nama stumbled from their dwellings only to fall before the Mausers. Women and children wailed and screamed and the men searched for their weapons.

Captain Hendrik Witbooi could not believe what was happening before his eyes. At first he thought it was the Hereros violating their peace agreement, but then he saw two Germans wresting a child from its mother and shooting the infant in front of her. Then one of them pushed his rifle against the groaning mother's chest and pulled the trigger.

"You bastards! Come here and fight against men!" shouted Witbooi. He shot the first one. The second one took fright and fled into the darkness.

Witbooi knelt by the woman and her child. Both were dead. He ran back to his house.

"Come Katriena, come Magdalena, you must flee. The Germans are here again. It is that Von Francois," he hissed angrily. "You must stay here at the house, Isak. Hide away behind that heap of wood and shoot any German that dares to come close to the house. I'll be right back."

He led Katriena, little Hendrik, Magdalena and Jesias out the back door into the darkness.

After he had seen his wife and children safely off onto the back road, Hendrik returned to his son Isak to help him shoot open an escape route. Hendrik shouted out instructions and the Namas began to summon their courage. They fought the invaders back. Bloodied corpses lay everywhere, mostly women and children. In the darkness chaos reigned.

At dawn the Germans retreated with a group of sixty wailing prisoners: men, *taras* and children. Amongst the war booty carried off by the Germans were three violins and a collection of bangles. And Captain Witbooi's diary.

Katriena Witbooi and her children slowly returned from their hiding place on the ledge of the precipice.

"Katriena, I cannot believe it. No civilized person can do this to women and children. Just last month Von Francois was here, in our house, supposedly to talk about our 'protection'. Against what did he want to protect us? Now is the time for the whole Nama nation to stand up to this treachery!"

Hendrik Witbooi and his men had to dig nearly one hundred graves at Hoornkrans. A bitter hatred took root in his heart.

Cornelius did not hesitate. Before Witbooi's messenger could dismount Cornelius stormed into the house. "*Totob ge khâi hâ!*[44] Father, I am going to help. They cannot do this to our people. I am going to make war. I am going to help the *Khowesin!*"

Josef Fredericks sighed. "*Nē //gâus !nâ du ra hō khoen ge toroba ǂgao tama hâ.*"[45]

The sight of white rows of crosses on fresh graves, like lines of washing on laundry day, met the eyes of Cornelius's small commando as they arrived just outside Hoornkrans. The realization that ninety-eight people had been massacred here surged through his arms, legs and chest like the fire of the scorpion's poison. He recalled Pastor Bam's aversion to rifles.

When he saw Magdalena standing in the doorway, his stomach churned. He let the reins fall to the ground in his haste to remove his hat from his head. They had no words for each other, but fortunately Magdalena's sad countenance changed into a soft smile.

"Cornelius. That is your name?" she teased.

"Correct. I came as soon as I heard. Were you not injured?"

---

44 *Totob ge khâi hâ:* It is war now.

45 *Nē //gâus !nâ du ra hō khoen ge toroba ǂ gao tama hâ:* The people of this house do not want war.

"Good afternoon Cornelius," he heard behind him.

"Afternoon, Captain. Afternoon Auntie Katriena," he greeted the two older people.

"Where is your father, Son?"

"No Captain, he is ill, Captain."

"Very well. How many men did you bring with you?"

"We are only twelve, Captain, but the others will also come, Captain."

Witbooi grunted. "That we will still have to see."

Like a jackal that had caught sheep, Von Francis kept returning to Hoornkrans. Each time the *Khowesin* drove the Germans back.

Then Witbooi spoke. "Men of the *Khowesin*, we cannot stay here longer and wait for Von Francois to attack us. We are going into the desert. It is the place we know but the Germans do not. There we will fight in our own way. And there we will conquer them. We will have to leave here for the time being. We will be moving on in a week's time."

The *Khowesin* packed up. The Captain had spoken. The *taras* broke down the *//haru oms*, bound the sticks in bundles and rolled up the mats.

Cornelius and Magdalena saw each other every day while the preparations for departure were under way. To him she became more beautiful, but he still could not pluck up the courage to ask her father the big question. Each time he saw the short little man, he became tongue-tied.

Witbooi sent the women and children south to Gibeon and Bethanien, to the protection of the Rhenish missionaries. For Cornelius and Magdalena it was a sad farewell.

"My *koekemakranka*,[46] you must look after yourself. We will be back soon," Cornelius promised.

"Cornelius, is it really necessary for you to go with my father? Can't you rather go with us to Gibeon? What about your own people down there in Bethanien?"

"Magdalena, we will never be happy if we have to keep wondering when Von Francois will be back again. Namaland belongs to the Namas. We have to stand together so that we can continue living in peace. Your father is angry with my father for selling Angra Pequena to the Germans. I owe it to him, your father, to you, and to every Nama, to fight against this injustice of Von Francois. I cannot take the route of a coward and sit

---

46   *Koekemakranka*: Edible plant with pleasant aroma, here used as a term of endearment.

with the *taras* at Bethanien or Gibeon and bake *aslêers*. I am a soldier, not a mouse."

Hendrik Witbooi and his men, with Cornelius and his *!Aman* volunteers, moved south-west, into the desert.

For months the *Khowesin* commandos played hide and seek with the Germans in the rocky kloofs and mountains of the Noukloof because this was Nama country. Time and again they let their bullets rain down from the towering rock faces onto the German patrols below.

The Namas humiliated the Germans. From Berlin, Von Francois was ordered to return to Germany. Witbooi laughed.

Soon a new commander, Major Theodor Leutwein, arrived and the whole process started again. After a protracted campaign in the arid mountains, Hendrik decided to talk peace. He and Leutwein signed an accord on condition that the *Khowesin* move back to Gibeon, away from their mountain fortress. In exchange Leutwein promised to keep the Hereros, as well as the other rebellious Nama clans, under control.

How did all of this happen? One day we were still fighting, and now we are friends. Leutwein was a real gentleman, Witbooi thought to himself.

!Korebeb //Naixab, Josef Fredericks, passed away at Bethanien on 20 October 1893. After the funeral Cornelius took over the leadership of the *!Aman*. Daniel wanted to stay away from politics. He preferred to make money in the German's shop.

"Cornelius, have you spoken to my father?"

Cornelius embraced Magdalena.

"Tomorrow is the day, tomorrow. Look, see the twinkling stars? They are telling one another how much I love you."

9

28 March 1906
The trek begins

Steam condensor, source of drinking water at Lüderitzbucht.
When the equipment was out of order the only alternative
supply was water shipped from the Cape Colony.

Joseph walked around his short-tent ox wagon, fully equipped with a
bedstead and side chests. It was freshly painted a leafy green with white
trim along the edges.

"Go! Go! All together! We are on the move!"

Joseph cracked his long whip over the team of oxen, the whip's tip high
above Johannes, the *touleier's* head. The combined strength of the oxen
managed to extract the fully laden wagon out of the sandy jaws of the

beach. Therese sat on the wagon chest with her arm around Charlotte. Joseph walked abreast of the left rear ox, clad in his flapping coat. The oxen, with Johannes at the front, strained as they pulled the load along the winding road. Joseph Luchtenstein was satisfied. In his mind's eye he could already see the large farmhouse he would build, now that his family was reunited. Now the government would allow him to purchase land - because his family was here.

Ernst, still in his soldier's uniform, walked right at the back, his head down. Every now and then he looked back across the bay towards the tortoise-shaped Shark Island. He bit his lower lip as he recalled the day's events. He had nearly drowned that morning. Something had hit him, there in the ice-cold sea. Salt water in his throat, people milling around, a hard knock to his chest, the strange brown people on the island. They looked just like this youngster, Johannes, walking up ahead. Real people, not creatures or animals; small, copper-coloured, like the coffee urn hanging from the rear of the wagon, real people. And the room with the strong odours, the bottles containing flesh, the doctor's eyes, his voice....

"*Aber er ist doch nur ein Jude...*"

And *Vater*? Is this land going to change me just as it has changed him? Who am I?

When the procession eventually reached the top of the double-strip track, Johannes brought the team to a stop on the landward side of *Hafenstrasse*.

"What's wrong, Johannes?" Joseph shouted.

"We need to get the water, *Baas*," Johannes replied.

"Oh yes, but hurry up. Take the *kleinbasie*[47] with you to help. Ernst, go with Johannes and bring the water back at once. No walking round or dawdling. Go, get a move on. Bring two barrels. Get ten marks from your mother, Ernst," commanded Joseph.

Therese handed Ernst the money.

"Why do we have to pay for water, Joseph?" she asked.

"Water is scarce here. The condensors[48] are broken again. The only water available is what comes by ship from the Cape. Our lives depend on that water. There is no water along the road."

"How much water are we taking with us? Two barrels, did you say?"

---

47   *Kleinbasie*: diminutive form of *baas*.

48   *Condensors*: Desalination plants for fresh water from sea water.

"Yes. Two. We will have to use it sparingly. Each of us will get only two mugs of water per day. No more. Tonight the oxen will drink at Boerekamp and tomorrow, after we have trekked a certain distance, we will have to bring them back, without the wagon, to drink again."

"Where is Boerekamp? And for how long will we have to struggle like this without water?"

"Boerekamp is close, not too far from here. And if we are lucky, we will be out of the desert in seven days, at Aus. There is plenty of water there."

"Seven days!" Therese exclaimed. "Where will we sleep? Are there guesthouses?"

"Guesthouses!" Joseph laughed. "A guesthouse in the Namib! No, my wife. Not here. We will be sleeping on and under the wagon."

Therese's shoulders sagged, and she sighed heavily. She hugged Charlotte closely to her and turned her back to the wind that was blowing with increasing ferocity from the south. They were going to sleep in the wilderness. Seven nights!

Joseph marched up and down, inspecting the oxen and the wagon. He adjusted the *jukskeis*[49] and strops and checked on each *lunsriem*, wheel bush, *ronge*, the *dwarsboom*, the *disselboom*[50] and the *langwa*.[51] He did not want any problems along the way. Within a year he must have sufficient money to buy the best farm in the Keetmanshoop district. Then he would build a house, lay out a garden – and give up this transport-riding business for good.

At last the two youngsters could be seen returning from the bottom end of *Bismarckstrasse*. They rolled the two barrels of water up to the wagon. Ernst loved this game of rolling the barrels. And he had made a friend. These copper-coloured people were just normal, real people like himself, he decided.

"Load up, you two! We have to move on!" Joseph commanded. The two youngsters wrestled with the heavy barrels but to no avail. Joseph had to lend them a hand and at last the barrels stood side by side on the

---

49 *Jukskei* (singular) or *skei*: wooden shaft fitted into the yoke on either side of the ox's neck.

50 *Disselboom* (singular) *disselbome* (plural): Central bar, thick and strong, attached to the front of the wagon, can steer to left or right, and affords a traction point to the team of oxen.

51 *Jukskeis, strops, lunsriem, ronge, dwarsboom, langwa*: parts of an ox wagon.

wagon, secured between a sack of maize meal and a few loose pieces of baggage. Therese and Charlotte watched the operation from a distance.

"Go! Go! All together! We are on the move!" Joseph Luchtenstein's voice boomed so loudly that everyone in Lüderitzbucht could hear him.

The Luchtenstein trek creaked slowly forward through *Bismarckstrasse*, past the office of the Woermann shipping line, owners of the Gertrud Woermann and the rest of the Woermann fleet. Slightly higher up, new houses with pitched roofs, turrets and decorative lead glass windows as colourful as finches adorned the steep inclines on both sides of the track, testimony to the new life the Kaiser's first pioneers were bringing to his colony.

A long-tailed mongrel with floppy ears barked and nipped at the leading ox on the right, Janbloed, who tried to butt him away, but Johannes checked the ox with a sharp jerk on the *leiriem*. Therese, sitting up front on the wagon chest, gazed fixedly ahead while the town passed her by.

Ernst now walked in front with his new friend, the *touleier*, Johannes.

1895
Cornelius and Magdalena
at peace

Hendrik Witbooi with one of his grandchildren.

Nē kuri //aeb ge !gâi //aeba[52].

---

52   *Nē kuri //aeb ge !gâi //aeba*: It is a good time.

Namaland flourished under Hendrik Witbooi. The rain fell and the veld yielded food in abundance. The *taras* were never short of mutton or venison. Cornelius no longer had to visit Magdalena with shabby footwear. Every couple of months he had new shoes made from kudu leather. The Germans brought prosperity to Namaland. And liquor. And rifles. The days of trekking to the Colony to buy ammunition or maize meal were over.

A dark-skinned stranger arrived at Gibeon. He brought with him only the clothes on his back and a Bible.

"Shepherd Stuurman," he introduced himself.

His voice sounded strange. Hendrik Witbooi had never heard such an accent before.

"Where are you from, nephew?" he asked.

The man pointed northwards over his shoulder.

"God has sent me to you, Captain Witbooi. To lead you."

Some said that Stuurman came from far away, from Abyssinia. Stuurman did not deny this. But he did not confirm it either.

Witbooi and Leutwein's luke-warm friendship and their official cooperation agreement obliged Namaland's diminutive general, leader of the *Khowesin,* to discipline the Khaus Namas, Bondelswarts, Ovambanderu, Swartboois and the Hereros from time to time. He was strict and intolerant of his countrymen's lawless behaviour, coming down on them hard. Wherever Witbooi and his punitive commando rode, the mysterious Shepherd Stuurman accompanied them. If the Bondelswarts had hidden the stolen livestock in the south, then the man of God would lead them directly to the herd. If the Hereros strayed into the mountains in the north, it would be Shepherd Stuurman who found them there.

When Cornelius finally got around to asking the big question, Witbooi felt he had to obtain a blessing from Stuurman.

"Captain Witbooi," said Shepherd Stuurman, "He is a good son, that one, a real Israelite in whom there is no deceit."

It was a grand wedding. It had to be. The leader of the *!Aman,* Cornelius Fredericks, married the daughter of Hendrik Witbooi. There was a mounted guard of honour, plenty of food and music. The *trapmesiek,*[53] mouth organ and violins set everyone dancing and soon they were all doing the *Nama-stap,*[54] including the captain.

---

53   *Trapmesiek*: Nama-Afrikaans word for mechanical organ, operated by a separate foot pump for air.

54   *Nama-stap*: Folk dance of the Nama people.

When the feast was over, the newly married couple were alone at last.

"Magdalena, my *koekemakranka*, I have two gifts for you."

From his coat pocket he took the *!uros* he had made from a tortoise shell, and from the other pocket he produced the bead necklace that he had ordered from the *taras* in Gibeon.

Magdalena clasped her two small hands to her wide mouth.

"Oh, my Cornelius, oh my beautiful big strong man, thank you! Thank you, thank you," she called out, dancing with joy. She drew him close and kissed him.

Witbooi read in the *Cape Times* of an unsuccessful invasion of Paul Kruger's republic by a doctor, Leander Starr Jameson, for whom they had to thank the Colony's Prime Minister, Cecil John Rhodes.

"The English are like the Germans, always wanting to take other people's land," snorted Witbooi over his coffee.

He also read of a new invention: a machine that could look inside a person's body. They called it an X-ray. Sounds like it comes from the devil, he thought. Elsewhere he read about the opening of the new opera, *La Boheme,* by a man with the strange name of Puccini.

Cornelius and Magdalena settled peacefully in Bethanien. Now and then he had to accompany his father-in-law on a punitive expedition. When he was alone in the mountains the longing for his wife settled on him like a dark cloud.

Magdalena was again with child – very happy, a good wife to Cornelius and a loving mother to their firstborn, Little Hendrik.

28–29 March 1906
From Boerekamp to Grassplatz

Offloading grass at Grassplatz

The team of oxen hauled their load along the dirt road that snaked its way up the hill, higher and higher, towards the blue and white sky. Man and beast had to screw up their eyes and walk with lowered heads in an effort to protect themselves from the blast of sand-needles driven by the strong south-easter.

Behind them the view of the bay, with its harbour and ships, gradually shrank in size. The sun, having burnt away the last vestiges of fog that lay over the sea and land, was now scorching the earth with oven-like heat. The wagon levelled out, then moved more easily downhill. Therese looked up. They were at the top of the first hill, on the outskirts of the town. In front of her there was an ants' nest of activity consisting of oxen, mules, horses, wagons, tents and people.

"Boerekamp. Whoa, whoa, stop!" Joseph called.

The Boers from the two old republics, the *Zuid-Afrikaansche Republiek* (ZAR) and the *Republiek van die Oranje-Vrijstaat*, had three or four years previously lost the war against the British, Johannes explained to Ernst. Many of the Boers had lost everything, some of them also their families in the English concentration camps. The transport business in German South-West Africa was a godsend to these men of the veld, men with ox wagons in their blood. It was a new beginning, a new adventure, with money from German South-West Africa being far more attractive than the Englishman's yoke.

Johannes outspanned the two front oxen, Hoogmoed and Janbloed.

"Come with me, Ernst! I am going to teach you how the life of a *transportryer* works."

They took the two oxen to the drinking place where people met to chat and gossip, and where the team leaders swapped stories and news about stopovers, springs and grazing along the different routes.

"Ukamas and Kaukausib's springs still flow freely, but Tschaukaib is already under strain," one *touleier* told the others.

"My *baas* lost his pipe and tobacco pouch at Rotkop. Please keep your eyes open for it when you pass that way," another mentioned.

Johannes explained to Ernst what lay ahead of them; eighty miles of Namib Desert between Lüderitzbucht and Aus.

"Ernst, this is a long, long road, and it's uphill all the way. It is also not a road like you would know. It is actually a river of sand with the east wind in your face and the sun blasting heat like the bellows over a blacksmith's oven in Keetmanshoop. Water is scarcer here than eland in Lüderitzbucht's main street.

"Only five teams per day are allowed to trek from Lüderitzbucht because the water at Ukamas, Tschaukaib and Kaukausib is not enough for any more animals than that," Johannes told him. "When we have travelled some distance into the desert, we will outspan the oxen and drive them back to Boerekamp to drink. Then we drive them back to the wagons and move on again. In this way we'll advance further and further into the desert every day until we are closer to the watering holes in the desert than to Boerekamp. There are three roads between Aus and Lüderitzbucht and the water at the watering holes will tell us which road to take. The good rains of last month might help us to take the shorter route through Tschaukaib."

They had to rig up a canvas to the side of the wagon to shield Therese and Charlotte from the merciless sun. Boerekamp's barren earth had no trees or shrubs, just as in ancient Israel. One of the Boers in the camp, noticing that Ernst was a recently arrived German immigrant, offered him some biltong. They were amused when he started chewing on the hard, dry meat and pulled a face, but he was soon enjoying the taste of this new delicacy.

Joseph checked the wagon and equipment again, inspected the oxen's hooves and readjusted the load. The safety of the entire trek depended on the state of the oxen's hooves. The heat of the Namib sand causes the hooves to crack.

"In an emergency we make shoes from the skin of a slaughtered ox," Johannes explained, while they drove the nine spare oxen they had left at Boerekamp the day before towards the wagon.

Therese was overjoyed when she was able to buy fresh bread and even a bucket of milk from the *smous's* mule wagon. She learnt from a lady, Johanna van der Merwe, how to brew tea over an open fire. Johanna explained in faulty German that she and her husband had arrived from the old ZAR, after all five of her children had died in the Volksrust concentration camp.

She could not keep her eyes off Charlotte. In tears she related how her own daughter of a similar age had been snatched from her by a British soldier, only to die later, alone in the camp hospital. Therese placed her arm around Johanna's shoulder and tried to comfort her.

Just after sunrise the next morning Joseph's bellowed command could be heard once more: "Go, go! All together now!"

The long whip circled and cracked through the air.

Ahead lay the bleached dunes of the Namib, as pale as a cadaver drained of blood. Therese held Charlotte to her side and hummed an old German song. Walking up front with Johannes, Ernst stared in awe at the vast, barren landscape around them.

The hushed atmosphere was broken only by the knocking of the yokes, the wagon wheels grinding through the sand and the intermittent cracks from Joseph's whip, high above the oxen.

For the first few miles they moved past hundreds of copper-brown people who were carrying railway tracks and sleepers and were digging in the sand. Soldiers, armed with rifles and whips, rode up and down next to the workers.

"They are making the iron road to Keetmanshoop for the new iron wagon," explained Johannes.

A vicious south-easter began to howl, stinging the weary group with millions of grains of sand. The oxen struggled and strained up the inclines. The wagon moved more and more slowly. Joseph cracked the whip and roared at the oxen. For a few seconds they pulled valiantly, then began to falter again.

Eventually, he whistled sharply.

"Whoa, whoa! Let's rest. Whoa, Johannes!"

The oxen stopped at once. Almost simultaneously they emptied their bladders. Joseph smelt the strong ammonia of their urine, but they all remained standing. If one of the exhausted animals were to lie down, it would spell trouble.

They moved on in the heat with the sound of thunder rolling towards them from the clouds on the horizon. Ernst's feet dragged on, ever more slowly. All there was to see was the white sand that he had watched for days on end from the ship. Joseph knew that they had to reach Grassplatz before the sun was too high, or man and beast would perish.

The day became a white-hot oven from hell. The wind blasted the sand right into the faces of the small group of people and animals. Joseph and Johannes sensed trouble. Again they had to call a halt in a patch of loose sand. Carefully Joseph opened the barrel of precious water and decanted water into a tin cup. He took a mouthful and held the cup out to Therese. She handed the cup to Charlotte. The little girl drank until she was out of breath.

In silence, everyone drank, careful not to waste a single drop. One of the oxen, smelt the water, and bellowed deeply. Joseph looked behind him. He realised that Roman, one of the oxen, would probably not make it to Grassplatz.

A pale fluttering movement on the stony sand caught Ernst's attention. A small upright bird scratched around on the ground, ran, scratched and ran again. He could not believe his eyes. Life! Could something be alive in this merciless hell? Impossible, he thought.

"What is that, this little bird, Johannes?"

"That? That is the dune lark. He stays here where other people and birds are too afraid to stay. He does not fear being alone. This is his land."

Ernst stared at the dune lark, amazed at the dull but brave sprite of life in this stark wilderness. He felt something like a spark of hope, like when Mother promised him a gift.

"We have to move. Get up, get up. Let's trek. Go, go! All together now!" Joseph called out.

His long whip cracked above the heads of the two front oxen, Hoogmoed and Janbloed. At first they responded feebly, but then, with Johannes's gentle words and Joseph's whip, the oxen were coaxed into making a brave team effort. They strained and heaved and the wagon moved an inch or two forward. They held the load but eventually Roman's hooves slipped and he buckled under the weight.

"Whoa, whoa," Joseph calmed the animals.

Roman, distressed, bellowed and tried to get up on his legs again.

"Johannes, untie Roman and Ligman."

He walked around the wagon, scratching his beard and muttering to himself.

"Ernst, help me. Do this. No, not right now, just wait, wait until I tell you to. Johannes, untie Roman and Ligman. Then replace them with Bergland and Witlies."

Joseph knelt at the right front wheel and dug furiously to remove the loose sand. Johannes was already busy at the left front wheel. Ernst started doing the same at the rear right wheel. The hot sand burnt his hands and the wind blew fine grains into his eyes, mouth and ears. He soon became exhausted, but if he gave up he would get it from his father. Eventually Joseph stood upright.

"Right. Everyone to a wheel. When I crack the whip, we push together. Right? Ernst. Left rear. Therese, you and Charlotte, stay behind the wagon. If Charlotte gets under the wagon or in between the oxen, she will be hurt. Everyone must help!"

Joseph talked to his oxen. Roman and Ligman, who had been outspanned, stood tethered to one side. The whip cracked, and the *trektou*,[55] a heavy, shining chain, tightened. With all their strength, Joseph and Ernst heaved at the wheels to get them moving while Joseph roared at the

---

55 *Trektou*: Afrikaans word for the heavy chain attached to the wagon's *disselboom*, leading between the two rows of oxen, and attached to each of the yokes. In earlier times it consisted of a thick, braided, leather thong.

animals, in between cracking the whip. At last the wheels broke free from the grip of the sand. The wagon started moving. The children cheered and Joseph and Therese exchanged a smile of relief.

Step by step and with lowered heads, the men and oxen ploughed through the hot, loose sand. It felt as if the few hundred yards to the top of the dune were endless, and stretched into heaven, but they had no choice but to continue uphill. The sun beat down and the east wind blew the sand against them, stinging them like thousands of bees. At last they reached the summit.

On the other side, the decline was so steep that the wagon quickly picked up speed. Joseph ran to the rear of the wagon. On the run he engaged the brake and whistled to calm the oxen to a slow walk. He hung on to the wagon, heels digging into the sand. Ernst immediately grasped the situation, grabbed hold of the railing and helped to hold the wagon back. Luckily the animals slowed down, and they resumed the trek down the winding track at a normal pace again.

Ernst felt something sting in his left thumb. He saw that a wood splinter must have broken off from the wagon's railing while he was helping to slow it down. He pulled the splinter out and watched as the blood oozed from his thumb and dropped onto the hot sand. The memory of blood trickling out of his arm onto a white sheet rushed back to him. What had happened there?

"*Aber er ist doch nur ein Jude...*"

Is that really who I am?

He looked around him and for the first time noticed the stones and hardy little shrubs clinging bravely to the dunes. He also saw the sand lying like waves of the sea on small and large dunes, with troughs in between. There were branches and stones, light and shade, and even what looked like the tracks or droppings of a strange animal here and there. He realised that the white sand was more than just white sand. Was this country perhaps home to something else besides hatred and fury? He drew in a slow, long breath until he felt as if he could taste the sand, animals, air and sun. Something felt new and strange and good to him, different from what he had experienced in life so far. Could it be that the unique quality of this country was bringing him some kind of quiet joy? he wondered.

When they crossed a low dune, they saw an unusual sight below in the valley: people. A group of men, six or seven, dressed in smart suits, complete with ties, jackets and boots, were gathered around a horse-drawn carriage. Joseph saw that the men were studying maps and documents.

"Good morning," he greeted them when the wagon came to a stand-still. "Luchtenstein," he introduced himself.

The leader, a short man with a black and grey goatee, approached and removed his hat. "August Stauch. Pleased to meet you."

Therese nodded and managed a smile from where she sat on the wagon chest.

"What are you doing in this forlorn place, *Herr* Stauch, if I may ask?" enquired Joseph.

"We are working on the railway line, so that you will no longer need to risk your lives for weeks in the desert. We want to be finished before the end of the year."

Without bidding farewell, Joseph cracked his whip. The railway line troubled him. How would he survive when the railway put an end to his transport business? With Therese and the children here, he would now be able to buy land. His trek took on even greater urgency. He must have a farm by the time the trains started rolling.

They passed a long row of half-naked, copper-brown prisoners, chained together and accompanied by a mounted patrol. The leader of the patrol had a stout riding crop in his hand. The open, swollen welts on the prisoners' backs demonstrated that the crop was being put to frequent and thorough use.

Ernst couldn't believe his eyes.

"What's going on, Johannes? What have these people done? Are they people, real people, I mean are they your people?"

"They are Namas who stood up to the Germans."

Johannes looked away.

"Good afternoon, *Hauptmann*[56]," Joseph greeted the officer astride a large brown horse.

The officer nodded. "Afternoon. You must be careful. Not too far from here, another group of natives are roaming around, causing trouble. This lot are on their way to the new concentration camp on Shark Island at Lüderitzbucht to work on the railway line."

Therese felt anxiety constrict her throat. She remembered the row upon row of copper-brown people, men, women and children they had seen, carrying rails and sleepers for the new line.

---

56   Hauptmann: Captain.

They moved on. Ernst was quiet. He looked back. Even the oxen pulling their wagon had a better life than these prisoners, he thought.

"We are nearly there. Can you see?" Joseph pointed at a crooked Bushman thorn tree surrounded by a few small shrubs and some stones below on the plain. On one side were four ox wagons and their out-spanned oxen.

The wagon descended the dune rapidly, and relief washed over them all. Joseph walked proud and tall, whistling through his teeth. Johannes had to jog to keep ahead of the oxen.

Since they had left the top of the previous dune, it felt as if the fury of the east wind had also abated. Therese pointed out to Charlotte the expanse of the rolling dunes, covered here and there with sparse shrubs like the stubbly beard of an old man.

"Joseph, my dear husband, it is good to see you again," she said with a smile, as he walked beside her.

Joseph looked at her.

"It has been long, Therese. I have worked hard, but it is better here than in Germany. Here one is free."

Joseph's eyes grew soft as he gazed at his family. He looked at his daughter with her blonde braids and blue eyes. He looked at Ernst, the one with the grey-blue eyes and the deep dimple in his chin, the one who spoke little and who was always on his own. What did the child think of all day?

Joseph returned his gaze to his wife. For a couple of seconds their eyes met, like in the old days. They reached the Bushman thorn tree and the circle of stones: Grassplatz, place of grass, their home for the day. The travellers from the other wagons lazed about while the animals crowded around the feeding trough. All the trekkers off-loaded a supply of fodder and a barrel of water, which was more precious than gold, every time they passed by here from the interior.

"Whoa, whoa, outspan!" Joseph called out, exhausted but happy and proud that they had made it.

Johannes bustled around to undo all the *rieme,* to remove the yokes and to free the tired animals. He arranged all the gear so that it was ready for the evening inspan.

Chivvying his touleier, Joseph said, "Johannes, you must get going; it is late and the road is long."

Johannes gathered the oxen together with a few sharp whistles, which were not even necessary. The patient animals knew the routine. They turned around in their tracks and took off in the direction that they had come from, back to Lüderitzbucht. Johannes took Joseph's whip, grabbed his bottle of water and trotted after the animals.

"Where is Johannes going, *Vater*?" asked Ernst.

"To Boerekamp. The oxen must drink there, because we are moving on tonight."

Ernst stared after the trusty animals and their *touleier*. He could not believe his ears. The oxen had trekked the entire day to get here, and tonight they had to move on again, but first they had to retrace their footsteps to Boerekamp, then return to Grassplatz, before trekking further into the desert, eastwards.

Joseph struggled to tilt the water barrel to decant water into a clay urn.

"Come here, Ernst. Lend me a hand."

Ernst clambered onto the wagon wheel. They filled the urn and Joseph sealed the precious barrel with the cork.

"Listen children, our lives depend on this water. You mustn't waste any. We only have two barrels and we can only fill up at Tschaukaib or Garub, if we are lucky," Joseph said.

"Joseph, apart from the water, what else can go wrong? Are there wild animals? Are there lions here? And natives?" asked Therese.

"There is nothing, my wife. No lions, elephants or natives…."

"And tigers and wolves?" she persisted.

Joseph evaded her eyes by fidgeting with the baggage on the wagon. "Don't be afraid, Therese. I have never seen a tiger or a wolf in Africa…".

"And the natives? The *Hauptmann* said…"

"How do you think a native could survive in this desert?" answered Joseph.

He was secretly concerned himself about the troublesome Namas. Cornelius Fredericks' *!Aman* were difficult. The Bondelswarts were also restless, always on the move, ahead of the *Schutztruppe*. Everywhere they went, they stole and murdered. Then there were also the Fransman people of Simon Koper, and the worst of the lot, Jakob Morenga, the Black Napoleon.

Even the east wind seemed to be tired, its incessant howling having subsided. The Namib sky was white as snow.

Ernst listened to the silence. He bent down, scooped up some sand and let it run through his fingers like water from an urn. When he looked up he saw an oryx, high up on the rim of the highest dune. He marvelled at the animal's beauty and spear-like horns. The oryx stood erect and proud, watching the human activity down below. Entranced, Ernst stared at the magnificent animal, surrounded by the stark desert. This desert had life in it, he thought, real life. The desert breathed, its heart beat and its hands had feeling.

The family set up camp. Joseph attached the large canvas to the wagon. The one side of the tarpaulin was secured to the upper beam to make a low shelter where they could rest.

"Bring wood, we want to boil water for coffee," Joseph ordered.

Ernst had to walk far and wide to find it, because there were no large trees. At last he collected enough dry *Boesmankers*[57] for kindling, so Joseph could start a small fire. Charlotte stared at the flames and pushed grass stems and twigs into it.

Therese scrabbled around in the food-box. She had no idea what her family would eat that evening. Next to the water barrels she found a hessian bag of coarse white meal. All she could find in the food-box were dry, rock-hard pieces of meat, a large salt ham in a cotton bag, a round cheese, a packet of salt, tins of sugar, coffee, tea and some strange fruit with hard prickly shells.

"Joseph, what is this dry meat and these hard vegetables? And this coarse flour? Must we eat this?"

"It is biltong. Good food. We have sufficient for two weeks. The flour is maize, mealie meal. We cook it in water. Then it becomes porridge. *Pap* the Boers call it. It is also good."

"I ate biltong in Boerekamp. It's really good," said Ernst.

Joseph took the three-legged cast iron pot from the wagon. He put five cups of water into it and placed it on the fire. He then added half a teaspoon of salt to the water and waited for the water to boil. Then he added some of the meal slowly whilst stirring it with a thick dry stick. Therese, hands on hips, watched the process closely. Joseph placed the lid onto the pot. He then fetched a *riempiestoel*[58] from the wagon for Therese to sit on.

"Sit down, Therese," he said. Then he went back to the wagon again and came back with a brown bottle. He poured a little of the contents into a tin cup for himself.

"What is that? What are you drinking?"

"Brandy. Like cognac. From the Cape. You also want to try some?"

---

57   *Boesmankers*: Namib plant used as fire lighter and candle

58   *Riempiestoel*: small folding stool with a seat of *riempies*.

"No thanks, but may I have a cup of water?"

"Ernst! A cup of water for Mother."

The family sat around the fire in silence, Joseph and the children sitting flat on the ground.

"When will Johannes return with the oxen, *Vater*?" Ernst asked.

"Later."

Joseph lifted the lid and stirred the thick white mixture.

Therese dished up small portions onto tin plates. The children looked at one another and began toying with their food. Ernst pushed his spoon into the *pap* and laughed when the spoon remained standing upright. Charlotte took a mouthful, tasted it without enthusiasm, but then took another one and began to enjoy this strange new food.

Joseph took a large piece of biltong from the food-box. He took his knife from the sheath on his belt and carved small pieces from the biltong, sharing it with Therese and the children. At first they chewed hesitantly, but then devoured the dry meat eagerly. All of them asked for more.

Suddenly a small dun-coloured bird with a black mask and collar appeared from nowhere. He stood bolt upright in front of Joseph and twittered cheerfully, hoping for something to eat.

"Father, what is that? A dune lark? No, it can't be. It's completely different," said Ernst, surprised. He remembered the dune lark.

"That is a *skaapwagter*, Ernst. *Schmätzer* in German, I think," answered Joseph. He told them there were many animals and birds in the Namib Desert.

Ernst repeated it in his mind: *skaapwagter, skaapwagter, skaapwagter.* He liked the sound. He also liked the cheeky little bird who lived so contentedly here in the dry wilderness.

Therese surprised everyone when she produced a tin of fine biscuits from the bottom of her trunk that she had brought all the way from Germany. Charlotte fell asleep on her mother's lap. Therese asked Joseph to pick her up. She climbed onto the wagon, arranged the blankets under the canvas tent, took Charlotte from him and laid her down gently. Then she made a bed for herself amongst all the paraphernalia.

Ernst lay down in the shade of the canvas and immediately fell asleep.

Joseph checked the yokes, and then lay down underneath the wagon to get a little sleep.

All was quiet. The east wind began to blow again. Joseph got up and walked around the wagon and saw to it that everything was secured. He knew that anything left standing out in the open would be blown away.

Then he heard the horns of two oxen crack against each other and Johannes's sharp, distinctive whistle. Johannes and the oxen were back. Joseph walked in amongst them and spoke to his animals.

"Afternoon, Johannes. Did you go well?" Joseph walked through the herd, here and there stroking their muscular backs.

"I went well, my *baas*. Very well."

"Did you hear anything about the Oorlams, Johannes?"

"Nothing, my *baas*. It is only the *!Kharakhoen*[59] that make trouble."

"They said the Fransmanne had slit the throats of the German soldiers at Kubub, my *baas*. And took their horses."

Joseph shuddered. This insurrection had been going on for too long. He had hoped that Von Trotha would make a difference. Leutwein before him was too soft and so the Kaiser's government decided to send General Lothar von Trotha to German South-West to solve the native problem. Von Trotha had quickly sorted out the Herero problem in the north. Why was he struggling so much with the Namas?

The exhausted oxen lay down to chew the cud.

"Johannes, there is still some *pap* in the pot. When you are finished eating, clean the pot before you go to sleep. We must move early. I don't want to be in the blazing sun again all day."

"Yes, my *baas*."

It was quiet in the Luchtenstein camp. The people and animals of the other treks also rested.

Just before turning in, Joseph removed his Mauser from the wagon kist and checked if there were rounds in the magazine.

---

59   *!Kharakhoen*: The Fransman Nama tribe led by Simon Koper.

12

1899–1904
Wars in Africa and a German soldier's dream

A group of German volunteers with the Boer forces during the Anglo Boer War 1899–1902. Photograph from the Ditsong National Museum of Cultural History, number HKF 128, 27/1

In Germany an old man called his son.

"Thilo, come here. Read this."

Young Thilo came from his room. In the hallway hung the portraits of five generations who bore the name Thilo von Trotha. The blood of a powerful military tradition ran in their veins. His uncle Lothar, too, was a soldier.

War in ZAR shouted the thick black letters on the front page of the *Berliner Morgenpost*. Paul Kruger's Republic in the south of Africa was on the road to a military confrontation with Britain, the paper said.

Thilo decided it was not a bad idea to go after a bit of an adventure in Africa. On board the ship taking German soldiers and nurses to Africa to help the Boers, fate forged a bond between Thilo and an attractive volunteer nurse, Margarethe. Their forced separation in Delagoa Bay cut into their two young hearts.

Thilo, as a member of the German corps, engaged in battle with the British who had advanced from Durban, but he had to flee from the Fifth Royal Irish Lancers at Elandslaagte. On the front in the battles of Colenso, Platrand and Spioenkop he quickly picked up the Boer language. The waving grasslands, blue cliffs, thick forests and bushveld enchanted him, but when an English bullet hit him for the fourth time in a few months, he was captured by the enemy. He became a Boer prisoner-of-war behind barbed wire on the island of Ceylon.

The war in the ZAR came to an end. The British took Paul Kruger's land. At the same time they helped themselves to the neighbouring territory, the Orange Free State, as well.

In Germany the two Boer war veterans, Thilo and Margarethe, walked under a guard of honour made up of the swords of Thilo's comrades who were dressed in ceremonial regalia, while the bells of the old church pealed and they were showered with grains of rice.

Both Thilo and Margarethe shared an obsession: Africa. They wanted to live on a farm, like the Boers, with sheep, horses and cattle. Their opportunity came in the form of another conflict: a war against the inhabitants of German South-West Africa, the Hereros.

"Margarethe, here is our chance. This time it will not take as long as it did for the English to conquer the Boers. This time it is the might of the Kaiser against a few thousand simple barbarians. Every officer who volunteers now will be allocated a farm. This is our chance. I am going over there now, and as soon as the war is over, you must come too."

"Thilo, my husband, that sounds like a good plan. I will wait for you. You must just write to me every day."

13

30 March 1906
The third day in Africa

Time to outspan and rest.

"Wake up! Get up! We must move on!"

It was still dark the following morning when Joseph's voice broke the quiet. The other *trekkers* already had their animals inspanned, all set to depart.

Ernst looked at Johannes sitting on his haunches, busy cleaning the *pap* pot. He admired this strong young man with his tattered clothes and handmade shoes.

"*Tita ge satsa ra tawede*[60]," Johannes greeted Ernst.

---

60   *Tita ge satsa ra tawede*: I greet you.

"Johannes, will you teach me to speak your language? Please? I want to talk like you and *Vater*."

"We, your father and I, speak the language of the Boers, but my real language is Nama. It is a difficult language and a youngster from Germany won't be able to speak it."

"But I want to. Please. Will you teach me? Both languages. I want to learn to speak the language of the Boers and your language."

"Well then, my Kaiser. Your wish is my command," laughed Johannes.

Johannes inspanned the oxen with Ernst hovering around him. Ernst quickly realised that it was no easy task to inspan oxen.

"*Titats ge ga hui*[61]!" Johannes called out. "Careful, Ernst. Never cross the *trektou*. If you scare the oxen and that chain is tightened while you are standing over it, you will be badly injured."

Ernst studied the long *trektou* that was tied to the *kramme*[62] on the yokes by means of the *teertrense*[63].

Just before the sun appeared from behind the dune, the wagon's wheels creaked across the sand again. The oxen's hides and eyes were duller than yesterday, and their sharp hipbones looked as though they would pierce their skins.

Ernst was walking next to Johannes in front with the leading oxen.

"Johannes, make sure that Ernst doesn't get hurt. And he is not to touch the *leiriem*, do you hear?" instructed Joseph from the rear.

"Right, my *baas*."

"Johannes, how long have you been working for my father?"

"It is now three years. Since he arrived here."

He told Ernst stories about their wanderings in the desert between Keetmanshoop and Lüderitzbucht, of hardships, heat and cold, hunger and thirst, as well as illness and pain. Ernst hung on his every word.

In some places twenty or more sets of tracks lay next to one another, indicating where other trekkers before them had taken different routes through the sand. Johannes chose the correct route, every time.

Ernst's language lessons drove away his exhaustion. He felt as though he was becoming like Johannes and beginning to think like him. As time went on, conversation between the two gradually ceased. Around them

---

61 *Titats ge ga hui*: Help me.
62 *Kramme*: rectangular brackets on the underside of the yoke.
63 *Teertrense*: strong leather thongs used to tie the *kramme* to the *trekketting*.

stretched the Namib's endless empty plains, blasted white by the heat of the sun, like iron in a forge.

Joseph drove the *trek* as hard as he could. He knew the desert well and was aware that it was a race against time, thirst, exhaustion, hunger and illness. No living being would be able to survive in this manner in the desert for much longer than a week. Joseph had planned this trip well. He knew that he had nine oxen in reserve. He could afford to lose as many as fourteen or fifteen oxen when they were still one day away from Aus. From Aus four or six oxen could pull the wagon. The great challenge was to reach Aus. From there onwards it was easy.

At a small depression in the desert, between two rocky outcrops, Johannes swung due south, away from the wagon trail, into the desert.

"What now?" Therese called out.

"Nothing, my wife, we will soon be there and then you can get down from the wagon and we can make camp."

Behind the dune, hidden from the wagon trail and the eyes of other transport riders, next to a lone thorn tree with low spreading branches, lay a pile of wood as high as the wagon. Johannes immediately outspanned the tired animals. They rushed over to the wood pile and began sniffing and trying to dislodge the pieces of wood. Johannes let them be while he dismantled the pile. Underneath the wood were two barrels of water and a pile of grass fodder that they had hidden there eight days before.

Johannes spread the bundles of dry grass out over a wide area with some of the animals following him and nudging him in the back. They began feeding on the grass, but soon stopped as it wasn't very tasty. Then they moved around bellowing and sniffing, heads lowered over the chalky, stony ground, before coming back to taste the dry grass again. The only water they would get that night would be from the two barrels of water. Johannes could not take the animals back to Lüderitzbucht or Grassplatz. The great distance would do more harm than good. The following morning they had to be close to Tschaukaib and the day after that they needed to push through to Tsirub. That is, only if there was enough good water at Tschaukaib. If not, they would have to get to Ukamas quickly or trek even further south, to Kaukausib.

Johannes inspanned the oxen again, but only to keep them under control. He filled the buckets with water from the barrels, and emptied them into the trough. Then he outspanned two oxen and brought them to the trough, repeating this process a pair of oxen at a time. He had to have his wits about him with the animals pushing and butting to get to the precious water, while the other oxen, still yoked, bellowed in their desperate need to drink.

14

Hereroland falls

11 August 1904, the day before the Battle of Waterberg. The German Schutztruppe prepare for the attack against the Herero stronghold.

Ever since the body of the great king of the Hereros, Tjamuaha Maherero, had been laid to rest under Okahandja's large camel thorn trees fourteen years before, there had been unrest in Hereroland. All the chiefs of the different Herero clans vied for his crown.

The Hereros were not afraid of running up debt in the Germans' shops. How else could the women afford the latest fashions worn by the English Queen? Tjamuaha's legitimate successor, his son Samuel, especially liked things that glittered. When the rinderpest of 1896 and debt eventually caught up with him, Samuel sold land to the Germans, land that belonged to other Herero chiefs. He later denied these transactions.

A shooting in the far south ended with two corpses: those of Lieutenant Walther Jobst of the *Schutztruppe* and the Bondelswarts' leader, Jan Christiaan. The governor, Major Theodor Leutwein, at the helm for the past ten years, intervened to suppress another Bondelswarts uprising. His mission to Warmbad took six weeks, during which time his junior officers were in charge of Hereroland. In the west Lieutenant Ludwig von Estorff scored a victory over the Hereros and made peace with Zacharias Zeraua's tribe, only to make a new decision, the next day.

"Zacharias, I have decided to take your people away from here because a great war is coming and you could get hurt."

"But Lieutenant, yesterday you said we could stay here?"

"You will be better off, Zacharias, believe me."

Zacharias Zeraua complied. He trusted the friendly, open-faced German. A Christian to boot, he thought to himself.

The young Lieutenant Zürn, acting commanding officer in Okahandja, devised his own plans for the stubborn Hereros.

"If they don't want to sign, then I will sign on their behalf," he decided.

He made three rough crosses on a 'contract', not knowing that the Herero chiefs who refused to sign could write very well. Zürn's avarice and audacity exceeded even that of the Hereros. He had a few old Herero skulls dug up and then sold them.

The spirits of the Hereros' ancestors were disturbed and provoked the people to conspiracy. Armed, rebellious gangs roamed everywhere, and rumours rolled through Okahandja's streets like tumbleweed.

Lieutenant Zürn forced all German citizens to go into the fort. Two spies left the fort to find out what the Hereros were planning. They saw one hundred armed Hereros saddling up and they then promptly raced back to the fort. Lieutenant Zürn telegraphed Berlin: "The war has started."

Shots. Chaos. No one knew who had fired first. Both sides blamed the other. The Hereros plundered the town. Years of frustration and plain greed gave birth to a revolution. They robbed stores, plundered, torched buildings and murdered two German couples. The German soldiers defended their positions courageously and according to military doctrine while the Hereros rampaged through Hereroland in a mad frenzy of destruction. They destroyed the railway lines to Windhuk.

Only six weeks later did Major Leutwein, the governor, return from his peace mission to Warmbad to resume command. In Germany the

Kaiser and the Reichstag were infuriated with the audacity of the black people. Two thousand new *Schutztruppe*, one of them Lieutenant Thilo van Trotha, disembarked at Swakopmund. The first real German army, in the true sense of the word, hoisted the red and black flag of Germany in a country now consumed with rage.

Thousands of Herero soldiers with their women and children barricaded themselves in the mountains of Okanjira, two days' journey on horseback from Okahandja. Major Leutwein, assembled a force of eight hundred men. He believed that he held two trump cards: one hundred Nama scouts under the leadership of none other than the legendary Hendrik Witbooi – once his enemy, but now his ally - and the other, the latest German artillery, comprising Maxim machine guns.

The Naukluft Convention of ten years earlier took effect again: Witbooi had to help. He was nearly seventy-four years of age, but the little general feared nobody, especially not a Herero. He still dreamed of a country in the north, in the Hoornkrans area, free from black enemies. One of Witbooi's confidants was his son-in-law, Cornelius Fredericks, captain of the *!Aman* of Bethanien, a brave warrior with a thorough knowledge of the veld. Also on commando and always at his side, was his personal prophet and mentor, Shepherd Stuurman, 'the dark man from Abyssinia', as they called him.

With the help of the Namas the Germans surrounded the Herero camp at Okanjira. Soon the bombs and machine guns of modern warfare exploded around the shocked Hereros. German technology scattered them but dozens of bodies lay strewn on the battlefield, among them women, still dressed in their finery, as well as children.

Cornelius's stomach heaved. He had to force down the nausea pushing up in his throat like brackish springwater in the Namib. Why was this necessary? he asked himself over and over again. He was sickened by the sight of the bodies, women like Magdalena and children like Hendrik and Martha, lying there with bloody, open wounds, dead eyes and mouths around which flies buzzed like bees around a hive. He was a soldier, but he hated the sight of people slaughtered like sheep on a Saturday morning before Sunday's *nagmaal* at Bethanien.

The Hereros retreated to Oviumbo with the Germans in pursuit. Governor Leutwein wanted to finish this, and quickly, but before they could unsaddle the first horse at the water, the Hereros' bullets rained down on them from the hills. Ambush. Defeat. Now the Germans fell like flies.

Cornelius was surprised that he felt no fear. He saw and heard the Herero rounds around him, but he did not care. He felt as if he were looking at pictures in a book. Surely people could not be doing this to one another, he wondered, as the thoughts went round in his head.

"Major Leutwein," Captain Witbooi said. "We're not going to make it tonight. I'm telling you. Shepherd also said so. The Hereros are going to wipe us out tonight. We must get away from here, now!"

"Captain Witbooi, yes, I think you're right. Spread the word. We are leaving just after dark. Quietly. I don't want the Hereros to follow us. That would be the end for us."

Throughout the night, what remained of Leutwein's force fled to the safety of the fort at Okahandja. Cornelius, riding at his father-in-law's side, felt dead already. The only thing keeping his spirit alive were the images of Magdalena and the two children. He wanted to ride into the veld and keep on riding until he fell off the edge of the earth, or ride into the sea so that the waves would swallow him up and erase all signs that he had ever existed, but he could not. Magdalena's broad smile broke through the mist of his heartache and shame. He rode with Hendrik Witbooi throughout the night, deaf, dumb and blind to everything around him, except for Magdalena's smile in his mind's eye.

Germany was furious, just as they had been when this same Witbooi, now the Emperor's ally, had humilated Von Francois at Naukluft, ten years before. Leutwein's little light had dimmed. The Kaiser appointed a new commander: none other than Thilo's uncle, the ruthless General Adrian Dietrich Lothar von Trotha, destroyer of German East Africa's Wahehe rebellion and brigade commander during the Boxer rebellion in China. General Von Trotha knew that military intelligence was the key. In his German East African experience he learnt that Africa guarded its secrets well. These Nama scouts were just what he needed.

Within a few days of his arrival in German South-West Africa, the general summoned his nephew, Thilo.

"Thilo, your father sends greetings to you, and Margarethe also, natu- rally. She sent you this parcel. Now, I have an important mission for you. Your experience in the Boer war will stand you in good stead. I want you to give me a detailed assessment, within three weeks, of the movement of all the Hereros. Find out where they are and where they are heading. You are not to get involved in skirmishes. There are others who can do that. Others who do not have young brides at home."

Embarrassed, Thilo fiddled with the parcel, neatly wrapped in brown paper and tied with thick cotton twine.

"Right Uncle Lothar...er... I mean General."

"You will be leaving on patrol tomorrow morning. You are in charge of Section One, Platoon Four of Alpha Company, but you will take with you only nine *Schutztruppe*, and four or five of the copper-brown ones, Witbooi's scouts. I hear they know the area and that the Hereros are their enemy. But beware, I don't trust them at all. I saw that in German-East. You can trust the people of this wild continent only as far as you can see them."

Thilo sensed that he was in the presence of a whole generation of brave fighters. They were his own ancestors, men like himself, fearless and loyal men of their word. They were men who paved the way for civilization, shaped the world, made history and so created the future. Germans. People who worked to bring control and order to everything around them in the service of the Great Creator. Thilo was proud of his heritage. They were here to bring civilization to Africa, to the honour of God and the Kaiser. They were here to conquer a new world and tame it so that Germany could hold sway over the entire earth.

General Von Trotha gave his orders: "In three weeks' time I want to know all that is going on. I want to know where the important natural obstacles are, the water sources, roads, mountains, valleys and rivers. And also, of course, the Hereros. As you know, water is the great problem. The one who controls the water wins the war. I will be sending out three more patrols like yours. You must communicate with one another. That's why there will be a signalman in each patrol with a portable heliograph. You must exchange information as far as possible."

The general prodded the map on his desk with a thick forefinger. "Initially this will be the area from where your platoon will operate. And here are the other platoon areas. Here, there, and there. There are high koppies or hills in each of these areas from where you can signal to one another. Look, here, here and here. Once a week you will send a man to Okahandja with one of the Witboois to collect provisions and to report to me personally. No shooting or skirmishes. Let the Hereros relax, let them become a bit tame. I want to launch one large offensive and finish the business before September. Something else. Your farm has been identified, son. Far in the south. Right here."

Thilo looked at the spot on the map above the pointing finger, saluted his uncle and walked out of the cool office. In the quadrangle of the fort the winter sun blazed down upon the group of Nama soldiers and their horses.

"*Feldwebel*[64], let the men line up," Thilo announced.

The proud Namas formed up in threes. A short, copper-brown man with grey hair and a tall, thin, serious-looking black man in a flapping grey jacket also approached them.

"Good afternoon, Lieutenant," the short one greeted. "I am Captain Hendrik Witbooi and this is my advisor and prophet, Shepherd Stuurman."

"Pleased to meet you, Captain Witbooi. I have heard so much about you. Afternoon, Mr Stuurman. My name is Thilo Von Trotha, nephew of the general."

Stuurman spat on the ground. Cornelius, who was standing alone at the rear of the platoon, saw the gesture. What does the Shepherd know that we don't? he wondered.

"Captain Witbooi, I need sixteen of your men for a reconnaissance operation. We need to spy on the Hereros' positions and report back to the general. We will be leaving in the morning in four sections. Each section will require four of your men. For tracking and to show the water sources. I myself will lead one of the sections."

"Very well, Lieutenant. Where did you learn the Boer language?"

"I fought with the Boers against the English, Captain. Until I was caught and sent to Ceylon."

"Oh. But then you are a friend of Africa? Cornelius, come here."

A lean, serious-looking soldier marched smartly up to the leaders. He saluted.

"Lieutenant, this is Cornelius Fredericks. He is the captain of the *!Aman*. He is the best scout in the land and also my son-in-law. I will lend him to you. You can trust him with your life. No one else knows the veld like he does. Cornelius, this is Lieutenant Von Trotha. Look after him for me. Take Abraham Morris with you even if he is a Bondel. It will keep him out of mischief."

Abraham Morris, a smart man from the far south in the second row, smiled with bulging cheeks under Hendrik Witbooi's angry frown.

"That's fine, Father," Cornelius said and saluted again. He trusted his father-in-law unconditionally. He would do anything the old man asked, but it could be a nuisance to have a Bondelswarts, particularly Abraham Morris, in this patrol. They were just too clever for their own good.

---

64   *Feldwebel*: Sergeant.

Shepherd Stuurman gave the three men a penetrating look. Then he spat on the ground again. Cornelius felt his blood run cold.

While the Germans believed they were using the Namas to gather intelligence, Witbooi, the great strategist, was playing his own political game. With Cornelius close to the young Von Trotha he was assured of intelligence from the closest inner circle of the *Schutztruppe*. And with the well-known Morris under Cornelius's wing, the Bondels would stop their nonsense for a while, at least until such time as the Hereros had been eliminated.

Late the following afternoon the heliographs flashed their first messages to one another.

For three weeks the four sections rode long distances over bushveld, across mountains and through ravines and valleys. They avoided all contact with the enemy. Cornelius and his men ensured that there was always fresh meat and food from the veld available. Porcupine, *dassie*, rabbit, guinea fowl, *kougoed*, *suurvy*, *ghaap*, ostrich egg, even tortoise and steenbok. They ignored large game such as oryx because they had to keep on the move and send signals. The general was waiting.

Late in the evenings Section One sat around a small fire, looking up at a sky studded with stars. Thilo told Cornelius about Margarethe. He spoke about his dream of a farm in Africa.

Cornelius told Thilo about the grazing land of Bethanien and showed him the tracks and signs of the veld.

"Look there, Thilo. See that little bird? The black one with the red breast. It looks just like your flag. We call it the German flag or the Kaiserbird, but its real name is the crimson-breasted shrike or hangman. It hangs insects on thorns, like a real hangman. But the little honeybird is cleverer, because she lays her eggs in the hangman's nest. Then the Kaiserbird, hatches the honeybird's eggs and raises its young. And when the German flag's own offspring hatch, the baby honeybirds kill them all. Here in our country it has always been like that. The people murder and steal from one another, almost from the moment they're born.

"You will still see. Herero against Herero. Herero against Nama. Nama against Nama. Bushman against Nama. German against Herero. German against Nama. And nobody ever wins. We all lose. I am tired of it. I just want to farm. I want to look after my sheep and teach my children the ways of God. I don't want to wage war any longer."

"Cornelius, I am the fifth generation Von Trotha with soldier's blood in my veins, but I feel the same as you. That is why I am here, to get away from war. And now I am still in a war. I thought that I would be coming to a little party in the bush. We all thought so, everyone who boarded the ship. And I admit we thought these Hereros were barbarians – not really people, not worthy to live – almost like animals…"

Cornelius remained quiet for a long time. The two looked at one another in silence. There is a great rift between us and these Germans, but then again, perhaps not, thought Cornelius.

When the Southern Cross was on it side, low over the horizon, the fire's last embers were glowing on their faces and the soldiers were already asleep, they returned easily to their conversation.

"Come, Cornelius, pour us a last coffee. Tell me again. How long have the Namas been living in this country? Were you or the Hereros here first? Or have you always been here? And why do you hate one another so? I mean, you are all from Africa and now you are helping us, the white people from Germany against your African brothers, these Hereros. How does this work?"

"Thilo, now you are ploughing amongst the stones. Those are difficult questions from a long time ago. Yet, also for today. You already know the story about the German flag, the Kaiserbird."

In time Thilo learnt that the Namas were the first people of this land of the south. He heard how Cornelius's and Hendrik Witbooi's ancestors had, hundreds of years ago, trekked southwards from the big water in the north. They were the first people, the Khoi-Khoin. Real people. They had moved south. Always south, further and further away from the black giants. Here in the south they found a paradise of game and veld, uninhabited and free. The only enemy were their own people, the robbers, the outcasts who banded together only to rob and plunder. The Khoi-San, the Bushmen. The bad people. They simply could not leave a sheep or a goat alone. They were always there, ready to steal. They trekked together, always a day or so apart, but still together. Often there were skirmishes between them and the real people. They shared the same beliefs and the same blood, yet were divided by their way of life. The real people had respect for the property of others, but these San robbers did not understand this.

Eventually, the real people, the Khoi-Khoin, found a new enemy: the white giants from the south, the Boers and the English. Then some of the Namas, the Oorlams, moved north again into Namaland. And, as always, the robbers, the Bushmen, were everywhere, ready to steal. And now they came into conflict again with the tall black people, the Hereros.

In Thilo Von Trotha's heart, Cornelius's country and people had already made a nest. Just like the honeybird in the Kaiserbird's nest, he realised. The Nama people had settled in the German soldier's heart.

The four heliographs and the despatch riders conveyed information to General Von Trotha. The general drilled and exercised his troops for the great offensive. He was going to destroy the enemy with one almighty blow.

A new report irritated the general. A smaller tribe consisting of both Herero and Nama soldiers was moving around continually, attacking the *Schutztruppe* on virtually a daily basis. They did not wait to be attacked. What was disturbing was that the captain of the tribe went all out to humiliate the leader of the *Schutztruppe*. He made the German bend over and gave him a severe beating like a schoolboy, in front of all his men. He then ordered all the other *Schutztruppe* to strip naked before chasing them into the veld, laughing as he rode behind them.

This captain's name was Jakob Morenga, a man of mixed blood, half Nama and half Herero.

General Von Trotha sent Lieutenant Zürn with one hundred *Schutztruppe* and twenty Namas in search of Morenga and his troops, but all they found were their women and children.

"Where is Jakob Morenga?" the young Zürn asked. They laughed at him. The Germans shot and killed eighty-eight women and children, while the Nama scouts had to stand by and watch.

In spite of his seventy-four years, Hendrik Witbooi, Supreme Commander of the Namas, was in the saddle with his men every day. He could shoot and ride with the best of them. He was a man of solid integrity. No false word ever came out of his mouth. Every morning and evening he held a church service for his men. When he spoke, everyone kept quiet and listened. He always had time for other people, but never for nonsense. When a woman entered a group, he would get up, lift his hat and greet her even if she was forty years younger than him. He loved children and would chat with them for hours, while his church committee waited for him impatiently. That's how he was.

Hendrik's head jerked up when he heard about the slaughter of the Morenga women and children.

He, with Shepherd Stuurman by his side and three bodyguards, went to address all the Namas in the veld.

Eventually he also reached Cornelius's section, greeted Thilo politely and requested to speak with Cornelius in private.

"Cornelius, son, I am disturbed. God revealed to me that we are fighting on the wrong side. These people, the Germans, are not civilized people. They are not real people. God showed me in a vision how the Kaiserbird is spreading over Namaland. It will bring great evil to this land. The hardship the Germans will inflict upon us will set the country alight. It will affect all our people, for a thousand generations. You, you Cornelius Fredericks, you must beware of the treachery of these children of the devil! We must cut the throat of the German flag, the Kaiserbird, whilst it still sits afraid and unfeathered in the nest, our nest."

Hendrik Witbooi gasped, short of breath, white flecks of saliva flying from the corners of his mouth. Then without taking leave, he mounted his horse and rode off, away from the staring eyes of Cornelius.

Captain Hendrik Witbooi travelled through Hereroland to warn the other Namas fighting under the German flag about the approaching calamity.

Thilo could not bring himself to look at Cornelius's questioning gaze from across his saddle. Instead, he kept himself busy with the saddle girth.

"I am taking the report myself today. You can take charge until I get back, Cornelius."

Thilo felt his friend's stare boring into his back as he turned in the direction of Okahandja. Am I a traitor? Then he comforted himself by remembering the soldier's eternal oath of loyalty to his supreme commander, the Kaiser. He had to report Witbooi's visit to the general. Although he couldn't understand what had been said, he could see that something was wrong. Hendrik Witbooi was angry.

Cornelius knew what he knew. Dismayed, he walked into the veld. Yes, he knew what he knew. Thilo was on his way to tell his uncle of father-in-law Witbooi's visit. Low in the branches of a sickle bush he saw the crimson-breasted shrike, a Kaiserbird, hanging a small lizard on the thorns. The wind had turned. The cold of the sweat evaporating on his back felt as though he was being grazed by the skin of a snake, but lightly, like a feather. At that moment Cornelius knew that the German forces would eventually also sink their claws into Namaland, like the sickle bush thorns in the lizard's body.

"All right then, son. I will arrange for someone to go and talk to Witbooi. We cannot afford to have a dispute with the Namas now. They first have to help us with these blacks. We can sort out the Namas later.

"And thank you for coming to tell us. That's exactly why I appointed you. Intelligence," Von Trotha thanked his nephew.

But Thilo wasn't proud of himself. He left the office, confused and worried. He felt that things were not progressing as well as he expected.

At the general's order Captain Von Burgsdorff sent a message to Captain Witbooi asking to see him urgently. A meeting was convened at Gibeon, home of the Witboois. Witbooi received the Germans cordially, but the young captain's manner was somewhat insolent. Witbooi confronted Von Burgsdorff with the tragedy of the massacre of the Morenga women and children.

Tempers flared. A young German soldier slapped the leader of Namaland, the revered seventy-four–year-old Hendrik Witbooi, in the face. The Namas jumped up and shouted in outrage, but the old man held up his hand, a gesture that prevented a bloodbath – for the moment. Hendrik Witbooi knew he needed time.

Winter was nearing its end by the time Cornelius and the four Nama scout sections returned from the veld to Okahandja.

General Von Trotha struck hard, with cunning and without mercy. The Hereros had to contend with scientific warfare and modern artillery, supported by accurate intelligence. They had to flee in the face of the might of Germany and the clever Namas.

At Waterberg, a natural fort formed by cliff ramparts, Samuel Maherero made his stand with thirty thousand Hereros, including women and children. One of the greatest massacres ever to occur took place there. The artillery and machine guns of the Germans were too much for Africa's cattle farmers. Man and beast fell until it seemed that the mountain itself bled and wailed with despair, like a weeping waterfall. The red blood streamed over the black rocks as if the German flag had been draped over the whole Waterberg. The stench of death rose from the bodies, and pieces of flesh, arms, brains and blood were strewn everywhere around. The *Schutztruppe* moved through the battlefield and shot at anything that moved. Just to make sure.

Cornelius and the other Nama scouts remained at a distance, as ordered. Every shot felt as if it was tearing through his own body. He knew what was happening. He felt the horror, fear and hatred of war crawl like an army of red ants up his legs, devouring every part of his body. He knew that every shot was cutting the throat of someone like Magdalena or little Hendrik or tiny Martha, like a sheep being slaughtered. His stomach heaved with revulsion and he wanted to throw up like a dog that had eaten a putrid rabbit in the veld.

General Lothar Von Trotha issued an extermination order. He did not want women and children as prisoners of war. He wanted the country free of Hereros. They either had to die or leave. German South-West Africa was now Germany's colony and nobody else's. Even if it cost rivers of blood, wrote General Von Trotha.

Cornelius and the other Nama scouts looked at each other. They knew what was happening, but could not believe their eyes. Surely, it couldn't be! We have fought side-by-side with these Germans. They wouldn't do the same to us, would they?

The remainder of the Herero tribe fled east, except for a few who fled south-west to the Kuiseb valley or south to Namaland. The majority, many of them the elderly and children, fled east towards Bechuanaland through the Omaheke desert, without food, without water. The Germans followed them, but remained at a distance. They let the Hereros go, knowing what lay ahead. They were fully prepared for a bloody pursuit into the waterless wasteland.

The fleeing Hereros spotted the approaching German cavalry. A great moan of fear and anguish rose from the defenceless refugees huddled together, totally exposed, without any protection. The soldiers came closer and closer. They shot and kept on shooting, left and right, front and rear. It made no difference if it was a woman or a child, they shot at anyone and everyone. Then they retreated, only to return and continue the carnage. The Hereros were not given the chance to bury their dead. They had to leave many wounded behind. They heard and saw the German snipers walk amongst the wounded administering final shots. In this way they were forced ever deeper into the Omaheke desert. Those who became exhausted were left behind. The weakest were the children.

After the second day the thirst became so intense that the Hereros died like flies. The Germans still came, but no longer shot. They played a cat-and-mouse game of chasing the people, then stopping and laughing at them. When the Hereros knelt down, pleading for water, they emptied their bottles of water onto the dry desert sand in front of their tortured, beseeching eyes.

A bewildered group of Hereros gave up hope in the Omaheke desert and turned back – into a German patrol. The *Schutztruppe* hung a copy of the general's proclamation around each prisoner's neck and drove them back east towards Bechuanaland. One emaciated old woman stopped to plead with them. They shot her dead.

As long as they kept walking, the soldiers did nothing, but as soon as a refugee turned around, they swooped down, forcing him to turn back, or they simply shot him. In this way they hounded the people further and further into the desert until turning around was no longer an option.

And then the Germans were gone, satisfied that they had seen the last of the Hereros.

A group of Bushmen approached the exhausted, parched Herero refugees. They talked and gesticulated, using exaggerated signs, grunts, groans and acting in theatrical display.

The Hereros watched them, but did not know what they wanted. One of the Bushmen stepped forward and pointed at himself. A Herero who understood their clicks and clucks came closer. He explained their predicament to the Bushman who spoke at length and told them that they had been following them for some time and saw what the Germans had done. The Bushmen believed that the Hereros were cursed and were ordered by Great Snake, Keinaus, to go into the desert to prove that they were loyal to him. They, the Bushmen, wanted to see if Great Snake was going to help them.

The Bushmen disappeared across a dune and soon returned with a dozen or so ostrich eggshells filled with water. The Hereros rushed at the water but let the children drink first. The Bushmen ran back and forth bringing shells full of water. The Hereros realised that the Bushmen were filling the shells somewhere and wanted to go with them to help. This displeased the Bushmen. They threatened to walk away and abandon the Hereros. So they gave the Bushmen their remaining calabashes, bottles and leather bags so that they could also fill those. In this way, everyone got a drink of water, but Bechuanaland was still far away. With only the ostrich eggshells of water they would never survive. But the Bushmen refused to show them the secret source of the water supply.

The sun went down over the refugees' backs. Approximately two thousand Hereros were left. The others had either died on Waterberg or in the desert. They held a huge church service. There were still a few believers among them. They prayed to the God of Israel, the same God the Germans believed in, and pleaded with Him to grant them another chance. They begged Him for deliverance.

The next day they trekked further into the rising sun. The Bushmen brought water: eggshell by eggshell. They still would not allow the Hereros to go with them. They did not trust them. By the middle of the day, with the sun at its hottest, they saw something on the horizon. As it came closer, they saw it was a mule wagon with a few people, coming straight at them. On the back of the wagon was a wooden barrel. Water was leaking from one joint.

Next to the wagon, a man on horseback and wearing a large hat stared at them. Then they recognized him. Jakob Morenga! The legend. Half Nama, half Herero.

The people fell to the ground in front of him.

"Thank you! Thank you!" they said over and over, but he ignored them.

He did not speak. Later they would find out that one of the Bushmen had gone to Bechuanaland during the night. At the border he had met up with Jakob.

He and his men spent the next two days travelling back and forth with the water cart to get them all out of the desert.

Jakob Morenga and a few Bushmen saved the Herero from extinction.

15

30-31 March 1906
Respite

Many oxen perished in the desert.

Joseph's whip cracked in the early dawn.

"Go, go! All together!"

Johannes, with Ernst next to him, led the willing team of oxen in front of the Luchtenstein wagon on the next stage of their journey. Behind them, nine skinny, untethered oxen plodded on with lowered heads.

The wagon passed Rotekuppe at midday, but Joseph knew they had to keep on going. They moved on under the scorching sun. It was going to be a long day.

At long last they reached a low rocky hill, scattered with stones and a few withered sickle bushes. Joseph whistled loudly. They would spend the night there.

Johannes gathered the oxen together. He hung a bag of water for himself around the neck of Hoogmoed, the left front ox. The oxen, now free of their load, walked off towards Tschaukaib, the *touleier* behind them.

The Luchtensteins made camp. Joseph took one of the hard, thorny fruits from the food box and made a small hole in it.

"*!Narra*, the food of the desert," he explained. He took a sip from the small hole and handed it to Therese.

"Drink, it is good for you. It prevents scurvy."

She hesitated and then took the fruit, looked at it carefully, brought it to her lips and let the acidic liquid drip into her mouth. She rolled it around in her mouth before swallowing. She looked at Joseph questioningly.

"The Bushmen and the Namas can survive on *!narras* alone for weeks. The ǂAonin or Topnaars, Johannes' people, make *pap* and fruit rolls from it. They live off it. It is food and water, and very nutritious. Eat it. It is your vegetables," Joseph told Ernst.

Ernst took the *!narra*. He sniffed at the small hole. He hesitated, and sniffed deeply again, drawing the aroma down into the back of his nose and throat. Its freshness surprised him, like the experiences he had in this new country over the last few days: bittersweet, fresh and strange. Then he drank the liquid and felt the power of the veld in his veins.

Quietly Ernst mumbled the new words and phrases of the Boer language that Johannes had taught him during the day, over and over: "*Die osse trek die wa deur die sand. Dit is warm in die woestyn. Ons trek Keetmanshoop toe. Ek is honger. Ek is dors. My suster is ses jaar oud.*"[65]

Later he began making up and humming little songs. This was easier than German, he thought. Everything is 'is': no *bin, bist, sind, seid* or *sein*. Johannes said that the past tense was also easy. You only add "*het ge-*" in front of the verbs. Just the guttural 'g'-sounds were strange. They did not exist in German.

"G – g, g – g, g – g…" he practised over and over again until Therese looked up in surprise.

---

65   *Die osse trek die wa deur die sand. Dit is warm in die woestyn. Ons trek Keetmanshoop toe. Ek is honger. Ek is dors. My suster is ses jaar oud:* The oxen are pulling the wagon through the sand. It is hot in the desert. We are trekking to Keetmanshoop. I am hungry. I am thirsty. My sister is six years old.

"What's wrong, Ernst. Is there something the matter with your throat?"

"No, nothing, *Mutti*. I am learning the Boer language."

"That's good my son, you must teach me too."

Joseph sat down on the ground with his back against the wagon wheel. From a bottle of brandy he poured a bit into a tin cup and then later a little more. He stretched his legs out in front of him so that he slipped lower and lower down. His head started to nod.

Everyone was asleep in the chilly darkness by the time Johannes returned with the oxen. Joseph lay beside the fire. He struggled upright, his eyes searching for the oxen. Without even looking at Johannes, he fired questions at him.

"Is everything all right? Are all the oxen here?"

"No, my *baas*, we went well. All the oxen are here but three are limping. Perhaps we need to rest them tomorrow, my *baas*."

"There is some grazing here behind this little hill. Perhaps they will get something to eat. Take them there and find a place for yourself to sleep."

16

3 October 1904 –14 June 1905
War clouds over Namaland

Governor Theodor Leutwein, Lieutenant Thilo von Trotha and his uncle, General Lothar von Trotha.

General Lothar Von Trotha boasted that he had killed sixty-five thousand Hereros, more than half of them women and children.

The Nama scouts who worked with the *Schutztruppe* understood the situation fully. They knew it was only a matter of time before Von Trotha's sword would be at their throats too.

Cornelius's horse started to gallop. It also sensed that they were close to Bethanien. Cornelius saw that the veld had been overgrazed, and was as barren as his own heart. The rainy season was still a long way off. When would the rain come this year? Would it ever rain again?

When he saw the dusty little town in the distance, he became a shepherd again – a child who only wanted to play, felt hunger and simply wanted to enjoy every moment of life.

Halfway up the street Magdalena came rushing up to him. He slid off the horse and embraced her quietly, with the two children tugging at her dress.

"My Cornelius, my Cornelius…".

He held her and whispered, "My *koekemakranka*, my 'krankie, my 'krankie…" into her neck.

Cornelius and Magdalena, each with a child on their arm, strolled down the street while the townspeople cheered and waved at them.

Cornelius wanted to talk, but could not get the words out. His love for his family left him tongue-tied and choked him up. He was unable to share the atrocities of Hereroland with Magdalena. How could he pollute this beautiful woman's thoughts with the realities of Okanjira, Oviumbo, Waterberg and the Omaheke? He lay awake deep into the night with Magdalena's body resting next to his and his chest moving up and down with every breath he took, like the waves of the sea. Then the fear of the future and the safety of his wife and children returned and choked him again. He clenched his hands into fists.

One fine day in September, father-in-law Hendrik arrived at Bethanien.

Cornelius thought it was a family visit, but when the short man alighted he immediately made the purpose of his visit clear.

"Cornelius, we must talk."

They walked towards the orchard. "Son, the Germans are planning something big. There are two large ships in Angra and more are on the way. We don't have time. They are going to murder us and chase us out of the country as they did with the Hereros. If we want to hit them we will have to do it quickly and hard."

Cornelius looked down and clenched his teeth. He was not keen on war, but was nevertheless strongly moved by the short man's powerful presence.

"You must do as you are led, my Captain."

Father-in-law Witbooi stared across the veld for a long time. Cornelius saw that he was tired and old, the troubles and hurt of many decades of war and treachery in the creases of the old weathered face, but when he turned around, he looked his son-in-law straight in the eye.

"Get your men together. Bring provisions for two weeks as well as fresh horses and report at Gibeon in four days." He then took his leave and rode off.

Four days later the largest assembly of Nama soldiers ever seen together in one place were gathered at Gibeon. Everyone was uneasy because they knew they were just as vulnerable as the Hereros had been at Waterberg. But Witbooi had set up scouts all around Gibeon to warn them of any German attack.

Witbooi removed his large hat. He closed his eyes and began to pray.

"*A da /gore!*[66] Almighty God, we stand here before You in humble dependency. God, the enemy has left us no choice. We have seen and we confess before You our guilt thereto. We participated in the murder of our brothers, the Hereros. God, we plead for forgiveness. We can only rely on your mercy, God, and today we stand before you and we plead, God, that you will protect us and our families on this difficult road upon which You have placed us. We place our hope and trust in You. Upon You we build and, if it is Your will, we will die in You. God, into Your hands we deliver ourselves. In Jesus Christ's name. Amen."

The sun beat down on the heads and hearts of all the men of Namaland. Cornelius looked at the crowd of Nama soldiers. These were his people, but did they realise what was happening here, he asked himself? Did they know about the nights in the veld, the cold, the gunshots, the suffering, the blood, the gaping mouths and dead eyes of the bodies, and the blow-flies buzzing around them?

He was sure of one thing. Never again would he have the privilege of just being a shepherd.

Witbooi replaced his hat and spoke.

"*Hub, //îb aits mâb ge a !anu.*[67] We stand here facing our greatest challenge. We moved out of the Colony as */gôada*[68] to escape the English swords of injustice. Our fathers and their fathers could no longer endure

---

66   A da /gore: Let us pray.

67   *Hub, //îb aits mâb ge a !anu*: The ground upon which you stand is holy ground.

68   /gôada: Young children.

living under them. They chased us away from our land, deeper into the deserts of Bushmanland and Namaqualand, the Kalahari and the Richtersveld. Every time our forebears found good pastures and water, the white man would come and drive us away like dogs from their food dishes. We decided to do what the Boers had done. We trekked with our ox wagons, mule carts and livestock to come in search of our own country, away from the Englishman's yoke.

"When our people moved through the Gariep River, like the Israelites through the Jordan, our country was as empty as the Namib, except for a few Khoi-San who trekked through now and then. We, the descendants of the Khoi-Khoin, the real people, the first people, had found our fatherland. We were the first inhabitants of Namaland, as the old Khoi-Khoin were the first people in the south, hundreds of years ago. We had our own fatherland, as did the Boers in the Orange Free State and the Zuid-Afrikaansche Republiek. We lived well here in our own land, Namaland.

"Then came the German flag. At first they came with smooth talk and then they came to buy a piece of land, but actually they came to steal the land with the crookery of the geographic mile. Now they are laying claim to the whole country. The Kaiser's army is raising the flag of the crimson-breasted shrike over Namaland, our country.

"We were sucked into the war against the Hereros. Some of you saw the outcome of that at Waterberg and in the Omaheke. Now the remnants of the Hereros are in a camp in Bechuanaland like the stubble in a mealie land after harvesting. There they will die. You also know how the Germans murdered the women and children of Jakob Morenga and his men.

"Men, you have another choice. You can decide to do nothing and lie down in front of the oppressor. I, Hendrik Witbooi of Gibeon, cannot walk that road. For me there is only one road, the road of the rifle: war."

A great cheer went up. Witbooi raised his hand and silence returned. "I, Hendrik Witbooi of Gibeon, hereby declare war against the German Imperial Empire and its forces in Namaland." He put his hand into the inside pocket of his jacket and took out an envelope.

"This letter is my declaration of war. Today it will be sent to the Germans in Keetmanshoop. It is an irrevocable declaration. May God be with us."

An icy wind cut across Cornelius's back and he hunched his neck deep into the collar of his jacket. He felt as if fear was going to make him fall over, but then he breathed slowly and deeply, squeezed his fists inside his jacket pockets and clenched his teeth. He must be strong today, for the sake of Magdalena. He frowned deeply and continued listening.

Father-in-law Hendrik had learnt a lot during the Herero war. He ordered his men never to be in groups of more than twenty in one place. Today would be the last occasion that such a large group would be together. They would never give the *Schutztruppe* a chance to do another Waterberg on them. If it happened that a group of Namas fell, then it would not be more than twenty of them.

According to father-in-law Witbooi's instructions, they should take the initiative without delay, terrorising the Germans wherever they came across them. Just as the Boers had done with the English for more than two years. They must concentrate on taking away the Germans' supplies and weapons so that they, the Namas, could use them. They must take the *Schutztruppe*'s horses and fodder, destroy their wagons, pour their water on the ground and confiscate their shoes.

"While you are fighting shoot as many as you can, but if a German surrenders, you are not to shoot him," ordered Witbooi.

Some muttered in protest at this, but Witbooi stood firm.

"If anyone harms a prisoner of war, I will shoot him personally," he hissed.

"The women and children, except the *!Aman* of Bethanien, together with the livestock, must take refuge in the mountains because this will be a total onslaught. Each group of women will be escorted by a small commando of soldiers. The soldiers must be rotated frequently, so that every man will have a chance to spend time with his family. These women and their children will move around in the Fish River Canyon, the Karas Mountains and the Naukluft Mountains. In order to get to fresh grazing regularly, they must not remain in one place for too long," ordered the leader.

"It is only in Bethanien where the *!Aman* women may stay under the protection of the missionaries."

Father-in-law Hendrik remained quiet for a long while, took a deep breath, gathered the reins from his adjutant and mounted his horse.

"*!Gâi as ge //gû !hûba //ōbasa!*"[69] he called out to his people.

The Nama soldiers' response was a proud roar coming from deep within their throats.

---

69   *!Gâi as ge //gû !hûba //ōbasa*: It is good to die for the fatherland.

The Nama nation trekked into the open veld, barely two months after the Herero war. Every captain went in his own direction with his soldiers. It was a strange feeling to fight against Germany and no longer on their side. The Namas knew the might of the white man. Had their forebears not fled from the English in the Colony? And did they not themselves see the German ships and cannons in the harbour at Lüderitzbucht? The ǂAonin[70] had told them how the Germans had offloaded horses by the thousand, Mausers and uniforms, food and meat at Swakopmund. What could they do against the Germans that the Hereros could not? The Hereros numbered far more than them. Before the war there were eighty thousand Hereros of which only fifteen thousand now remained. There were only twenty thousand Namas. How many would survive this war? On his way back to Bethanien all these questions buzzed like horseflies round and round in Cornelius's mind.

"Magdalena, your father sent a despatch rider to Keetmanshoop with a declaration of war. It is war. Tomorrow I will take some of the *Khowesin* of Gibeon to the Fish River. Your father asked me. I will return to see that you and the children are well. I want you to stay here with the missionaries. You will be safe here."

"Cornelius, my Cornelius, you must be careful."

Magdalena grabbed her husband by the shoulders. "I love you so much, so much, I love you more than life itself!"

Cornelius felt as if he was being lowered into the ground like a coffin when he withdrew from Magdalena's embrace. His mouth felt dry and tight and closed like an old *!narra,* his heart was in tatters, but he managed to turn away and mount his horse before nausea and pain overcame him.

Wherever one looked, it was just ox wagons, horses, sheep, goat wagons, dogs and children. Cornelius trekked in a wide arc to avoid Kubub with its many Germans, always southwards, towards the Fish River. He had plenty of time to think about the difficult times ahead. Father-in-law Hendrik said that they had no other choice. Whether or not they wanted to wage war, the Germans were determined to do so. The Germans would not rest until the Namas were exterminated, like the Hereros, and driven out of the country, this country that Vogelsang had stolen from them. That devil, General Von Trotha, had spelled it out: he was not interested in prisoners of war, not even women and children. Even if it meant rivers of blood.

---

70 ǂAonin: The Topnaars, Namas of the Walvis Bay area.

Father-in-law also said that God would use the Nama nation to punish this wickedness. The Germans did not know the veld like the Namas did; they did not know where the waterholes were and there were no longer any Hereros who could show them. Father-in-law said that the Namas' knowledge of the veld would always give them the advantage to outwit the Germans. The horses of the Namas also knew the desert. The Germans' horses had to rest up and feed in camps every week.

Cornelius tried to encourage himself with the wise words of Hendrik Witbooi. Father-in-law knew best. He would not let them down. He would rescue them. Father-in-law often spoke about the Boers of the two republics who had thrashed the English in the first war and who would have done the same in the second war had the English not thrown the women and children into their camps and destroyed the homes, livestock and crops of the Boers. He believed that the Namas just had to ensure that they had sufficient supplies of water and food, and the women and children remained out of the clutches of the Germans. Then the Almighty would preserve them and give them victory. The Nama nation stood behind its leader.

At last Cornelius and the trek reached the Fish River. The open mouth of the canyon swallowed the *Khowesin* and a few *!Aman,* enclosing them in its safe interior.

The general looked up from behind his desk in Keetmanshoop. The centre of the war was now here, in Namaland.

"Uncle Lothar, there is something I wish to discuss with you."

"Yes, son?"

"You may remember that during the Herero war I had a loyal scout, Cornelius Fredericks."

"Yes?"

"Well, he has become like a friend to me. I would like to see that he and his people do not come to harm, even though they are now fighting against us. I ask for leave of absence to find him and to ask him to lay down his arms. I want him to move to my farm. I need good labourers there. The farm is close to their village of Bethanien."

The stern general thought for a while.

"Very well, then. You have three weeks. Total surrender and nothing less. Then they can go and work on your farm – as labourers."

"Thank you very much Uncle Lothar… General."

Thilo von Trotha trekked southwards in search of Cornelius. The Namas of Berseba, the #Hobexab who were neutral, had told him that Cornelius's warriors had passed there two days before on their way to the Fish River Canyon. At Bethanien the missionaries had told him that most of the Namas had left and that Thilo, if he found them, should convince them that they would be safe at the mission station. There was no reason why they should flee from the mission station, even though there was a war going on.

Thilo set off alone to the Fish River Canyon. He realised that time was running out. He had to convince Cornelius to surrender before his uncle's amnesty expired.

He was still ashamed of his report to his uncle regarding Hendrik Witbooi's visit. He knew that Cornelius was aware of it. He also knew that Cornelius's people knew of the massacres at Waterberg and in the Omaheke. He was ashamed of those too, although he would never admit this to his uncle or his own father. He could not even think about it. He had never seen such barbaric cruelty in the Transvaal or Natal. Not on the part of either the Boers or the English. Now, however, he was a party to those horrendous atrocities, the worst massacres of all time. And he was bitterly ashamed of them, ashamed to death.

Abraham Morris stood on the edge of the Fish River Canyon with his small group of *!Gami-#nun*[71] women, children and men - the end of the earth, a desolate place where not even the Bushmen wanted to stay for long, but that had now become a refuge for the Namas. Abraham knew that his comrade of the Herero company, Cornelius Fredericks of Bethanien and the *Khowesin* and *!Aman* were here, somewhere in the canyon.

The Bondelswarts hid their wagons, carts and trek equipment, along with the women's extra clothing and better items of furniture which they had been reluctant to leave behind at Warmbad, on the rim of the canyon under sickle bushes and monkey thorn branches. Now they had to descend into the safety of the canyon where no donkey cart or mule wagon could go.

The sheep bleated and the horses' ears hung downwards. The descent went at a snail's pace. Some places were so steep that the small children had to be carried down.

---

71   *!Gami-#nun*: Bondelswarts/Bondels, Nama tribe of the far south.

Their knees took strain but they eventually reached the water on the canyon floor. Very few people had ever been down to the river. Apart from the difficult terrain, the distance and the heat, the Fish River was also home to Great Snake, Keinaus. There was no wind and no sound. Even the cicadas were quiet. Water and grazing were excellent, an ideal hiding place for man and beast. The Bondels knew they could survive the winter here, but Abraham wanted to get out as soon as possible to tackle the Germans. But first they had to take care of the women and children.

A pleasant two weeks went by. The women erected *//haru-oms* while the children played in the sand. They built sand castles and the women baked bread. The men enjoyed fishing. Soon they were busy constructing fish traps that consisted of huge funnels into which the fish were diverted and then killed with *knobkieries*.

The Bondelswarts were afraid of Great Snake, but after a few days they relaxed because there was no sign of the creature. The old people told many tales about this god-like snake but perhaps not everything was true:

"Long, long ago, before the time of the first people, the Khoi-Khoin, the king of the Karas Mountains had a beautiful daughter. The king of the Black Mountains had a young son who wanted to marry the beautiful daughter of the king of the Karas Mountains. He gave her a crown with a huge shiny white stone on it. She was so proud of her crown that she wouldn't take it off her head. The bad prince of Holoogberg wanted the princess's crown. One evening he went to visit Keinaus, Great Snake, down in the vlei.

'If you give me the crown belonging to the princess of the Karas Mountains, I shall worship you for ever, and every year bring you four young girls,' he promised Keinaus.

"Keinaus spewed and hissed and a strong whirlwind started to blow and kept blowing until the moon and stars disappeared. Keinaus flew with the whirlwind to the Karas mountains. When the princess saw Great Snake, she became so frightened that the crown fell off her head. Keinaus swallowed the crown, but the shiny stone penetrated through the skin of his head and grew onto his head. He flew back to Holoogberg, but he could never remove the shiny stone from his head to give to the bad prince.

"The bad prince cursed Keinaus.

'You will wait for the young girls at the water holes forever, but I will not bring them to you until you bring me the shiny stone. And the day the shiny stone comes off your head, that's the day you will die, and with you all the people of the Karas Mountains, the Black mountains and Swartmodder, the whole of Namaland.'

"The princess cried so bitterly over her crown that her tears washed away the earth and that is where the Fish River canyon came from – from the tears of the princess. From that day on, Great Snake with the shiny stone on his head has been waiting at the waterholes of Namaland for the young girls, his fate intertwined with that of the people of Namaland."

The *!Gami-#nun* moved often, staying in one place no longer than four days. In this way they conserved the grazing and the fishing holes. Abraham Morris also knew it would take a German patrol longer than four days to get the news from a secret scout and then to reach them.

Abraham did not want unnecessary shooting, but one day they encountered a herd of zebras. That evening they ate fresh meat and Abraham's wife began preparing the skin for a fine *karos*.

Because it was so quiet, the smallest noise could be heard. Each day four guards were posted high above the camp to warn of approaching Germans. Each guard had his own call so that the people would know who was calling. One called like a francolin, one like a guinea fowl, and one like a fish eagle, while another barked like a zebra.

Abraham sent out scouts in several directions to find Cornelius and his people. He finally got word that Cornelius was in the Auchab, a tributary of the great Fish River. After riding for one and a half days, Abraham found his friend. The two comrades embraced.

"Abraham, my friend. Where on earth have you come from now?"

"From the Karas Mountains. It became too uncomfortable there. So I decided to look for you."

After a few hours of talking and eating together, Abraham returned to his people to lead them to Cornelius's camp. It was a slow trek, since all the *!Gami-#nun* cattle, sheep, horses, women and children had to go along with them. It would take them at least three days to reach Cornelius's camp.

Two days after Abraham's visit, Thilo stood on a rise. Through his binoculars he could see the smoke of the fires in Cornelius's camp. He left his rifle under a thorn tree and used his vest as a white flag.

From afar Cornelius's scout saw the white flag and waited for him.

"I come in peace. I am looking for my friend Cornelius Fredericks of Bethanien," Thilo said politely in the Boer language.

The scout lowered his rifle.

"Come," he said and motioned towards the narrow game track. Thilo rode in front of the scout, all the time aware of the rifle pointed at his back.

Cornelius squinted at the two riders as they approached, the one in front a *Schutztruppe* with a white flag. When he recognized the German, he gaped at him. They stared at each other for some time, both unsure of what to say, until their mutual sense of true friendship broke through their uncertainty. Then they broke into laughter and slapped each other on the back so that puffs of dust rose from their clothing. The Namas stared in amazement: the scene appeared absurd to them.

The conversation was strained at first, but after a while their old friendship triumphed again and they broke into comfortable banter. Cornelius was amused at the new medal on Thilo's chest, awarded for his role in the Herero war.

"You Germans really like the shiny stuff, just like the Hereros. Don't you know that the zebra and the eland can also see it from a distance?" he said.

"Cornelius, I am here with a proposal."

They talked far into the night, with only a small campfire for company, almost as they had done in Hereroland, but the other men in the camp muttered among themselves. Cornelius also had his doubts. Could he trust the German? He remembered the sweat chilling his back when Thilo departed to deliver his report of father-in-law's visit to the general. And what about Oviumbo and Okanjira and Waterberg? The Herero massacre was still foremost in Cornelius's mind.

It was late morning, after breakfast in the Bondelswarts camp. Abraham Morris wanted to get to Cornelius's camp before the sun became too hot. All the mats and poles of the //haru-oms had been fastened to the backs of the oxen, ready to begin the last stretch to Cornelius's camp.

Suddenly a salvo of shots exploded around them. The Bondels took fright. The women and children fled and scattered into the hills. The cattle and sheep stormed down the winding game track into the canyon, away from the shots. Abraham and a few men ran after the animals, because they knew that the herd would now race in the direction of Cornelius's camp, with the *Schutztruppe*'s patrol who had fired on them, right behind.

Around the last bend in the ravine the Mausers of Cornelius Fredericks's soldiers waited, ready to shoot. They had heard the shots and the thundering noise of the stampeding livestock. Abraham Morris and his men appeared out of the cloud of dust and ran behind the large round boulders where Cornelius and his men were hiding. Abraham got the surprise of his life. Lieutenant Thilo Von Trotha, his previous commander in Hereroland and now his enemy, was right next to his friend and confidant, Cornelius Fredericks.

"My God. Lieutenant! What in blazes are you doing here, Thilo? And who is shooting at us from behind? Are they your troops? What's going on here? Is it a trap? Or did you catch him, Cornelius?"

Cornelius peered along the barrel of his rifle in the direction from which Abraham and his livestock had just come and from where he expected the attackers. All around them lay Nama soldiers, peering over the sights of their rifles.

"What the hell is going on here, Lieutenant? What are you doing here? Did you come to betray us?" Abraham demanded again, furious.

"I swear Abraham, on the life of my wife Margarethe and in the name of everything that's good, I do not know what's going on here. I arrived here yesterday to talk peace. Ask Cornelius. He and I were talking just now, then your livestock stormed here and we heard the shots. I know nothing about this. I swear."

It was dead quiet in the canyon. The shooting had ceased, but Cornelius and his men kept themselves hidden, because they knew the enemy was still out there. Thilo jumped up and ran, bent over, to one side.

"What are you doing now, Thilo?" Cornelius asked.

"I am looking for my pen and paper. I want to write a letter."

He knelt next to his saddlebag, wrote something and then showed it to Cornelius and Abraham: *I am Lieutenant Thilo von Trotha, German Schutztruppe, an envoy of General Von Trotha and I am here to negotiate peace. Cease fire immediately and withdraw.*

He handed the letter to Cornelius, who raised a dirty white shirt attached to the stock of a whip and sent a young man ahead with the letter. Silence hung over the valley. Nothing happened. After a while Thilo stood up again and ran back to his saddlebag. He knelt again, slightly behind Cornelius and Abraham.

Abraham watched Thilo kneeling and searching in his saddlebag. Cornelius ignored him and stared in the direction of the attackers, from where he expected the return of the young man with the white flag at any moment.

Two shots were fired behind Abraham and Cornelius. They spun around, just in time to see Thilo fall to the ground with both hands clutching at his chest and blood oozing through his fingers. Cornelius dropped everything, ran to his friend and held him in his arms.

"It hurts, it hurts...I didn't even have a rifle..." Thilo whispered.

It was over. The last drops of blood trickled through Cornelius's fingers onto the hot white sand of the Fish River.

And then Cornelius wept. It felt as if his own life, his blood and his wife and children's, was flowing away with that of Thilo into the sand of the Fish River.

"*//ōb hâ*[72], *//ōb hâ, //ōb hâ...*" he groaned over and over again.

Cornelius's nephew, Christopher Lambert, strutted around. "I shot the traitor," he boasted.

Cornelius looked at him. "Son, today you have signed the death warrant of the Nama people."

Cornelius knew that the Germans would never forgive this crime, that they would now hunt the Nama people to the ends of the earth, with far more deadly intent than they had with the Hereros.

Now they had the excuse, the reason they needed. They would exterminate the nation and chase survivors into the desert as they had done to the Hereros. They would show no mercy. Thilo was here, on the direct orders of the supreme commander and under the white flag. Now he was dead. The Namas were to blame, the Germans would argue. At the same time the Namas would believe that it was Thilo who had betrayed them. The irony of war tasted like bitter aloes in Cornelius Federicks's mouth.

He turned and walked away in the direction of the attackers, without his rifle, his arms hanging limply by his side.

It was very quiet again. Nothing and nobody moved. Cornelius wanted to see if he could make contact with the Germans to give a true account of what had happened, but the *Schutztruppe* section had already prepared to move on and were saddled up. He was just in time to see them gallop away. Thilo's letter had reached them. They had obeyed the instruction to suspend shooting and to withdraw.

---

72   *//ōb hâ*: He is dead.

After a long while Cornelius walked back. Then he noticed two of his men had already plundered Thilo's body. They had removed the pocket watch with the golden chain and small photo box, his wedding gift from Margarethe, his medal and wedding and signet rings and strutted around showing them off. He felt as if he could vomit with anger, fear and heartache.

Cornelius issued orders for all the women and children to trek across the Gariep River to the Colony and to stay there till the war was over. His own Magdalena and children were still at the mission station at Bethanien, where they were safe.

"Not tomorrow, now. You must trek tonight. You, Lambert, you go with them. Your life is worth nothing any more. Not to me either."

Abraham Morris agreed that the women and children would be safe on the other side of the Gariep River. Warmbad was very close to the river. His people could easily move back and forth from there.

Cornelius saw to it that Thilo's body was washed. He did not want to bury him in the river bed. He wanted a grave higher up where scavengers would not easily reach it and the river would not wash it open. He found a high stone ridge where the rocks formed a small crevice that would be an ideal grave. Cornelius read Psalm 121 and prayed for forgiveness for this dastardly act. He then started singing the words of Psalm 146. One by one the men joined in. When they were finished, Cornelius wept again.

The grave was sealed with sand and stones. On a piece of wood they burnt Thilo's name and the date of his death with a hot iron. They knew that the Germans would find the grave, but Cornelius wanted them to know with certainty who lay there.

When the late moon rose over the deserted grave, a lone jackal crept closer, sniffed at the heap of fresh ground, gave a mournful howl, and trotted on.

A few months later a great tragedy befell the Nama nation at Vaalgras. Hendrik Witbooi was fatally struck by a German bullet.

His two sons buried him in the veld, without a coffin, with his Bible on his chest. They fled the scene but slowly enough for the Germans to follow them, away from the grave.

Shepherd Stuurman disappeared over the horizon, alone, forever.

17

31 March–1 April 1906
The little hare and the moon

A camp site in the desert

To escape the scorching heat of the sun they *trekked* at night and rested during the day.

Ernst walked up front with Johannes, where he continued learning the language of the Boers and was learning to speak longer and longer sentences. He also mastered a few dozen Nama words. The tongue pops and clicks, the back-to-front sentence construction, the *ra* and the *go*, the *ge*, *nî* and *nîra*, made him tongue-tied and muddled his head, but helped to shorten the journey through the endless, desolate wilderness.

After an icy night's *trek*, everyone was relieved to see the golden glow of the horizon in the east. In the late morning they called a halt at the water pool on the Tschaukaib plain. Johannes outspanned the oxen. Heads down and bellowing, they stormed the low stone wall encircling the precious *bankwasser*.[73]

One red ox with downturned horns, Skinker, was limping. When he lay down, Joseph tried to make him get up, but the animal was exhausted. Joseph drew his knife from its sheath and grabbed the ox by the one horn.

"Hold on, Johannes!"

With one stroke he severed the animal's main artery. The dark red blood spurted out in a thick warm stream onto the rocky ground.

"Come, let's take out the liver, my boy."

Three more limping animals caught his eye.

"Let us put shoes on their feet, Johannes. Bring Donker first."

He returned to the carcass and skinned the dead animal.

The oxen disliked having their sore hooves worked on so Joseph, Johannes and Ernst had to tie them up and turn them over onto their backs. They then tied pieces of the fresh skin to their hooves with *riempies*.

"Johannes, now fetch the *teerputs*.[74] We should already have greased the wheels yesterday."

Johannes crouched down under the wagon to retrieve the small barrel filled with lard. Joseph greased the wheel bushes, the *skamel*[75] and the wagon's brake. A small bird appeared and darted around Johannes's head, then perched a few feet away, chirping its happy song.

"Another bird, like the *skaapwagter* bird," Ernst said. "What bird is this?"

"*Spekvreter*," answered Joseph. "Like Johannes. Where the fat is, there are the *spekvreters*. Wherever people work with fat, there they are. Also at the *teerputs* on the ox wagons, just like the *touleiers*."

Ernst frowned. Johannes stared at his feet and smiled.

---

73   *Bankwasser*: Literally bank water, a natural collection of rain water on hard ground in the desert.

74   *Teerputs*: small barrel, usually hung below the ox wagon and filled with Stockholm tar, used for smearing working parts of the wagon. When Stockholm tar was unavailable animal fat (lard) was substituted. The *spekvreter* birds were partial to this lard and followed the wagons.

75   *Skamel*: steering block attached to the *disselboom* of the ox wagon.

"Johannes, are you a *spekvreter*? Is that a good name?" Ernst asked.

"No, Ernst. What are you, a *skaapwagter* or a dune lark? Or do you perhaps think you are a Kaiserbird?" Johannes retorted.

Ernst considered Johannes's question for a while with the *spekvreter's* song ringing in his ears: "Who am I? Why am I here? Who am I? Why am I here? Who am I? Why am I here?" The *spekvreter's* cheerful little song resonated with the questions in his heart.

At dusk the wheels turned again. "Go, go! All together now!"

The *spekvreter's* chirpy song continued to echo the questions in Ernst's heart.

Johannes pointed to the moon descending in the west: "Ernst, what happens when a man dies?"

"If he had lived a good life he goes to heaven, otherwise he goes to hell. That's what *Mutti* said."

"Where is that heaven? Tell me, where is it?"

Ernst looked at the thousands of bright stars twinkling above. "I don't think anyone knows where heaven is, Johannes, but it must be above there. Somewhere among all those stars, I think."

"And what do all the dead people do? Do you think they work, or do they play? Huh?"

"No man, how would I know? You tell me, you are very clever and know everything."

"Right. Let me tell you a story about a big fight. Look, do you see the moon? Do you see those marks on the moon's face?"

"Mmm yes. What about them?"

"Do you know *Hasie's*[76] lip?" That split lip of his?"

"Yes, you also get people with those cleft lips. In Prussia, in my school was a little boy with such a lip. The other children called him *Haas*. He cried a lot."

"Alright. Now, do you know where that comes from? That cut in his lip?"

"*Haas's* or *Hasie's*?" Ernst asked.

"*Hasie's*, the desert hare." Johannes held his fingers behind his ears, crouched and jumped in long leaps like a hare. Ernst laughed, and then Johannes said:

"Long, long ago, before you and I were born, *Hasie* and Moon had an

---

76   *Hasie* (diminutive) or *haas*: hare or rabbit.

argument. Moon said 'People are born, die and return and are born again, die, return again, are born again, die and return and so it carries on, just like me, the moon. Humans are better than you, little *Hasie*. When you die, you rot away. Forever."

"But *Hasie* mocked Moon: 'Rubbish man. People die and rot just like a fish or a hare. They do not return. Never!'

"And so the fight began. *Hasie* scratched and scratched Moon's face for two days in a row."

Johannes adopted his hare stance again and scratched the air so that Ernst laughed once more.

"And then? And then?"

Johannes stretched out and continued.

"Then Moon picked up a small springbok horn and struck *Hasie* on his lip so that blood squirted everywhere. Today *Hasie* still has that wound on his lip and Moon has those scratches on his face. And today, people still do not return. When they die they stay together with the Great God and with the stars in the west."

It was a long night, but without incident. Again and again Joseph walked around the wagon inspecting the wheels, spokes, *lunsrieme*[77] and axles, the *skamel* and the animals. He knew they could not afford a breakdown. The next morning they had to be close to Tsirub, their last opportunity to get water between Aus and Tschaukaib. From the next day on Johannes would have to go ahead to Kubub and back with the oxen until they had eventually got through the desert.

Mile after mile, the barren plains, rough dunes and low stone ridges stretched ahead, with patches of dry, sparse bushes and shrubs the only vegetation. The only consolation was that they were now out of the wind belt.

Johannes stopped.

"What is it now, Johannes?" called Joseph.

"Tracks, my *baas*," and he pointed to the ground.

Even Ernst could identify the tracks as hoofmarks, horses without shoes, the riding horses of the cruel copper-coloured Nama fighters.

Joseph stared at the horizon all around them.

"Count them, Johannes, how many are they?"

---

77 *Lunsriem*, plural *lunsrieme:* Small *riem* acting as cotter pin to secure wheel on axle.

"It's the *!Aman*, my *baas*. These horses' hooves still carry the lines of Bethanien's rough ground. I count fifteen or sixteen, *baas* Joseph."

Joseph climbed onto the wagon. He took his Mauser from the wagon kist, opened the lock and inserted five rounds in the magazine. He put a handful of rounds in his trouser pockets.

"What's going on, Joseph?" Therese asked.

"Nothing, my wife, nothing. Some native tracks."

They *trekked* further in silence, but the atmosphere was tense.

It was morning when they stopped. Early evening, by the light of the moon which had grown a bit larger, the trek moved on again.

They met another wagon on its way to Lüderitzbucht, but Joseph did not waste time talking. The *trekkers* exchanged only the most important information. The Namas had not caused too many problems in the area recently. Only a few isolated gangs had harrassed the *Schutztruppe*, here and there, but they were pursued and eliminated. Von Trotha had done good work.

Another *trek* day ended at sunrise and they outspanned the wagon. Johannes straightaway took his water bag and whistled. Within minutes he and the team of oxen had disappeared in the direction of Tsirub and its water.

Johannes and the oxen returned early in the afternoon, exhausted.

Later, Joseph could not stand the wait any longer.

"Ernst, go and wake Johannes. It's getting late, we have to move."

Half an hour later the whip cracked.

"Move, move! All together now!"

They trekked to Tsirub where they allowed the oxen to drink before moving on to an old campsite with a fireplace that was neatly laid out with stones. A blackened, broken kettle and a shard of rusted corrugated iron told a tale of long nights around the fire in the desert. A little further on the wind was blowing desert sand over the skeleton of an ox, its skull grinning grotesquely for the last time.

Johannes outspanned and prepared to move on. The ravenous span of oxen had to push on to Klein Kubub that day.

Joseph held his hand in the air, thought for a while and then sighed. "Wait. Listen, Johannes, the oxen must graze, they look bad. Let them graze in Klein Kubub's pastures, but no longer than two or three hours."

While Johannes and the oxen disappeared in the distance, the Luchtensteins continued with their normal activities. They made a fire, cooked food, put up their tarpaulins and unrolled their blankets. Joseph crept underneath the wagon to inspect the axles and wheels. He explained to Ernst that he was concerned that the left front wheel might be out of alignment.

"Bring me the *teerputs*, Ernst"

The little *spekvreter* instantly appeared.

"Look *Vater*, Johannes's little bird."

Who am I? Why am I here? Who am I? Why am I here? The little bird chirped incessantly in Ernst's head.

PART TWO

THE POISON OF THE KAISERBIRD

18

1 April 1906
Doom and mercy in the desert

Place of rest in the Namib Desert

A sharp sound pierced the silence at dusk. The family froze. Joseph looked around. The sound grew louder – a sharp, irregular sound of hooves on stony ground. The rumble increased in volume as it came closer.

Joseph grabbed his Mauser. He searched his pocket for the rounds, but his hands shook so badly that he could not open the lock. He knew what was coming. Fear overwhelmed him. He wanted to give instructions, but didn't know what to say or do. He sat down, flat on the ground. His mouth, dry as the sand beneath his fingers, opened and closed. He could not speak.

A mounted Nama commando, the riders wearing wide-brimmed hats, rode into the camp. Fourteen riders, upright in their saddles with Mausers at the ready, *velskoens* in the stirrups, and with saltpetre showing white on their horses' flanks. The horses, foaming at the mouth, came to a standstill.

The soldiers stared at the forlorn little group before them while the dust settled. At the front of the group the leader, a tall lean Nama with a gaunt face and wearing a black jacket, sat proudly on his horse.

Therese rushed up to the brown stranger. She fell to her knees in the dust and folded her hands together in a gesture of prayer.

"I beg you, sir. I plead with you in the name of everything that is good and pure. Sir. Please, I cannot speak your language. But I ask you humbly, please, sir… Do not harm my children. We have not been in your country for more than a week."

The leader looked down at Therese on her knees in the dust front before him. Then he lifted his hat and responded in perfect German.

"Madam, kneel before God alone! Not before me!"

With a quick movement he was out of the saddle. He extended his hand and helped her to her feet.

"My name is Cornelius Fredericks. I am captain of the *!Aman*, the pride of the Nama people. We do not wage war against women and children."

Blushing, Therese brushed the dust from her dress and tidied her hair.

"Sir…uh sir, *Herr* Fredericks, pleased to meet you. Uh-uhm, my children and I have just arrived from Prussia in Germany and my husband…".

Ernst walked forward and looked the tall man in the eye. Then he greeted him in the language of the Boers in his heavy German accent.

"Good evening, sir. My name is Ernst Luchtenstein, son of Joseph and Therese. Leave us in peace. You are frightening my mother."

The group of Nama soldiers cackled with laughter.

"Indeed, little General, you say your name is Ernst? And where did you suddenly learn to speak like a Boer? Eh? Tell me?"

He advanced a step closer. Ernst stood his ground.

"Johannes taught me. He is my friend. Johannes is our *touleier*. He has gone to Kubub to let the oxen graze."

Fredericks's thirteen soldiers dismounted their horses and unsaddled. In an instant they had clambered all over the wagon. It did not take long for them to find Joseph's brandy. With their narrow eyes half closed, they gulped down the warm brown liquid. The bunch became merry, but the mood soon changed and they started to curse and swear. The leader, Cornelius, sat apart. He did not drink with them.

The Luchtenstein family sat on the ground. Charlotte pressed her face into her mother's neck and Therese rocked her back and forth.

"Joseph, what are they going to do to us?" whispered Therese.

Joseph swallowed. "Nothing. I don't know….". The corners of his mouth were white, his hands shaking.

"But what will they do? This cannot be happening? Where are the police ... isn't there law and order here, Joseph? How can they threaten and rob us just like that?"

"Until two years ago, all was quiet. The soldiers will come and shoot them as they did with the Hereros."

A cold darkness descended over the camp. Thirteen noisy, inebriated Namas were stumbling and falling over one another around the fire.

Cornelius sat next to the fire with his legs apart, sober and alone, his back resting against his horse's saddle. He gazed into the fire, unaware of his soldiers' crazy shouting. The flames from the fire glowed and flickered over the wrinkles on his face. For him, this evening was just another senseless episode in this senseless war. He knew it was only a moment of respite in their eventual defeat. Just as his ancestors had had to flee the Colony, so would they, the Namas of Namaland, come to a tragic end. They would be humiliated in the same way. The power of the whites was just too strong. He had seen this in the Herero war.

He spat angrily into the fire and slid down lower against his saddle. He recalled the nights around the fire with his friend, the young Lieutenant Thilo von Trotha, Abraham Morris and their other companions. Pursuing the Hereros. How many nights had they sat like this around a small fire and spoken about their future dreams and of the country and all the problems, he wondered. Why did everything have to turn out like this, Cornelius asked himself over and over again.

He looked at the German family. What was he to do with them? The images of Magdalena, little Hendrik and Martha came before his eyes. He hadn't seen them for such a long time. He looked at the German woman and her two children sitting on the other side of the campfire, people like himself. These Germans, who had left their own country to pitch their tents in the world of the Khoi-Khoin and who now threatened to wipe out his family and people, as they had done in Hereroland. These people were moving across Namaland like a swarm of birds and placing every inch of land under the German flag. It was all the fault of his father,

Josef Fredericks. It was he who had sold Angra Pequena to the Germans. He remembered very well how one of them came out of the church that afternoon and hung the red and black flag from the camel thorn tree. He also recalled how his father had staggered home as a result of too much German firewater. He looked to one side and saw how his men were gulping down the firewater now.

Pastor Bam was right. The temptations of the firesticks and the firewater were the beginning of the end for Namaland. Cornelius sighed and rested his chin on his chest. He was too tired to be angry, afraid or anxious. He only wanted to be at Bethanien and lie in the arms of his *koekemakranka*.

It was getting late. The drunken Namas stumbled and fell about aimlessly. The *trekker* family, huddled in blankets, sat on the ground, trembling with fear and cold. Ernst watched the bizarre scene in front of him. He noticed some movement around the Nama leader. Four of his men were involved in an altercation with him. Ernst did not understand what they were saying, but he knew that the brown people were arguing about his family.

Cornelius Fredericks's tall figure towered over the family.

"Get up, take only what you need and leave. Come, come! Immediately. My men are after your blood. They want to kill you. Move, quickly, get away. Please! In a couple of minutes all hell will break loose here. Remember a bag of water, otherwise you'll die tomorrow, in any case."

Therese and Joseph scrambled up.

"Thank you Mr Fredericks, thank you very much, sir," said Therese.

"Madam, I gave you my word and I'm keeping to it, but this bunch of mine are drunk. Please go now."

Ernst came forward.

"Thank you, Mr Fredericks. I can see that you are a man of honour." He offered his hand to Cornelius. Cornelius shook his hand. The tall copper-coloured man's face softened. How he missed his own family.

Within minutes the Luchtensteins disappeared into the darkness. Therese had no more tears, only fear; terrible, intense fear. She could not see anything, hear anything or feel anything, not even Charlotte's small hand in hers. Her mouth was dry and her skin ice cold. It was dark, but the half-moon and the stars lit up the sand around them. Soon it was dead quiet. They heard only their own footsteps crunching in the sand. Every now and then Therese looked back and saw the fire at the camp receding into the blackness of the night. Joseph walked faster and Charlotte had to run to keep up with him.

"Joseph, she can't go on anymore. Slower please, walk a bit slower," pleaded Therese.

Johannes, returning, stumbled into the military camp at Aus. He knew something was wrong when he saw the strange tracks that led towards the wagon. Leaving the oxen behind he drew nearer, crouching, only to see the drunken soldiers raising hell around the wagon. He then turned around, and for the second time in twenty-four hours, walked back to Aus with the oxen.

Johannes told the German officer everything that had happened. When he was finished, the big man stared at him for some time, sighed deeply, and then barked his orders.

"Von Rosenthal, take fifty men and sufficient provisions for three days. Arrange for a wagon and two teams of oxen and six men on horseback to follow you. Follow this *touleier's* tracks, in the direction of Lüderitzbucht. When you come across the enemy, kill them all except the leader. We are still searching for that Fredericks. The general wants him alive. Bring him to me. And bring the German family back to the camp with you."

An hour later fifty mounted German soldiers under the command of Lieutenant Von Rosenthal, as well as Johannes, also on horseback, rode out into the bright morning sun with an icy wind at their backs. An ox wagon, two teams of oxen, additional provisions and six mounted riders followed behind them.

The fleeing Luchtensteins stumbled on through the night and dropped to the ground in a frozen heap in the early hours of the morning. A light breeze accompanied the rising sun. Joseph knew he had lost everything the previous night. His wagon, oxen, food, water, *trekking* gear, everything. Tears rolled uncontrollably down Therese's cheeks, but she made no sound.

Why? Why? Why? she asked herself over and over again.

She found no answer. Joseph drank deeply from the bag of water.

"Here, my wife. Drink. We are almost at Aus."

But Therese heard nothing.

Joseph's head jerked up. He jumped to his feet, looked around and then began to laugh, as he danced around.

"Look there! Here they are! The soldiers are here! They have come to rescue us! They have come to rescue us!"

The commando surrounded the family. Therese could not believe her eyes when Johannes dismounted and bowed in front of her.

And then she wept and laughed at the same time. She kissed Ernst, Charlotte and then Joseph. The soldiers watched the drama playing out before their eyes.

Lieutenant Von Rosenthal gave instructions that the family, Johannes and four soldiers were to remain and wait for the wagon to take them to Aus.

"Lieutenant, when you find them, shoot them all dead, right there on the spot. Just bring my wagon back with you."

Joseph walked tall again.

The *Schutztruppe* disappeared over the dune in the direction of the sea.

19

2 April 1906
Blood in the desert

Cornelius Fredericks after his capture.

It was a cruel massacre. Cornelius Fredericks's inebriated gang lurched around open-mouthed, their heads swaying, when Lieutenant Richard von Rosenthal's soldiers struck. Fredericks was the only one who was not drunk.

Cursing and shouting orders, the soldiers herded the drunk and confused Namas together, while two soldiers handcuffed Cornelius's hands in front of him. Von Rosenthal's soldiers cocked their Mausers. Without another word, they opened fire. They loaded and fired, loaded and fired without stopping. Some of the Namas fell immediately. Two tried to flee before they were gunned down.

"No, no! What are you doing! No!" Cornelius Fredericks screamed.

Then he became sick and vomited all over his chest. Just in front of him a German soldier vomited too.

The dust settled. It was quiet. Von Rosenthal dismounted from his horse. He walked amongst the dead Namas. One lay struggling for breath through a bloody hole in his throat. Von Rosenthal removed his pistol from its holster and shot the Nama behind the ear. Then he retched and walked into the desert.

The soldiers inspanned Joseph's wagon. They left the scene with the Nama rebels' bodies lying in the sun, just as they had fallen. Cornelius Fredericks, with his hands still bound and barefoot, had to run in front of the horses. Now and then a crop would hit his face or shoulders. He stared straight ahead, not uttering a sound.

Late that evening the patrol rode into Aus. Cornelius Fredericks of Bethanien was locked up in a cell, without food or water.

20

Aus. From the fingers of the desert

Aus, a place of rest for man and beast, circa 1906.

The ox wagons and mule carts ground the dirt roads of Aus into powder. Transport riders, *Schutztruppe* and business people abounded in this busy, friendly town with the best pastures in German South-West Africa, situated just outside the arid Namib. Here all travellers could pause to recover from or prepare for their dangerous treks in the desert. Most of the oxen and mules waited south of the Aus Mountains, at Klein Kubub's strong spring.

Wide plains of grass, broken by dozens of larger and smaller hills, an abundance of camel thorn trees, shepherd's trees, sickle bushes and waving bushman's grass made it seem like a paradise compared to the barren stretches of sand of the Namib Desert.

"From here to Keetmanshoop it is easy," said Joseph.

Therese walked past the enormous hospital tents. She was surprised by the rows of neatly made beds she saw through the open tent flaps. Perhaps Joseph was right, she thought. Perhaps their hardship was over. Perhaps they had a future here; perhaps civilisation was indeed breaking through in this wild country.

At the entrance to the military camp she asked permission from the guards to see the commanding officer. One of them escorted her to the office where a young man in uniform received her. He introduced himself as Lieutenant Von Rosenthal. He looked a pleasant young man, she thought.

"Lieutenant, I am concerned about the man who is kept here as a prisoner, Mr Fredericks. May I see him please?"

"The native who nearly murdered you? Cornelius Fredericks? And why would you be concerned about him, if I may ask, Madam? You must know that he is held responsible for various deeds, among others for the death of Lieutenant Thilo von Trotha, the previous commander of the German *Schutztruppe* in German South West-Africa, General Von Trotha's nephew?"

Therese's eyes widened.

"No, I did not know that, but I do know that he treated us very well under the circumstances. In fact, he protected us from his own people. Particularly when they became drunk, and some threatened to harm us."

"Madam, Cornelius Fredericks is as good as dead. The only reason he did not die in the desert, as the other rebels did, is because the general wanted him alive. To make him pay for the death of young Von Trotha."

"Please, Lieutenant? I ask you. Only for five minutes."

The young man thought about it for a while. "I'll see what I can do. Please return in an hour's time."

Therese left and quickly went back to put some leftover meat, bread and dainty biscuits, which she had brought with her from Germany, in a basket. She was determined to get to the truth, personally.

"Ernst, walk with me and carry this basket," she said.

She knocked on Von Rosenthal's door. A sergeant and two soldiers escorted her to a low building, hidden away behind the barracks. The sergeant opened the lock holding the thick chain together.

"*Heraus!*" his voice boomed into the cell.

Cornelius Fredericks bent down to exit the low door. He screwed up his eyes against the sharp glare of the sun. Therese started when she saw him. He was only wearing tattered shorts. His face and back were covered with wounds.

Shocked, she looked at the sergeant. "What did you do to him? Why did you beat him up like this?" she asked.

"Madam, we are in a state of war and this man got close to wiping you and your family out. And he murdered General Von Trotha's nephew."

"That is not true," said Fredericks, defensively.

One soldier aimed the butt of his rifle at Cornelius's head, but the sergeant stopped him.

"Wait, wait. Madam, you have five minutes."

The three soldiers moved some distance away.

Therese and Ernst stood closer. "*Herr* Fredericks, I am so sorry and wish to thank you for what you did for us there in the desert. You enabled us to get away. I am just so sorry that you're now… well, that you're now sitting here. I am sorry…".

"Madam, I told you on the first day, and I'll say it again: the Namas do not wage war against women and children. We are not like you Germans."

"What do you mean? Like us?"

"Madam, it is your people that kill innocent people. Women and children. We don't do that. Never. A Nama criminal perhaps yes, but not a Nama soldier. We can never receive the blessing of God on our wars if we become as barbaric as the German soldiers and the Bushmen. I did what a Nama soldier does, Madam."

"But surely a German soldier would not do a woman or child any harm?"

"Madam, your people, your soldiers do terrible things here. We, I, fought on your side with the *Schutztruppe* against the Hereros. We helped you to conquer them, to exterminate a nation. To kill women and children until the Waterberg itself wept blood. Today I am full of shame and regret. We thought that we were closer to you white people than our enemy, the black Hereros from darkest Africa, but today we know that the opposite is true. If this is what civilised people do, then I would prefer to be a barbarian. Then I would rather perish in the desert than live inside your Kaiser's palace."

"But Mr Fredericks, please, what are you talking about? What do you mean? In Germany there were stories of cruelty, but we never believed them. Are they actually true? If I had known they were true, I would never have boarded that ship. I need to know, Mr Fredericks. We have been in this country barely two weeks and do not know much. Tell me. What is happening here? Please? What is the truth?"

"Madam, I have reached the end. You, your… these *Schutztruppe* are going to kill me. That is a certainty. Do you not know what happened to my men back there in the desert when you were gone already? Did nobody tell you?"

Therese looked away.

"Allow me to tell you, Madam. They herded my men, who had been fighting side-by-side with your German *Schutztruppe* for the past two years against the Hereros, like sheep into a kraal at dusk, and opened fire with their Mausers, killing them all. Then this same Von Rosenthal walked amongst the dead and wounded and shot those who were still alive with his pistol. Just like that, Madam. Like wounded oryx."

Therese pressed her fist against her mouth. She felt dizzy. Ernst's mouth was dry, his hands clenched into fists and his ears were ringing.

"Mr Fredericks," he asked. "Sir, did the soldiers kill all your friends? Really?"

Cornelius Fredericks regarded the young boy for a long while. Then he sighed deeply. "Yes, my little General, yes. They shot them like animals, one by one, until the last one was dead."

Ernst swallowed with difficulty, his throat thick and dry.

"But how is all this possible? And what's going on in this country? Why do people hate one another so? Please tell me. I have to know. Tell me. I want to know everything," begged Therese.

"Madam, it is a long story. It has come a long way and I want someone to know the truth when I am no longer here. But they are not going to give me a chance to give a proper account of what happened.

"The Namas and the Herero's never got along with one another. We came from the Cape and they are from the place they call the Congo. We are Khoi-Khoin, brown people, and they are black, as different as you and I, just more so."

"I was raised on a German mission station, Madam, Bethanien, home of the *!Aman*, two days' ride on horseback from here. My father was Josef Fredericks the second. And Madam, it was he, my father, who was robbed by your Adolph Lüderitz of our own land. I was there, a young lad, just old enough to serve water to the important guests from Germany. I saw it with my own eyes. Although I did not realise what I was witnessing, I did see it and I mourn that incident every day of my life.

"Just as I regret many other things. Like helping you Germans to slaughter thousands of Herero women and children until the Waterberg ran with blood, and allowing others to die of thirst in the desert."

"Madam Luchtenstein, this is now enough, Madam. We have to lock up the prisoner again," came the voice of the sergeant.

The three soldiers stood closer. They dragged Cornelius back. Cornelius desperately clung to the gifts from the white woman, but when the visitors were out of sight, the soldiers took them away from him.

Ernst walked back to the ox wagon with his mother. The *spekvreter's* old questions rang in his mind.

"Mother, we must help him. I don't want the soldiers to kill him."

"I beg your pardon? What did you say, my son?"

"Oh, I'm sorry," said Ernst, half embarrassed.

He realized that he was thinking and speaking like a Boer. He had spoken to his mother in the Boer language. What was happening to him?

"I only said that I don't want them to kill him, *Mutti*."

"Me too, my son," she replied, but fear and doubt lay like a great weight on her chest. "We need to remember this story and tell it to the world. The worst evil cannot survive if a light is shone upon it. We must tell the story. I will write down everything Mr Fredericks told us. We are Germans, civilised people, but if we act like barbarians, we have no right to look down on the indigenous people. They are people, real people, just like you and me. Never forget that, as long as you live."

"I know *Mutti*. I know."

Late into the night, Therese used Ernst's best pencil to write in his exercise book. She hid the book at the bottom of her trunk.

21

Cornelius narrates and Therese writes

Therese Luchtenstein

The next morning Therese rose early. She baked bread and made a flask of coffee. The fears and doubts of the previous day had given way to a firm decision. She knew what was right and what was wrong.

"Come, Ernst, I need to talk to Mr Fredericks again."

Von Rosenthal relented. He could see in her eyes that she was determined. He personally fulfilled her request to meet with the prisoner in the shade of the camel thorn tree. She went and sat there, with Ernst beside her.

"Did you enjoy the little gift I brought you yesterday, Mr Fredericks?"

"They took it away from me, Madam, but I'm not complaining. It is good to see you again."

"You must talk, Mr Fredericks. We don't have much time. I want to know everything, but today you must sit here in front of me and eat all the food I've brought. Please, eat and talk."

She opened Ernst's exercise book.

"I will write everything down, because the world needs to know. I will send a letter to Germany at the first opportunity I get. My brother works for a newspaper there, Mr Fredericks."

"Very well, Madam."

He bent his head, whispered a prayer, and began to chew.

The prisoner sat flat on the ground, his hands still cuffed, a brown canvas coat covering his upper body to hide the wounds. Blood from the cuts and sores on his feet dripped onto the grass and sand. Ernst stared, horrified. He saw the drops of blood mingling with the sand and leaves, and then setting into a thick substance like the filling in the little tarts his mother baked. Then fresh blood fell and the process repeated itself, while the older coagulated blood hardened and blackened and sand covered it, like the carcass of an animal in the desert. Absentmindedly Cornelius moved his feet, destroying the silent, ugly evidence of his bleeding wounds. Then again, the blood reappeared through the sticky sand covering the soles of his feet, dripping onto the ground. Ernst's whole body shuddered. This thirsty country drank blood, the blood of its people, to quench its anger. It will also drink my blood, as well as Mother's, Father's and Charlotte's, he thought.

The vision of a row of bottles with pieces of flesh and a dry skull came to him and he heard the voice again:

"*Aber er ist doch nur ein Jude...*".

And he saw Dr Fischer's cold grey eyes right in front of him.

Who am I? Why am I here?

Cornelius ate in silence for a while, and then continued speaking.

"We children only found out years later what had really happened that day. I remember that the adults signed papers. My father made a large cross on the paper. Everyone stood up and went outside where one of the Germans hung your flag, the Kaiserbird, as we called it, from the camel thorn tree."

"Please eat some more, Mr Fredericks," Therese urged. She held out a plate to Cornelius.

"Thank you, Madam," he said and took a piece of bread.

"What happened that day was the beginning of why I am sitting here today, Madam. That day my father, Josef Fredericks, captain of the *!Aman*, the Nama of Bethanien, sold his birthright for a pot of lentil soup. That day he signed a paper that made Adolph Lüderitz the owner of Angra Pequena and the five miles surrounding the bay."

"Sorry, Madam. Your time is up. You have to leave." The young sergeant stepped forward.

"But Sergeant, what is the problem? What is so urgent?" Therese argued.

"Madam, I have strict instructions. There is a war on, you know," he answered.

"You! Get up, on your feet, on your feet!" He aimed at Cornelius with the butt of his rifle.

"No, Sergeant! Please don't harm him. We are leaving."

Therese stood up. She closed her book.

22

Five minutes for the prisoner

A German soldier with three Nama prisoners

The Luchtenstein family rose in the early dawn, to find a small Nama woman seated next to the wagon: Cornelius's wife Magdalena, daughter of Hendrik Witbooi, and her two young children, little Hendrik, who was six and Martha, four years old. Magdalena was an attractive woman with the coppery-red complexion, wide mouth and small hands of the Nama women. She appeared fresh, without any sign of the previous two days' travel from Bethanien in the company of a transport wagon of Maltahöhe.

"I have no work or alms for you. What do you want?" Joseph asked Magdalena when he saw her.

Therese remonstrated with him and addressed Magdalena directly. "*Frau*, can I help? Who are you?" When she heard who Magdelena was, she said "But come, sit here, oh, I am so sorry…".

Therese learnt that the news of Cornelius's capture had reached Bethanien. She immediately gave the two children food and milk. Charlotte and her two new friends, Hendrik and Martha, played together in the sand under the camel thorn tree while the two women made plans to see Lieutenant Von Rosenthal as soon as possible.

"Therese, today is the day that we move on. We have spent enough time here just doing nothing. I want to get home," Joseph said from inside the wagon tent.

Therese did not answer him.

Just after eight o'clock Therese and Magdalena were in the office of Lieutenant Von Rosenthal. The German woman's continued interference with the prisoner frustrated the young officer, but he was fully aware of the controversy in Germany over the current phase of the war. Many questions were being asked in the Reichstag. General Von Trotha had been replaced the previous week because of his harsh actions in the Herero campaign. If this woman were to send news to Germany, it could only lead to problems again.

"Madam, I already told you that this Cornelius Fredericks is being held responsible for the murder of Lieutenant Von Trotha, the previous general's nephew. The lieutenant was unarmed, under a white flag as special envoy to negotiate peace, when this man shot him from behind. A telegram was received last night from Keetmanshoop. They apprehended an eyewitness in possession of the lieutenant's medal and his watch. He told them everything."

"Lieutenant, that cannot be true."

"Madam, I was there. I tracked them for weeks. I was there, down in the Fish River canyon in command of the patrol, on the verge of capturing them, when a young boy carrying a white flag came out. We stopped shooting. The boy gave me a letter from the lieutenant, the young Von Trotha, in which he told me of his secret mission. I immediately left the scene so that he could continue with his negotiations, but then they – he, this woman's husband, Cornelius Fredericks – shot the general's nephew. Madam, we have an eyewitness. He is being held in the jail in Keetmanshoop."

"Lieutenant, please. Listen to me or to mr Fredericks. He will tell you what really happened there. Please, Lieutenant," pleaded Therese while Magdalena stared at the officer in silence.

"Madam, I have my instructions. The prisoner has to go to Keetmanshoop today where he will be tried. We are leaving in half an hour."

Just then the handcuffed Cornelius came around the corner with two soldiers escorting him. Magdalena jumped up and grabbed at her husband whom she had not seen for months, but the soldiers kept her away.

"Cornelius! Cornelius! What have they done to you?" she called out, tears streaming down her cheeks. She clung to his ankles.

"Magdalena my 'krankie…. Stand up my wife. Do not crawl in the dust in front of these Germans, please! We need to remain strong, my 'krankie."

Tears welled up in Therese's eyes, but she continued to plead: "Lieutenant, this man has not yet been found guilty by a court of law. I am begging you with all due respect and humility. I implore you in the name of everything that is good and right: please give the two people a few minutes together."

"Very well, five minutes. That is all. Then we have to leave." He turned and left the office.

"Mr Fredericks, you must please listen to me. They are taking you away from here today, I do not know where to, but I must know what happened here. This is your and your people's only chance. The whole world needs to know. Can you write?" Therese asked Cornelius.

He raised his chin. "Of course, Madam. Not all people in Africa are barbarians."

"Good. Please write down the whole story just as it happened. I will come looking for you and I will come and get it. Either myself or my son Ernst here."

She tore a few blank pages from the book and handed them to him with the pencil. Cornelius shoved the items into his pants underneath the canvas vest. Fighting back her tears, Therese turned away, leaving the two forlorn creatures, Cornelius and Magdalena, to look into each other's eyes.

"Lieutenant!" Therese called to Von Rosenthal, running after him.

"Yes, Madam, what is it now?" he said over his shoulder, without stopping.

"We are also on our way to Keetmanshoop today. Could we possibly travel with you? It is so dangerous."

"Madam, that is completely out of the question. You are too slow. We are travelling on horseback. We have to be in Keetmanshoop in four days. It could take an ox wagon another four weeks."

The two women sat on the wagon kist, talking about their children. Therese promised Magdalena that she would speak to the commanding officer in Keetmanshoop, but privately she wondered if Cornelius would still be alive by the time they got there.

"Move. Move! All together!" The command rang across the vast plains every now and then.

The countryside beyond Aus was beautiful, unlike the merciless desert they had now left far behind them. The pastures were lush and green, with grazing in abundance and many sparkling springs with fresh water. Herds of springbok, ostriches and oryx appeared from time to time, only to disappear over the hoizon or behind the hills again, away from the danger of the rifles.

Ernst's command of the Nama language improved every day and he now also spoke the language of the Boers fluently. He also learnt more of the history of Johannes's people; of the *!narra* fields in the Kuiseb valley and how Johannes had lost the birthright to his ancestral land when he absconded; of the wonderful properties of the fruits of the veld and all the songs and stories about them. In good times these Namas made *!narra* rolls, like dried fruit rolls, and survived on them for months.

Ernst often gazed in silent wonderment at this young man, the man of Africa. Ever present in his mind were the vultures of Cornelius's tale. He thought about Cornelius's fate, and the cruelty and anger raging in this harsh land.

He drove out of his mind the images that came back to him of that terrible day in Luderitzbucht's water, and the lights afterwards in the hospital, as well as that voice. He would whistle the song of the omnipresent *spekvreter* whenever these dark visions intruded.

"Who am I? Why am I here?" he whistled the tune with the words spinning round and round in his head, like the squeaking sound of the wagon's left front wheel as it turned more and more crookedly.

They now *trekked* in the daytime. At dusk they outspanned. It was a comfortable life, very different from the scorching desert. The women had ample time to prepare food and wash and mend clothes. The animals had time to graze and drink. The track was firm, clear and well trodden. Because the going was good, the oxen's hooves no longer cracked and often only three or four pairs were needed to pull the wagon. They were swapped round frequently to spare their strength or to allow them more time to graze.

The evenings around the campfire were pleasant. Johannes taught Ernst about the stars of the southern heavens and what each group of stars meant to the Namas.

"Look there. There is the Copper star; that little reddish one. He tells us how long we have been *trekking* during the night."

Although it was cold at night, winter had not yet arrived. Everyone slept peacefully except for one night when a leopard's deep growl was heard near the oxen, causing them to bellow nervously. Joseph shot randomly into the night. It became quiet again, but Therese could not get back to sleep.

23

Cornelius in prison at Keetmanshoop

Colonel Berthold von Deimling

Cornelius's hands remained bound. He sat on a mule tethered to the horses of the soldiers riding on either side of him. He did not speak. Every night, tied to a tree, he thought of his family. When they rode down the wide main street of Keetmanshoop after four days of travel, all the townspeople stared at the emaciated prisoner.

They knew he must be an important Nama captain.

"It is Hendrik Witbooi. So he never died," some whispered.

"It is Simon Koper. If they have him, then the war is over," others said.

Cornelius held his head high. At the German camp two soldiers dragged him to a neat stone building. They stopped in front of the entrance. Two steps led up to a brightly polished stoep. On either side grew bright, cheerful beds of daisies.

A large man with a dark moustache drew aside a dark red curtain at a window. His eyes met Cornelius's direct gaze. Then he made an impatient gesture. The soldiers shunted Cornelius through a heavy iron gate to another vaulted steel door in a huge sandstone wall. They forced him down a long passageway of cells to one at the end which a warder unlocked. At last a soldier removed the cuffs. While Cornelius rubbed his wrists where the metal had chafed him for four days, he was shoved into the cell. He looked around him. It was dark with only one small window high up in the corner, where he could see a fragment of Namaland's vast blue sky. A bucket stood in one corner, a rumpled, dirty blanket lay in the other. He smelt the strong odour of rats and heard the door being locked behind him.

After two days of bread and water, the key turned in the lock.

"Up *Hotnot*[78]! On your feet! Out! The *Herr Oberst*[79] wishes to see the snake who murdered General Von Trotha's nephew!"

Cornelius stumbled down the passage accompanied by two soldiers. He squinted against the bright light. First they took him to an outside room, some kind of a bathroom, and gave him a bucket of water and a block of blue soap.

"Go on, wash your stinking body. You cannot appear in such a disgusting state before the *Oberst*."

Cornelius washed himself as best he could. He had to dry himself with a hessian bag. Again they chased him down the passage, at the end of which there was a door. They pushed him into the large, nearly empty room. Inside were only a small desk and two chairs.

"Stand there!" bellowed one of the soldiers, pointing to a spot in front of the desk. Cornelius waited and waited. After an hour or two he heard hurried footsteps approaching in the passage. Then a group entered the room. The large man with the dark moustache sat down. He tossed down his cap on the desk. Cornelius guessed that he was Colonel Von

78 *Hotnot*: From Hottentot, a derogatory term, politically incorrect.
79 *Oberst*: Colonel

Deimling, new supreme commander of the Kaiser's defence force in the colony of German South-West Africa.

The colonel was red-faced, his thin lips pressed tightly together.

"Who are you?" he hissed at the prisoner.

"Cornelius Fredericks, captain of the *!Aman* of Bethanien, son of Josef Fredericks from whom Adolph Lüderitz stole our land."

The soldier behind Cornelius hit him with the butt of his rifle so that he almost fell over on top of the Colonel but the other soldier grabbed him by the neck and hauled him upright again.

"What were you doing there in the Fish River canyon? Why did you murder an unarmed envoy of the Kaiser?" barked the Colonel.

"Thilo was my friend, Colonel, the best German I ever knew. We fought together against the Hereros. I did not murder him," answered Cornelius.

The Colonel looked up sharply.

"You are lying to me now!"

"Why would I, Colonel? I know my death sentence has been signed. I do not care any longer. Do as you want, but only know that I never, never would have murdered my friend. I am sorry, really sorry, especially for Margarethe."

Von Deimling's head jerked up.

"What do you know about Margarethe?" he hissed.

"I told you Colonel, we fought together. Thilo, Lieutenant Von Trotha and I. Margarethe was his wife. For weeks he and I and our men slept under the stars, hunted Hereros and dreamt of peace and our families. He was a good man. He did not want to wage war. Just like me, he wanted to farm with sheep and cattle, and to be with his wife and children."

Von Deimling leant back in his chair.

"Tell me more!"

Cornelius told him about all the sadness of the past two years while Von Deimling fidgeted in his chair. Without Cornelius being aware of it, the man in front of him was under orders from Germany to suspend the cruelties of his predecessor, General Lothar von Trotha.

Von Deimling could no longer issue a summary command that a high profile prisoner be hanged. The liberal tide in Germany was turning. It had already claimed the head of Von Trotha. He had to watch his step. There was still Shark Island in Lüderitzbucht, the German defence force's secret project. This project provided the opportunity to deal with the Empire's enemies in a way the newspapers knew nothing about.

Cornelius's account fascinated Von Deimling. He instinctively knew it was the truth.

"Yes, Fredericks. Be that as it may, but why did you attack this German family's *trek* in the desert and rob them? Why was that necessary? And then send them into the desert in the middle of the night?"

"I don't know Colonel. I have no explanation. After two years of war, murder and death, I suppose you lose perspective and then do stupid things. When the war started we made very sure not to make trouble with civilians. Our war was against people like you, soldiers of the Kaiser. We hunted soldiers to kill them, but not farmers or civilians and definitely not women and children. Unlike you Germans who thought nothing of wiping out thousands of Herero women and children and Jakob Morenga's women and children. Or letting them perish from hunger and thirst on Shark Island."

When Von Deimling heard the name Shark Island, he jerked his head up sharply.

"What do you know about Shark Island?" he demanded.

"That is the place where the mighty Germany sacrifices the Nama people to the Great Snake," Cornelius answered.

"Take him back!" Von Deimling barked. He left the room to send off a telegram.

24

One day too late

Keetmanshoop during the Nama war with
a few //haru-oms dwellings.

Three weeks after departing from Aus in their wagon, the Luchtenstein family with Magdalena and her two children spent their last night in the open veld, half a day's journey from Keetmanshoop. At last they were nearly at home. By now Therese had learnt some words and phrases in the Nama language from her friend, Magdalena. She was almost beginning to feel part of this new world.

The oxen and the wagon had survived. Joseph was keen to get to Keetmanshoop to deliver Hesselman's goods so that he could depart again immediately. He had no time to waste on visiting. The accursed railway line was creeping across the land like the black plague. He did not know how long he would still be able to work as a *transportryer* before the train finally delivered its fatal bite. What would he do then? He had no idea.

He had to make enough money to buy land before the railway was completed.

The trip from Aus had been easy. At the Fish River everybody had to put their shoulders to the wheel to get the wagon through the drift, but it was a great victory for the family.

The wagon now stood under a shepherd's tree. Some distance away there were a few sweet-thorn trees and beyond them some camelthorn trees.

The sun lingered like a drop of blood among the feathery, pink-orange clouds above the horizon. In the distance the Karas mountains enclosed the scene like the carved frames of Therese's portraits.

Ernst marvelled at the wonder of yet another sunset. He knew tonight that he loved this country with his entire being. He knew that he was already part of it, this harsh, free world with its hardy people, and that he wanted to remain here – always. He knew it was a cruel land that could take one's life in an instant and that he did not understand it all. Those people on the island. The prisoners alongside the road, the people that assaulted them and shot them dead. Cornelius in jail. He did not yet understand all the pain and anger, but he felt the blood in his veins pulsating in harmony with the heartbeat of the desert's sand, grass, camelthorn trees, mountains, springbok, oryx, eagles, larks, *skaapwagters*, *spekvreters*, Namas, springs, sun and blue sky.

Tomorrow they would be in Keetmanshoop. He hoped his mother would speak to the German soldiers about seeing Cornelius. He had to see him again. He wanted to listen to more stories. To try to understand what he still did not know.

That evening was a feast. Therese delved deep into her trunk for the last of the fine biscuits with the icing sugar. The children laughed and played.

Early the next morning Therese awoke and walked into the darkness. Suddenly, something hit her with a mighty blow. She could only make choking sounds while she struggled feebly on the ground. Next to her was a leopard with its powerful jaws clamped tightly round her throat. The large spotted cat had leapt on her from behind, grabbed her by the neck and pulled her down. Mercifully, she was quickly overcome by deep darkness. She never knew what happened to her.

After a while Joseph went outside to see what was keeping her so long. In the darkness he could make out the outline of a leopard, sitting on Therese's body, twitching its tail. Instinctively he seized a *jukskei* and threw it at the animal.

He charged up to where she was lying. Too late. He could do nothing to help her. Mute with shock, he sat with her body in his arms. He rocked to and fro, and cried for the first time in thirty years.

Later he woke Magdalena. He instructed her to take the children away. Magdalena tried to explain to them what had happened. Ernst could not believe what had happened. He wanted to see his mother but Joseph forbade him from doing so. Charlotte did not understand what was going on.

Joseph and Johannes dug a grave under the shepherd's tree. They cut and fashioned a shroud from the wagon tent's canvas, sewed Therese's body inside it and lowered her into the grave. Then Joseph called Magdalena and the children.

Ernst noticed that a thin trickle of blood had seeped through a tear in the canvas and fallen to the ground. Why did this country have such a thirst for the blood of its people?

With everyone gathered round the grave, Joseph tossed in a small bunch of wild flowers and began shovelling it closed. Tears ran freely down Ernst's cheeks and his body shook as he helped to push the soft, warm sand onto his mother's body with his bare hands. In his head he heard the *spekvreter*'s questioning song again.

Charlotte understood little of what she saw.

Later, when Joseph was not looking, Ernst searched in his mother's trunk for the remains of his exercise book with Cornelius's story. He wanted to complete her work.

"That is what she would have wanted", he mumbled to himself. That was the only way he could make sense of the senseless death that had shattered his family.

Late that afternoon the wagon with the tattered canvas rolled into Keetmanshoop. That was the end of the Luchtenstein family, as it used to be.

Mrs Gertruida McKay, Nama wife of the rich Scotsman Robert McKay, a strong woman with bosoms as large as two *tsammas*,[80] arms like *disselbome* and a smile as wide as the Namib, had heard of the tragedy. She insisted on taking Magdalena and the children under her wing.

Joseph was silent and listless. He lingered a night in the town. The next day he trekked to McKay's farm.

Gertruida did not allow the grass to grow under her feet. She accompanied Magdalena to the prison.

---

80 *Tsammas*: a fruit of the desert.

"*Leutnant*[81], you have Cornelius Fredericks here in your prison. This is his wife, Magdalena, daughter of the late Hendrik Witbooi. She is here to see her husband, now!"

"*Frau*, this is irregular, I don't know...".

"Irregular, my foot. Where is your *baas*, the *Herr Oberst*? Call him. Tell him Gertruida McKay is here to see him. Go on, what are you waiting for?"

"Madam, please wait. Just wait here. Alright? I'll be right back."

After a while he returned. He told Magdalena to go with him.

"My *koekemakrankie*, Magdalena, my love," Cornelius called out when he saw her. His heart contracted painfully when he heard that a leopard had killed Therese. He felt as if even nature had turned against him, because the only white person alive who had cared about him, was now gone.

He and Magdalena talked about the children, of better days, and of Bethanien.

Magdalena stayed in a small back room in McKay's shop. She was allowed to visit Cornelius and take him food every day.

During each visit a small piece of paper changed hands, unnoticed.

Magdalena put all these letters into an empty soap tin, just as she received them from Cornelius. She would keep them for him until his release, even if it took six weeks. She was so proud of her Cornelius, the captain who could write so well. She knew her father, who was an important man, had loved Cornelius very much. And her own father had loved writing too, just like Cornelius.

A few days after their arrival Joseph and Johannes left Keetmanshoop with an empty wagon on their return trek to Lüderitzbucht. Ernst and Charlotte remained behind on Robert McKay's farm, *Paradys*, outside Keetmanshoop.

One day, when Magdalena arrived at the prison again, the young lieutenant avoided her eyes. He busied himself with a file of papers and stared out of the window.

"I am sorry. He is gone. To Lüderitzbucht. They took him away from here."

Magdalena felt a cold shudder run down her back. It felt as if Great Snake was twisting its coils around her and was forcing all the breath out of her body.

---

81   *Leutnant*: Lieutenant.

25

Beautiful days at Paradys

An orderly ox wagon trek.

Robert McKay, short and stocky with only one eye, over which he wore a black eyepatch, was a successful *transportryer*. He had eight ox wagons and four full teams of oxen in service. Whether his reddish complexion was due to his Scottish genes, the sun or whisky, was not clear or important. Everyone liked him, even the German soldiers. He treated his workers well and his trek equipment was always in immaculate condition. His general dealer's store in town was a busy meeting place.

To have two more children was not a problem to him or Gertruida. Their home was spacious with large rooms, a broad, shiny red veranda and many outside rooms. The two elder children worked in the Keetmanshoop shop while the other two attended *Meister* Grünow's school on the farm.

Charlotte, Martha and Hendrik played in the shade of the camelthorn tree or on the veranda. Now and then one who was teased would run to

Gertruida to complain in the hope that a hard sweet would appear from her apron pocket. They called her 'Ma Gertie'.

When the tearful Magdalena arrived at Paradys with the bad news, Gertruida realised that she intended to leave for Lüderitzbucht at once and on foot, but she stopped Magdalena from doing so. Because of her elevated status as Mrs McKay she was regarded differently from the common Nama women and was immune to brutal German treatment. She would often take advantage of her position, but that morning Gertruida realised she could do nothing. Stories about the concentration camp on the island in Lüderitzbucht had reached her. The two Nama women wept quietly on each other's shoulders.

McKay listened to the story. He, an ordinary citizen, was also powerless against the Germans, especially since he had done so much business with them. Secretly he wondered whether this Fredericks was not just another troublemaker, but was too afraid of his wife's tongue to share his thoughts with her.

"Mister Mac," Magdalena asked, "Please, I want to go with the next wagon to Lüderitzbucht. I want to go and see my husband."

McKay did not know what to say. She could also be seized by the soldiers and end up in the camp.

Nothing the McKays said could change Magdalena's mind. A few days later she, with little Hendrik and Martha, left on a transport wagon while Robert, Gertruida, Charlotte and Ernst stood on the front veranda and waved until the wagon disappeared around the corner.

Joseph returned from a trip to Lüderitzbucht with a strange look in his eyes. He hardly noticed his children. Johannes told Ernst that Joseph had not spoken to anyone, not even to him. Johannes said they had met the Fredericks' wagon along the way, but they had only waved to one another. Ernst was privately relieved when Joseph and his wagon disappeared over the horizon in the direction of Maltahöhe.

Ernst discovered McKay's workshop. He spent time there with Uncle Lewies, the Boer from the Transvaal who was also the local blacksmith. They adjusted and repaired the wagons, because Mr McKay did not tolerate shoddy equipment. Every wagon was brought into the workshop after a trip. The *transportryers* then took a wagon that had been serviced for their next trip. A broken wheel could leave a wagon with its load stuck in the desert for weeks on end. The oxen could not survive long in the desert and would have to be taken out while the wagon and its precious load had to be left behind. Someone had to stay with the wagon, and someone had to take the oxen out. It created a lot of problems. A broken-down wagon was the favourite prey of Nama gangs.

Ernst learnt how to repair tent canvasses, tan skins, cut lashes for the whips, make thongs, *kort*[82] the wheels, grease wheel bushes, paint and even replace *disselbome*. He learnt how to work with a plane and how to use the bellows. To Ernst the ox wagon became the symbol of manhood, freedom, independence and a means of earning money. He dreamt of owning his own wagon and oxen and working for himself. He also learnt how to work with the animals and use the whiplash.

The hard work during the day kept the ghost of the *spekvreter's* questions at bay, but late at night the little bird intruded into his dreams.

Who am I? Why am I here?

The two Luchtenstein children lived like the McKay's own children in the spacious house. Gertruida loved Ernst. Early on she sensed that there was something special about the quiet, sensitive young boy. Nothing escaped him. He never complained or bothered her and always worked hard. In the evenings he helped to wash the dishes of his own accord. He did his own and his sister's laundry. Gertruida wondered why her own children were so spoilt. She always had to shout at them to pick up their clothes and wash themselves. Now and then, in a fit of anger, she would take the large leather swatter from behind the kitchen door and get stuck into the youngsters, but it was never necessary to row with Ernst. It was probably the Nama blood in her brood that made them so lazy, she thought. The young Adriaan and Lambert McKay often mocked Ernst by calling him '*baas* Ernst'.

Adriaan and Lambert took Ernst on long walks into the veld around Paradys. They taught him how to live off the veld and how to track. He learnt how to set traps for guinea fowl, how to look for water, to identify edible veld mushrooms and how to make poison for arrows from the yellow fluid of beetle larvae and the gum of thorn trees, just like a real Bushman. He learnt how to skin animals and tan the hides, and also how to slaughter a goat so that he could make a *!hob*, a skin bag to carry food in. The secret was to make as few cuts as possible, so that the skin could literally be peeled off the carcass. This took hours of patient work.

---

82 *Kort*: Afrikaans term for the process of tightening the metal band on the external surface of the wagon wheel.

The three boys competed with one another with their catapults and slingshots. Later on they managed to shatter a *karkoer*[83] at fifteen metres. When they tired of stationary targets, they threw stones into the air and attempted to hit them with their slingshots. Ernst learnt fast and sometimes beat the other two. They taunted and teased one another, laughing all the time.

Gertruida praised Ernst when he arrived home with a plucked francolin or a slaughtered hare. She told him of the love between a man and a woman and taught him about respect and loyalty and the traditions she had learnt from her aunts and her mother. She also taught him how to clean the shell of a young tortoise and to prepare it as a powder box for the *!uros*, every Nama woman's treasure, the body powder that could cast a spell over a man.

"Look here, Ernst. Here we plug the underside with the gum of the sweet-thorn tree. Then we fashion a plug for the top from jackal skin. Look, like so."

She also told him what was needed to make the body powder.

"We need the roots and the leaves of the shrubs I showed you yesterday, the moss that grows on the rocks and the seed of the mushrooms. We mix all of that together with the powder from these stones. Go now and grind the stones there on the veranda for me until we have enough powder. It must be very fine. Then bring it to me."

Ernst often walked in the veld, deep in thought, looking for the ingredients that would gladden Ma Gertie's heart.

He learnt how to make bangles for Charlotte. She was allowed to wear her bangle until she was ten years old, after which she could wear a beaded necklace, because then she would be almost grown up.

Over time, the Nama culture, its legends and tales, were transferred to Ernst. He heard the stories about Great Snake with the shiny stone on its forehead and of the great city, but even Ma Gertie evaded his questions.

"Go and play, Ernst, you are bothering me this morning with all your questions. There isn't a big city, it is only old people's stories," or "Leave your nonsense with the olden days. We don't live in reed houses anymore. We now live in decent homes in towns, no longer in reed houses. We do not believe in Great Snake and all that stuff. It is actually all nonsense. There, here's a sweet for you. Go now, off with you."

---

83   *Karkoer*: Afrikaans word for a fruit of the veld.

Ernst could now roll and click the sounds of the Nama language in his mouth until he knew every word and expression as well as he knew German and the language of the Boers.

The three boys also learnt to shoot. McKay brought them a BSA air gun from his shop. They spent hours on end shooting at targets, sparrows and weaver birds. Naturally, they nagged Mister Mac to allow them to shoot with his Mauser, but he was very strict. He allowed them to shoot with the big rifle only under the scrutiny of his one good eye.

At night the same questions came back again. "*Aber er ist doch nur ein Jude…*". Who am I? Why am I here? German? Jew? Nama? Scotsman? *Spekvreter*? *Skaapwagter*? Kaiserbird?

26

Shark Island, cradle of delusion

Dr Eugen Fischer

The *Schutztruppe* looked for the slightest excuse to lash out at Cornelius with their crops. They liked to aim for his face. If his mule moved out of step, they would use the crop. If he said something they did not like, they would hit him.

If he got onto his mule too slowly, he felt their crops. Later, even his quiet anger left him. He just tried to concentrate on surviving the next moment.

From Aus, the ox wagon trail met the new railway line where hordes of Nama and Herero prisoners of war toiled, including women and young children. They used picks and shovels and had to pull ox carts themselves. Ever present were the guards with their whips. Cornelius saw that it had become sport to the guards to hit them in the face. At first he was shocked at their cruelty, but later became used to the brutality.

When he saw the first lifeless body next to the road, he was shocked again, but after seeing other bodies lying every couple of miles along the way, he got used to that too. He saw how the German *Schutztruppe* had broken the spirit of his people, like the Egyptian slave masters in the Bible. The prisoners did not even look up when the commando passed them.

At Boerekamp the transport people stared open-mouthed at the bloodied prisoner with his lacerated and swollen face.

At the summit of the last hill, Cornelius saw the bay, Luderitzbucht, for the first time again after many years. He recalled how they had collected the rifles from the Vogelsang ship. He also remembered Pastor Bam's warning about the instruments of death, and felt an ice-cold shiver run through his body.

The mounted commando halted in front of a double barbed-wire fence. Two guards in black uniforms and black boots came out of the small guardhouse with its yellow and black pitched roof. Cornelius saw that the guards wore caps, instead of the *Schutztruppe*'s broad-brimmed hats, turned up on one side. Above the entrance gate, metallic letters pronounced the motto:

Wissenscaft ist Weisheit[84]

The guards swung the gates open, but allowed only the lieutenant and Cornelius in, on foot. From a large building behind the fence six soldiers, all in black uniform and shiny black caps, arrived to receive Cornelius. They frogmarched and shoved him right into the camp. The lieutenant walked to the nearest office where he completed a number of forms and immediately returned to the gate, under escort.

The soldiers took Cornelius to a room where four guards with pistols in their holsters and with short, braided leather crops in their hands

---

84   *Wissenschaft ist Weisheit*: Science is Wisdom

stood in the four corners of the room. A drum with a lid stood in one corner. Next to the drum was a red cylinder with a handle and a length of pipe attached to it.

One of the soldiers stepped forward. "Undress!" he barked.

Cornelius hesitated. The soldier moved forward and hit him in the face. He fell forward. The soldier struck blows left, right and centre on Cornelius's back with his crop. They burnt like the stings of a scorpion.

"Undress," he repeated. "Everything!"

Cornelius had no choice. He undressed.

"Throw everything in that drum!" the soldier shouted. Cornelius obeyed.

"Stand still!" commanded the soldier.

One of the other soldiers came closer with the red cylinder. He sprayed an acidic liquid over Cornelius's naked body. If he dared move, the soldiers lifted their crops.

The four soldiers pointed to the door. Cornelius walked through it. He found himself in another room. The face of a sad-looking soldier with grey hair stared at him through a hatch.

"Name?" asked the soldier.

"Cornelius Fredericks."

"Date of birth?"

"9 September 1870."

"Tribe?"

"*!Aman* of Bethanien."

The soldier took something from the shelf and handed it to Cornelius. "Put this on."

It was a short canvas gown with three holes: two for the arms and one for the head. The soldier took another stack of canvas from the shelf and handed it to Cornelius.

From there they took Cornelius and his canvas bedding to a small room where he had to wait while the four soldiers stood guard over him. After a long while a soldier in a white apron and wearing gloves, opened the door.

"Doctor Fischer is ready," he announced.

The four soldiers pushed Cornelius towards a door at the end of a long passage. There were strange odours, bright lights, shelves with rows of bottles, flasks, shiny instruments and a long high bench right in the middle.

On both sides of the bench stood three men wearing aprons and gloves. One of them had steely grey eyes, a pointed beard, thin hair and a sharp nose. They directed him to the corner of the room where two feet were painted on the floor.

"Stand there. No, turn around man, are you stupid?" shouted one.

He stood on the foot marks. The men in white stood closer. They measured every part of his body. One of them recorded the measurements in a file. Then Cornelius had to step onto a scale.

The man with the grey eyes instructed him to climb onto the bench and lie down. Two wooden planks were swung out from beneath the bench and his arms were tied to them with leather belts. They also tied his legs to two steel rings at the bottom end of the bench. The man with the steely grey eyes approached. In his hand was a small sharp knife. Cold naked fear overwhelmed the Nama sheep farmer of Bethanien. He let out a primeval scream of terror with all his might, until one of the men in a white apron stuffed a bundle of rags into his mouth.

The man with the knife lifted the canvas gown. With a deft cut he penetrated the writhing Cornelius's scrotum for a biopsy of one of his testicles. An indescribable pain shot through Cornelius's body until, mercifully, a black cloud enveloped him. Fischer sutured the wound with two stitches and collected a blood sample from one of Cornelius's bulging neck veins while he gasped hoarsely and slowly regained consciousness.

When he came to, he felt the throbbing, burning, stabbing pain between his legs. He roared like the young bull calves did when they were castrated in the kraal. When his breathing slowed down they undid the leather belts while the four soldiers who had entered again, held him down. The men in white aprons disappeared and the guards dragged him down the long passage, through an open quadrangle, up some steps and through a steel door. There they threw him down on the floor.

He heard the door slam shut, and the key turn in the lock. He lay on the floor for a long time, curled up from the pain and with tears running silently down his cheeks. All he was aware of was the unbelievable pain shooting through his body like a red-hot spear. After a while the pain subsided slightly to be replaced by shame and anger for the humiliation he had been subjected to. He could not believe that such barbaric treatment could still be practised at the beginning of the twentieth century.

"Oh, Jesus! Oh, God! Oh, God! Why did You forsake me?" he kept groaning, half unconsciously, until he blacked out completely.

He was woken by a vicious kick from which he recoiled.

"Up! On your feet, *Hotnot*! Get up!" a strange voice shouted. He crawled to the wall and pulled himself up.

"Out with you! Get out, out, out. Outside!" Cornelius walked out the door with difficulty. It was dark outside. There was now only one soldier. The soldier shoved him through another door. He heard the click of the lock. He looked around. It was a small cubicle. In one corner sat something resembling a human being. When his eyes grew accustomed to the gloom, he saw it was indeed a human being, curled up on a small heap of something.

"Evening," he whispered softly. Silence. "*Tawede, tita ge Cornelius, taritsa?*"[85]

"Were you also there with the white aprons?" he heard the person mumble.

"Yes, I was. You too?"

"Never have I felt such pain. The bloody bastards. I hate them."

"Who are you?" Cornelius asked the man in the dark.

The man sounded like a Herero. He remembered the months when he and Thilo hunted Hereros.

"I am Zacharias Zeraua of Otjimbingwe. I am the sole survivor of my family, the only one…", he whispered hoarsely.

Cornelius remembered the name as one of the Herero captains.

"I am Cornelius Fredericks, captain of the *!Aman* of Bethanien, and I was part of the war against you. I am sorry. How long have you been here, Zacharias?"

"I don't know any more. I think it could be ten months, but it could also be six."

"What the hell is going on here? What kind of a place is this? Is this a slaughterhouse for people or what? What are they going to do with us?"

Zacharias laughed quietly, choked on his saliva and then coughed for a long time. At last the coughing fit ceased. He struggled to breathe, his chest heaving before he spoke again. "This is the entrance to hell. This is the residence of the devil himself. His name is Eugen Fischer. He is a doctor, but a mad one."

"Then it must be him who cut me to pieces in that room with the many lights and bottles. There where a man does not want to be hurt, you know?"

"You mean he also cut open your balls?" Zacharias asked in a loud voice. "That's their way. What did you say your name was again? Cornelius, yes? Well, Cornelius, you must be glad that you are not a woman. The pigs do

---

85   *Tawede, tita ge Cornelius, taritsa?*: Evening, I am Cornelius, who are you?

worse things to women. They are crueller than the worst animals. Far more cruel than that Von Trotha general who hunted us like dogs."

"Zacharias, I know I will not see another sunrise over Bethanien. I must tell you how I hunted your people with the selfsame Von Trotha's nephew. If you can, forgive me. Please? Forgive me?" pleaded Cornelius softly.

Zacharias laughed softly again, careful not to cough again.

"Not to worry, my *Hotnot* friend. *Hoada ge a //ore-gao*."[86]

Cornelius raised his eyebrows.

"Yes, I know your language. We caused this trouble ourselves over many years. It was because we had robbed and murdered each other for so many years that you and I are here where we are now. It is because we did not allow the sun to shine on one another's backs that we now sit here like chickens waiting to be slaughtered. That is why. How can I be angry with you? Must you and I now continue the fight? It was stupid of me to be caught out by that snotty-nosed Lieutenant Von Estorff. He promised he would leave us in peace if we stopped waging war and handed in our rifles, but when we did that, they came for us the very next day. The others are already all dead. I am the only one still alive, if you can call this life. Nothing came of Von Estorff's promises. No, and that is why I'm sitting here now, because I trusted a German."

"I also trusted a German with my life once, and he trusted me with his life too. And in the end it cost him his life. He was Thilo von Trotha. Yes, that Von Trotha, nephew of the great general. The one under whom I had fought against you."

Cornelius related the tale until far into the night, at times drifting into sleep, but then being woken again by the horror of his surroundings.

"But it was not your fault that your men shot Von Trotha. He wanted to take you in. Then you would have ended up here anyway, just like me. Von Estorff made the same promises to me that your Von Trotha friend made to you but it did not help me much. What does it matter, Cornelius? We've lost everything. Even the last remains of our self-respect. If we had only known… Go and ask Hendrik Witbooi. He will be able to tell you. He tried everything. He tried to fight the Germans and he tried to be their ally against us. In the end he too saw that it helped nothing. Now he's fighting against them again."

"Hendrik Witbooi is dead. He was my father-in-law."

---

86 *Hoada ge a //ore-gao:* We are all sinners.

"Dead? No! I didn't know that. Your father-in-law you say? What happened? I have been sitting and rotting here in jail. I know nothing. Tell me, please?"

"Yes, I married his daughter Magdalena and my son's name is also Hendrik. Last year there was a fight at Vaalgras. Father Hendrik died there."

"You know, that father-in-law of yours warned Maherero not to connive with the Germans. If we had listened to Witbooi then, the first time, and chased the Germans into the sea, then the two of us would not have ended up here. It would have been so easy then. There were only a few of them then; now they are swarming like jackals all over the country."

The next morning the two prisoners were handed one plate of *pap* and a tin mug of water. They stayed locked up for the whole day, and the following thirty days, as well.

One morning the heavy door of the cell swung open. Two soldiers stood in front of Cornelius.

"Up, *Hotnot!*" one of them shouted and kicked him with the toecap of his shiny leather boot. Shaking, Cornelius got up. They had to help him.

They pointed towards the door and pushed him from behind. He fell and tried to get up, then fell again. When they realised that pushing and kicking would not help, they grabbed him by his upper arms and dragged his emaciated body through the door. Cornelius had to squint against the bright sunlight he had not seen for a month. He saw that he was again being taken to that dreaded room with the many lights. His bony frame shook like that of a sheep being slaughtered.

"What are you going to do with me?"

"Aha, the captain is not so brave now, hey?"

He was first taken to the bathroom where they handed him a bar of blue soap and a bucket of water. Despite everything, he enjoyed the water and the sharp soap on his skin. Slowly he felt his circulation returning. He then walked by himself and concentrated on the horizon of the sea just visible from underneath the iron roof of the passage. Far away he heard the groaning of a woman.

When he got to the room with the lights he was again weighed and measured and with a nod directed to get on to the examining bench. His whole body was soaked in sweat. He had to fight the cold naked fear threatening to overwhelm him. He was too weak to get on to the table by himself. They had to lift him. Again he was tied down with the leather belts, and the lights were switched on. Like a nightmare the steely grey eyes bored into him. The man inspected him from head to toe. When he shivered too much, a soldier slapped his face. Then someone brought a funnel and a tube. The man with the eyes placed a block of wood between Cornelius's teeth. Then he pushed the tube down his throat and right down into his stomach, or so it felt. They poured a bitter liquid down the funnel into his stomach. Then it was over. The soldier undid the belts. They chased him back to his cell.

Cornelius felt a burning sensation in his stomach. He tried to vomit, but without success. Zacharias came closer. He looked anxiously at the figure doubled over on the floor.

"What happened, my friend? What did they do to you?"

Cornelius's eyes grew dull. It became dark in front of him. After a long while he woke up. It felt as if a horse had kicked him between the eyes.

"Where am I? What happened?" he mumbled.

"Do you want some water?"

Cornelius nodded.

Zacharias brought the mug closer and held Cornelius's head in his arms.

27

"I would rather be in prison with my husband than free without him."

Father Emil Laaf

Four weeks later Magdalena arrived in Lüderitzbucht. She immediately went to the small Roman Catholic church and knocked on the door. A lean grey man opened the door. He noticed the two children hiding behind her.

"What can I do for you, *Frau*?"

"Pastor, Reverend, I don't know what to call you….".

"Call me Father, Madam."

"Thank you, Pastor. Sorry, Father. I have come from far away, from the mission station at Bethanien and the soldiers have captured my husband. Sorry, I am Magdalena Fredericks and my husband is Cornelius and these are our two children, Father, Hendrik and Martha. Yes, Reverend, I have just arrived from Aus, there where they took my husband for the first time. Now, I wondered if it would be possible to see my husband. There in Keetmanshoop it was possible to see him every day and the soldiers were friendly. But you see Reverend, I do not even know where they are keeping him here, Reverend, so I thought I would come and ask you, Reverend."

Father Laaf took a long look at the woman in front of him. He said nothing. Then he invited her in.

"Ah, my apologies, Madam, please come in. I am so absentminded."

He led her through the rows of upright benches in the church, past the pulpit to the door on the right which he allowed her to enter first, with the two children behind. Six chairs were arranged round a table in the small room.

"Please sit down. Tell me again, what have you come here for?"

Magdalena told him. Everything.

"Pastor, I mean Father, my husband is now in the German jail, and my father, he was Hendrik Witbooi, the leader of the Namas, my people. He fought on the side of the Germans for ten years until the year before last, but then he turned against the Germans. Then last year, there at Vaalgras, they shot and killed him. But for ten years he fought against the Hereros and the Bondelswarts, side-by-side with the Germans. And now I thought, if I could only see the *baas* of the soldiers and plead for my husband, they would perhaps show a bit of mercy," she finished.

The German priest thought a long time before he replied. "Madam, it is war and war is never a pleasant affair. This war is very ugly and I doubt that it would be possible for you to see your husband. I don't know how to say this to you, but the truth is that many of the prisoners of war have already died from the diseases in the camp. We see them every day, because they work on the railway line, but we know that … well, that many of them don't make it. What you ask is out of the ordinary. I am really not aware of any visitors that have been allowed into the camp. The best would be for you to return to Bethanien at once. In fact, I do not think that you are safe here. You yourself could be arrested. This is war, Madam."

"Father, I am not going home until I have seen Cornelius. If they take me, then they must take me, but I will remain here until I have seen him. I'd rather be in jail with him than free without him."

Laaf looked at Magdalena. "I will see what I can do, Madam," he replied after a while.

He took Magdalena and the children to a small outside room with a bed and a chair.

"Make yourself at home, Madam. This is all I can offer you."

"Thank you so much, Father."

That afternoon the spiritual leader walked to the island. He told the guard at the gate who he was and that he wanted to see the commanding officer. Eventually he was received by the man, Captain Von Estorff, and offered a cup of tea. They talked about the war. Von Estorff explained that the camp was there because of the colonial government's policy to keep the different fighting Nama and Herero factions separate from one another. Also to keep the women and children, who had been left defenceless while the men were fighting, in a safe area, for their protection. They were hoping to end the war soon. The camps – there were also camps at Swakopmund, Okatumba, Omburo, Otjosongombe and Okornitombe – had the added advantage that they prevented the men from receiving supplies from the women.

"*Hauptmann*, tell me, is it true that so many detainees die here? Last week, I think it was Wednesday evening, I came across a mule wagon in town with four bodies on it."

Von Estorff shifted uneasily in his chair. "Yes, Father. It is a problem. These people are so different to us Europeans, very different. A well-known researcher from Berlin is now busy researching the problem. Their bodies function differently from ours. There is even a school of thought that they, er, actually, how can I put it? ... that they are the missing link, if you understand what I mean?"

"You are surely not serious, *Hauptmann*?" Father Laaf stared at Von Estorff.

"Yes, Father. I mean I don't really know. I also do not understand it properly, but the researcher is quite sure of his case. Everyone is entitled to his opinion. No, I don't know. What I do know is that they are weaker than us, less resistant to illnesses and so on. Perhaps the research could do something to help, you know."

"As long as you know they are people created by God, like you and me, *Hauptmann*."

Von Estorff remained silent until Laaf spoke again.

"*Hauptmann*, I have a Nama woman back at the church. Her husband is a detainee here. She would like to visit him. Can you help me, please?"

"We have a problem, Father. We cannot allow it. You see, that is how illness is spread. We cannot allow people to come in and out of here every day. The doctor, the researcher, says they bring diseases in with them. If they come in, they will have to remain here. She is most welcome, because we look after the inmates well. There are also many children here."

Laaf was sceptical, but remained polite. After he left, Von Estorff put his head in his hands and sat in that position for a long time.

Back at the church Father Laaf explained the position to Magdalena.

"Madam, I still think it best for you to return to Bethanien."

But Magdalena remained determined.

A day later the heavy, double barbed-wire gate with the words "*Wissenschaft ist Weisheit*" above it, swung closed behind her and her children.

28

The new touleier finds a friend

Jakob Morenga, the Black Napoleon (centre), with his men.

Ernst and Charlotte thrived at Paradys. The large farmhouse with its thick walls, broad surrounding veranda and spacious kitchen, warm from the Aga stove, was a friendly haven. The farmyard was alive with chickens and ducks, and even had a lawn, flowers and farm workers to tend it. There were also cattle, horses, sheep and a tame springbok.

The McKays were fond of their two new children. Gradually the trauma of the horrible events on the wagon trek faded into distant memory, but every now and then Charlotte was woken by a nightmare of a leopard grabbing her by the throat. Ernst had to comfort her until she fell asleep again.

Dinner was a feast around the large Cape yellow-wood table, groaning under the weight of Ma Gertie's *!kom*, tripe, sheepshanks, oryx steaks, springbok ribs and vegetables. She took great pride in her vegetable garden.

Ernst and Charlotte only saw their father, Joseph, when he visited Paradys during his travels to Maltahöhe, Mariental, Keetmanshoop and Lüderitzbucht. Each time he seemed older and stranger. Johannes said he walked in the veld at night, talking to himself.

Joseph told McKay that the south of German South-West Africa would still be needing ox wagons for several years to come because the train would only travel as far as Keetmanshoop. He had acquired a small contract to move building material to Duwisib, a farm west of Maltahöhe, where a German Major, a certain Von Wolff, was building a castle for his American wife. The money was good and grazing more plentiful than it was between Aus and Keetmanshoop.

One day McKay called Ernst. "Ernst, I want you to learn how to be a *touleier*. Are you up to it, my boy?"

"Why, Mr Mac, of course, yes please! I have wanted to do it for a long time."

"Well then. Tomorrow I am sending a wagon to Keetmanshoop for a few goods from the shop. You have to be back at Paradys by nightfall. I am sending Gerhardus and Andries with you. You must listen to Andries. Gerhardus will teach you about the *leiriem*. You must try to take it on your own on the return journey."

"Sure, Mr Mac. Thank you, sir."

That evening Ernst was excited. He overheard Ma Gertie arguing with Mr Mac for wanting Ernst to walk so far.

"Robert, you know the war is not over yet. Anything could happen. Some of these Namas are real *hotnots*."

"But Gertruida, the youngster wants to learn. I did not pressurise him, my wife. Ask him yourself."

"All right then, but what about proper shoes? Those boots that he arrived here with are finished, and too small besides."

"Oh, goodness. What about Adriaan's and Lambert's shoes? Don't they have any that would fit him?"

"I will quickly go and look, but when he gets to Keetmanshoop he must buy himself decent shoes. Be sure to give him enough money."

It was still pitch dark when Ma Gertie placed a cup of hot, sweet coffee and a rusk next to Ernst's bed.

"It's time to get up, Ernst."

Ernst instantly flew out of bed.

"Where's my hat, Ma Gertie? And my shoes? We have to *trek*."

"Wait, wait, wait, Ernst. Relax. Nobody is going anywhere without you. Drink your coffee. Go on now."

She sat down on the bed beside him. "You be careful, do you hear, my child? If somebody confronts you on the way, you tell them that you are Gertruida McKay's adopted child. They must leave you alone, do you hear? And when you get to Keetmanshoop, go straight to the shop and buy yourself two pairs of shoes. Nice soft shoes made of kudu leather. Here, here is the money."

She took a roll of notes from her apron pocket and put it into his hands. In the kitchen she had already prepared a basket filled with food as well as two flasks of coffee.

"Thank you, Ma Gertie, thank you for everything." He folded his arms around the large woman and hugged her tightly. "I love you, Mother. See you this evening."

When he hurried outside clutching the basket under his arm, tears ran down her cheeks. She sniffed noisily.

"Go, Go! All together, now!"

The crack of Andries' whip woke the whole farmyard up. Gerhardus took up his position at the front with Ernst by his side.

"Come on, my mates. Rooiland, Draaikop. Take the strain! Come, we are going to Keetmans. *Die pad is lank en swaar en die mense wag al daar.*"[87]

Gerhardus talked to his animals all the time. He knew the *touleier's* job was to keep them calm. He also knew Andries's whip could only do so much. If the oxen lost their spirit, no amount of force would get them to Keetmanshoop and back. As he walked, he whistled and sang and turned now and then to stroke the heads of the two leading oxen. Ernst saw that Gerhardus was an expert in his way of handling the oxen, and he was surprised to see what a difference a gentle hand and a kind word could make. The oxen walked on steadily and the miles slipped past.

Along the way they saw herds of oryx walking proudly over the dunes and springbok leaping and *pronking*. Sometimes an ostrich appeared. Ernst's fingers itched. How pleased Ma Gertie would be with some venison, he thought to himself. After two hours of *trekking* they halted to give the oxen a rest. The men drank coffee.

---

87   *Die pad is lank en swaar en die mense wag al daar*: Phrase from old Afrikaans folksong about life on the *trek* path literally meaning, the road is long and difficult and people are waiting for us.

Ernst knew he never wanted to live anywhere else. He understood why father Joseph wanted to live here. Father Joseph? Since when had 'Vater Joseph' become 'father Joseph'? Am I now becoming a real Afrikaner?

Suddenly, a mounted commando appeared out of nowhere on the wagon trail ahead of them. Gerhardus stopped, looking tense.

"Whoa!" Andries brought the team to a halt.

For what felt like an eternity, nobody said or did anything until the commando leader, a man wearing a big hat, gestured to Andries to come closer.

Andries hesitated. "Stand still and keep quiet. I think I know who this man is. He hates Germans because they murdered his wife and children," he whispered to Ernst.

Then Andries approached with outstretched hands, pleading.

Ernst saw how the horseman with the big hat talked to Andries and how Andries, with eyes downcast, nodded and shook his head. It was too far for Ernst to hear what they were saying. Then his curiosity got the better of him and he walked up to them.

"*Gao-aob, tawede*,"[88] he greeted in Nama, with a trace of his German accent.

"Ernst!" Andries called out and tried to come between him and the leader. The other riders in the group urged their horses closer. Andries had to give way but he still tried to keep Ernst behind him.

The leader gave some sort of signal. Two of the riders came forward and pushed Andries out of the way while the leader nudged his horse right up against Ernst. The leader leaned down on his horse's neck with his arms folded comfortably. He fixed his gaze on Ernst.

"Who are you, little German?"

"Ernst Luchtenstein, from Paradys, sir, and my mother..." he swallowed and continued, "... my mother is Gertruida McKay. But I was born in Germany. My real mother was Therese and my father is Joseph."

The man shifted on his horse. "And where are you travelling to with these two tame baboons?"

"To town, sir. My father, Mr McKay, sent us to fetch stuff from his shop, sir."

"And where did you learn to speak Nama?"

"From my father Joseph's *touleier* and from the McKays, sir."

---

88   *Gao-aob, tawede*: Nama greeting to a senior person.

"Do you have two fathers then, young man? Do you know about Keinaus, who lives over there in his Great City?"

"Yes, sir. I do know."

"And what do you know about Great Snake?"

"Only that he reigns over Namaland and that if the Namas don't behave, he will swallow all of them, one by one."

The leader laughed.

"Yes, son, watch out for him. Always only speak the truth. Then he will leave you alone. Only speak the truth. And now I have a little job for you. Are you going to help me?"

"I will gladly help you if I can, sir. What is it?"

"You are on your way to Keetmanshoop, to the shop of McKay, that one-eyed pirate stepfather of yours, right? Good. Today I need one hundred rounds of ammunition from you, otherwise Great Snake will come for you tonight. Understand?"

Ernst nodded vigorously.

"Will that be all, sir, only one hundred rounds?"

"That's right. No, try for two hundred, but you need to speak to the young McKay yourself, the one with the small spectacles. He will not give it to these two baboons, because it is not in his father's letter, that letter there in your pocket. You tell young Robert that his father forgot to add it to the letter and that he only told you when the wagon was already under way. Do you understand?"

"Right, sir, I understand. Sir ...?"

"Yes?"

"Who are you?"

"Me? You want to know who I am? Why? So that you can tell the Germans?"

"No, sir. With respect, sir, if I were to do that, they will come, with or without your name, sir."

The man looked down so that his hat covered his face. He shot a side-long glance at his adjutant and his body shook with laughter.

"Smart, this little Nama-German hey? Or what are you, actually? Nama, German, or what?" he snorted.

He raised his head. "Jakob Morenga of Namibia is pleased to make your acquaintance, Mr Luchtenstein," and he held out his hand in a formal gesture. Ernst did the same and looked Jakob straight in the eye.

"Pleased to meet you, Mr Morenga. Are you the Black Napoleon, sir?"

Morenga burst out laughing. "No, Mr Luchtenstein. Napoleon was the white Morenga, only uglier."

"And Namibia, where is that, Mr Morenga?"

Again Morenga laughed.

"Look around you, young man, as far as you can see. Everything you can see, is the land of Namibia. So it always was and so it will always be. *‡Au du niga ta ra miba du.*"[89]

"Mr Morenga, you will have your rounds this evening. May we move on now, please? Keetmanshoop is still far."

"Yes, be on your way. We will see you this evening, somewhere. Then you must also tell me who you are, do you hear?"

The whip cracked. "Go, go! All together, now!" Andries got the *trek* on the move again.

Gerhardus wiped the sweat from his brow. "Come, Rooiland. Come, Draaikop. Come on, my beauties. *Die pad is lank en swaar en die mense wag al daar,*" he whispered shakily.

Ernst could not fathom why Andries and Gerhardus were so afraid, because the Black Napoleon had stirred something different in him. Morenga had looked right through him, deep into his soul.

The sun was high by the time they came to a halt in front of the Quiver Emporium in Keetmanshoop. They left the oxen inspanned because they were pressed for time. Andries handed McKay's list of requirements to Robert McKay Junior, who managed the shop. The staff scurried around loading everything onto the ox wagon. Ernst realised that he was on the horns of a dilemma. He was a man of his word and he had made a promise to Jakob Morenga, but now he would have to tell a lie to keep that promise. If he told the truth, he would not get the rounds. If he lied, he would be deceiving his benefactors. He waited until he had Robert McKay Junior's attention.

"Robert?" he whispered urgently.

"Yes, what is it, Ernst?" responded Robert with mock-seriousness.

"Robert, I have a problem, but I cannot discuss it with anyone. Will you trust me?"

"Trust? Why? I don't know," he teased Ernst. "Trust? You?"

"Yes, I'm serious Robert, please. Will you trust me?"

---

89   *‡Au du niga ta ra miba du:* I say this to you that you must know it (a kind of emphasis)

Andries watched the conversation out of the corner of his eye some distance away.

"Right, Ernst. What can I do for you?" Robert asked. He put down the list and pen, folded his arms and focussed on Ernst.

"I promised someone two hundred rounds of ammunition, Robert, and I cannot tell you who it is. I am obliged to keep my word not to betray him, but I am equally obliged not to deceive your father. All I can do is to ask you to trust me. As soon as I return to Paradys I will explain to your father and I will repay him. I give you my word."

Robert McKay thought for a moment, realising the implications. He knew, with a war being waged, that these rounds were destined for the Nama gangs. He, Robert, would have to account for that, but he was struck by the youngster's integrity. He had been in charge of his father's shop for two years and he had heard more lies from debtors on a single day than most other people in three years. He turned around, went into the office and returned with a package.

"Ernst, here are the rounds Father requested. Please deliver them into his own hands. Do you hear?" he said in a loud voice so that everyone around them could hear.

Ernst realised that Robert had understood. He murmured a quick thank you, took the heavy package and hid it inside the side kist under a few bags of sugar Gertruida had ordered.

For Ernst the great moment had arrived. Since the Lüderitzbucht *trek* he had wanted to take charge of the *leiriem*. Today was his opportunity. This was why he was here, he told himself.

"Andries, please, I'm asking you nicely, don't use your whip too much. I want to work gently with my oxen. And please, just give me five minutes before we start?"

He then turned and placed his hand on the shoulder of Opperman, the *haaragteros's*[90] shoulder and looked at the animal. "Opperman, my big man, my handsome man, today we must work together," he said softly.

"Pistool, today Ernst is in charge, we will all pull together," he told the *haarnaasagteros*[91] , Pistool, with his stumpy tail.

---

90   *Haaragteros*: rear right ox, the last ox in the team on the right hand side.

91   *Haarnaasagteros*: second last ox on the right hand side.

Then it was the turn of Hoogmoed, the *haar-op-ses*.[92]. In this way he walked and spoke to each *haaros*[93], Wiegman, Lekkerland, Jintelman and Vastrap up to the *vooros*[94], Janbloed.

Ernst hesitated close to the two *voorosse*. He noticed that Andries and Gerhardus were surreptitiously sniggering. Then he walked to the left-hand side and started with the *hotvooros*[95].

"Potberg, master of the yard, we all pull together!" He moved towards the back and spoke to each ox in turn, Bakker, Vlakveld, Swartland, Riemland, Kappie, Ryperd and Rinkhals.

By this time the other two were snorting with laughter, but Ernst ignored them. He walked to the front, took the *leiriem* in his left hand, removed his hat, and whistled loudly, first on one note and then on a lower one.

"Go, go! All together!" he called as loud as he could.

Andries and Gerhardus still stood aside, splitting their sides at the amusing scene. Andries deliberately kept his whip silent, not because Ernst had asked him to do so, but because they wanted to play a trick on him. The oxen pulled straight and in unison at Ernst's whistle and shout. And off the *trek* went, down the track with Ernst having to jog to stay ahead. The two experienced *transportryers* looked at each other, impressed. He had won the trust of the oxen without using a whip. He had proven that these soft-natured, brave and patient animals had a spirit of their own, a spirit that could be won over with love. The two Namas jogged behind the wagon.

At dusk, when the fire at Paradys was already visible in the distance, Jakob Morenga and his commando appeared from the bushes around them.

"Whoa," Ernst called the trek to a halt.

"You probably thought that old Morenga wouldn't come, hey little German, or is it little Nama or Scotsman or Jew?" Jakob asked.

Ernst walked forward and held out his hand.

"Good evening, Mr Morenga. I was wondering, yes. Do you still want the rounds?"

---

92   *Haar-op-ses*: the sixth ox from the front on the right hand side.

93   *Haaros*: right hand ox, as opposed to hotos, left hand side ox.

94   *Vooros*: leading ox, Voorosse: plural

95   *Hotvooros*: leading ox on the left hand side.

"Now why would I not want them? Of course I want them. Do you have them here?"

"I gave my word and now I want to ask the same of you, please Mr Morenga?"

"What do you want, big man?" Morenga said, with a straight face.

"Please, Mr Morenga, you have placed me in a difficult position. I had to deliver on my promise to you, but I could never lie to the McKays. I got the rounds without having to lie to Robert junior, but I will now have to tell Mr Mac the truth. Is that in order with you?"

"There is no problem with that little German. It is in order, speak the truth, always. And one day when you are big, remember it, do you hear?"

Ernst took the rounds from underneath the sugar and handed them to Jakob. Jakob removed his hat and bowed his head.

"The Nama people thank you, Mr Luchtenstein."

Then he beckoned Ernst to come closer, bent down low in the saddle and held his hand close to Ernst's ear.

"Thank you, son. Listen carefully. If you want to find out who you are and where Namibia is, then you need to climb into the heart and marrow of Namaland. Then you will find out why we love this land so much. That is where we Nama people found our freedom, where our nation was born. Go and live there until you have learnt the great secret of Namaland's spirit. From here ride south-east for two and a half days, and look for the Bak River. Ask the Bushmen if you are not sure. Follow the river's course. Then quietly whisper to the wind: *'//Khauxa!nas, //Khauxa!nas, //Khauxa!nas.*[96] "Don't say it aloud, ever. The honeybird will come to lead you. Follow him. He will bring you to the Great City of the Namas where you will be safe. There is always food and water. Nobody will ever find you there. This is our secret. Do you hear?"

"Yes, sir, I hear, *//Khauxa!nas,*" the flustered Ernst replied in a whisper.

The commando disappeared into the night. No further words were needed to coax the tired oxen on the last mile to Paradys.

Gertruida rushed out of the house, wiping her hands on her white apron.

"Ernst, are you back, are you safe?" she called out. "I was so worried, my child." She hugged him tightly. "There were soldiers here today. They told us that that our Black Napoleon was in the area and they were

---

96   *//Khauxa!nas*: Place name of the ancient fortress city of the Namas, south-west of Aroab.

looking for him. I was so afraid that something might have happened. Sometimes people go mad when there is a war going on."

McKay followed on his wife's heels. "And? And? Is all in order? How did our new *touleier* do, Andries? Was he able to take the *leiriem*?" he asked, tousling Ernst's hair.

"Mr Mac, he nearly walked us off our feet today. He and the oxen seem to have a language of their own. No, we went very well, Mr Mac."

"Come in, Ernst. Andries, you can offload tomorrow. Just outspan the oxen so they can drink. Sleep well and thank you. You did well today."

Charlotte skipped all around Ernst. "Did you bring me something from the shop, *Boetie?*[97] Did you?"

McKay did not even bat his single eyelid when Ernst owned up to him about the rounds of ammunition. "Those are the last kicks of a dying sheep. I feel very sorry for these people. Come, let's find you a plate of food and then you can tell us all about your *trek*."

"Mr Mac. It was so good. I want to do it again. Please? When can we do another *trek*?" he asked.

That evening Ernst wrote the words "Bak River, //Khauxa!nas and honeybird" below the last sentence his mother Therese had written in his exercise book. He was wary of writing the word "Morenga."

Before he fell asleep, he thought about Cornelius and wondered if he was still alive.

---

97   *Boetie*: Afrikaans, diminutive form of the word 'brother' as a term of endearment.

29

In the name of science

German soldiers packing human skulls for shipping to Berlin.

Magdalena sat on the single chair in the empty room, her small hands folded in her lap, her lips pressed tightly together, waiting. She was used to waiting: it was a woman's lot, but in a short while she would see Cornelius again. The two children were playing at her feet. A rank odour like the smell of Father's horses after a long trip in the desert hung over the quiet room.

A blonde soldier entered at last. He looked down his nose at Magdalena. "What do you want, *meid*?"[98]

---

98   *Meid*: derogatory, racist, term for a non-white female.

"Oh, sir, I told Father Laaf that I wanted to see my husband because he was here and they said that I could only see him if I also stayed here, me and my two children. He told me that you said you would look after us well and that you have now built a hospital for the sick people, and so on."

"*Ach so*," he said. "What is your name and your husband's name?"

"I am Magdalena Fredericks, daughter of the late Hendrik Witbooi. My husband is Captain Cornelius Fredericks, whom you have here."

At the mention of her husband and her father's names, the officer raised his eyebrows. He turned on his heel and left without a word.

This was indeed a strange request, the first and last time he would hear something like this. But this was a well-known bloodline and the woman and her children were evidently in good health. Perhaps the doctor would be interested, he thought.

He stayed away for a long time. The children became restless and Magdalena had to reprimand them.

Four soldiers entered the room. They instructed her to leave the children behind and to accompany them.

"Be quiet now. Mommy is going to see Father. I'll be back soon," she told them.

Three minutes later two soldiers took the two children to a room with many lights, held them down on a bench, kicking and screaming, and murdered them with injections of phenol. Doctor Fischer dissected their bodies completely and placed the organs carefully in bottles of formalin to be shipped with the skulls to the Kaiser Wilhelm Institute in Berlin. At last he had the perfect controls he needed for the great research project: healthy organs of this unique species. Nobody needed to know where they came from.

The four soldiers first took Magdalena to a bathroom where she was handed a bar of blue soap and a bucket of water.

"Undress!"

"What do you mean, sir? Undress? All my clothes?"

A lash fell across her back. She cried out in pain. And then the next blow fell. And the next. She fell, and groaning, tried to crawl to the door, but a booted foot came down on her neck.

"On your feet, *meid*! Up!" She trembled like a reed and stood up.

"Undress, I said," the one soldier said, lifting the crop. Magdalena undressed completely, but tried to cover her private parts.

"Go on, wash yourself." She scrubbed and washed under the scrutiny of four pairs of eyes whilst her whole body trembled and shuddered in fear.

They then pushed and shoved her to the next room where another soldier squirted an acrid liquid over her naked body with a red pump. Then they raped her, one by one. When they had finished, they gave her a canvas smock and ordered her to put it on. She was too weak to walk and they had to drag her down a long passage to the rear of the building. A guard unlocked the door and they dragged her across a bare sandy patch up to a large barbed-wire gate which was unlocked by another guard. They hurled her through the gate. She just lay there, crying and groaning for a long time until her tears and runny nose had turned the soil under her face into a puddle of mud.

"Where are my children? Where are my children? My children, my children..."

After a while a pair of shiny boots appeared beside her head. The little soap tin containing Cornelius's letters fell next to her head. She clutched it tightly with her fingers.

Curious eyes of people in brown canvas smocks approached. A woman crouched beside her. Magdalena felt her hand on her shoulder. No one spoke. They just let her cry.

At dusk, hands picked her up and moved her into a low shelter resembling the shell of a tortoise. She stayed there through the night and the following day and night, shivering and weeping in the cold and terrible wind. Every now and then faces appeared in the opening to stare at her. One brought a can of water. Nobody brought food. Not that she had any desire to eat.

The second day she crept out of her shelter. She could – or would – not walk. Behind her she saw a high structure with five ropes hanging from a beam. She knew what it was. She also knew that she would never again see her husband or her children.

She sat in one place the whole day, staring in front of her. Around her numerous people crawled in and out of their tortoise-like shelters. These were built with sticks and mats like her people's //haru-oms when they trekked with their sheep seeking grazing in the wide plains. Except that the reed mats were now dirty old pieces of canvas and tattered clothing. The putrid stench of death and excrement enveloped the place, because the whole area was used as a toilet. The people were quiet. She saw that some were Hereros and others were her people, but in this place they were all regarded as lower than animals. All around them she could see the sea. Behind her, beyond the gallows on the ridge and the barbed wire fence, was Lüderitzbucht, and still further were the Namib and Bethanien and Gibeon, she knew. She was raw and broken and wept for days on end, until there were no more tears left.

Then they fetched her again and took her to the bathroom with the blue soap and then to the room with the many lights and the bottles … and the bench. She had to get onto the bench where her arms and legs were bound with leather belts and they inserted things into her before the soldiers mounted her again. Four times. She no longer wept. They fetched her every week and repeated the process. She just lay there. Each time they enquired whether she was pregnant. They also made her urinate into a tin and drew blood. Later she began to realise that they were not coming for her anymore.

In their cell, less than one hundred yards from Magdalena, were Cornelius and Zacharias. Every week the soldiers took Cornelius to the room with the many lights and bottles and force-fed him the awful poison with the funnel and long hose. Then they took blood from his veins and inspected his body from head to toe. He was becoming weaker and weaker, and, over time, his hair and teeth had started to fall out. His mouth was as dry as a dead steenbok's skin after it had lain in the sun and sand for six months.

The two never knew how close to each other they were.

With the passing of time Magdalena began to understand the routine on Shark Island. Early in the morning some twenty guards in black uniforms made the prisoners assemble. Then they marched them through the gate to the railway line to work. The weakest prisoners, those who could no longer walk, remained behind. Sometimes the soldiers walked through the camp to find anyone who feigned sickness. Then they used the riding crop to test the prisoner. If he or she remained lying down, they would be left alone. In the beginning new prisoners arrived from time to time, but later that stopped. She did not know why.

Later in the morning, a mule cart came – to collect the bodies of those who had died the previous day and night. Sometimes there were many bodies, and sometimes only one or two. She watched the mule cart disappear around the rocky outcrop jutting into the sea at the point of the bay. Prisoners with shovels over their shoulders followed behind it.

She whiled away the days sitting on the rocks gazing at the rippling waves and waiting for Great Snake, Keinaus. She often saw him. She had learnt that Great Snake was always there when a large whaling boat entered the harbour towing a fat whale carcass. Sometimes she could see how Great Snake had attacked the carcass and ripped off chunks of meat. Great Snake then swam around the island and sometimes it would stick its head, with its huge eyes and rows of sharp white teeth, out of the water in the shallows right in front of her. Once it seemed as if it were talking to her. She did not know if it was reprimanding her for all her sins or whether it was trying to encourage her. She spoke to the others about Great Snake. One had suggested that Great Snake was some creature from the Book of Revelations, but she had never understood Revelations. Actually, she was too scared to read it, but she loved the Psalms. Especially Psalm 23 because her father, brothers, husband and all her people had been shepherds. She did not have a Bible with her anymore. The soldiers must have taken it with all her other stuff, but what did it matter now, anyway?

Some of the people laughed at her, saying she was stupid. Did she not know that it was only a fish swimming around the island? She started to doubt it herself, but then she remembered again the nights around the campfire in Gibeon and the tales of the old people and her father, as well as the clever Hendrik Witbooi's and the prophet Stuurman's prophecies. Then she knew that these scoffers were wrong. But the doubts came back regularly. They unsettled her.

In the evenings most of the dirty, dusty people with their broken hands and faces and their backs covered with lacerations from the whips, returned through the barbed wire gate of the camp. They brought with them some of the *pap* the soldiers had given them at the railway line. They gave it to prisoners who had remained behind, like her. Some prisoners never returned from the railway line.

There was a Herero, Samuel Kariko, a man of God, a pastor, who tried to encourage the prisoners with the message of Good News. He was a tall black man and the soldiers ignored him. He had his own Bible. He wrote many letters and gave them to the soldiers to post. He held services in the evenings, but few cared to listen any more. Magdalena always went. She just sat there. She heard the words, but they made no sense to her. She waited till they sang. Mostly there were four or six of them and on one occasion, eleven. Magdalena enjoyed the singing. She sang and for a short time managed to forget. The next day she would hum the previous evening's Psalm over and over again.

Sometimes a prisoner would attempt to escape. At other times the soldiers caught one who tried to attack a guard. It was usually a prisoner who had gone mad, because many went insane. Once ten prisoners charged at a group of soldiers and tried to overpower them. Others tried to steal or smuggle food, and they were also caught. The outcome was always the same: the gallows. They were already imprisoned and the only other punishment was hanging. Early in the morning the soldiers brought the condemned prisoners from the death cell behind the barbed wire, with their hands tied behind their backs. Some screamed and kicked. Those still wanted to live. The others were quiet. The convicts were dressed in trousers with the legs tightly bound around their ankles, because they often soiled themselves and the soldiers didn't want to deal with the mess.

The condemned were shoved up onto the scaffold, and those who would not climb up themselves, were dragged up onto the standing beam where they had to balance on their toes and try not to fall off.

Samuel Kariko stood right at the front and read from his Bible. Nobody listened to him. The ropes were placed around their necks and pulled tight. A soldier walked behind them and pushed each convict off the standing beam so that they hung there from their necks, kicking wildly. The moment they fell off the beam, they stopped screaming, because the rope constricted their airways. After a while they stopped kicking.

All the other prisoners had to stand there and watch the executions. The bodies hung there till evening.

Then the mule wagon came.

30

The great trek

The Schützenhaus at Keetmanshoop

A messenger from the commander of the *Schutztruppe* arrived at Paradys requesting Robert McKay to report urgently to the German camp at Keetmanshoop. The Scotsman was concerned about Ernst's subversive deal with the black Napoleon, but said nothing. Early the next morning he left Paradys on his horse, Campbell, with his Mauser at his side.

"Good morning, Mr McKay," greeted colonel Von Deimling. "Please sit down. Coffee?"

Robert realised that he was safe here, in the tiger's lair, at least for the moment.

"What can I do for you, *Herr Oberst*?"

"Aha, thank you for responding so promptly, Mr McKay. We urgently need your assistance. You know that the war has been dragging on for quite a while and shows no sign of letting up. It is such a nuisance and the Kaiser is keen to develop the country and let it grow to its full potential. But the cursed natives, these *Hotnots* ... uhmm ... er ... Namas are so persistent. They just don't want to stop fighting. We've tried everything.

"Now, a large consignment of cargo from the Fatherland is expected in Lüderitzbucht in the next three weeks. Needless to say, we have to get it here urgently. The Brits in the Colony have closed the border posts again ... for the sixth time this year. They said we have used up our quota for imports overland.

"Last time they claimed it was because of the rinderpest, but we know what it was all about: Politics. Your people, the British, are sensitive about the opinion of the coloured people, after the war against the Boers. The Namaqualand Border Scouts and the Bushmanland Border Scouts – all coloureds – helped England in the war against the Boers and England does not want to upset them now. There are spies everywhere who are monitoring the relationship between Germany and Britain. This war against the Namas has won Germany no friends amongst the coloured people.

"To be brief: we need you to smuggle in our own cargo. Imagine that! But it is the colonial government's requirement. They are refusing to transport the goods through the normal channels, or even to send them by road because they are afraid of a reaction from their coloureds. You have the perfect profile, with your Nama wife and all."

With his one eye over his coffee cup, McKay eyed the German. His mind was already doing the sums. It sounded to him as though Christmas was going to come early this year, thanks to this turn of events. Official assignments were usually lucrative, McKay thought, but this one was special.

"But of course, *Herr Oberst*. How many wagons and what type of cargo, if I may ask?" he enquired encouragingly.

"Actually, you are not allowed to ask, but it would be the normal sort of merchandise: weapons and ammunition, telephone cables, uniforms and a lot of other things. All of it well camouflaged as civilian cargo, of course, bags of maize, bags of cement and so on."

"You obviously know the Namas will not just ignore such a cargo, *Herr Oberst*? There are risks associated with this," the Scot said without hesitating. In his mind he pushed his fee up another couple of notches.

"Yes, Mr McKay, I know. In a few months the railway track will be completed as far as Aus and a year or so later the train will run from Lüderitzbucht to here in less than three days."

"But until then you will still be dependent on us, *Herr Oberst.*"

Von Deimling laughed. "Yes, yes, yes, I know. Name your price McKay, the Kaiser is paying."

That evening, back at Paradys, McKay broke the news to Gertruida and Ernst. His four best wagons and teams would go to Lüderitzbucht and he would accompany the expedition himself. The most important news was that young Ernst was chosen as the *touleier* for one of the teams.

"Hooray! Thank you, Mr Mac! Thank you, thank you, thank you!"

"Robert, how can you? He is still too young," Gertruida said.

"No Mother, that isn't true at all. I am big enough. Thank you Mr Mac, thank you Mother!" Ernst grabbed Gertruida around the neck and hugged her tightly.

The next two weeks saw the Paradys people working late into the night. They plaited new *rieme* and *stroppe*[99], carved new yokes, filled the *teerputse*, replaced the *lunsrieme*, fitted new metal bands over the wood of the wheels, repaired the canvas tarpaulins and painted the wagons. Gertruida cooked and baked so that her people would not go hungry. Ernst spent as much time as possible with the oxen. He had to assemble his teams, but this was difficult, because Mr McKay wanted to show off. He insisted that all the oxen in a team should look the same. There would be a black team, a red team, a multi-coloured team and a winning team. The winning team, according to McKay, would be two *voorosse* and two *agterosse*, each red with white backs. The oxen between these *voor-* and *agterosse* would be black with white backs. Each team would consist of twenty-four oxen, that is, twelve pairs of oxen in front of every wagon.

Ernst knew oxen had minds of their own. Some refused to pull in the same yoke with certain individuals. Nowhere was the selection of yoke partners more important than the *voor-* and *agterosse*. He tried many different combinations to find compatible pairings that would also meet Mr McKay's colour preferences. He used the water cart to inspan two oxen at a time, until he found a pair who could work well together. In the evenings he was exhausted. He went to bed early and at dawn was back among the animals again. He talked to them constantly until he got to know each one's whims and peculiarities.

---

99   *Strop*, singular, *stroppe*, plural: Special leather thongs.

"Mr Mac, Hangkop refuses to pull *haar*[100], he should go *hot*[101]. Rooiland used to be *vooros*, but he isn't so lively anymore, may I try him out at *haaragter*[102]?"

The district was full of stories about McKay's great trek. Everyone knew McKay had always wanted to set the record, but this would be one of the last *treks* between Lüderitzbucht and Keetmanshoop. Bets were even made, and a report on the event appeared in the newspaper in the Cape Colony.

In the dark early hours of an August morning, Paradys was bustling with activity. Everyone was awake and at their posts. In front of the wagons the trek equipment lay spread out on the ground.

With calls of "Hoi-hoi-hoi" the oxen were summoned. They grouped themselves in a herd to the left of their wagons and waited for the *touleier* and driver to fasten the *stroppe* to their horns. Ernst scurried around to make sure that the right animals got to the correct teams.

When the oxen had been inspanned, the drivers cracked their whips.

"Out!" The call resounded across the farmyard.

The teams strained forward until the *trektou* that was attached to the *disselboom* straightened across the backs of the *haarosse* and the animals fell into line.

In the east the first rays of the sun lit up the darkness with an orange glow. McKay hesitated.

He had heard from Andries and Gerhardus about Ernst talking to the oxen and he was curious.

"Ernst, come here!" he called and the youngster came running, his new *velskoens* on his feet.

"Yes, Mr Mac?"

"Ernst, go and say goodbye, then talk to your team, like you did at Keetmanshoop."

Ernst ran to Gertruida. He kissed and hugged her quickly.

"Look after yourself, Ernst. Look out for the oxen and ... and ..." she called after him nervously.

"*Boetie*, please bring me some seashells? Remember!" begged Charlotte.

Ernst hurried to the rear team's *agterosse* to begin his ritual. The other three *touleiers* and their drivers were half-annoyed but also curious about

---

100 *Haar*: In the ox wagon context, right.
101 *Hot*: In the ox wagon context, left.
102 *Haaragter*: Right rearmost position.

this interference in their teams. Knowing that he was delaying the *trek*, he talked fast and urgently to the animals. He called each ox by name, all ninety-six of them, including the three other teams, and he moved quickly. McKay walked behind him. He could not believe what he saw. It was obvious that the oxen understood and responded to Ernst's encouragement. As the boy moved forward, everyone sensed a growing tension.

When he got to his *leiriem*, tied to the horns of the *voorosse* of the team in front, the red team, he drew a deep breath and shouted at the top of his voice:

"Red team! Black team! Mixed-colour team! Winning team! We are on our way to Lüderitzbucht! Go! Go! All together now!"

The four whips cracked together and the four teams of twelve pairs of oxen started forward and as one team in the early morning sunshine. The eight men – *touleiers* and drivers – waved goodbye to the people of Paradys.

Ernst's team pulled the long-tent wagon. His driver was Andries. Then followed Gerhardus as *touleier*, with Petrus as his driver and the black team pulling the short-tent wagon. Next was Albertus and Joshua with the winning team and lastly Kerneels and Koos with the mixed-colour team. The two last teams pulled open transport wagons with no tents.

Mr Mac, mounted on his horse Campbell, departed half an hour later and took a shortcut through the veld so that he could admire the splendid sight of the procession from the top of Kieriekop. He had never before been so proud of his wagon teams. It was going to be a hot day, but nobody cared. McKay joined up with the trek and rode right up to the front.

"How are you doing, Ernst? Are your feet holding out in those new shoes?" he asked from the saddle of the grey horse.

"All is fine, Mr Mac! How are we doing with time?"

"Not to worry, our record only starts from Keetmanshoop!"

Even as far as two miles before Keetmanshoop the first curious spectators lined the road. All knew McKay's record *trek* was on its way. They cheered and applauded the magnificent sight. The McKay *touleiers* and drivers were fit to burst with pride. Ernst felt as if he had hardly covered any distance despite the fact that Paradys was far behind them.

Children ran alongside, dogs barked and women waved from their doorways. It was not yet half past eleven but the town's menfolk were already heading in the direction of the Schützenhaus to quench their thirst. First though, they strolled around the *trek* and expressed their views on McKay's chances.

"Hmf, too many oxen are not good. They pull sideways," said one.

"They should have used only red Afrikaner oxen. These multi-coloured animals don't last," said another.

"I have never seen a more beautiful sight in all my life! He is going to smash the record!" said another.

McKay rode to colonel Von Deimling. The officer came out of his office to view the spectacle.

"McKay, I must say that this is a wonderful sight. I would have loved to show the people in the Fatherland what it looks like. Come, let me give you your deposit."

The *touleiers* and drivers took turns to run into McKay's shop to buy boiled sweets, tobacco, an extra blanket or two, a secret little bottle wrapped in brown paper and other odds and ends.

Ernst walked up and down between the rows of oxen. Here and there he adjusted a yoke or a chain or tightened a wagon tent. He knew they faced a tough and long journey ahead, but he was looking forward to it. He was a true Afrikaner now: he spoke their language, wore the same clothes and thought like them. When he had disembarked from the ship he was fresh out of Germany. A German who did not know the difference between an ox wagon and an oryx. He was retracing his footsteps now, but as another person. For a moment he wondered if he would come across his father on the way. He also knew that their *trek* would pass right by his mother's grave.

McKay returned from the German camp with a thick brown envelope in his trouser pocket.

"I have to remain here for business. I will meet up with you this evening. You must trek to *Amoskop* on Mr Schneitmann's farm, Slangkop, and set up camp there. I have arranged it with him. I must first attend to important matters before I can join you, but I have faith in my men. You know your work and you don't need me to supervise you. Men, the time has come."

Robert McKay took his gold watch from his pocket, opened the lid and announced, "Men of *Paradys*, it is half past twelve on 30 August 1906. Our record *trek* starts now!"

He waved his broad-brimmed hat in a wide circle.

This time Andries was the first to shout. "Go, Go! All together now!"

The spectators started clapping and cheering when the finest trek in the history of Keetmanshoop surged down the main street. McKay waited until the wagons disappeared from view before he walked to the post office. A few minutes later he entered the brand new Schützenhaus.

"Whisky for all, *Whisky für alle.* Today it's Robbie McKay of Paradys's round!" he called to the jovial group gathered there.

He sat down on a shiny stinkwood stool at the bar and started chatting.

"Robert, you old bugger. Where did you find all those good animals? Probably smuggled from Bechuanaland, hey?"

"Hey, Robert, how about a small loan there? You seem to be loaded."

"You wily old Scotsman, that was good, really good. Congratulations, mate. I hope you smash that record."

Everyone wanted to have a word with the generous Scotsman with the big heart. The conversations revolved around the drought, the Namas, the karakul industry and the coming railway line. The men in the transport business were very unhappy about the iron track that was creeping ever closer. It was going to rob them of their work, and what then?

Just before sunset McKay excused himself. He stumbled slightly as he got up from the high bar stool and reached for his hat where it hung with the other men's on a row of springbok horns on the wall.

"Right, my friends. Time to go. See you again in less than four weeks. This exact spot, for more of the same. Cheers!"

The men of the Schützenhaus cheered and shouted their farewells at the top of their voices.

Outside Campbell had been waiting patiently. McKay tightened the girth, mounted and rode off. Once outside the town, he gave Campbell his head in a slow trot westwards while he pulled his hat low over his one eye and dozed with folded hands.

Ernst stood next to his mother's lonely grave beneath the shepherd's tree. All that was left was a small heap of gravel and a Star of David Father Joseph had fashioned from a few *skeis* on that fateful day. He would have *trekked* past it if Andries had not pointed it out to him.

It had cost his mother her life for him to live in this beautiful land. He knelt and without thinking, he whispered. "*Es tut mir leid, Mutter.*"[103]

The men left Ernst alone for a few minutes. Then they gathered closer, removed their hats respectfully and stood in a small circle. Seven

---

103 *Es tut mir leid, Mutter*: I am sorry, Mother.

voices were lifted in a melancholy Namaland version of "Nearer my God to Thee".

Ernst gazed at his friends, one by one, "Thank you," he murmured when they had finished.

They built a neat stone cairn and placed a wooden cross on the Jewish lady's grave, right next to the Star of David.

Late that evening McKay reached Slangkop, the farm of his great friend Schneitmann. The trek was resting at Amoskop, some distance away from the homestead. Some of the men rested on their elbows in a circle around a camelthorn wood fire under the stars while others had curled up under grey blankets, on or under the wagons.

"Good evening men, what do you say now?" McKay greeted them.

"Evening, Mr Mac," they answered. One walked to the wagons to wake those that slept and another led Campbell to the watering place.

"We have to *trek*, resting time is over. We will never break that record by resting! *Inspan*[104]! *Inspan*! Let's go, men of Paradys."

Soon the hoi-hoi-hoi calls sounded over *Amoskop*.

Ernst Schneitmann stumbled from the house, dressed in his white nightshirt, complete with a soft nightcap on his head and a storm lantern in his hand, like a sailor at sea.

"Robert, you idiot, where have you been? I've been getting myself drunk waiting for you!"

McKay instructed Andries to *trek* as far as the Fish River and wait there, before he and Schneitmann staggered arm-in-arm into the farmhouse for a shot or two.

The *trek* made good progress in the cool of the night. Towards the middle of the morning they reached the large pool in the Fish River just below the shallow drift. It was a beautiful campsite with plenty of shade beneath the camelthorn trees and deliciously clean, fresh water. McKay only arrived just before dusk, he and Campbell equally thirsty.

Just after midnight the Scotsman bellowed up the Fish River Canyon: "*Inspan*, men of Paradys, *inspan* I say!"

Ten days later they outspanned at Klein Kubub, south of Aus. The two transport wagons were laden with freshly cut grass. They filled the four barrels on each wagon with water at Klein Kubub's spring.

---

104 *Inspan*: Afrikaans order to tether, inspan, a team of oxen to the wagon.

Tension now lay over them like a heavy blanket. Some of the men became grumpy. Mr Mac decided it was time for a party. He sent Andries to buy a sheep at Geider's butchery in Aus and a bottle of cheap brandy.

Ernst watched in amazement as the *touleiers* performed the *Nama-stap*[105] and the *riel*[106] in the light of the huge campfire.

---

105 *Nama-stap*: Traditional folk dance of the Namas.

106 *Riel*: Another folk dance of the Khoi-Khoin people.

31

Ernst and Cornelius on Shark Island: a lesson in the Namib

Shark Island in the background with the mission
church to the right in the foreground.

When the four ox wagons rounded the foothills of the Aus Mountains, the outstretched expanse of the Namib Desert lay laughing before them, almost like a lady of the night in all her nakedness. It was as though the desert was enticing them, knowing she would soon have them in her power.

That first day everyone spoke in a low voice, softly, even to the oxen.

"When you look at the Namib as a stranger from the outside, she strikes fear into your heart but from the moment you become one with her, you fall in love. You discover that she is full of mercy. She will provide you with food, sometimes water as well, but you dare not take chances with her. She will turn you inside out and leave you to dry like the Kaiserbird with a lizard," Andries told Ernst.

The wagons rolled slowly westwards through the stark and barren landscape. Ernst often walked with his head down, the *leiriem* in one hand, caught up in his own thoughts, for an hour or longer. Every time he looked up, it looked exactly the same, as if he hadn't moved at all: the same hard, stony, calcareous sand covered with multiple wagon tracks, and a shimmering horizon dancing with the blue-white sky. Here and there small hills rose from the desert floor like ships on the sea.

They outspanned when the midday sun was at its fiercest. Nobody spoke. The oxen lay, without food or water, their eyes closed against the sandy onslaught of the east wind.

At midnight they *inspanned* the oxen and *trekked* again until eleven o'clock in the morning. Then the task of driving the tired but now un-burdened animals back to Klein Kubub to drink began. As soon as they had drunk their fill from the big, wide troughs there, it was time to turn around and head back to the waiting wagons and the yokes.

Immediately after their arrival at the wagons, the oxen were *inspanned* and they trekked to the next stop in the coolness of the night.

Outspan. The oxen driven on to Tschaukaib to drink again.

Again at nightfall they *trekked* deeper into the Namib. The next day man and beast again drank at Tschaukaib before they moved on. At a secret hiding place they offloaded half the grass fodder.

On the fourth day they veered south-west to Ukamas, because the direct route westwards was dry and Tschaukaib did not have sufficient water for the oxen to be taken back there. The oxen sniffed hesitantly before drinking Ukamas's brackish water.

On day five they swung back in a north-westerly direction and offloaded the remainder of the grass at Grassplatz. The oxen were taken ahead to Boerekamp at Lüderitzbucht to drink. McKay went with them. He was relieved to see people and lights again and to breathe in the salty air of the sea. The whisky on the veranda of Woermann's Shipping Line tasted a lot better than the south-easter, the sand and dry *pap*. He returned to Grassplatz and his *trek* late that night.

The closer they got to Lüderitzbucht, the more Ernst thought about Cornelius and Magdalena.

"What could have become of them?" he asked Mr Mac.

"Oh, that woman who arrived with you in Keetmanshoop when you first came? Cornelius Fredericks's wife and children? No, I heard there is a camp where people are being held, but no, I don't know."

When the four wagons rolled into Boerekamp, Ernst remembered his first arrival there. So many things had changed. He had a new family now and he was happy. He felt a bit guilty when he thought about his parents, but the struggle for survival had taught him that it did not help to dwell on the past. It was just this thing of Cornelius and his family that bothered him. What could have happened to these people? And that voice under the lights: "*Aber er ist doch nur ein Jude...*".

Once the oxen had been watered and fed the expensive fodder McKay had bought from the *smous*, Ernst wandered around the campsites. He even recognised the Boer who had taught him to eat biltong. He walked straight up to the man.

"Evening, *Oom*[107]. Do you still remember me?" he said and offered his hand politely. The shaggy-bearded Boer, sitting on his haunches at his fire, pipe in mouth and deep in thought, looked up and recognised Ernst.

"Wait, you are that little German who nearly drowned, not so? And now here you are speaking our language? Where are your mother and father, young man?"

"My mother passed away, *Oom* and I don't know where my father is. I am living with Mr Mac at Paradys. I came with him to load cargo. I am a *touleier* now, *Oom*."

The Boer frowned.

"Your mother is dead? Sorry to hear that. What happened? What is your name again?"

"My name is Ernst Luchtenstein, *Oom*. And it was a leopard that took my mother, *Oom*. The last day, the morning before we were due to arrive at Keetmans, my mother woke up early and the leopard grabbed her at the back of her neck."

"Sorry to hear that. I really am sorry. There are many leopards between Aus and Keetmanshoop. We always see their tracks. And tell me, your father? You say he is gone. What do you mean? But sit down. Here, have some of this excellent fresh biltong."

Ernst hesitated. "Thank you, *Oom*. No, *Oom*, I don't know about my father. He left just after it happened. He left us with Mr Mac. We only see him now and then."

"Mmm, Luchtenstein, you say. Is your father tallish with a black beard? His touleier is Johannes, a Topnaar?"

---

107 *Oom*: Afrikaans word for uncle, generally used as a term of respect for an older man.

"Yes, yes *Oom*, that's them. Has *Oom* seen them? How is Johannes? He taught me your language – as well as Nama."

"Yes, I saw them at Duwisib. I offloaded stuff for that baron and his American wife. Your father also offloaded. I think it was cement or something. No, he is well. Strange, he didn't say anything about your mother."

"And Johannes, *Oom*? What did he say?"

"I did not speak to him, but it seems he is well too. You know how it is."

"*Oom*, I want to ask you something, please? *Oom*, it is about an important Nama captain. His name is Cornelius Fredericks. I got to know him when we first arrived here. The soldiers caught him. We heard that he was brought here to some camp. His wife and two children also came here later, to be with him. Now, I was wondering if I would be able to see him before we go back again. Do you know anything about such a camp?"

"We only see the prisoners who work on the railway line. In the evenings we see them walking back to Shark Island, but nothing more than that. You know that our wives and children were also kept in such camps there in the Transvaal. Tens of thousands perished in those camps. Why do you think I am here alone? But go and ask around in town, and also at the harbour. Perhaps someone will know."

"All right, *Oom*. Thanks, *Oom*."

Ernst said goodbye and walked on, deep in thought. His thoughts revolved around Cornelius.

"Mr Mac, may I please go to town?" he asked later.

"But of course. Wait, you surely need some money."

With hands deep in his trouser pockets, clenching his first month's pay, Ernst walked down Bai road to the intersection with Bismarckstrasse. Builders were at work everywhere, mixing cement, passing bricks, plastering walls, fitting doors and windows and putting up roofs.

Below in the harbour he saw a few ships to the right with the tortoise island to the left. From this angle he could see two rows of barbed wire fencing and a low, flat-roofed, corrugated iron building, and behind that, a few of the tortoise huts. It must have been in that corrugated iron building that he lay that morning after he had so nearly drowned. Beyond, far in the distance, he also saw the silhouette of the wooden construction. All the memories of that morning came rushing back. What was it that had bumped into him? What had actually happened that morning? Suddenly, for the first time in weeks, the song of the *spekvreter* was alive in his mind, screeching louder and louder: 'Who am I? Why am I here?' The questions and doubts were back.

He turned right into *Hafenstrasse*. At the harbour he saw seven ox wagons being loaded. He also saw that a new quay was being built. The ships lay at anchor near the deepest point of the new quay. The small, dangerous rowing boats would soon not be needed anymore. He then turned left, as if drawn by a magnet, to the barbed-wire gates. On this side of the barbed-wire gates, on the mainland, were a guard hut with two armed guards and their German shepherd dog. He looked at the smartly turned-out guards, in their black uniforms, shiny boots and military caps, so different to the *Schutztruppe*, and then plucked up all his courage. Before he could venture closer to the guard hut, the two guards advanced straight towards him, rifles at the ready, half threatening. He stopped.

"What do you want, boy?" the one asked.

"Excuse me, sir. I am looking for my friend. His name is Cornelius Fredericks and he is a Nama. I heard that you have many prisoners of war here. Do you know someone by that name?"

"Go away! Immediately. If you love your life!"

"Please, sir, I have to speak to him."

Ernst looked the large guard directly in the eye. The two stared at each other for a long while, but Ernst stood his ground. The few months he had spent in the new world had made a man of him. The soldier's resolve began to weaken. He turned around.

"Wait here!" came the order.

He waited for a long time. Then two soldiers appeared.

"What do you want, boy?" one of them asked.

"I want to talk to my friend, sir. His name is Cornelius Fredericks."

The soldier's chin lifted slightly and he narrowed his eyes as looked down at Ernst. "Who are you and why do you want to talk to him?"

"My name is Ernst Luchtenstein and I have been here for only a few months. I came from Prussia with my parents and now live in Keetmanshoop."

"But aren't you the youngster who nearly drowned when you disembarked from the ship?"

"Yes, that's me, sir. And someone rescued me, here, in this same place."

The soldier was silent for a while and then asked: "Tell me first what your interest is in this criminal, this Fredericks? Why are you so eager to see him?"

Ernst realised he had to be careful. "Sir, this Mr Fredericks helped me and my parents a lot when other people wanted to do us harm. I just want to thank him. That's all, sir. I ask for only a short while. Please, sir?"

"Well, alright, but you will have to wait. He is a bit ill. I will first have to ascertain if it is possible for him to see you."

"That is fine with me, sir. I will wait."

While he waited, Ernst's mind was occupied with the images of glass bottles, the skull, Dr Fischer's eyes and the words, *Aber er ist doch nur ein Jude....* He looked around to see if he could spot the doctor.

Perhaps all of this was just a dream, he thought.

Cornelius looked up when the door was unlocked. "Up, *Hotnot*! Get up! You have a visitor."

He fell when he got up.

"Come on! Walk!"

The guard pushed Cornelius forward in the direction of the familiar bathroom with its bucket and blue soap. He steeled himself for the cruel pipe with its poison, but to his surprise the guard gave him a clean shirt and trousers and a pair of shoes.

"Go on, put them on! You cannot look like this when people come visiting!"

Cornelius's trembling fingers struggled to fasten the buttons. His mouth hung open so that the saliva ran from his mouth. He was unable to fasten his laces.

"Come on, man! We don't have all day."

The guard motioned Cornelius down the passage. At a closed door the guard stopped and knocked.

"Come in!"

Cornelius was ushered inside. His eyes were screwed up even more against the harsh light. Behind the desk sat a dark-haired man in uniform. The room was empty except for rows of files against the walls.

"Fredericks, there is a visitor for you. I have decided to make an exception. For his sake, not yours. You may see him, but you are not to speak about the research work being done here. It is top secret and classified. Do you understand?"

Cornelius only nodded. His will had left him. His spirit had been broken. The guard led him to the next room and ordered him to sit down on a chair. After a long while the door opened again. Ernst walked in and gasped. He knew this was no dream.

"Mr Fredericks! What's wrong? Is it really you? I mean … uhm … I … I … Is it really you?"

Cornelius recognised the young boy. His face creased. "Is it you, my little General? Did you come to look for me? You have grown up. You're tall."

"Yes, sir. It is me, Ernst Luchtenstein, sir."

Ernst stepped forward and held out his hand. Cornelius took his hand in both of his. He gazed at Ernst for a long time without saying a word.

"Your mother is dead, Ernst. Magdalena told me. There in the jail in Keetmanshoop she told me. I am sorry. She was a good woman, for she wanted to help us. I am really sorry, son."

"Thank you, Mr Fredericks. The leopard killed her. We were almost in Keetmanshoop."

"And now, what are you doing here? I mean here in Lüderitzbucht? Are you returning to Germany?"

"No sir. I am a *touleier* now, in Mr McKay's employ, but Mr Fredericks, I have come to hear the story from you. The story you told me and my mother. I have the book in which she has written it down. I want to know what happened afterwards. Tell me please! Before they take you away again. Please! I want to finish my mother's work," Ernst begged.

"Alright. Where were we last time? Where did I stop?"

"You spoke of the time when Mr Vogelsang bought Angra Pequena, this place, Lüderitzbucht, for Mr Lüderitz, in Bethanien."

"Oh, yes. Oh, yes. Did I tell you about the second sale as well?"

"No, I don't think so, Mr Fredericks. Please tell me again."

The guard had left the room. They were alone.

"Good. I will tell you, but there are other stories also, little Ernst. These stories must be told, because my nation is being massacred here in this place. The world needs to know, but the Namas are not book or newspaper people, my little General. We cannot tell the stories to the world. We are shepherds, not clever people who work in offices."

"I want to know everything, because I want to help you, like my mother wanted to. I really want to help."

Cornelius stared at Ernst. "I will tell, but it's going to take a lot of time and my time is nearly over, for ever. I wrote some things on your mother's pieces of paper as well as I could, and gave them to my wife Magdalena. Find her and tell her to give them to you so that you can tell the world."

"I do not know where she is, Mr Fredericks, but I will look for her. I promise. I thought she was with you on the island."

"No, my little General. Not that I know of. I hope not, but go and ask her for my little letters."

Cornelius talked, in a somewhat incoherent and confused way, about the geographic mile scam, the tragedy in the Fish River Canyon and the courage and power of his father-in-law.

The door opened. "Now, that's enough, young man," said the guard. "The prisoner has to leave now." Ernst could do nothing but obey.

"Mr Fredericks, thank you. Thanks for everything. I will visit again, and I will convey greetings to Mrs Magdalena when I see her again. Goodbye."

"Goodbye, my little General and thank you. Please finish your mother's work."

"I promise, Mr Fredericks, I promise."

That evening Ernst wrote in his exercise book again.

The following morning it was the turn of the McKay trek to enter the harbour. But before they turned in at the harbour, Mr Mac sent the transport wagon of Albertus and Koos to purchase four barrels of water at the condensors. It was expensive – forty marks.

Meanwhile the Professor Woermann, a huge steamship boasting new blue paint and shiny windows, docked at the quay. The bags of mealie meal and boxes, clearly marked in red letters: "Produce of the Cape, R. McKay, Paradys, District Keetmanshoop," were swiftly brought ashore. The sailors packed the heaviest cargo, marked as maize, over the front and rear axles of the wagons. McKay's men arranged the rest of the cargo around the barrels from which the expensive water was dripping.

Ernst knew that the steep climbs, the searing heat, the stinging wind, the freezing nights and the scorching, thick sand lay ahead of them. His team talk to the oxen had become a prayer for him, because he spoke to One greater than himself.

The *touleiers* and drivers stood quietly while Mr McKay inspected the cargo. He walked around each wagon and pulled and pushed at the bags and barrels, checking if everything was firm and stable, but this was unnecessary. Then he climbed onto the back of the foremost wagon, took off his hat and cleared his throat.

"Men of Paradys. Today we are at the start of our journey back home. You know about our record, but today I want to tell you, forget about it. We only wish to get home safely. If we do break the record, then it will be a bonus. I wish each of you a safe journey. Are all of you ready?"

"Yes, Mr Mac," they all replied in unison.

"I can't hear you."

"Yes, Mr Mac!" they roared together.

"Well then. Ready. Go! Go! All together now!"

The Scotsman's voice reverberated across the harbour. Four whips swung and cracked cheerfully. The oxen strained in line. The wagons moved forward, slowly but surely. The first stage, to Boerekamp, was short but steep. The people of Lüderitzbucht were used to ox wagons, but this *trek* was something else. The discipline and smartness were impressive and four teams of twelve pairs each – on top of it in matching colours – were exceptional. The Buchters[108] gawked at the spectacle.

At Boerekamp the *touleiers* led the oxen to the water. The real *trek*, away from civilization and into the desert, would begin at midnight. When the wind blew over a kettle and a tin mug the men around the small campfire looked at one another. Everyone feared Lüderitzbucht's wind.

Shortly after midnight the wheels rolled eastward, right into the angry wind. The oxen squeezed their eyes closed, and the heads of the *touleiers* were bowed, their hats hanging down. The sand stung wherever there was a patch of bare skin. The east wind created sand dunes where the day before there had been none. McKay frowned.

At the first dune, just beyond the flat ground outside Boerekamp, Andries's team came to a standstill. McKay rode up to them immediately.

"What's the matter?" he yelled so that Andries could hear him above the howling wind.

"The wagon, it is stuck, Mr Mac."

When McKay knelt down beside the wheels, he saw how they had cut into the sand like the sharp edge of an axe into a tree stump. Albertus, Koos and Ernst also came to see what was wrong. They started shovelling the sand away, their faces and hands constantly peppered by the stinging grains of sand driven by the easterly wind. They worked away all the sand in front of the wheels, but the sand had also packed against the *disselboom*. They had to dig in more deeply. McKay walked around the wagon once more before he gave the signal.

"Go, go! All together now!" rang out across the Namib. The oxen strained and the *trektou* straightened. When the wagon started to move forward, McKay got onto Campbell's back, but the wagon stopped again. He could not believe it. All that hard work for nothing. They repeated

---

108 *Buchters*: nickname for the inhabitants of Lüderitzbucht.

the whole process again. Dig dig, dig, while trying to dodge the needles of sand.

Ernst talked to his team, starting at *haaragter*. One by one he spoke to them until he reached *haarvoor*, and then he started again at *hotagter* until he reached *hotvoor*. Then he signalled to Andries who gave the order and cracked his whip and the oxen strained forward. Slowly the wagon inched forward. It was free.

Kerneels and Koos followed them but Koos swerved too far to the right. Now their wagon was stuck. To make matters worse, it was one of the most heavily laden ones. The sun's first rays struggled through the cloud of sand enveloping them.

The day was white-hot by the time Kerneels and Koos's wagon joined the others. McKay knew that since midnight they had progressed a mere two miles. The east wind still howled into their faces. He himself was exhausted from all the stress, but rest was out of the question. He had hoped to be at Grassplatz by the afternoon, but that would not happen now. Tonight his oxen would have to eat sand. They were close enough to Boerekamp to easily return for water, but there would be no time for them to graze.

They *trekked* parallel to the new railway line. Just after daybreak they saw a strange monstrosity on the track: a wagon rolling on the line, pulled by a group of Namas dressed in canvas prison garb, followed by four soldiers on horseback, holding crops. The wagon, loaded with sleepers and rails, slid past the ox wagons as McKay and his team stared.

Further on, they saw that the railway wagon had come to a stop. When they got closer, they saw why. Up ahead the railway line was buried under layers of sand, four, five, six feet deep in places. The prisoners shovelled furiously to clear the line. No sooner had they cleared the line ahead, when the wind was closing it behind them with more sand.

The Paradys ox wagons got stuck twice more before noon. They had not even reached Coleman's place yet. McKay called a halt; his men were exhausted. They placed the wagons in a semicircular formation and put up canvas in an effort to shield the cooking and sleeping areas from the vicious wind.

It was again poor Albertus and Koos's task to drive the oxen back to Boerekamp to drink. Fortunately it was not far and they returned long before dark. McKay remained concerned because the wind was not letting up. They were powerless against this baking hot wind blasting the Namib sands.

At midnight McKay bellowed to the camp to wake up. There was sand, sand and more sand everywhere. The coffee kettle and the three-legged pot with the charred remains of the previous evening's *pap* were gone. After some digging, Albertus retrieved them. The windward side of the wagons was covered by three feet of sand. It took more than an hour's digging and clearing just to free the wheels from the unyielding sand.

Man and beast had barely struggled forward for half a mile when Ernst's wagon got stuck again, right up to the *disselboom*. The more they shovelled to free the wagon, the deeper it seemed to sink. They eventually took off the wheel jack and lifted the entire wagon, cleared the sand away on one side, placed canvas under the wheel and then lowered the wagon onto it. They did the same with the other wheels. This time the three wagons at the rear end chose a different route, bypassing the stranded wagon. McKay let them get ahead to prevent further loss of time. Soon afterwards, two other wagons became trapped.

At first light they could still see the place they had camped at the previous night in the distance. McKay's throat constricted and he had the feeling of a looming disaster.

At last Andries and Ernst managed to free their wagon from the sand and arrived where Albertus and Koos were still wrestling with their bogged-down wagon. When the sand was cleared and the wagon was free, McKay ordered two extra teams of oxen to be hitched in front of the existing team. He gave the word and the three teams pulled the wagon as if they were on the main street of Keetmanshoop. McKay let the wagon run for a good half-mile before the additional teams were outspanned.

That day they progressed only a short distance. Only in the middle of the third day did they outspan at Grassplatz.

"Today's trip to Lüderitzbucht and back with the oxen will be tough and I know you are tired and exhausted. I will be going with you on Campbell. Who is going to help me?" Ernst's hand was up first.

They arrived back at Grassplatz well after dark, the oxen exhausted and famished. McKay had no choice but to start the next shift a bit later.

Kruisman, from the coloured team, did not want to get up. Could not get up. He paid the ultimate price.

The trek moved on, away from Grassplatz, towards Aus. An hour into the trek, it happened again. Stuck. Shovel, shovel, shovel. Jack, dig, dig. Move jack, shovel, shovel, move jack. Outspan, inspan, pull, outspan, inspan, pull, stuck, dig, dig, and dig again.

On one occasion Andries and Ernst were stuck so badly that all the shovelling, jacking up and even three teams of oxen could not free them. The wagon remained where it stood. McKay watched from a distance, but did not show how despondent he was feeling.

"Right men, outspan!"

When the exhausted animals were standing with their backs to the wind and eyes tightly closed, McKay spoke again.

"Alright, men, unload!"

They removed all the cargo and packed it to one side.

"Hoi-hoi-hoi!" Again they inspanned three teams. Ernst spoke to the oxen. With a huge effort the empty wagon broke free and a loud cheer erupted.

"Go, go, go, don't stop, keep on walking!" shouted McKay. Everyone walked with the wagon to help push if it showed any signs of getting trapped. Only after a mile did McKay call a halt.

By this time only the tops of the other wagons protruded from the sand; the lower parts were completely buried. All the cargo that had been offloaded had also been covered with sand. And still the wind howled from the east and the sun scorched from above. Dig dig, dig. The shovelling began all over again. The cargo had to be carried, rolled and dragged by hand all the way to the wagon. Back again to the other wagons. More shovelling. "Hoi-hoi-hoi!" Inspan. Pull. Load. Pull. It was a day from hell.

By late afternoon the wind had subsided. It became quiet. For the first time since they had left Lüderitzbucht, there was not even a breeze. A full moon rose above the dunes. Despite all their hardship, the nine men marvelled in silence at the beauty of the Namib twilight.

The next day the wagons changed direction, south of the new railway line. As they looked back one last time, the transport riders saw the rail truck approach, pass and disappear behind the dunes. The prisoners must have managed to clear the tracks eventually.

The heat of the Namib sand caused more and more of the animals to limp. As Ernst had learnt from Johannes and his father, they made shoes for these animals from the freshly slaughtered hides of the oxen that were unable to stand upright any longer.

After eight more days of battling, the loss of twelve oxen and eighteen others with cracked hooves, they were out of the Namib's sand belt at Ukamas, the place of brackish water. McKay was worried. The slightest error would mean the end of them all. Aus was still far away. They were barely half way on their return journey. All they had in their favour was the fact that the sand was now behind them. But the oxen were in the last stages of exhaustion and there were four heavy cargoes to move. And there was only the brackish water of Ukamas for them.

McKay summoned Ernst and Andries.

"Men, we have no choice. You see the state the animals are in. I think two or three more days and they will all die, to the last one. Then it will be over for us, my business, the whole lot. I am going ahead tomorrow with two wagons and all the oxen. I am going to leave half the cargo of the two wagons behind in order to make the trek easier. You two must remain here to guard the wagons and the cargo. As soon as I get to Aus, I will make a plan to fetch you with fresh oxen. All right?"

McKay knew that he could not leave the wagons and their valuable cargo in the hands of two Namas, no matter how long they had been working for him. Ernst's presence would ensure that nothing went missing and that Andries remained at his post.

McKay and the others left them with a barrel of water, the maize on the wagon, a bag of sugar and a few things to barter with. The two built themselves a sturdy shelter, a place to cook and began the long wait. Days passed. All they could do was talk and wait.

After a few days Ernst began to realise something strange was happening here in this endless, empty, deafening silence of the desert. It felt as if he was hovering above time, looking down onto the beginning and end of everything. He was seeing more sharply and hearing more clearly; he smelt the air and the sand; saw the eagle in the sky and felt the breath of the gecko. When he drank from the precious supply of water, he tasted the anger of the earth in it, the love of the people over centuries, the golden colour of the sun on the wagon's tent and the granular texture of the sand.

A visitor arrived. A small, quick, grey bird. A dune lark, the dune lark. It scurried around, scratching and searching for food amongst the stones, and when the sun had climbed high, it rested in the shade of the wagon. Then suddenly, there was another one, the female. Ernst found their new nest, right underneath the wagon. He was enchanted by their tenacity and adaptability. He made sure that they had water and a little maize, but he never saw them drink.

Sometimes he would sit and stare at the grains of sand being blown about, the ants crawling over little sand mounds, falling off, crawling up again, falling off again, crawling up again, being covered by twelve or twenty or thirty grains of sand, only to crawl out again, fall off again, or be blown away by the incessant wind. And always his eyes would return to rest on the lark's nest, the only sign of hope in these desolate plains.

At other times he would just sit and smell the wind. He would draw air in halfway, wait a moment, then inhale very deeply and wash the air deep down into the back of his throat. He began to feel that he could even smell the breath of the animals. He thought he could smell the polish on the veranda of Paradys or the smoky atmosphere of the blacksmith's workshop.

Sometimes the young boy thought he was dreaming or becoming a little like his father, but actually he was experiencing for the first time in his life that he could truly see. Could hear. Could smell. Could taste. Could feel. He felt alive for the first time. From the ship the sandy beaches had seemed like sheets on a washing line, naked, empty and devoid of life: but now he knew that the desert was filled with small grains of sand, each with its own shape, colour and texture. Together with the millions of other grains of sand this desert lived, breathed, its heart throbbed, and it spoke to him in the language of the larks.

He realised the desert had changed him – from a child into a man. He felt the power of centuries of dawns pulsing through his veins. He rejoiced in his energised spirit because he now knew that he could do or achieve anything he wanted.

The blade of his Joseph Rodgers pocket knife was thin, blue-grey and as sharp as the white sun. He looked at the marks the sharpening stone had made on the metal blade during many hours of sharpening. He scratched out the bit of oily grit from the finger-nail notch. There were four grains of sand in the mixture of oil, stone and metal. He wiped them off on his upper arm. The black handle was slightly dull in one place. He started polishing it with the palm of his hand. Later he used some of the oil from the skin on the bridge of his nose and polished the vulcanite with it until it shone like a quiet dam in the moonlight. He looked at the knife, smelt the sharp odour of the metal, tasted the iron, and tapped the blade against the edge of his front tooth. To his left, about ten yards away, Andries sat in silence, as if he was not seeing, hearing, thinking or dreaming of anything. Ernst wondered what was going on inside his head.

Then Ernst slowly closed the knife and reopened it. He took the blade in his right hand and held it like a pencil. With the sharp point he slowly made a small cut in the middle of his left thumb until a drop of blood welled up from it, like a whale breaking the surface of the sea. He turned his thumb downwards so that the blood could drip onto the sand in front of him.

He smelt his thumb, tasted the saltiness of the blood and saw its shiny redness in the bright sun. Two drops of blood fell next to each other beside the shadow of his head and spread quickly from one grey-white grain of sand to the next until the last grain in the circle was only half-covered in red, its other side still grey-white. Then he pressed on his thumb so that another drop appeared and fell half an inch from the other two, in direct sunlight. He watched the blood spreading again, from one grain of sand to the next, sparkling and glistening like a ruby.

He felt how his soul and spirit penetrated the innermost nature of the Namib, germinated and grew there. The Namib's dry, warm breath blew into his nostrils down deep into the back of his throat where he inhaled its aroma and experienced the power of the sun, sand and heat like a waterfall of energy.

Often, without warning, like a dark cloud before the sun, the images of glass bottles, the skull and the grey eyes entered his mind and the words "*Aber er ist doch nur ein Jude...*" filled his mind.

"No," he said out loud, so that Andries looked up in surprise.

"What did you say, Ernst?"

Ernst did not reply.

He saw wagons with their *touleiers* and drivers come and go, hurrying past, always on their way to somewhere, but never finding it. He came to understand that people were always driven by someone or something and were never satisfied with what they had or where they were.

He came to a decision. He would always be content with what he had, while he worked hard to build an even better life. He knew that all he really had, at that moment in eternity, was now, the present. He realised that every moment, every heartbeat, every second of every day was a precious gift and he would practise for days on end to enjoy and appreciate it.

He saw how the transport riders passed by with set faces just like *wabrieke*[109], how they strained with every ounce of strength to reach Lüderitzbucht or Aus because it was there that happiness in the form of money, food, drink or just a little water waited, while he sat here, content to wait. Day after day. Night after night.

Ernst learnt the secrets of the Namib. He loved the Namib desert. He knew it had made a man of him and taught him more about himself than he would ever have learnt in Germany or at Paradys.

---

109 *Wabrieke*: Afrikaans, literally the brake fitted to the rear of an ox wagon, implying grim, unyielding determination.

Andries taught him about the *horingsman* and one day they even caught one of these horned, poisonous reptiles and cooked it. Ernst ate slowly, relishing the strange taste of the viper while Andries watched him surreptitiously. Whenever a wagon passed Ernst checked to see if it was his father's wagon, but it never was. The *transportryers* helped where they could with water and now and then something to eat.

From people on wagons coming from the interior they learnt that McKay had indeed arrived at Kubub after four days of travel, but that he had lost a further twenty oxen on the way. The other animals were in no condition to return to the desert. McKay let them know that he was busy planning a strategy. They just had to keep up their spirits: he was coming!

Ernst and Andries had little more to eat than *pap* and sugar. At times they had to dig away the mounds of sand starting to cover the wagons. The sight of a passing springbok or oryx made their mouths water. They devised all kinds of plans to get hold of some fresh meat, but to no avail.

One day the baby larks hatched. Their grey speckled shells lay to one side. Ernst was overjoyed and watched them grow every day, even fearing later that McKay's workers would arrive and he would have to take leave of the little birds.

On a quiet evening about two weeks after they had been left behind there, they heard the sound of horse's hooves. They got a fright. Jakob Morenga and his men stopped in front of them.

"Aha. Ernst Luchtenstein? My little smuggler, aren't you? Good evening, my young friend. Evening to you too," Jakob nodded towards Andries.

"And what are you two doing here all alone in the Namib?"

"Evening, Sir. Yes it's me. */Uru te tamats kom hâo.*[110] We have been here for longer than two weeks. Mr Mac has gone to Klein Kubub with the other wagons. We had a terrible struggle and the oxen started dying. So then he took all the oxen that were left. Now we are waiting for him to return."

"Is there anything I can do for you?"

"No, sir, we just have to wait. That's all. But perhaps, perhaps there is something. Mister, you don't perhaps have biltong or fresh meat with you? We are dying for meat and the springbok walk right past us here, but we don't have a rifle."

Morenga laughed. "Now why don't you have a rifle? In this country one should always have a rifle and water with you. No, sorry my young friend,

---

110 */Uru te tamats kom hâo*: You have not forgotten me.

we have nothing with us. We will say goodbye now. If those German soldiers come past here, tell them the black Napoleon was here and he had twelve German scalps and penises attached to his saddle bag, you hear?"

Morenga shook with laughter. His little commando disappeared into the night.

The next morning when they woke up, a freshly slaughtered haunch of springbok and ribcage, with its hide still on, and the bloody initials JM clearly carved out in the skin, hung from the side of the wagon.

After about twenty or thirty days, they had lost count, they saw a cloud of dust rise in the east. It came closer and then they saw it was a herd of fifty-odd oxen, unknown to them. They jumped up and down, laughed and danced when they recognized Kerneels and Koos. Mr Mac had not forgotten them! Kerneels handed over the gifts: food, fresh *!narras*, cheese, ham, potatoes and even some boiled sweets.

"Now what oxen are these, Kerneels?" Ernst asked. "They are not ours?"

"No, Ernst. Mr Mac thought our animals would recover at Aus after the troubles we had in the desert, but there is still no grazing round Kubub. The German horses and oxen finished all of it. So he had to take them to Bethanien to fatten them up. Then he had trouble finding fresh oxen. You know, it isn't easy. Nobody wants to give away their oxen, especially to come here and be slaughtered. But four days ago this lot arrived from Bechuanaland. Hardy animals, I tell you. They took to the Namib as if it was a proper road. A man by the name of Smith, Scotty Smith, turned up with them. He said he was looking for Mr Mac. The Black Napoleon, Jakob Morenga had sent him. They spoke and then Mr Mac told us to come and get you immediately. That's the story."

Ernst remembered his larks, but when he looked under the wagon, they had gone. The whole family had left the sanctuary of the wagon to continue their harsh lives in the desert.

The Bechuana team was wild, but strong, with hard and healthy hooves. They were a real bunch of *skeibrekers*[111]. You couldn't talk of *voorosse* or *agterosse*. It was a struggle to *inspan* them and to get them to pull as a unit, but with Ernst on the *leiriem* and three drivers, they were on their way that same evening. Andries and Ernst would not hear of outspanning.

---

111 *Skeibrekers*: literally breakers of *jukskeie*, the straight wooden slats fitted on both sides of an ox's head in the yoke. The term indicates a person or animal of wild, untamed disposition.

They had had enough of the desert. The wind was in their favour, the road hard. They rested during the heat of the day, but trekked throughout the next night. Two days later they arrived at Kubub. Mr McKay was pleased to see them. That evening the men of Paradys celebrated. Ernst did the *Nama-stap*, his travelling companions roaring with laughter.

The next morning McKay announced that he would leave the two wagons at Kubub. He was going to use the Bechuana teams to trek to Keetmanshoop. He would return for the other wagons. This time Albertus and Joshua stayed behind with the wagons to watch over the cargo.

It was November. Every afternoon huge white clouds piled up in the blue sky like a giant cauliflower. The men knew they had to be out of the veld by Christmas because the ground of Namaland became as thick as toffee in the rain. If the Fish River burst its banks, they would be stymied for a long time.

Two weeks later they arrived in Keetmanshoop, a subdued little bunch compared to the four proud wagons, animals and men that had left there three months before. Andries and Ernst were instructed to leave immediately for Paradys, on foot.

Gertruida laughed, wept and danced. She clasped Ernst in her embrace so tightly that he could hardly breathe. Tears ran down her cheeks. Charlotte danced around excitedly.

"Did you remember my seashells, *Boetie*, did you?"

"How you have grown, Ernst" Gertruida exclaimed. "You are taller than I am. Oh man. How old you make me feel. And look at your hands, and those feet of yours! Those new shoes are probably too small again!"

Ernst was startled to hear from Gertruida that his father had been there, looking for him. Gertruida said he did not even greet Charlotte when he saw her. He only wanted Ernst.

Meanwhile, Gertruida sold all Mr Mac's old trek-oxen to a German who had come to her with a sob-story. McKay had said for a long time that the oxen were past trekking. That is why he had left them behind, but now he needed them. All that he now had in his possession were a bunch of youngsters that still needed a lot of training.

The following morning it was a struggle for Ernst and Andries to *inspan* the young oxen. They decided to use a pair of the Bechuana oxen as *voor-* and *agterosse*. With great difficulty they managed to reach Keetmanshoop where an impatient McKay was waiting for them in the Schützenhaus.

Just before Christmas the four empty wagons arrived back at Paradys. That evening the rains came.

32

The end on Shark Island

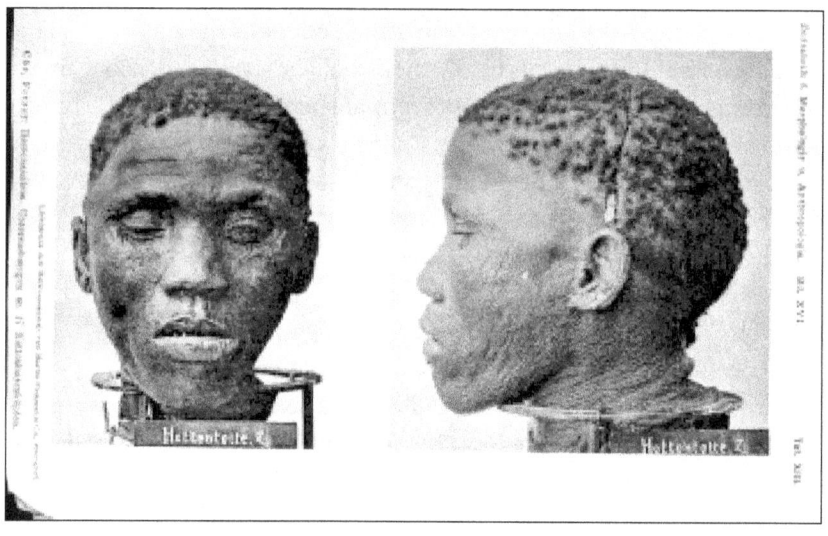

The head of a Nama prisoner at Shark Island.

On Shark Island Captain Ludwig von Estorff received an official envelope with good news. He was appointed as the new commanding officer of the *Schutztruppe,* setting him free from the accursed prison.

He had one remaining and unpleasant task left, one he had been postponing for six months, but now it couldn't wait any longer.

He rang the bell. His secretary entered and jumped to attention.

"*Herr Hauptmann.*"

"Bring me the Herero prisoner, Zacharias Zeraua of Otjimbingwe, the one that is in the cell with Fredericks. Bring him here, into my office."

"*Jawohl, Hauptmann.*"

A few minutes later the soldier knocked.

"Inside!" barked Von Estorff. Zacharias shuffled in, followed by the soldier and a guard with a rifle. Zacharias's eyes narrowed when he recognised Von Estorff.

"You! You devil! Is it really you? What are you doing here?" he hissed at the German. "You traitor! You promised us our freedom. And just the following day you fetched us and brought us here. You are pigs!" Zacharias spat at Von Estorff. The guard lifted his rifle.

"No!" ordered Von Estorff.

The alarmed soldier lowered his rifle.

"Please leave us alone. I will call if I need your assistance," said Von Estorff.

"Go on, out with you!"

"Sit here Zacharias. On this chair. Please."

Von Estorff pulled out one of the two chairs in front of his desk. He sat on the other.

"Now what's with all this friendliness, after your treachery? After you have wiped out my whole family and half of Namaland as well, here in your slaughterhouse? What's this now? Do you first want to have a good look at me before you also hang me or let me drink more of the doctor's poison?"

Von Estorff listened to the Herero prisoner's accusations with bowed head. He lifted both his hands.

"I am guilty, Zacharias, guilty. I don't deny it. Everything you say is true, every word. But I didn't know...".

"You did not know! You swine! Didn't you know when they cut my balls to pieces? When they fed us the poison? When they hanged my people every second or third morning? When you let our women and children die of hunger? You say that you didn't know. I sat there in that dark hole and I knew everything going on here, and God also knew, but you say you didn't know? What exactly do you mean, you German pig?"

Zacharias was breathing fast. It was dead still in the office.

"I will have to live with this for the rest of my life, Zacharias. God knows, I will have to. That will be my punishment, but all I wish to do, all I want, is that you must know, that I really did not know. That is the truth. *Oberst* Von Deimling betrayed me. I believed you would be allowed to return home. I did not intend to deceive you. My commanding officer deceived me. I had no choice but to carry out his instructions," Von

Estorff said. "Up to the day I spoke to you, I really believed I was telling the truth. The command to arrest you came through the next day."

"And what about this place? This slaughterhouse of yours? Didn't you know about this either? All the time you were here, how long has it been? Didn't we arrive here at the same time?"

"Yes, and no. I mean yes, we did arrive here together, but no, at first I did not know what the plan was with this place. But yes, I did find out later. By then it was too late."

"Too late? For what? For all the hundreds of people who perished here? Yes, for them it was too late, but for you? For you it was the right time. Looks like they now promoted you to the rank of *Hauptmann*. It wasn't too late for that!"

"Zacharias, I say to you again, I am sorry. I never intended to bring you here. I also do not expect you to forgive me, but…"

"But what?"

"All that I want to say is that I never knew…".

"Yes, and when you found out, what did you do then?"

"What could I do? Write a letter and complain to the very people who gave me my orders? Report them? To whom? All I did was to try and protect you personally and to carry out my orders."

"Oh yes. Like the time they slashed open my balls? Thank you for that protection, *Hauptmann* or *Leutnant* or whatever the hell they call you now."

"Ludwig," murmured the German.

"Well, thank you, Ludwig, for looking after me so well. Thank you. And thank you for letting my friends be hanged one by one, and for letting the others starve to death. Thank you very much."

"I did not know what kind of experiments the doctor was doing. I was glad when he came here, because they said the Kaiser himself gave the orders for the hospital to be built. But when I found out what kind of hospital it was, well, all I could do was to say they had to leave you and keep you in a separate cell. That was all I could do."

"And all the others had to die? Just as long as your conscience was soothed by keeping me alive. It was alright for the others to die! Tell me *Hauptmann*, Ludwig, how many of my people perished here? How many?"

Von Estorff remained silent.

"So, tell me, how many?"

"I don't know. It is official policy not to keep count."

"Official policy? Why? Because we are animals? Less important than whites? Is that why it was not important to keep a record?"

"Zacharias, I am tired of this place. I have been transferred and all I can still do is to ensure that you are treated well. That I will do, I swear it. I think this war is almost over. Then you can all go home. But I will speak to my successor to ensure you receive only the best treatment."

"The last time I believed you was the last time. To me it doesn't matter any longer. It is too late, I have lost everything. There is nothing left."

"Zacharias, I promise you, in the name of everything that is good and true, I will close this camp after I have taken over final command. I promise."

Shark Island never changed. The new commander, Stuhlmann, still bent his knee to Dr Fischer's programme. The doctor remained untouchable, the Kaiser's favourite. The experiments to develop new medicines and contraceptives had their sponsors in Switzerland writing out huge cheques, but Dr Fischer was more interested in his racial and genetic studies, convinced that he had unearthed a great truth. These copper-coloured individuals were the missing link between man and animal. What huge implications this had for the world!

The daily removal of bodies by mule wagon was an embarrassment and raised uncomfortable questions. The soldiers buried the corpses below the high water mark under cover of darkness. High tide uncovered some of the bodies, but fortunately there were more and more sharks, thanks to all the whaling boats in the harbour.

One of the soldiers came up with the idea of feeding the bodies directly to the sharks from the island. The secret was not to toss too many bodies into the sea at once. It also helped if the bodies were cut into smaller pieces and then thrown into the sea. There were many prisoners to do this work.

The strongest were selected for this task. They had to take the bodies to the feeding place, cut them up and then hurl the legs, arms, heads and torsos into the sea, piece by piece.

The feeding spot attracted more and more sharks until the water boiled. Some sharks leapt halfway out of the water, jaws wide open, displaying row upon row of white serrated teeth. Now and then they jumped out of the water completely, exposing their whole bodies. When there were lots of sharks, the soldiers allowed the prisoners to toss in whole bodies. Then the sharks did the dismembering themselves while the Namas had to witness how their friends, children, parents and family were turned into fish fodder.

No one except Magdalena believed it was Great Snake.

Fischer required more skulls and brains for his research. He ordered the soldiers to bring the bodies of the condemned prisoners directly to his examination room after the executions. There he decapitated the bodies and carefully opened up the skulls with a special electrical saw he had brought with him from Germany. He removed the brains skilfully, transferred them into special bottles filled with formalin, and marked them carefully. Hundreds of bottles containing organs would be shipped back to Germany to determine what side effects resulted from the various experiments he had carried out. The bottles included those containing the organs of little Hendrik and Martha Fredericks, the healthy, perfect control organs without which any of his research was useless, particularly since this was a new species.

To strip the skulls properly till they were completely bare of flesh, was a time-consuming and unpleasant task. When he instructed the soldiers to clean the skulls, they refused, knowing it was an unlawful instruction even a German soldier could disregard. Before, Fischer had boiled the skulls of the two Fredericks children himself, but now he was too busy. The soldiers commandeered a group of Herero and Nama women to clean the skulls. They gave the heads and shards of glass to the women with the order to remove the soft tissue from the bone. The women sat next to the water, discarding the small pieces of flesh, skin and eyes into the water where the small fish could fight over it.

Some of the women went mad. One ran straight into the sea. She was soon ripped apart. Two lay on the ground and screamed incessantly. One just sat, folded her arms around her knees and swayed to and fro while she wept, for days on end. The soldiers locked them up until Fischer could decide how to handle the problem.

Magdalena offered to help when she saw the women's terrible suffering. She sat to one side and hummed the previous night's Psalm. She scraped and scraped until her skulls were as white as snow. She kept the craniums that had been cut open to one side and scraped the jawbones till they were immaculate, without causing the teeth to fall out. If one did fall out, she would put it back neatly, without losing a single one. She also made sure that each cranium was matched with the correct jaw. The soldiers thanked and praised her for a job well done.

"'Charias, 'Charias," whispered Cornelius in the dark.

"What's the matter?" asked Zacharias.

"Water…" was all Zacharias heard. He shuffled on hands and backside over to where Cornelius lay. He saw that Cornelius was short of breath and that his mouth was wide open. Cornelius lay flat, his head askew. He choked when Zacharias tried to get him to drink from the tin cup. Zacharias picked up Cornelius's head and shifted underneath him. He sat with Cornelius's head in his lap and trickled drops of water from his fingers into Cornelius's mouth.

"Zacharias, remember those letters, for the little general. He will return, he will," mumbled Cornelius.

Zacharias was sitting in the same position when the first light of day crept under the door of the cell, his tears streaming down onto Cornelius's lifeless face.

The experiments with the new product for the treatment of stomach ulcers were not the success the Swiss companies had hoped for, but at least they had sponsored his travel costs, thought Fischer. He had been waiting a long time for this death. He had known about the children from the start and he couldn't have risked them becoming ill. He had to have perfect controls. It was necessary for the products' possible side effects to complete their full cycle in order for unambiguous conclusions to be reached. He couldn't intervene and terminate the subject early because this could give rise to criticism. At times the demands of research could be tiresome, as in the present instance. However, this death suited him well. His ship was leaving in two weeks' time and he could use an additional skull. The statisticians always demanded large samples. In addition, there was the issue of blood relationship with the children. He would be able to draw some conclusions regarding heredity now that he had all three skulls. Was the mother still alive, he wondered?

The soldiers brought Cornelius's head to Magdalena.

"Here is another one for you, *meid*. The last one. Clean it properly, just like the others."

Magdalena took the thin, shrivelled head into her hands and turned it round and round.

"*Cornelius sats ge? Toa go xawe. Hoara ti ûib ge rēba.*"[112]

---

112 *Cornelius sats ge? Toas go xawe. Hoara ti ûib ge rēba.* Cornelius is this you? It is finished. This is my whole life.

Later, while cleaning the skull, she wept and hummed a Psalm. She sang more and more loudly until she was singing and laughing and crying at the top of her voice. The other women stood at a distance and stared at the woman who had clearly lost her mind. Later she just sat there, stroking the skull softly.

"Cornelius, my little Cornelius," she groaned again and again, her tears falling onto the skull she was caressing.

33

Uncomfortable questions from the Cape Colony

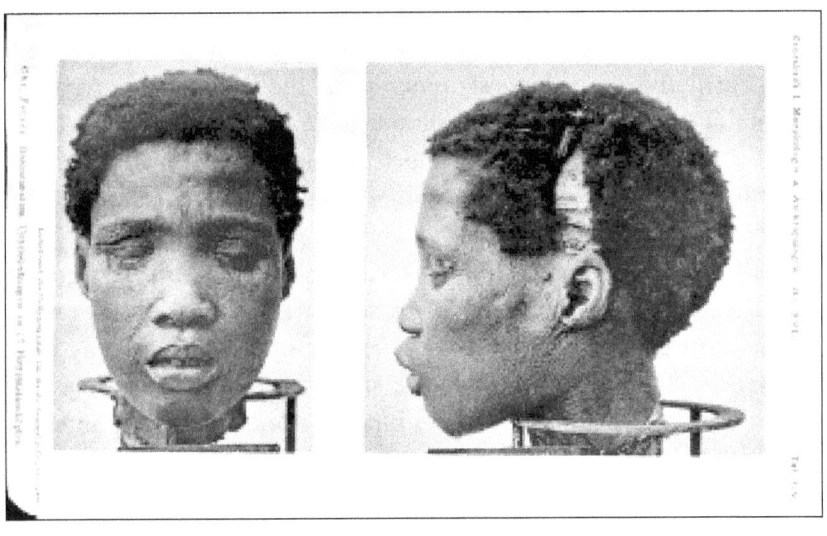

Photograph of Nama head from the Zeitschrift
für Morphologie und Anthropologie.

The young man walked along Lüderitzbucht's quay. His eyes darted everywhere, searching. He knocked on the door of the small church. It took a while for the door to open.

"Good morning, Father. You are Father Laaf, not so? Griffiths, Percival Griffiths of the *Cape Argus*. Pleased to meet you."

"Oh yes, come in please. I wondered when you would arrive."

Laaf looked up and down the street before quickly closing the door behind Griffiths. They talked until late in the afternoon. Laaf offered Griffiths accommodation in the outside room, the same room where Magdalena and her children had stayed. He asked Griffiths to be discreet by leaving early in the morning and returning only after dark.

That evening Griffiths wrote his first report, based on his discussion with Laaf. He handed it to Laaf for safekeeping.

The next morning he left early and strolled through the town again, avoiding eye contact with people. He wanted to remain anonymous. If his information was correct he was onto the scoop of a lifetime. Time and time again his eyes turned to the island, but all he could see were the double barbed wire fence and the low corrugated iron building. When he went closer, he also saw the guard house and the fence barring access to the causeway. He saw the low, round, brown structures in the distance and the structure at the highest point beyond the sides of the corrugated iron building. That must be the gallows, he thought.

His curiosity grew. He had obtained the news tip-off in the Cape. It had required a great deal of pleading to get the editor's approval and money to undertake the trip.

"Please remember Griffiths, Britain's relationship with Germany is fragile since the old Queen is no longer with us. She always, out of respect for Albert, ensured that her ministers remained on a sound footing with the Huns, but now it is different. We are not even entirely sure which part of the desert belongs to whom. It is not worth creating an international incident over sand. Even if they occasionally kill a few natives, do you understand?"

"I understand completely, Mr Symonds."

He was disgusted by Symonds's remark, but chose to say nothing.

Late in the afternoon Griffiths loitered around the harbour, trying his best to be unobtrusive and look innocent while asking questions. He walked up to a small fishing boat and introduced himself.

The fisherman tending his nets hardly looked up. "So what is this you want me to do for you, Mr Griffiths?"

"Are there fish in these waters?"

"Fish? Here? Now what do you think I, old Rooi Piet, am doing here? Because I am enjoying it? No, Mister, it is to put food on the table that I work here. And you ask if there are fish here? Let me tell you, this is where they invented fish, Mister. Plenty of fish here! It is the place of fish, crayfish and oysters, Mister."

"Oh, I see. And you say your name is Rooi Piet. Now, Rooi Piet, how much will you charge me if I ask to go fishing with you?"

The following morning before daybreak Griffiths was on the boat with Rooi Piet. He did not bother with fishing, but kept his eyes trained on the island.

"What's your problem, Mister? You just keep looking at the island."

"Rooi Piet, can't we go around the island a bit, to the other side perhaps?"

"No, Mister. That island belongs to the Germans. Nobody is allowed to go around the place."

"But then can't we go closer on this side? I would like to see what is going on there, please?"

Rooi Piet shook his head, but rowed closer. An enormous shark broke the surface of the water and stuck its head so high that even Rooi Piet got a fright.

Griffiths saw the hordes of people on the island and the low shelters they stayed in. They were made of canvas and fabric and had room for only one person. All the people were dressed in canvas smocks and even from a distance it was evident that they were emaciated.

What was going on here?

For the rest of the day he was seasick, while Rooi Piet pulled out one kabeljou[113] after another. He lay on the bottom of the boat and tried to think of ways he could get onto the island.

That evening he came to a decision. He informed Laaf of his findings. He wrote down all he had seen and gave the document to the quiet gentleman with precise instructions – just in case.

At sunrise the next morning, Griffiths pushed Rooi Piet's boat into the water. He knew it was theft, but he also realised it would be better not to involve Rooi Piet in this mission. Rowing was more difficult than he had thought the previous day. Soon his arms ached. He kept a constant lookout at the water's surface, fearful of the sharks, and it was not long before the first shark circled the boat. It swam away when he hit the water with the oar. The sun was hot on his back by the time he got close to the island. He saw no soldiers or guards, only the copper-brown people staring at him. He knew he would be a dead man if he set foot ashore. He rowed to the closest group of prisoners. The light south-easterly wind

---

113 *Kabeljou*: Fish of Namibian coast, erroneously called cod or salmon.

kept pushing the boat off course, and he had to row strenuously just to remain in one place.

"Morning!" he called out in a low voice when he came within earshot. He looked up to where he expected guards to be. Nobody replied and he rowed closer. He greeted them again and this time he received a few nods.

"My name is Percival Griffiths. I work for a newspaper in the Cape. I heard of this place and I want to tell the world about it. What place is this? What's going on here?"

The prisoners stirred and started talking to one another. After a while he saw them disappearing one by one, until only one remained, a woman.

"What's your name, Madam?"

"Magdalena, my Cornelius always called me. But he is gone now."

"Please tell me, Magdalena, tell me everything that's going on here. Please!"

Griffiths sat rowing in one place while Magdalena, almost incoherently, told of people who suffered hunger and such cold that their teeth rattled, and of a great snake that had devoured the body of her husband, Cornelius. She told of her children who had disappeared on the island. She kept on coming back to the people's heads she had cleaned so well that the soldiers praised her. Griffiths found it impossible to distinguish between the truth and the confused visions of a disturbed brain.

"Magdalena, tell me, do they hang people here?"

"Yes, sir, if they are naughty."

"Magdalena, do the German soldiers inject people here?"

"I think so, sir."

"Magdalena, did they rape you?"

"Many times, sir, until it no longer bothered me."

"Do you get food, Magdalena? Do you have to work? Do they beat you?"

After a while a grey-haired old man shuffled towards them. He had just woken up. He walked slowly and unsteadily up to Magdalena and folded his arms around her.

"Morning, sir. I am Samuel Kariko. I am the pastor of these people. Whatever Magdalena has told you cannot be worse than the truth. This is a living hell, sir. The living hell from which no one has escaped and never will. Sir, hundreds of people, no thousands, have died here of hunger and the wicked experiments of the doctor. Many have been hanged. This woman, and a few others, had to sit here, just here, and clean their husbands' heads which the Germans had cut off. With pieces of broken glass, sir. These people are prisoners of war, they are not thieves or murderers, sir. Their only crime was that they didn't want to give their land to the Germans."

The next moment four German soldiers with guns appeared behind the old man and Magdalena.

"Woman, listen. This is your last chance. Jump into the water and swim to the Englishman. Now, go!" Samuel Kariko said softly to Magdalena when he turned and saw the soldiers.

"Keinaus, my Great Snake, Keinaus, I'm coming!" Magdalena screamed and lifted her arms. She rushed forward, fell in the water, splashed with her arms, came up again, and then her head disappeared beneath the waves.

"Help her, help her!" Griffiths shouted at the soldiers while he tried frantically to row closer. "Help the woman, help her, you bastards! Don't just stand there!"

The soldiers stood frozen and watched the large fin racing towards her. The surface bulged and boiled. The soldiers and the Englishman stared at one another across the large red spot that was spreading all the time. Griffiths saw a small soap tin bobbing on the red water. He grabbed it from the water and rowed vigorously to the beach, away from the island. He looked for a deserted spot and aimed at a rocky outcrop opposite Penguin Island. There he wrote a brief report on his writing pad. When he had finished he remembered the little soap tin and inspected it from all sides. Inside he found a small bundle of papers, still relatively dry. He put everything back neatly into his pocket. Then he copied his report, word for word, and placed it in another pocket. He walked to the Post Office and mailed the report to his editor. The copy he kept in his jacket pocket.

After dark he made his way to his room. Within five minutes Father Laaf knocked on the door. Griffiths handed him the copy of his report, with clear instructions. Just after midnight Griffiths heard voices outside his door. Father Laaf was protesting but was powerless against the twenty soldiers who led Griffiths away, in handcuffs.

34

A difficult affair in the colony of the Germans

Jakob Morenga

A cloud of gloom hung over the Groote Schuur estate and the office of Dr Leander Starr Jameson, Prime Minister of the Cape Colony. This morning's news had upset him.

The first news was from Gordonia:

A patrol of German *Schutztruppe*, tracking a group of Hottentots, crossed the border into the Colony. The local commander of the colonial police confronted the Germans, but the Germans complained that the

British were not doing enough to check the cross-border insurgency of the Hottentots into German South–West Africa. The British commander drove the Germans out of the Colony. He then went after the Hottentots and requested them to accompany him. They are now in a temporary camp near Prieska, awaiting the release of their leader, one Jakob Morenga, who has been detained in an internment camp for the past month. The Hottentots want to take him back to German South-West Africa. He appears to be some kind of hero amongst his people who are waiting all over the south of German South-West Africa for his return.

The German Consul-general, Dr Dieter Humboldt, arrived at Groote Schuur shortly after receipt of the telegram announcing the incident, to hand over a diplomatic note of protest.

"The German government would prefer that Morenga remained interned," the note stated.

"The audacity! It was they who had violated the border and now they deliver notes of protest," grumbled Jameson.

Less than an hour later the secretary placed another telegram on the Prime Minister's desk. It was a message from Father Emil Laaf, a preacher at Lüderitzbucht. It read:

"Highly confidential.

To: The Prime Minister, Cape Colony.

British correspondent Griffiths apprehended. Condition unknown.

Detailed report regarding German atrocities in concentration camp here mailed to the *Cape Argus*."

Jameson knew the first article had already appeared in the *Argus* that morning. It contained little information and was based on flimsy intelligence. What could there be in the detailed report that was of such importance that it led to the journalist's arrest? It was probably just a bunch of prisoners moaning and complaining. What else was new?

He thought long and hard over the matter, but remained undecided. He phoned the editor of the *Cape Argus*.

"Symonds, my friend. How are you? I read the report of that Griffiths chap of yours this morning in the *Argus*. What more do you know?"

"Prime Minister, only that there are many irregularities going on and that the Jerries are a bit cruel. You know, their usual thing?"

Two days later another telegram from Father Laaf arrived.

"Situation critical. Please contact Germany."

Jameson dictated a short note to Berlin in which he expressed his dismay at the border violations. At the same time he enquired about the British subject held in Lüderitzbucht. Late that night he sat alone in Groote Schuur. We should not irritate the Germans, he decided.

The following morning Humboldt was there again, highly agitated.

"Prime Minister. Firstly: the Morenga case. We have now been waiting a number of days for a reaction and still nothing has happened. When are you going to act?"

"Consul-general, please be patient. These people are interned near Prieska and they can go nowhere. Patience sir, please."

Humboldt took a sharp breath. "Secondly, Prime Minister: our government in Lüderitzbucht is detaining one of your subjects – on suspicion of espionage. He was caught spying on a military installation."

"What? Espionage? What nonsense is this? And what is his name? I assure you, Consul-general, I know nothing about it!"

Humboldt watched Jameson carefully. "His name is Percival Griffiths."

Jameson recalled the name of Symonds's reporter, but maintained a thoughtful silence.

"Well?" Humboldt asked, after a while.

"I know of Griffiths. I have known for a long time that you are holding him. I also know that he is not a spy as you allege, Consul-general, but a journalist of the *Cape Argus*. We also know that he possesses explosive information. Information that could cause great damage to the German Empire, Dr Humboldt."

Humboldt went white in the face.

"Prime Minister, if any further lies were to appear in the Cape newspapers regarding our programmes in German South-West Africa, we will regard it as an insult. My consulate will be closed. Your people will have to leave German South-West Africa and Berlin. Then you can forget about any cooperation between your Colony and the mighty German Empire and German South-West Africa."

Humboldt turned and stormed out of the office without another word.

The next day Jameson sent a telegram to Prieska: Morenga's internment has been extended. Griffiths was released, but the *Cape Argus* did not publish any further articles about his conversations with Magdalena and Samuel Kariko.

The following morning Father Laaf's cleaner found Griffiths's body in his room. It appeared that he had hanged himself, but the investigating officer studied the cut on Griffiths's face for a long time, before closing the file.

Later Father Laaf found a rusty soap tin containing a collection of small papers hidden underneath Griffiths's possessions.

In April 1907 Von Estorff, the new commanding officer of the *Schutz-truppe*, closed the concentration camp on Shark Island two weeks after Dr Fischer's departure. He had the inmates moved to the abandoned site at Boerekamp.

A FORGOTTEN PEOPLE'S LEGACY
AND THE POWER OF LOVE

35

A thing of beauty and a city in the Kalahari

//Khauxa!nas, fortress of the Namas.

The seasons came and went, bringing prosperity to Ernst and Andries's business under the guidance of Mr Mac's single watchful eye. They employed small groups of Nama refugees to cut grass because grass was their business. The land was teeming with horses and cattle which all needed grass. They transported it to the military camp at Keetmanshoop with one of Mr Mac's wagons and made good money.

Ernst soon learnt about bartering, and regularly brought goods to the Namas in the veld. He quickly realised he could make even more money if only he had another wagon. He knew he had to become independent as soon as possible and work for himself, but he was unable to do anything without money. So he saved and worked like a trek ox, step by step and penny for penny, day in and day out. Many a night he had to sleep out in the veld when they were too far away from Paradys. Sometimes, in the autumn and winter, they had to trek a long way to find good grass. Then they stayed away for days on end.

Ernst got to know the veld like the back of his hand, and learnt how to survive by living off it. He fell in love with the camel thorn and shepherd's trees, the sweet thorns, the rocky hills with the quiver trees, the deep crevices and secret valleys packed tightly between the Namib and Kalahari deserts. Every day he fell in love afresh with the golden light of dawn, the pale white heat of midday and the purple tints of sunset.

Ernst the hunter could kill a francolin for the pot with a carefully aimed stone. No kori bustard or korhaan was safe when he took out his slingshot. After good rains he ate *tsammas* and wild mushrooms.

Once, also after good rains, he and Andries trekked eastwards towards Aroab in search of grass for the soldiers' horses. Andries showed him some strange cracks in the ground. They dug under the surface and found a brown tuber that looked like donkey droppings. Andries told him these were called *!nabbas*. That evening they enjoyed this delicacy. Ernst collected a bag full for Ma Gertie.

They trekked further, right up to Aroab. Just after midday they saw someone on horseback racing towards them, but there was something about the figure that seemed strange. Ernst's mouth became dry and he could hardly move his tongue when the rider stopped next to them. He had never seen anything as beautiful as the sight before him. Struck dumb, he pulled his hat from his head and stuttered a greeting.

"Morning Missus, I mean Miss."

Regina Klube sat out of breath on her horse, laughing so that her white teeth flashed in the sunlight. Her thick blonde ponytail tumbled out from under her *Schutztruppe* hat. She wore men's khaki trousers tucked into her riding boots and a plain blue shirt.

The black mare stood still while Ernst rubbed her soft muzzle.

"What is your name? Excuse me, mine is Ernst Luchtenstein. We are collecting grass for the troops' horses."

"I am Regina. I work at *Hauptmann* Göttiger of *Haus* Streitdam here in Aroab. Let me show you where there is plenty of grass. Oh, yes, this is Heidi and she is mine," she said, rubbing the mare's neck gently.

Ernst could not keep his eyes off this wild girl. Andries, who had to lead Heidi, recognised the telltale signs. Ernst walked next to Regina, completely oblivious of his ox wagon. He stared at this vision of beauty with her lithe body, soft skin and pale blue eyes like the morning sky over Keetmanshoop.

"How old are you?" Ernst enquired, blushing.

"Fifteen, and you?"

"Nearly sixteen."

Regina told Ernst she grew up in Keetmanshoop as one of two daughters of German settlers. When the time came for the two sisters to go to school, their parents took them to Cologne in Germany. They were six and seven years old, respectively. After enrolling them at the school, their parents had to undertake the long journey back to Keetmanshoop. She and her sister cried so much that the teacher had to wrench them away from their mother.

From Lüderitzbucht her parents had to travel by ox wagon, just like Ernst and his family, but at Aus they both contracted typhoid fever, died and were buried there. The people of Keetmanshoop collected money to fetch the two orphans from Germany. She was then placed with *Hauptmann* and *Frau* Göttiger and her sister with somebody else, but they had not seen each other since. She told Ernst that *Frau* Göttiger was very good to her, but she had to work hard in the house. In the afternoons she could ride her horse and play until dark.

Ernst's life had changed in an instant. He gave Regina the whole bag of *!nabbas* he had collected for Ma Gertie and that evening around the campfire Andries teased him about his clumsiness.

"When you look into that girl's eyes you become like a *kierieboud*[114]. You don't look where you walk, you step here, then there, yes, you with your red shins![115]"

"Ag, Andries man! Promise me you won't tell Ma Gertie, please Andries?"

Late into the night Ernst tossed and turned. When sleep came he dreamt of the girl galloping towards him and racing clean past him without so much as a backward glance. The next morning Andries was up early and made a fire for coffee.

---

114 *Kierieboud*: Nama-Afrikaans for ostrich, literally: "haunch looking like a walking stick."

115 *red shins*: refers to the appearance of a breeding male ostrich's shins.

"Wake up, young lover!" he yelled in Ernst's direction. "We need to go and offload the grass and they are looking for more."

When they had offloaded their wagon, they immediately led the oxen back to the veld, in the direction Regina had indicated the previous day. A honey guide appeared and fluttered ahead of them.

"*Lek-ker, lek-ker, lek-ker,*[116]" called the little bird with the large bill and white throat.

"What is that, Andries?"

"No, I don't know it. Never seen it before. But I know that in Bechuanaland there are birds that show people where the honey is. He takes them straight to it. Then the people give some of the honey to the bird, but if you crook the bird out of his share, next time he will take you straight to Great Snake."

Ernst recalled Jakob Morenga's words.

"Let's follow the bird, Andries. Let's see where he takes us."

"Man, I am not keen on being stung by bees, Ernst."

"Oh, you're only scared of the snake. Come on, let's just walk a little way."

Ernst followed the honey guide. He whispered softly into the wind.

"*//Khauxa!nas, //Khauxa!nas, //Khauxa!nas.*"

The little bird darted around, flitting forwards and backwards. They followed him down an overgrown footpath, rounded a bend and saw a massive, steep rock face, higher than Keetmanshoop's church steeple, blocking the footpath. There was no way they could continue with the wagon and oxen.

They wanted to turn around when they found themselves staring down the barrel of a gun. A Nama with a wide-brimmed hat, bandolier over his shoulder and a red neckcloth was aiming a rifle at them. More Nama soldiers with rifles appeared. Ernst looked for Jakob Morenga's face, but realised it was a different group, unknown to him.

"What do you want here?" the leader snapped.

"We are looking for grass, Mister, and are now following the little bird."

"Who told you about the little birds?"

Ernst realised that this was a critical moment. He thought fast.

"Jakob Morenga, Mister, the Black Napoleon, it was him, Mister. One day I helped him to get ammunition from Mr Mac's shop at Keetmanshoop.

---

116 *Lekker*: Afrikaans adjective and adverb with multiple meanings, mainly indicating sweetness, pleasant taste, enjoyment and goodness.

That's when he told me. But he told me that I should come here if I…well, if I wanted to find out who I am."

The leader, a short, strong man with a big white moustache, a coppery-red complexion and strong forearms relaxed and lowered his rifle. "Oh yes, you are the little transport rider who works for McKay. Gertruida is a distant relative of mine. Come with us, leave your wagon here, one of my men will look after your stuff."

He stepped closer and held out his hand. "Simon Koper, pleased to meet you."

"Ernst Luchtenstein, and this is Andries. Pleased to meet you, Mr Koper."

One of Koper's men led them along the footpath, close to the rugged rock face. Ernst kept looking upwards and saw the pigeon nests and small shrubs clinging to the clefts in the surface of the cliff. They came to a thick, tangled shrub growing close up against the rocks. The guide drew the shrub's branches aside and motioned to Ernst and Andries to enter. They looked at each other and then climbed into a crevice concealed by the shrub. When they looked up they saw a small steep footpath twisting upwards between two rocky cliffs. They had to clamber up on all fours and pull themselves upwards by tree roots and branches. Simon Koper and his men followed behind. The curved surfaces of the two rock cliffs matched so closely that they formed a sort of tunnel. At the top two dirty brown hands reached out, took hold of them and pulled them up over the last piece of rock.

When the whole group was at the top, Koper's men formed a circle around Ernst and Andries. An elderly man, bent with age, with grey frizzy hair and a skin *karos* folded around his body, offered Ernst a calabash filled with a white, milky liquid.

"Drink!" commanded Simon Koper.

"What's this? Poison?"

The soldiers laughed. "To make you forget how you got here. It's the old man's medicine. It's not poison. Drink!"

Ernst closed his eyes and drank. The concoction was both bitter and sour, but quite refreshing. When he had swallowed, the taste immediately disappeared, in a way that was strange. He handed the calabash to Andries who looked at it suspiciously before taking a small sip.

"Drink, you tame *Hotnot*!" one of the soldiers ordered while the others laughed.

The old man with the skin *karos* went and stood on the edge of the cliff. He began to hum in a Nama dialect neither of the visitors understood. The old man babbled and gesticulated, pointing at the sun and making all sorts of gestures with his hands. When he had finished, he turned around and walked down the footpath with the soldiers and the two visitors following behind him.

Before them, the view opened up to a strange sight: a town built from stone and surrounded by a ring wall that extended to a sheer drop at the edge of the cliff. A mysterious aroma of burning herbs hung over the settlement. From these heights, the view stretched away in three directions as far as the eye could see, right into Bechuanaland. Below the rock face, on the opposite side to where they had left their wagon, Ernst saw a large water pool and a river feeding it on the northern side. Some of the stone buildings had thatched roofs, some had roofs made from animal hide, while others only had reed mats stretched across them. Chickens, dogs and children ran around everywhere. There were kraals with sheep and horses inside them. A big building stood in the middle.

Ernst walked to the ring wall.

"Watch out for the bees!" shouted Simon Koper.

When he got to the wall, Ernst saw many bees' nests wedged in between the blocks of rock.

Straight away Ernst understood the role of the honey guide and how it was natural that they would lead people to the bees' nests.

"These bees give us food and guard over us," he heard a voice say behind him. It was Simon Koper. "This place is the great church of the Nama nation, //Khauxa!nas. It is the birthplace of the nation. This is where the Afrikaners and the others before them came when they fled from the Colony across the Gariep River after the Pienaar business."

"What Pienaar business, *Oom* Simon?"

"Young people of today know nothing about history," Koper answered and spat on the ground.

"It started more than a hundred years ago, in the Cape. Those Hollanders put old Ram, the great-great-great-grandfather of the *Oorlams* in jail along with his son Afrikaner on their prison-island; Robben Island, I think they call the place. Old Ram's other son, Klaas Afrikaner, did business with a Boer, Pieter Pienaar, for many years. But Pienaar became difficult and crooked. He cheated Klaas and Klaas killed him. Klaas and his two sons, Jager and Titus with all their families and livestock fled to this place, //Khauxa!nas, with all the Colony's police after them. The police hunted them, without success.

"The Colony sent three expeditions. They never found the Afrikaners or //Khauxa!nas. When Klaas and Jager died, Jonker, Jager's son, became tired of the loneliness. He trekked north from here and established the place Winterhoek which the Germans now call Windhuk.

"It was here, at //Khauxa!nas where the Khoi-Khoin, our ancestors, lived a long time before they even saw a Dutchman. This is the place where Great Snake lives, down there in the water pool in the Bak River. He is still there and you must never swim in that water. He guards us. He and the bees. And this river is our river. It is the only river in Namaland that never dries up. There is always water here. But, the best thing about //Khauxa!nas is that the Germans don't know how to get here. They have tried, believe me, they have tried.

"As long as we live in peace with one another and nature, the Nama nation will endure, no matter what the Germans do. This is our fortress and the Germans will never remove us from it, no matter how hard they try.

"A few years ago the priest, Father Malinowski, came here and pleaded with Jakob Morenga. The holy man had a German with him, Lieutenant Von Koppy, along with six of his men. Instead of peace, Von Koppy only spoke about surrender. It was then that Morenga chased him and his six *Schutztruppe* away like troublesome pests. Not long afterwards another lieutenant, Von Stempel, with a hundred *Schutztruppe* came to apprehend Jakob, but they couldn't find their way here. You see, Von Koppy and his six men also had to drink the forget medicine before Jakob took them up, just like you. Jakob saw Von Stempel and his troops from afar, wandering on the plains, looking for the way to //Khauxa!nas. Jakob's men shot Von Stempel and three of his men. The rest fled. Von Stempel's grave is just down there. You will see it when you go home. If you remember.

"From that day onwards the Germans have been looking for this place. We often see them come and go. Some days I wish they would find us, because here they will not defeat us. We will beat them here, every time, because this is our place. Ours, together with the bees and Great Snake. If any stinking German dares to cross this wall, the bees will get him, and Great Snake waits below. This is the place we run to when we have been injured. When we become ill. When we are tired. When we are heartbroken. This is the place of the Namas' heart."

"And why don't the bees sting you?"

Koper laughed. "I am telling you of all these important things, and you ask why we don't get stung by the bees? You are weird people, you Germans."

"I am no longer a German," Ernst replied.

"Now what are you, then?"

"I don't know, but I think I am an African, a Boer. But why don't the bees sting you?"

"*Boertjie*[117], can't you smell? Don't you smell the aroma of the red *vygie*[118] that we burn? Every Nama who lives here burns the red *vygie* in his shelter and when we want to take honey from the nest we take a smoking branch with us and then they don't sting us. See all the small fires around us?"

Ernst looked around and saw the smouldering wood fires in the joints and grooves between the stones, at each shelter and all over in the ring wall. The smoke carried the strange aroma and calmed the bees.

"We have a meeting in a short while. Come, let me introduce you to some of the people. Come on, *Boertjie*," Koper commanded. He set off towards the large building in the middle of the village.

It was dark and cool inside and smelled of pipe tobacco.

"Friends, see what the south-easter has blown in here. A Nama-speaking German-Jewish *Boertjie,* with a Nama for a stepmother. No wonder he got lost. He does not know who or what he is."

The group of elders smiled from behind their pipes. "This is Ernst Luchtenstein, Gertruida McKay's stepchild, and this is Andries, his servant," Koper said.

"Good day, gentlemen," Ernst greeted them, with a little more confidence. Andries stood to one side, crumpling up his hat.

One by one the elders came forward and greeted him with a handshake. "Abraham Morris, pleased to meet you. My father was also a Scotsman like McKay, but my mother fortunately was a genuine Bondelswarts."

Everyone laughed.

"Johannes Christiaan, pleased to meet you."

"Wilhelm Ortmann."

"Dawid Fredericks."

"Klein Hendrik Witbooi."

"Abraham Rolf."

"These are the diehards, this lot. The last of the Nama heroes, the hope of our nation," Simon Koper explained.

---

117 *Boertjie*: Diminutive form of Boer, here used with affection.

118 *Vygie*: *Mesembryanthemum* species.

"I know Cornelius Fredericks, *Oom* Dawid. He is married to Magdalena. *Oom* Klein Hendrik, is she your sister?" Ernst asked, looking from one to the other.

The seven legends raised their heads.

"You say you know the Fredericks family, son? Then you are not aware that they have all passed away?" asked Dawid.

Ernst's ears buzzed. His heart became cold as ice and he trembled. "Are they dead? But how, *Oom* Dawid? What happened?"

"We have heard many stories, too many. We ourselves do not know what the truth is. But we do know that they have died. And their children as well. They were in the concentration camp on that island at Lüderitzbucht. Thousands of our people died there. Many worked on the railway line and just died there next to it. Others died on the island. There are many stories about the island. People say they hanged people there, women were raped, others were fed poison, some were lashed with sjamboks and there are even stories that Great Snake had eaten many of them, but we know he is here with us, down there in the pool in the Bak River. But, tell us what you know and how you know the Fredericks family."

Ernst told how he had been on the island, on his first day in Africa. He was hesitant to relate how the woman had saved him because he didn't remember it clearly. He also spoke of his last visit, when Cornelius was still in the land of the living.

"But where is Jakob Morenga? Why is he not here with you?" Ernst wanted to know.

"We are waiting for him," Simon Koper and Abraham Morris both answered together.

"The whole of Namaland is waiting for the Black Napoleon's release from jail. He was at first held in the jail at Prieska and later in Tokai in the Cape. The English freed him two weeks ago on condition that he never sets foot in German South-West Africa again. That dog, Von Estorff, issued a decree that he may not cross the Gariep River, but we know and every Nama knows and the Germans know: he will come. Can an oryx stop eating *tsammas* because the English made a law? Can a horse stop eating grass because the Germans commanded it? We are waiting for him. The moment he is here, all hell will break loose. We know Jakob Morenga. He will drive the Germans into the sea," Koper informed him.

"If I may ask something," Ernst began. "I was, as I said, with Mr Fredericks in the jail on that island not so long ago. I wanted him to tell me the story of how Namaland came under German rule. He said he was innocent and that he didn't shoot the nephew of the great German general. But the Germans decided he was guilty and they were going to kill him. And now you tell me he has died? Is there somebody who knows the truth?" Ernst looked each man in the eye.

"And for what reason do you 'want to know the truth', young man?" Simon Koper asked, slightly irritated.

"It's my mother, Mister, my real German mother. She wrote down the story, but she is dead now and I want to finish her work. She said the whole world should know."

"Come here, young man. What is it you want to know? I was there, with Cornelius Fredericks," said Abraham Morris, leader of the Bondelswarts, taking him to one side.

That afternoon Simon Koper and a few of his men escorted Ernst and Andries to their wagon and oxen. After saying their goodbyes, they trekked further, each of them lost in their own thoughts. Along the way they saw a grave and Ernst read the name painted on the weathered wooden cross. Von Stempel, was all he could decipher.

"Wonder who he was?" Ernst said.

"Never heard of him," Andries replied.

Later, around their campfire, they recalled the day and what had happened to them. It was as if the whole day was shrouded in fog.

"Must be the medicine of that old man," Ernst concluded.

"What medicine?"

"No, I don't know either."

36

The Black Napoleon returns

Jakob Morenga and two of his deputies.

The news of Jakob Morenga's release spread throughout the Cape Colony. He was a hero, a symbol of freedom, not only to the Namas of Namaland but also to the Namaqualand Namas, the Malays, the Cape Coloured people and even the Xhosas. They all applauded the colonial government for taking this courageous step. At long last something had united the country.

Berlin was not so impressed. Humboldt delivered one note of protest after another. Jameson sighed more and more deeply.

"Prime Minister, the Berlin government is deeply disturbed by the colonial government's action. It is proof of your insensitivity to the interests of the German people and the Kaiser. Moreover it is proof of the British government's lack of insight regarding the development of civilisation here in Africa. Dr Jameson, the time has come for you and your government to realise what we have to contend with on this continent. This is not Europe and these natives are not Europeans like us," Humboldt said in an accusing tone.

"But they are people, Consul-general, people like you and me," Jameson replied wearily.

"But that is exactly the problem, Dr Jameson! Can't you see? They are *not* like us. Just look at them. The noses, the hair, their culture, their hygiene. That is the problem you British have. You are so preoccupied with your humanism that you fail to see the plain reality in front of your eyes."

Jameson's face showed no emotion, but he wished the man would leave. "Dr Humboldt, I assume that the German government agrees with your point of view?"

"But of course, Doctor! In fact, this is not my point of view, as you call it. These are hard scientific facts, confirmed by our researchers. Our government supports the laws of science. Surely you know the maxim *Wissenschaft ist Weisheit* – Science is Wisdom? This is our only position, what we live by. We live in and through science."

"Tell me more about this research, Dr Humboldt. What precisely does it entail? Would you like another cup of coffee?"

"Thank you. That would be nice."

"Dr Jameson, our government has sponsored several anthropology research programmes in our colonies over the last few years and recently a number of interesting publications have emerged. New ideas have developed which are helping us to manage the colonies more efficiently."

"You do research in German South-West Africa, that we know. Where else, if I may ask, Doctor?"

"Cameroon, Togo, China and German-East Africa, amongst others. But you will understand if I tell you the results are confidential and to some extent, yes well…, potentially explosive by nature."

Humboldt choked a little on his coffee and cleared his throat.

"Doctor, I understand, but what is the essence of the findings? What are you trying to tell me?"

Jameson enjoyed seeing the way Humboldt shifted uncomfortably in his chair.

"Prime Minister, let me spell it out for you," he said and put his cup down on Jameson's desk.

"These natives are not people in the normal sense of the word, you understand, like you and me. They are different. Their tissues look different, their skulls have different dimensions, and their hair is different. They are simply unlike normal people."

"Really, Doctor?" Jameson found the conversation amusing, but he kept a straight face. "Tell me more."

Humboldt took a deep breath. "It is the God-given task of the German people to tame the wilderness and to bring western civilisation here. It is therefore necessary to wipe out criminal elements like this Morenga and his gangs."

"And their wives and children? What about them?"

"Dr Jameson, the history of the world sometimes requires people to make sacrifices in order to make progress. If it is necessary for them to go, then so be it."

"Tell me, Dr Humboldt, you have many missionaries there in German South-West Africa. How do you reconcile their work with the…well, the findings of your research? Is it not by implication a waste of time and energy? Should you not rather send the missionaries back to Germany or perhaps to America?"

Jameson struggled to keep his expression serious.

"Yes, the church problem." Humboldt sighed. "We are in the process of formulating a discussion document, but yes, I concede we have not yet managed to get full co-operation from the churches."

"Consul-general, you will have to excuse me. I have another appointment, but first tell me what exactly you want me to do regarding the Morenga case. Please bear in mind that he is a hero amongst the coloured population and at the moment they worship the ground I walk on for setting him free. How do you propose I handle the problem?"

"Prime Minister, it is simple. It is your choice. Do you want to build a future with this bunch of barbarians, or with the mighty German Empire with all its wealth and science? That is the question. When you have decided, then you will know what to do. As far as we are concerned, we do not want him to ever set foot on German soil again and if he does, he will be summarily shot. The Kaiser has put a bounty of twenty thousand marks on his head. We will pay that to you if he is shot in British territory. Concerning your political problem with the natives, it is the same as ours. As soon as Morenga is gone, calm will return. They will forget about their supposed hero when the country starts to grow and they find money in their pockets. Economic growth is what is needed, not dubious black heroes."

Later that afternoon Jameson issued an instruction to the commander of the police in Upington to keep him abreast of Morenga's movements. He also requested Humboldt to send an envoy of the *Schutztruppe* to Upington. Lieutenant Hahnfeldt departed from Keetmanshoop to Upington on the same day.

Jameson phoned Humboldt a few days after.

"Dr Humboldt, I am sorry, it's too late. Apparently Morenga crossed the border last night. We suspect he could be in hiding close to the Bak River in the south of your colony," said Jameson. "It is now outside our jurisdiction."

"Thank you Prime Minister. Just promise me one thing, please?"

"Yes, what is it?"

"If he runs back to the Colony again, please allow our *Schutztruppe* to assist you to settle the problem once and for all."

"Yes, very well then. Do what you have to do."

Jameson sighed and put the phone down.

Ernst and Andries saw the mounted commando from afar.

"Morning, son. Who is he?" asked the captain and nodded towards Andries.

"Morning, *Hauptmann*. This is Andries. And I am Ernst. We work for Mr McKay of the farm Paradys, close to Keetmanshoop. We cut grass for the Germans' horses."

"Oh, oh yes, the Scotsman with the one eye. You did not perhaps see any of the Nama rebels? We are searching for Jakob Morenga."

"No, *Hauptmann*. We haven't seen anyone," Ernst answered, quick as a flash.

"Good, but if you notice anything untoward, please notify the police or *Schutztruppe* at Aroab or Keetmanshoop. We think we know where he is heading. Go well."

The commando disappeared in a cloud of dust.

"That's the last thing I would ever do," Ernst spat out.

Minutes later Jakob Morenga and eight men on horseback appeared from behind a rocky hill.

"Aha, if it isn't my smuggler friend? It has been a long time. How are you?"

Ernst laughed. "Morning, Mr Morenga. I am very well thank you, and yourself?"

"The same, but tell me, what did those Germans have to say? Are they looking for me again?"

"Yes, sir. They asked if we had seen you, I said no and then they said we should let them know when we do."

"And are you going to do so, Ernst?"

"Never, sir. They will shoot you or take you to that island."

"Thank you, my friend. One day I will make you Minister of Transport," Morenga said, cackling with laughter.

"Mr Morenga, the German *Hauptmann* said they knew where you are going. You must be careful."

"Thank you, my little friend."

That night the wily Black Napoleon slipped across the border again. He wanted to join Simon Koper at *//Khauxa!nas* but realised it was dangerous and that his presence could betray the secret hideaway. He changed his plan. Twenty-two of his men joined the little band. It felt like the old days again. He knew he would be safe on the other side of the Gariep River, where he could order a consignment of weapons from Scotty. The time in the jail had softened him, so that he wasn't as sharp as he used to be. He wanted to speak the language of the veld, shoot and ride and drill his men before he took on the Germans again. This time he would drive the Germans into the sea, no; only to that island of theirs. They could stay there for a few years before boarding a ship back to Germany.

"Hallo Scotty, how are you?"

"Morning, Jakobus. Nice horse you have there. Where did you get it from?"

"Oh no! It seems I'll have to lock up my horse tonight. Where Bles comes from there are more. How many do you want? "

Scotty Smith, also known as George St Leger Gordon Lennox, was a man of many talents. He had qualified as a veterinarian in Perth, Scotland, but preferred to steal horses from rich people and especially from governments, either German South-West Africa's or the Colony's.

"You know Jakobus, the Colony's people are on your trail."

"Yes, Scotty, I know."

The two men discussed their business and said goodbye. The following morning Scotty phoned the police in Upington.

Forty policemen and Lieutenant Von Hahnfeldt surrounded Jakob Morenga and his men where they lay sleeping in between shrubs on the farm Eensaamheid. Along with Jakob Morenga, his brother, a brother-in-law and three nephews were killed.

The whole Nama nation mourned. Across the Gariep River in the Cape Colony huge anger arose over this betrayal by their own government. One by one the Nama captains left *//Khauxa!nas* and returned to their people in the veld…and a dark future.

37

Simon Koper –
an undefeated bittereinder[119]

The Kalahari expedition with Captain Willeke in
front on their way to attack Simon Koper.

Koper knew it was the end. What once had been the stomping ground of
his people, the *!Karakhoen,* the Fransmanne[120], now stretched across two
international borders. The governments of Germany and Great Britain

119 *Bittereinder*: Afrikaans for soldier who refused to surrender, notably during
the Second Anglo-Boer War, 1899-1902
120 *Fransmanne*: Equivalent term for *!Kharakoen,* literally meaning Frenchmen,
yet with no reference to men of France.

had not yet formalised the boundaries between their two colonies, German South-West Africa and the Cape Colony, but one thing was certain: there was no place for Simon Koper's *!Karakhoen*. Previously, the Fransmanne had roamed across the plains of the Kalahari, east of Aroab and *//Khauxa!nas*, across the area between the Auob and Nossob Rivers and further east towards Bechuanaland. They were hunters who lived off the veld. They could survive for months without water as long as they had a supply of *tsammas*, the wild cucumbers the oryx loved so much. The *tsammas* were their water and their food. Their movements depended on nature's *tsamma* harvest. After good rains they could roam far and wide, slaking their thirst with the fruity juice, but when it was too dry or too early in the *tsamma* season the scarcity of *tsammas* forced them to stick close to the watering holes.

"Good morning Consul-general. What is it this time?"

Jameson sighed and moved the documents on his desk aside without meeting the German's eyes.

"Good morning Prime Minister. Thank you for the opportunity to see you this morning. It is my pleasant duty to convey to you the Kaiser's congratulations," said Humboldt.

"Oh, and what for, if I may ask?"

"Your handling of the Morenga case, naturally Dr Jameson!"

"Oh yes, that." Jameson looked up briefly and busied himself with his documents again. "Anything else, Consul-general?"

"To tell the truth, Prime Minister, there is something else. We are still experiencing problems with a few Hottentots who regularly cross the border into German South-West Africa and rob our settlers."

"So why don't you catch them, Dr Humboldt?"

"Well, Prime Minister, the problem is that the border has not yet been surveyed. Our *Schutztruppe* do not know where they can and cannot operate."

"That apparently did not stop your *Schutztruppe* from pursuing Morenga when he took refuge in the Colony, or did it, Dr Humboldt?"

Jameson regarded Humboldt with an icy stare and thrust his chin forward. "Are you asking us to do Germany's dirty work again? Wasn't it enough that we eliminated Morenga for you?"

"No, Dr Jameson. It is only that the eastern border between the two colonies is not clearly demarcated. From time to time our soldiers may find themselves in British territory. Unwittingly, of course."

"Of course. Naturally, unwittingly, Dr Humboldt. But tell me, who are you looking for these days? Another Black Napoleon?"

"No, Dr Jameson. That was Morenga. The person we now are looking for is Koper, Simon Koper. He is one of the last diehards."

Dr Leander Starr Jameson was relieved when the door closed behind the Consul-general. The arrogant German irritated him.

Aroab Captain Friedrich von Erckert, commander of the *Schutztruppe* in the north of Namaland, was testing Lieutenant Oberg's latest camel saddle. Von Erckert had developed an obsession. If there was one person he hated, it was Simon Koper, the Nama captain of the Fransmanne. The war against the Namas was supposed to have ended a long time ago, but Koper persisted with his raids. They mainly kept to the Kalahari Desert across the border to the south-east in the Cape Colony, or to the northeast in Bechuanaland, but regularly carried out incursions into German South-West Africa. Just recently Koper had attacked and robbed a wagon at Hoachanas and a week later another at Kowi-se-Kolk. Von Erckert had initially posted *Schutztruppe* at each watering hole but they never encountered a Fransman there. These Namas survived without water. He hated them, because they had the audacity to challenge the might of the German Kaiser and thus made a fool of him, Von Erckert.

Von Erckert came to the conclusion that the only way to take action against Simon Koper would be to pursue him to the ends of the earth. The problem was water. Normal people, like his *Schutztruppe*, became constipated from eating *tsammas* and there was simply no water where Simon Koper was hiding. Von Erckert decided that a large camel patrol was the only way around the problem.

Von Erckert dismounted slowly from the camel and walked around the kneeling animal.

"Very good work, Oberg! Very nice."

"Thank you, *Hauptmann*. I also thought so."

"How are you progressing with the camels? Will they be trained in time?"

"Yes, *Hauptmann*. It just takes time."

"Well, *Leutnant*, the success of this operation depends on the camels. Without them we will never get into that desert."

"How much time do we have, *Hauptmann*?"

"We need to wait for the *tsamma* supply to be depleted, *Leutnant*. The Hottentots would then have to remain close to water. I am planning to pursue them with the camels at full moon in March next year. By April, the next *tsamma* harvest will be ready again and then we would have lost our chance. You have exactly four months to prepare the camels and saddles."

"Very well, *Hauptmann*. That is in order. "

In his office von Erckert scrutinised the photograph of Simon Koper taken by a Cape policeman at Grootkolk. This short, brown little man was an enemy of the Kaiser, an illiterate barbarian who challenged and undermined the might of the German forces. He, Von Erckert, would shoot him without batting an eyelid.

He planned and worked day and night on his operation without rest or sleep. By the end of January, his preparations were almost complete. All he had to wait for was the full moon in March – and grass. The camels needed grass.

"*Hauptmann*, there is a young German boy who cuts grass around here to supply our camp at Keetmanshoop. I will ask our patrols to find him."

"Thank, you *Leutnant*. Do what you must. We simply have to be ready in a month's time."

Ernst and Andries trekked all over the Aroab region. There was good grass to be harvested as well as the added attraction of the wild girl, Regina Klube, on her horse. In the mornings she had to work in *Haus* Streitdam, but in the afternoons she saddled her horse and rode into the veld, following the wagon tracks. When Ernst heard the sound of her horse's hooves or saw the plume of dust on the horizon, his heart leapt in his chest, his throat became dry and he forgot about cutting grass and driving oxen. He left the whip on the wagon and waited for Regina and Heidi. Andries watched the two young lovers and grumbled to himself that he had to cut grass alone while they took long walks along the rugged ridges.

When the *Schutztruppe* stopped next to the wagon, Ernst thought they were in some kind of trouble.

"Good morning. How can I help?"

"We need grass, plenty of it. *Hauptmann* von Erckert Aroab sent us."

"Yes, well, you know the grass is scarce this year and we need to supply Keetmanshoop," Ernst hedged.

"The *Hauptmann* will pay extra if you bring us the grass."

"What is the urgency?"

"Secret operation. In a month's time."

"Oh, I see."

This turn of events was a bonus to Ernst and Regina. He did not need to travel to Keetmanshoop with his loads of grass. His market was right here, almost at Regina's front door. Aroab. They saw each other every afternoon and the love between them grew. Later Regina helped to cut grass. At dusk she saddled Heidi up and rode back to *Haus* Streitdam.

It did not take long for Ernst and Andries to fathom what the objective of the secret operation was. It was to catch or kill Simon Koper. While offloading one load of grass after another at the camel camp, Ernst's thoughts veered in several directions. He often thought of Cornelius and had heard about Morenga's death. Now the same fate awaited Simon Koper. And here he was assisting the *Schutztruppe* in their hunt. He knew it was wrong. How could he sell Simon Koper's life for the money he made out of the grass? He considered not returning to the camel camp Aroab, but in the eyes of the Germans it would be wrong, even treasonable to do so. Was he not a German? What was he? On whose side was he? Who was he? Regina's stepfather was a German police officer. If he worked against the *Schutztruppe*, would that be a betrayal of her, or not?

It was not difficult for him to make up his mind.

"Andries, we have to warn Simon Koper," Ernst said one evening as they sat next to the campfire.

"Hau, what are you saying? This isn't our war. I don't want trouble with the Germans. They are the ones that put the jam on my bread, you understand?"

"Andries, you can go home if you wish, but I am going to warn him. Or help. Or something."

Andries sighed. He knew his friend. He saw trouble ahead.

Ernst and Andries's network of Nama grass harvesters had also expanded, but the Namas knew nothing about Koper. Whenever Ernst asked any questions about him their only response was to remain silent and stare at their shoes. The Namas were tired of fighting, tired of fleeing, tired of just surviving and tired of struggling. They had built their last hope on the Black Napoleon and that had also been blown away by the east wind. They now only wanted to survive, eat, sleep and drink, even as slaves if need be. They had lost everything, they who had been the first people, the real people, the Khoi-Khoin.

Something drew Ernst eastwards like a magnet. They cut and loaded grass further eastwards until they came to a stretch of veld that seemed familiar. They rounded a hill and came upon a lonely, open grave, partly overgrown, under a sickle bush. The wooden cross was old, but the heap of earth indicated that the grave had been dug open recently. They peered into the grave and shuddered. Down below, bones protruded through the sand. The name painted on the small rusted nameplate was still decipherable: Von Stempel.

Oh yes, that was the soldier that was killed by Jakob Morenga when the German patrol came looking for him at //Khauxa!nas, Ernst remembered now.

He knew they had to be close to the place or in the vicinity and he was on the point of whispering "//Khauxa!nas," when they noticed a small //haru-oms some distance away between the shrubs.

They walked closer, crouching beneath the low branches, and saw a bent, grey figure dressed in rags, sitting next to a small fire and staring into the flames. The dead eyes looked up, but past them. The old man was blind. He looked vaguely familiar. Next to him a human skull lay in the ashes.

"*Sakhom ge ra //khā //khā-aob tawede*,"[121] Ernst greeted him.

The old man nodded his head. Ernst greeted again and began speaking, but the old man held up his hand. Then he started humming, swaying to and fro while he chanted in a language that sounded like Nama yet was quite different.

Ernst remembered. This was the old man from //Khauxa!nas, who gave them the medicine to drink. After a long while the old man fell silent. Tears trickled down his cheeks. His nose ran.

Ernst and Andries exchanged glances. Andries shook his head. He wanted to get away from here. Ernst gathered all his courage. "//Khā //khā-aob," he began again.

The old man turned his head towards him. Ernst spoke about Simon Koper and the Great War and eventually asked him to warn Simon Koper of the danger. He spoke his best Nama, but did not know whether the old man had heard or understood him.

After he had kept quiet for a long time and while Andries hung around nervously, the old man started humming again, louder and louder. This time he groped around with his left hand until he grasped the skull and lifted it high above his head while he sang louder and louder, then got up and slowly walked off in the direction of the bush. Ernst and Andries followed at a distance, speechless with trepidation. After a while they

---

121 *Sakhom ge ra //khā //khā-aob tawede*: We greet you, Teacher.

reached a deep pool of water beside a high cliff. The water moved as if a large animal, fish, monitor lizard or other creature moved in it.

The old man turned towards them, spat on the ground and waved his arms wildly. Cruelty and evil radiated from his face. They both decided that they had had enough and turned back the way they had come. He did not want them here. That much was clear.

"Oh, my God, save me from this place. Take me far away from here," Andries groaned aloud. Ernst looked at him and sniggered, but nevertheless looked over his shoulder in the direction of the old man.

He narrowed his eyes. "What is that, Andries?" he asked and pointed in the direction from where they had just come.

In the distance they saw a brown column of dust, spinning in the air. A gigantic whirlwind raced closer, became larger and directed itself towards the old man, and hovered over the place. They stared at the spectacle from a safe distance. Then the column sped away again. It was all over.

"Let's go and see, Andries."

"You're mad, Ernst."

"Very well then, I'll go by myself."

"*Ai*, Ernst."

Andries followed behind his friend. At the place where the *//haru-oms* and the water had been, there was nothing now, not even the water. Only a dry mud pool remained. The column of wind had taken everything. The old man was gone as well. Everything was gone. They got away from there as fast as their legs could carry them.

Late in the afternoon of 7 March 1908, nearly four hundred *Schutztruppe* with some one hundred servants, seven hundred camels, two horses, five mules, eleven riding oxen and four machine guns under the command of Captain Friedrich von Erckert departed from Arahoab[122], north of Aroab, eastwards, towards the Kalahari.

Von Erckert could hardly contain his excitement. He had been waiting a long time for this opportunity to destroy these barbarians. He divided his commando into two companies. *Hauptmann* Grüner led the Auob section, the sharp end of the operation, and *Hauptmann* Willeke the Nossob section, the support troops.

---

122 *Arahoab*: Present day Aranos.

Two days after their departure from Aranos the Fransmanne shot and killed Sergeant Jaeger and six men in an ambush. The Namas fled back to their base in the Kalahari, making a fatal mistake: they left clear tracks behind.

Von Erckert called Grüner.

"*Hauptmann* Grüner, I think we are on British soil now. We cannot delay too long. This is the moment we have been preparing for. From here on there will be little time for rest. Do you understand?"

"Yes, *Hauptmann.*"

Grüner's section departed and waited at Grootkolk for Willeke to arrive. From Grootkolk Von Erckert sent out scouts. They returned with good news.

"*Hauptmann*, we found the tracks of the Namas who massacred Jaeger's section. They went past here, up ahead, back eastwards."

"Excellent. They will lead us to their leader's camp. Now we have them."

"Look, Simon! A light flare!"

Simon Koper saw the flash of light across the dark sky. The Germans were after him again.

"Go and see how many they are. Quickly now. Don't shoot," Simon ordered.

An hour later the two scouts were back.

"It's a small group. Six of them, on camels."

"Oh, then I'm going to sleep for a while. I want to be in Bechuanaland by early morning. There are no *tsammas* around here. You need to remain here with the rest of the people until I find water or *tsammas.*"

Simon Koper slept restlessly. In his dreams something like a blind old man warned him to get away from here, but he was reluctant to leave the others behind. There were too few *tsammas* for all. He would have to locate a supply before he could let the rest of his people join him.

Simon's commando of approximately forty men had gone quite a distance by the time the first shots were delivered. At first light the Germans opened fire on the sleeping Namas who had remained behind in the camp.

Von Erckert led the advance party. Fifteen minutes into the battle, a Nama round silenced him forever. Lieutenant Ebinger and ten more German soldiers fell as well. Fifty-eight Nama soldiers died, but at least twenty-five escaped. They followed their leader into the desert of Bechuanaland.

"One small matter, Prime Minister," Humboldt said.

"Yes, and what might that be?" sighed Jameson.

"Germany is delighted that Simon Koper now lives in Bechuanaland. We earnestly hope that he and his people never come back. We are prepared to pay an amount of four thousand marks per year so that he remains there. But there is one condition: Simon Koper must never know where his four thousand marks come from each year. Will you arrange for him to receive the money, Prime Minister?"

Jameson could not help laughing out loud.

"Certainly, Consul-general."

"Another thing, Prime Minister."

Jameson sighed again.

"Yes?"

"The press must also know nothing about this. Please."

"But of course not, Consul-general.

Germany never defeated Simon Koper.

38

A son parts from his father

Joseph Luchtenstein

Ernst immediately noticed the strange wagon arriving at Paradys.

"Do you know that wagon, Andries?"

"No."

"But Andries, that's Father's wagon, look there."

Ernst frowned, wondering what this could mean.

In the front room everything was quiet. Gertruida sat upright, staring at the floor. Opposite her sat Joseph Luchtenstein in an armchair next to her husband.

"Hello Ernst!" Gertruida called out when he came through the door.

"We heard you were on the way," said Mr Mac.

"Hello Ma Gertie. Hello Mr Mac. Hello Father."

Ernst looked from Gertruida to his father Joseph.

"Hello, Ernst. You must go and get your things. I have come to fetch you. And that woman is not your mother, do you hear? I am your *Vater*, understand?"

Ernst was completely taken aback.

"But…but why? I live here with Ma Gertie and Mr Mac. I don't want to…"

"Don't want to what, young man? Come on, get your stuff, I've been waiting for you all day."

Ernst at stared at the McKays, his eyes full of unspoken questions, but they both avoided looking at him.

"I purchased a farm close by. As soon as I have built a house, I will fetch Charlotte as well," stated Joseph.

Late that afternoon the wagon drew up at the camp of Hariros, Joseph's new farm, which consisted only of a tent, a drum of water and a fireplace. Andries came too, refusing to let Ernst go alone.

"Very well, *Hotnot*, but I cannot pay you," said Joseph.

Hariros was a magnificent farm, Ernst realised. It had excellent grazing for sheep, cattle and also had abundant game.

Ernst became Joseph's slave. The old man ransacked Ernst's belongings. When he came across the tin trunk with the boy's money, he took the lot.

Ernst whiled away the days by thinking of Regina upon her horse. He did not know if he would ever see her again. Aroab was far away. His father drove him from early till late. He had no way of informing Regina of his situation. He felt as if he would go mad if he didn't see her again soon. Would she remember him, he wondered. Was she still staying at Aroab? Perhaps she already had another boyfriend? He often considered writing her a letter, but his elementary German from Tilsit primary school was not good enough for a declaration of love.

Joseph lay in his tent for days on end, drinking and coughing. Once he sent Ernst to shoot a springbok and gave him three rounds of ammunition. When he returned with the springbok but without the other two rounds, the old man was upset.

"What did you do with the other rounds?"

"Missed, Father…*Vater*."

Joseph grabbed the sjambok and tackled Ernst.

Ernst fled into the veld. He charged through the *swarthaak* and *sekelbos* without feeling the sharp thorns. The tears burnt his eyes and his body shook. What had happened to his life? Why did he tolerate it? He ran. Stumbled. Fell. Got up again, and ran blindly into the veld once more. He just wanted to get away. He had nothing with him, but he ran without stopping, without thinking.

Eventually he went and sat under a shepherd's tree, his head hanging down and his arms around his knees. Tired. Thirsty. His clothing was torn to shreds, and there were red scratch marks all over his legs. After a while his tears dried up.

Then he heard a well-known sound. As he looked up, he saw, right in front of him, a flimsy, crooked, wooden cross, a splintered Star of David knocked together with yokes and a small heap of stones. On the ground next to the wooden cross sat a *spekvreter* chirping its song. Some distance away he saw Amoskop and realised that his blind flight had brought him right next to his mother's grave. Close to the old wagon trail.

"I am sorry, Mother," he mumbled brokenly. "I am sorry, I am sorry."

He walked to Amoskop's watering hole to drink water in the coolness of the early evening, but returned to the shepherd's tree and the cross, where he kindled a fire in the way of the Bushmen. He stared into the flames and saw the copper sheen of the scratch marks crisscrossing his bare legs like Namaland's wagon trails.

Why did his wagon trail end here? Why did *Mutti* die here? Where must he go from here? When would he see Regina again? He became scared when he thought of her, of the roads they still had to travel. He recalled his mother's death and how senseless it was. And of Cornelius and Shark Island. High above in the sky he saw the moon's craggy face, like the scratch marks made by the sickle bush on his legs and he knew: human beings are cruel. *Mutti* was not like that. She was soft like the fresh, warm bread from Ma Gertie's oven, her voice like the whispering wind in the branches of the shepherd's tree.

He remembered his mother's concern for Cornelius and Magdalena and their story in his exercise book. He had to complete that task, for the sake of *Mutti*…and Cornelius and Magdalena…and this angry country…and Regina.

He slept peacefully without nightmares or fear, even when he heard the growl of a leopard in the distance. Early the next morning he walked back to Hariros.

Joseph acted as if nothing had happened. He sent Ernst to Keetmanshoop to fetch a wagon wheel. Ernst and Andries walked the twelve miles. On their return that evening, Joseph swore and gave Ernst a tongue-lashing.

"You idiot! Can't you see that it's the wrong wheel? Go back and fetch the correct one! Now!"

Ernst walked. To Paradys – and did not return again. Andries went with him.

At Paradys there was great joy. "If that man ever sets foot on this property again, I will shoot him, if you don't, Robert McKay!" spat Ma Gertie over her shoulder where she stood in front of the Aga stove.

Mr Mac just laughed.

Ernst's heart was filled with joy and his throat felt like the dry skin of a long dead steenbok scorched by Aroab's sun. He recognised the approaching horse and rider. The whip fell from his hands to the ground next to the wagon.

"I thought that you had forgotten about me, Ernst." She looked down from her horse at him. Ernst's face turned red and his breath got lost somewhere in his stomach. Fortunately Regina's face broke into a smile before he could die from embarrassment.

Regina dismounted and handed the reins to Andries. He knew it was going to be an afternoon of harvesting grass by himself. He didn't mind. He understood his friend's enchantment with this wild horse-girl with a smile as wide as the Kalahari.

"Hello! Yes! No! I mean, how could I, Regina? Sorry, it was my father. Let's talk about something else. It's been a long time. I came as soon as I could."

As they walked away, a quiet happiness surrounded Ernst. He knew he was in love with this beautiful creature of the veld, his Regina. One day he would marry her. But how would he tell her? And both of them were still far too young.

39

Love grows

A camping site east of Keetmanshoop

Ernst worked harder than ever and slowly but surely the bottom of the tin trunk disappeared under the notes again. Now and then they would rest up at Paradys to do some repairs on the wagon but soon they would be off again.

The harder he worked, the more he thought of Regina.

He constantly made his way back to Aroab. That was where his heart was. Andries objected that they had already denuded the veld of grass around Aroab. Every time Ernst saw Regina and Heidi galloping across the plains after a period of absence, his heart soared.

They shared all the details of their everyday lives, the veld, the oxen and the horses. Ernst had to stop himself from gazing at her too long. In the evenings when Ernst and Andries slept in the veld, he asked Andries about the ways of love, but the young Nama would only scratch in the fire with a dry twig.

"Ernst, those are the things of adults. We must work and make money. That's what we have to do."

One day McKay called Ernst. "How about it? Do you want to go on a trip with me?"

"As long as it is not to Lüderitzbucht again, Mr Mac."

McKay laughed. "No, no, no. Not soon again. In fact, never again. No, I want to fetch some goods in Windhuk."

"Windhuk! Yes! When are we leaving?"

Ernst's thoughts immediately turned to Regina. He had to tell her that he would be going away, but he was too embarrassed to discuss it with Mr Mac.

"Ma Gertie, I need to speak to someone, but please first promise me you will not laugh."

Gertruida's Nama heart beat warmly when she listened to the young man's plea. She was happy about her foster-child's young love.

"Don't you worry. Ma Gertie will make sure she knows the situation. But tell me, what is her name?"

They *trekked* for almost two months, but never lost a single animal. Ernst thought of Regina constantly. He dreamt of her and when he awoke she was still floating around in his thoughts.

One evening after Andries and the others had gone to bed, McKay told Ernst "I want to discuss something serious with you."

"Yes, Mr Mac?"

"Ernst, we live in strange times. The world is changing and I don't know what lies in the future. Things don't look good and there is a possibility that the Germans will take my farm one day. Because of Gertruida, you know. Because she is a Nama."

"But they wouldn't dare do that, Mr Mac. How could they?"

McKay kicked at a burning log in the fire. "No, I don't know Ernst, but weird things are happening. All I want to ask is this: you must promise me here this evening that when I'm no longer here, you will look after my children. And after Gertruida."

"I promise, Mr Mac."

McKay looked up at the heavens. "See how beautiful the stars are this evening. Is there still some whisky in the bottle, or should I open a new one?"

The day after they returned to Paradys, Ernst and Andries *trekked* eastwards with their wagon, oxen and sickles. Three days later, in the veld west of Aroab, two young people embraced each other for the first time.

40

Diamonds, grass and love

Lüderitzbucht before the discovery of diamonds.

There was a knock on the door of Jameson's office.

"Come in."

His secretary opened the door. "Mr Oppenheimer to see you."

"Please show him in, immediately."

Jameson stood up and walked around his desk to greet his old friend.

"Ernest! What brings you here? Welcome, welcome. How are things in Kimberley?"

The two men embraced each other.

"I have news for you Leander, great news, old friend."

"Take a seat, I am all ears."

"No, Leander, not here. The walls…you know. They have ears. Come – let's go to the club."

They went by coach. At the Cape Town Club everyone stood to attention. The two gentlemen were ushered into the private lounge where they reclined on comfortable leather chairs and lit their cigars.

"What is this great news, Ernest?"

"Leander, what would you say if I told you of a place where there are hundreds of thousands of diamonds just lying around on the ground?"

"Well, first I would tell you that you are lying through your teeth. Then I would kiss your backside."

Jameson shook with laughter.

"I came immediately. I received a telegram from a Dr Peyer. He lives in a small place in German South-West Africa, Aus, but he knows diamonds. He is convinced that the find is ten times bigger than Kimberley's."

Jameson raised his eyebrows. "Who else knows about this?"

Oppenheimer chuckled.

"In the Colony it is only myself, and now the Prime Minister."

"When are you leaving?"

"The ship sails tomorrow."

"If the rumours are true, buy everything you see, particularly the diamonds. Buy everything, land, horses, ox wagons, houses, shops, and diamonds. Everything. Buy everything you see," were Jameson's parting words.

The discovery of diamonds at Coleman's *koppie*[123] reverberated around the world. Germany's stepchild colony became a prized jewel in the Kaiser's crown. Fortune seekers from across the globe swarmed to the little town like flies to a carcass. Lüderitzbucht was bursting at the seams and the economy exploded. The Nama war was forgotten.

There were only three problems in Kolmanskuppe: too little water, too much wind and no labour. The town depended on the desalination plants in Lüderitzbucht for water. Labour had to be imported from Ovamboland, nine hundred kilometres to the north. The Ovambos had to walk for three months from Ovamboland to work at Kolmanskuppe. Against the wind everyone was powerless.

The country was awash with rumours. Prospectors hammered their pegs in everywhere. Great finds were made at Elizabeth's Bay, Pomona and Charlottental, all a stone's throw from Lüderitzbucht. The Namib Desert became the centre of the universe.

---

123 *Coleman's koppie: Kolmanskuppe* or Kolmanskop

All this passed Ernst by. He had no interest in little stones, however pretty they may be.

Paradys had a frequent visitor: Moses Rosenstein, but everyone called him the Wandering Jew. Nobody knew where he came from. He came every few months, stayed for a couple of weeks and then disappeared again. He always had a suitcase with him.

One day he told Ernst of a place where there were more diamonds than at Kolmanskuppe.

"They lie on the beach, right next to a large river mouth," he said. "Come with me, I will show you where and you will never have to inspan an ox again. That I promise you."

Ernst flatly refused. He would much rather go to Aroab.

The two lovers realised, without having to put it into words, that their individual paths were converging and becoming a single road.

Regina knew when she could expect him back after his trips to Keetmanshoop when he had to offload his goods. Then she asked to be excused from *Frau* Göttiger earlier and earlier in the afternoon. She saddled Heidi and galloped across the plain to the top of Kannenberg and looked eagerly in the direction of Straussennest and Brakpan, searching for a small cloud of dust that would signal Ernst's wagon. When there was nothing, she returned to *Haus* Streitdam with a heavy heart, only to follow the same routine the next day.

Ernst and Regina walked hand in hand for miles through the untouched and uninhabited hills and ravines of the Kalahari, while Andries loaded grass onto the wagon. They discussed the game and Regina's horses, and gathered edible plants from the veld.

Gradually Ernst taught Regina all about the secrets of the veld.

The years came and went. Ernst's little tin box became so full that he had to buy another one at Hesselman's shop. He knew for whom he was working and why. That made the long days and nights in the veld worthwhile.

The Wandering Jew left with a suitcase filled with diamonds. No one ever saw him again, but the legend of a suitcase full of diamonds, hidden somewhere in the Karas Mountains, captivated many hopefuls in search of a fortune.

41

1914 – 1916
Alone in the Karas Mountains

A painting by Johann Blatt, commisioned by Ernst
Luchtenstein in later years, showing the young
fugitive's hiding place in the Karas Mountains.

In Sarajevo a bullet hit Prince Franz Ferdinand in the neck and shattered
the hearts of two lovers in Keetmanshoop and Aroab.

In German South-West Africa German citizens everywhere queued to
register for military duty. The twenty-one-year-old Ernst had to report
at the German camp in Keetmanshoop. There wasn't even time to say
goodbye to Regina.

First he and Andries went for a last walk in the veld at Paradys. Ernst told Andries to bring along a sheet of old canvas and plenty of oil. They buried Ernst's Mauser in a secret place.

"If they shoot me, you can have it," Ernst said solemnly.

Andries grasped Ernst by the shoulders while tears rolled down his brown cheeks.

"No man, stop talking like that."

Ernst signed and put the pen down in front of the sergeant.

"Luchtenstein, go and have your hair cut. Then join the queue at the quartermaster to get your uniform. *Heil der Kaiser*!"

"*Heil der Kaiser*," Ernst mumbled.

In his heart he was a man of the veld, a Boer because he spoke their language, a white Nama, an Afrikaner, Jewish by birth, but from now on Germany would determine his destiny and perhaps cost him his life too. He was trapped in the tentacles of a web stretching to the war rooms and battlefields of Europe – another world, a world without dune larks, *spekvreters*, *skaapwagters*, honey guides, kudu and oryx. Without lonely, dry rocky hills, deep ravines and desolate valleys.

Scarcely nine months later the Supreme Commander of the German forces, General Victor Francke and the governor of the territory, Theodor Seitz, sat at a small table in the icy wind on the farm Khorab, with General Louis Botha, Prime Minister of the young Union of South Africa and leader of the South African forces. They were signing a simple document. All German troops were to lay down their arms and would be held in concentration camps until the war in Europe was over.

Ernst was not prepared to go to a concentration camp. He would escape. He knew exactly what he would do, and how, but kept it to himself. He remembered the stories about the camps in the Transvaal and the Orange Free State and what took place on Shark Island in Lüderitzbucht.

The train with the prisoners steamed southward, closer and closer to Ernst's world, past Komukanti, Okaputa, Otjikango, Okave, Heuningberg, Otjiwarongo, Erundu, Kaalkop, Otuwe, Omaruru, Erongo and Usakos. At Usakos they changed trains. Karibib, Albrechts, Vogelsang and Okazize. At Okahandja Ernst saw German prisoners of war behind a barbed wire fence, marching against a backdrop of rows and rows of bell tents and high watchtowers with Union soldiers armed with rifles: a concentration camp. No, never, never!

He saw workers in blue overalls replacing place name signs. Windhuk became Windhoek and Kolmanskuppe became Kolmanskop, Lüderitzbucht became Lüderitz, a sergeant told him.

The train whistled and halted at Windhoek, letting off steam. Hundreds of people milled about on the platform. The soldiers ordered the prisoners to get off the train. They were allowed to buy beer at the small café under the watchful eyes of Union soldiers.

On one side Ernst saw a group of women and children standing behind a rope barrier. They had large suitcases with them. A Union soldier stood with them, a file tucked under his arm and a pencil in his mouth. Ernst realised that these were German women and their children on their way to a camp somewhere. Something drew him closer. And then he saw her. Regina! He charged towards them, past the soldier who only shook his head and muttered something to himself.

"Regina! Is it really you?" he called out, his voice hoarse with disbelief and fear.

Regina's clear blue eyes focussed. "Ernst, what…?"

He stood in front of her and stared at her, oblivious of the other women and their children. Then he stepped even closer, took her in his arms and held her against him.

"All these months, all these months. Regina, you were all that kept me going throughout these months."

"Ernst, do you know how I longed for you? Where have you been?"

The soldier came closer. "Please, I beg you. This is my girlfriend. Give us a couple of minutes. Please?" pleaded Ernst.

"All right," he agreed. "Just don't try to run away."

"I promise. Thank you, thank you very much."

The soldier turned and walked a short distance away.

"Ernst, please come and meet my stepmother, *Frau* Göttiger."

The short, plumpish woman held out her hand. "I wish it was under better circumstances, young man, but I am pleased to meet you. Regina has told me all about you."

"*Frau* Göttiger, Ernst Luchtenstein, pleased to meet you, Madam. I realise that this is strange, but all I have been able to think of since I saw her last, was Regina and there is something I want to ask you now. Please do not laugh at me, but Madam, *Frau*, I wish to marry Regina. We have known each other for a couple of years. Do I have your approval?"

Regina drew her breath in sharply. "Ernst, what on earth?"

"Sorry Regina, I still wanted to ask you, but I just had to know. May I? I mean there isn't another man?" Behind his black beard, Ernst's face turned redder and redder by the minute.

"Young man," *Frau* Göttiger answered. "I understand. Believe me. Heaven knows, I understand. The war will be over soon and then you must come and visit us at *Haus* Streitdam. You know the way. You are most welcome, then we'll talk again."

"Very well Madam, and thank you."

"Ernst, but you haven't asked *me*, yet."

Regina enjoyed the moment.

"Regina, will you marry me, please?"

"I will, Ernst. Yes, I will." Regina's eyes shone. She clasped her fingers together and rocked on her heels.

The women around them stared openly at the little drama and a few tears were shed.

The Union soldier allowed the young lovers to walk down the platform hand in hand.

"How did it happen that you arrived here?" Ernst asked.

"We went on with our lives as usual. Housework, horses, everything. Uncle Bruno, *Hauptmann* Göttiger, reported the latest news at home every day. He had been expecting the invasion by the Union for a while. He was very despondent. Then one day Aroab was teeming with Union soldiers. They first went to his office at Aroab. They were courteous and allowed him time to pack up his files and books. They also allowed him to come home to fetch his clothes and say goodbye to us. Then he left with a group of other men. Apparently they will remain at Aus until the war is over. They think a couple of weeks, perhaps two months. I don't like that place Aus at all. Both my parents are buried there."

"I know," said Ernst.

He shuddered for he knew his train was also on its way to Aus, to the concentration camp there.

"And you? Why are you here at Windhoek?"

"The Commander of the Union decided that it was too dangerous for women on the farms. He, General Botha, said that he would personally see to it that we would not be harmed. He wants us to remain here in Windhoek so that everybody can see we are not being ill-treated the way the English treated the Boer women and children."

"Regina, I wish I could tell you of all the nights, the yearning of so many days and months, the loneliness and of the hopelessness of being a soldier. I wish I could begin to tell you."

"One day you must. One day you must tell me."

"Regina, listen to me. We only have a few minutes before the train leaves. Whatever happens, I am not going to sit in a concentration camp. When the train gets to Keetmanshoop, I am going to disappear until the war is over. Then I will fetch you. I will not wait a day longer than the end of the war. Promise me you will return straight home as soon as the war is over, promise?"

"I promise Ernst, I promise."

They kissed, while a few soldiers whistled and laughed.

He was alone again on the train, but now with a new dream.

In the early hours of the morning, just outside Keetmanshoop, he jumped off the train. He walked the short distance to where he and Andries had hidden the rifle and ammunition. With the Mauser over his shoulder, he walked south-east without stopping at the McKays. He did not want to expose them to the consequences of his escape.

Ernst walked to Schneitmann's farm Slangkop because he was thirsty and knew he had to get water for his long journey. He first walked right round the homestead, keeping to the dense *swarthaak* and *sekelbos* surrounding it, while carefully surveying the place. The farmyard was deserted. He moved closer with caution, saw nobody, and found the house locked. The Schneitmanns had also been uprooted by the war.

"What are you looking for, *Besembek*[124]?" he heard behind him. When he turned around, he saw the small, pathetic figure of a shrivelled old Bushman woman.

"Good afternoon. I am Ernst Luchtenstein and I am running away from the war. Where are Mr Schneitmann and the other people?"

"They all left. The war took them. The *Oubaas*[125] is in the camp at Aus and the old lady went to Windhoek."

"Could I have some water, please?"

"Sit here," she ordered. He sat down on Slangkop's veranda wall. After a while she returned with a calabash of water.

---

124 *Besembek:* literally "mouth like a broom." A rather rude name referring to an unshaven face.

125 *Oubaas:* term referring to master, boss, with the added meaning of an older man.

He drank slowly and looked at her. "Thank you. What is your name?"

"My name is !Oma. I am hungry."

Ernst realised she was the only person on the farm, waiting only for death. He could not leave her like this, but he also could not take her with him.

He went into the veld and shot a springbok with one of his precious fifty rounds. After the shot, he lay and waited to see if anyone would come to investigate who had fired a shot. Just after dark he slung the springbok over his shoulder and went back to the homestead. He put the carcass down in front of !Oma. She clapped her hands and laughed with an open mouth, displaying very few teeth. She disappeared around the corner and when she returned she was leading a thin, brown, long-tailed dog on a rope.

"Here, you helped me. Take the dog. He is very nice."

Ernst bent down, untied the dog, and picked it up. The dog began to lick him. Ernst realised that the animal was on the brink of starvation. He asked the old woman if he could take a piece of meat for himself and the dog.

"But you brought the meat. You can take everything," she said, laughing.

With the animal's head, its four feet, and two ostrich egg shells filled with water in his rucksack, he called, "Come, boy."

The dog trembled and hesitated, and then managed to gather enough courage to follow his new master, only to fall over his own feet. Ernst picked him up and tucked him under one arm, shouldered his rifle, slung his rucksack on his back and set off on the road he knew so well, into the darkness.

"What should we call you, boy?" he asked the dog. "I know, let's just call you Willie."

Willie nudged his nose against his new master's warm body. After a while he stopped shivering.

Ernst walked a couple of miles and then turned into the veld. When he was far enough from the road, he made a small fire. He placed the springbok head and feet, skin and all, into the hot ash. He unrolled his bedding next to the fire and slept with Willie in his arms.

Early the next morning he took the springbok head and feet from the ash and removed the skin. Willie was frantic with excitement. He trembled and fell over his own feet, while he waited for Ernst to give him some meat. Everything was eventually consumed. Afterwards Willie drank water stored in the ostrich eggshell from his master's cupped hand.

Ernst obliterated his tracks with a branch, collected everything and headed south, in the direction of the highest peak in the Great Karas Mountains, Lord Hill. He saw herds of ostrich, springbok and oryx, but he was too afraid to shoot. He could survive for another day or two, but he had to get Willie something to eat. He walked on, only stopping at a spring where he and Willie drank and where he filled the ostrich eggshells.

Late that afternoon, just after sunset, he shot a springbok. That night he and Willie had a substantial feast.

Ernst did not sleep well because he wanted to reach the mountains as soon as possible. Before sunrise they were on their way again. Willie was much livelier. He walked and trotted behind his master. When he got tired, he sat down and looked at Ernst. Then Ernst had to carry him again.

Lord Hill came closer. "Tomorrow evening we'll be there, Willie. Then we can rest."

The next afternoon Ernst and Willie climbed halfway up Lord Hill. The barren landscape of the Karas Mountains with their towering hills, massive rocks, deep ravines and dark gulleys rose from the land like an island deep out at sea. Everywhere Bushman paintings adorned the rocks where the small people had sheltered for generations.

There was still abundant food in the veld after the previous season's good rains. Game was plentiful. Ernst and Willie did not go hungry. It was seldom necessary to shoot, because Ernst used his slingshot to hunt *dassie*. It did not take long for Willie to master the art of stalking and catching *dassie*. One *dassie* was enough food for the two of them for two days. He slept against his master's back and warned him if a scorpion or snake came close.

At full moon porcupine was on the menu. The clumsy animals emerged from their holes and one blow to the snout with a *knobkierie*[126] settled matters. Then Ernst and Willie feasted on the fatty meat from the back of the porcupine.

Ernst set traps with a stick, a large flat stone and a long string. He placed seeds under the flat stone and waited. As soon as a guinea fowl or

---

126 *Knobkierie:* Primitive weapon or arm in the form of a walking stick with a thick, blunt end, used for bludgeoning man or beast.

francolin took the seeds, Ernst tugged the string, and their meal was secured.

Springs and pools with clear, fresh water were all around but he kept his ostrich eggshells full in case they had to leave in a hurry.

He came across an old kraal made from tree branches, with horsehair stuck in the twigs, signs of an old Nama commando outpost. He plaited the horsehair to make strong drawstrings for snares in the paths trodden by game.

On occasions he shot a springbok, steenbok, oryx or kudu, but he always fired only one shot. He knew that sound travelled far in the veld. One shot may sound like a breaking branch or a falling rock, but two or three shots in quick succession would give away the presence of a person.

The days and weeks became months as the seasons changed. He was alone with his thoughts and Willie's company, and with the image of Regina's face constantly before him. He knew he could live there forever with her at his side. He did not need other people. He was content to study the veld, mountain, animals, insects, stars and the orbits of the sun and moon.

His senses became so sharply honed that he could distinguish between the smell of klipspringer and duiker droppings. He became acquainted with every *spekvreter*, francolin, black eagle, Kaiserbird and *dassie* on Lord Hill. He searched for his old friend, the dune lark, on the slopes of the mountain, but found only one of its brownish cousins, and another one with a long beak. The dune lark preferred the hard life of the Namib Desert. Luckily the familiar old *spekvreter* with his little song and questions was always present to keep him company. When Ernst shot a fat springbok, the little bird joined in the festivities. Why were the *spekvreters* of the Karas Mountains so brown and those of the Namib so dull in colour, he often wondered.

He knew when and where every kudu would drink water. When he woke, he knew whether or not it would rain that day. He knew where to find wood for his fire when stocks dwindled. He only hunted to provide for his and Willie's needs. After he had executed two successful hunts on one group of *dassie*, he left that group alone for a month. Then they would rather look for porcupine or steenbok, or find a different group of *dassie* elsewhere. In this way he maintained a steady supply of meat for himself as well as for other hunters such as the black eagles, jackals, wolves, and the leopard whose tracks he came across now and then.

He would often sit and gaze at the splendour of nature until his eyes burned. One day, sitting like this, lost in thought, he took his Joseph Rodgers knife from his pocket. He opened and closed it several times. He studied the blade. After years of constant use and sharpening it was now a miniature of the original. Without thinking, he took the blade in his right hand as if holding a pencil, and with the tip of the blade made a thin cut in the rough skin of his left thumb. He watched the blood well up, fall down onto the rock in front of him and explode into one large drop with a dozen other smaller ones. The edge of the large drop was somewhat ragged, but the small drops formed perfect circles. Another drop fell onto the smaller ones to one side and then melted into the first large drop. He cut the end of a blade of grass into a sharp point and drew a straight line through the blood. Then he dipped the blade of grass into the second large drop that was still fluid and drew a line to the right from the upper edge of the first line. He wanted to curve the right end of the second line downwards, but the blood was finished. He dipped the grass in the drop of blood again.

He began to draw again where he had stopped, but the blood had already begun to coagulate. He compressed the cut in his thumb with the thumb and forefinger of the other hand to force blood from the cut, and let it fall a little apart from the other red drops. He dipped the blade of grass into the fresh blood to complete the letter R. He stared at the letter, with passion and pain in his heart and his eyes burning.

Visions of the glass bottles, the doctor's grey eyes, his words and Cornelius's face appeared before him. He saw the handcuffed prisoner with blood dripping from the cuts on his feet and falling onto the sand of Aus to be covered by the ceaseless east wind. In his mind's eye he also saw Andries sitting wordless and sightless, staring out in front of him across the Namib Desert. He saw the vulnerability of man, the brevity of his existence, the urge for survival, the longing for peace, the love, the fear, the hate, the selfishness, the greed, the desire for possessions and money, the eternal quest for the purpose of everything, for truth. He suddenly felt that perhaps he had discovered something of the greater truth, right there in the Karas Mountains.

The Bushman rock paintings reminded him that for centuries this country had witnessed the dreams, love, hate, procreation, wars, murders and survival of people, many people. He had become part of this eternal circle of life, here, where he was now. He saw the moon with its scratched face come and go, come and go. Yet the Karas Mountains remained undisturbed, eternal. Long after this war was over, he knew the moon would continue to sail over these same rough mountains, animals, trees and plants. Nothing would change, not even man's avarice and hatred. It would continue to come and go like the phases of the moon. At the same time he knew he had only one opportunity to make a difference to this relentless, routine of life. He realised that he could only do this through the power of the love that burnt in his heart and soul. That he needed Regina as a partner; she was the spark, the rudder, the fire, the blade, the *disselboom*, the *leiriem* of his existence. With her at his side, he could turn this country around and drive the momentum of the hatred and selfishness in a different direction. An old Nama proverb swirled round and round in his head: *A i tarita-i hoa-e //î-i !gasab di !ga kai re!*[127]

The mounds of game skins became higher. He used the knowledge he acquired at Paradys to tan them until they were as soft as velvet. He made a beautiful *karos* from *dassie* skins, but would Regina ever sleep under such a *karos*? He made a pair of kudu leather shoes for himself and a stock of whips – for one day.

From his hideout high in the mountain he had a view across the plains which stretched into infinity. He knew he would see any intruder or enemy long before they saw him, but nobody came. Gradually he became more relaxed.

It was another good year for rain. Ernst noticed something strange: it always seemed to rain in the same places while in others it remained dry. He also saw how, over centuries, the vegetation and the game had adapted to this pattern and how it had changed the appearance of the environment. In these ways his knowledge of the Karas Mountains developed and expanded. He knew no civilized person had had to live so long in this rough environment before he came. He recalled the legend of the Wandering Jew, Moses Rosenstein, who had visited Paradys a number of times. He was the one who had, according to legend, hidden a suitcase filled with diamonds somewhere here in the Karas Mountains, but he never gave a thought to looking for it. He would rather have a bag of potatoes or a bottle of milk than a suitcase filled with diamonds.

He had plenty of time to appreciate the beauty of the Karas Mountains, whenever he sat and contemplated life. He had no desire for money, the company of people or the life of luxury in Keetmanshoop, as long as

---

127 *A i tarita-i hoa-e //î-i !gasab di !ga kai re!*: May each of us become our brother's servant.

he was free and could gaze into the distance. Now and then he became rather tired of his unbroken diet of meat. Then he longed for Ma Gertie's sweet potatoes, potatoes and beans. Each time after the rains he looked for mushrooms in the veld. In April he found *!nabbas* on the plain west of the Karas Mountains, reminding him of his first meeting with Regina. Everything reminded him of her.

To him the sunset over Lord Hill was the most beautiful view he had ever seen. He sat for hours, Willie lying fast asleep across his feet, staring at the shades of blue and orange that lay like velvet over the hills and valleys while the night and its silence descended. Then the longing became intense and brought back the nagging questions of the war.

When would it ever be over? he wondered day in and day out. Sometimes he convinced himself that perhaps the war was over already, while his bride sat and waited for him. Then he quickly realised that such thoughts were just wishful thinking. He would know when it was safe for him to leave his mountain refuge.

At times he noticed smoke rising from the Little Karas Mountains in the far west: Namas, he presumed. They would know the state of the war, he thought. One day the urge for news, to know what was happening overwhelmed him. He decided to take a chance and cross the plain.

On the plain he felt very exposed. After a year in the Great Karas Mountains where he could disappear into the crevices and ravines within moments, it felt as if he was standing there naked. He knew he must look like a barbarian with his long hair and beard.

The foothills of the Little Karas Mountains enveloped him and made him feel secure again. He saw smoke in the air some distance ahead of him. Cautiously he edged closer. The horses, sheep and the *//haru-oms* confirmed that it was indeed a Nama settlement.

They saw him. The women fled into the mountains and some of the men fell to the ground. They had to be armed, he realised. He raised his hands in the air.

"*Tawede. Tawede!*"[128] He shouted as loudly as he could. "I come in peace, do not shoot!" No one answered. He walked closer.

Abraham Morris, leader of the Bondelswarts, got up from the ground, dusted himself off and placed his rifle against a shrub. Three other men followed him.

---

128 *Tawede:* Hello.

"*Ernst, sats ge!*[129] Where did I see you the last time, young man? But are you not Cornelius's young friend? Just look at you now! Where did that dog find you?"

"*/Uru te tamats kom hâo*," Ernst answered.

The two laughed and shook hands.

"Do you still remember Abraham Rolf? And Wilhelm and Johannes? From *//Khauxa!nas*? Or did the forget medicine work too well?" chuckled Abraham.

"No. I remember. Well, sort of."

The women started bringing food. There were still leftovers from the previous evening's *!kom*, the morning's fresh *askoek*, boiled *anyswortel*, *raaptol* and even *bergkambro*. For the first time in a year Ernst spoke to people, sat in a chair, ate from a plate, laughed and drank goat's milk. He realised how much he had missed the love and friendship of other people.

"No, man, the English and the Germans are still at it. Not here, but up there in Europe. They say millions have already died and many more will die. Good, let them die, the bastards!"

"And what are you doing here in the mountains with your rifles Abraham? I thought that your war was over a long time ago?"

Abraham's mouth twisted and he narrowed his eyes. "Ernst, for most of the Namas the war is over, but not for the Bondelswarts. We will fight to the last drop of blood. "

"But who are you fighting against now, Abraham? The Germans are all in jail."

"No, Ernst. We are waiting for our chance. A company of Union soldiers is now stationed in Warmbad. The first thing they will want to do is to confiscate our rifles. Once they have our rifles, we are slaves. That is what they want, but they will first have to kill Abraham Morris before they can get his rifle. I'm telling you, while the war is still going on in Europe, we do nothing. We will wait, but we want our country back. We want to live like our ancestors before us have lived for hundreds of years. With our sheep and our horses on our own land. We were the first people in Namaland, long before the Kaiserbird moved across Namaland and long before the Boers and the English moved in here. We still do not know what the Union is going to do. Are they going to follow the route of the Germans and steal our land, or are they going to walk the path of the Lord? You tell me."

---

129 *Sats ge:* It is you.

"No, how would I know? I have never been in the Union in my life. I only know the Boers I became acquainted with on the transport trail and *Oom* Lewies at Paradys. They appeared to be good people because they honour God's commandments. We will just have to see. But Abraham, do you remember the time I was at your place, *//Khauxa!nas*?"

"Of course I remember."

"Do you remember the story you told me? The one about Cornelius and Thilo von Trotha?"

"Yes, I remember. Why?"

"Please tell it to me again. For some reason I seem to have forgotten most of what you told me then."

"But you remember the medicine the old man gave you?"

"Yes I do, but I still don't remember what you told me."

That evening Abraham told him the tale again. Ernst made sure of each fact.

"But you still know the tale of the Namas and Great Snake, or don't you?" asked Abraham.

"Yes, I know about Great Snake, Keinaus, and that he lives at Aus and in the Fish River and at *//Khauxa!nas* or wherever, but what about it? Other people say he devoured the dead people at Lüderitz, but I don't believe that. I have never seen him. Have you?"

"No, I haven't seen him, but others have. He is huge with gills on the sides of his head and a large shiny stone in the middle of his forehead. As long as he lives all will go well with the Namas, but if we harm him it will signal the end of our nation."

"Do you really believe that, Abraham?"

"I don't know. I don't know what to believe. Once I found his tracks in the Kalahari Desert, here near *//Khauxa!nas*. The peculiar thing was that each spoor was about one hundred yards away from the next, as if he could fly or jump. The spoor consisted of large drag marks on the ground, each one on a slight incline. You could see clearly where he was heading. When you walked in that direction, you came across the next spoor. We followed the tracks up to a cave, but were too afraid to enter. So we turned around. All we know is that he guards over us. There is an old story that every ten years he wants a young Nama girl as a wife, but I am not so sure about that. What I do know is that we should not look for trouble with him."

Ernst gorged himself on all the delicacies that the women served, especially the fresh milk. When he was preparing to leave, they poured two calabashes of milk for the road.

"Please remember to let me know when you have news of the war. Just walk towards Lord Hill. I will see you long before you see me."

Ernst returned to his lonely existence on the Karas Mountains. The Bondelswarts continued their nomadic lifestyle on the plains and mountains of Namaland, the Fish River Canyon and on the other side of the Gariep River in Namaqualand.

A week later he saw oryx far below him on the plain. He moved downwind and crawled to a series of rocks from where he planned to fire. When he knelt down on his knees to rest his Mauser on the branch of a dead tree, he stared into the face of a hissing, black spitting cobra, two yards away from him. He froze, lost his balance and his rifle went flying down the cliff. The butt of the rifle was shattered and the bolt was bent. After this he and Willie had to settle for a diet of *dassies*, francolin and occasionally porcupine.

The days passed. His yearning for Regina intensified. How would he ever find out whether the war was over?

One day he saw people on the plain. It was a small horse commando. As they came closer he did not know whether to flee or remain. He counted three horses, but something appeared to be out of place. The leading rider was carrying a large object on his saddle. He recognized Abraham. He clambered down the mountain and walked towards his friends.

"Hallo, Ernst! How is it going with the hermit? We thought you were too lonely and hungry, so we brought you a gift."

Ernst laughed when he unloaded the live *orrabok*[130] from the horse.

"Many thanks."

"Bella is her name. Her lamb died," Abraham said.

There was time to talk and reminisce.

"Ernst, one of our youngsters, Moses of Small Koos, was in Karasburg the other day. The police there enquired after you, but Moses said nothing. Just that he would keep a lookout for you."

Ernst went cold. He would go mad if he had to be locked up in jail.

"And the war? What do you hear?"

"No, nothing man. All still the same."

"You must remember to let me know, please my friends."

---

130 *Orrabok:* a goat ewe whose lamb has died

Ernst now had a fresh supply of fresh milk, kindly donated by Bella, his *orrabok*.

Willie and Bella became good friends. They slept together, but one night there was an unearthly commotion and growling. Willie fled to Ernst's side, trembling and whining. Ernst set a dry twig alight to see in the dark. He saw Bella was missing and he saw a large pool of blood. Ernst knew at once. Leopard!

They did not sleep again that night. Ernst made a large fire. All he could think of was the cruel turn life had taken with his mother. Early the next morning he and the trembling Willie set off on the tracks of the leopard. It was not difficult. The trail was covered in blood. An hour later he saw the remains of Bella in a shepherd's tree. All he had with him was a large stone in his right hand and his *knobkierie* in his left. His knife rested in its sheath on his belt. He knew the leopard had to be close and he missed his Mauser.

Ahead of him was a large group of boulders, the size of ox wagons. The track disappeared behind the boulders. He edged closer, little by little, his nerves as taut as a *trekketting* in the Namib sand, the sweat on his back icy cold. When he rounded the last rock, he saw the spotted cat ten yards ahead of him. The leopard bared its teeth. He saw it tense the muscles of its front legs and lower its hindquarters, preparing to jump. Ernst flung the stone and hit the leopard between the eyes. The leopard fell over and tried to stagger upright again, but Ernst was there in a flash and rained blows on it with his *knobkierie*. He kept on hitting until the animal's body became limp and its eyes closed, only to fall half open again in a death stare. Ernst remembered the morning when they buried his mother and the small assembly of singing Namas around her grave.

Willie stormed forward, grabbed the leopard by the tail, growling and barking furiously.

"Yes, now you are brave but last night you were scared, weren't you?" he told Willie. He slaughtered the leopard, and found its meat wasn't bad at all. He tanned the skin with the naked spot between the eyes. Each time he rubbed the soft pelt, he thought of Bella's lovely milk and his mother's gentle eyes.

Ernst lay asleep in the heat of the January midday sun. Too late he heard Willie growl at voices just outside his shelter. He hoped it was Abraham's people, but when he looked out through opening he saw the uniforms. He realised that it was the end.

"Aha, Mr Luchtenstein, not so?"

"Yes, Ernst Luchtenstein, that's me," he replied and stared far across the plain to the Little Karas Mountains.

"We have come to fetch you. Captain Tilley is waiting for you at Keetmanshoop. Are you ready?"

"Yes, I think so. Let me just get my things together. Come Willie. Our time here is up."

Constables Francois de Vos and Bertus van Zyl of the South African Police had brought a mule with them for Ernst. They rode on horses. This time Willie was strong enough to run alongside.

"Do you have news about the war?" he asked.

"No, nothing. Everything just carries on. Why do you ask?"

"No, I am only asking, because my girlfriend is in Windhoek. She is a German. She has to remain there until the war is over."

The trip to Keetmanshoop took two days. All the while Ernst made plans to escape. At night the two inexperienced constables struggled to sleep. There was no chance of escape then. He also knew the horses would overtake him. Later he accepted his fate. He made friends with the two easygoing policemen.

In Keetmanshoop they took him straight to Captain Tilley's office.

"Morning, morning, Mr Luchtenstein, pleased to meet you," greeted the young man. "My, look at you! How long were you there in the mountains? I can see there weren't any barbers there," he joked.

"I think it must have been about eighteen months, Captain. Where are you taking me now? To the concentration camp in Aus?"

"Concentration camp? Good gracious, no man! Why would I want to do that?" a surprised Tilley asked.

"But isn't it the case that all Germans have to be in the camp?" an equally surprised Ernst asked.

"No man, only the permanent *Schutztruppe*. You are a civilian, are you not?"

"Yes, Captain, I am. Before the war I was a transport rider. I was conscripted when war broke out."

"Well, then you are a free man. You can do as you wish," Tilley replied.

"You mean I never had to go to a camp in the first place?"

"That's what I am saying, yes."

Ernst realised that he had spent eighteen months roaming in the Karas Mountains for no reason at all, but he also knew that he did not regret it one bit.

"But now, if I may ask, Captain. Why then did you come and fetch me?"

The captain smiled. "Man, I am so sorry. Please forgive me. Van Zyl and De Vos aren't the best cartridges in the packet. They should have told you. I require your services. I want to go hunting and I need a good guide. Can you help me?"

Ernst smiled. "Of course, Captain, I will gladly help, but first is there a gunsmith who could perhaps fix my rifle?"

"Yes, certainly!"

"And tell me, Captain, the Göttiger family from Aroab. Are they still in Windhoek?"

"I believe so, but I'll find out."

They agreed to depart in two weeks. Ernst went to Paradys. Gertruida burst into tears when she saw him.

"Ernst! Ernst! O, Ernst I thought you were dead!"

Andries was overjoyed and Charlotte's face shone with excitement. He laughed and greeted everybody.

"Here, little sister. Before you row with me again, I have a gift for you! Look here!" he said and held the leopard's skin up. Charlotte's face stiffened as she stared at the skin.

"It is not the same…". She did not complete her sentence "Thank you, *Boetie*. It is very nice. It will always remind me of Mother."

They talked and laughed far into the night. Ernst told them of all his adventures. He heard that his father had come looking for him again during his two-year absence.

He devoted the next two weeks to preparing an ox wagon and training a team of oxen. He reported to Captain Tilley, with Andries at his side.

They *trekked* towards the Karas Mountains with the ox wagon filled with tents, chairs, tables, dishes, crockery and cutlery as well as three servants from the Cape. They rode on horses. Ernst felt like a king. He and the captain had long conversations. Tilley went to school in England and was used to only the best. He enquired about the country and its people. This man was different, thought Ernst, a person who cared.

"Do you know of the Nama uprising, Captain?"

"No, tell me?"

Ernst told the captain about Josef and Cornelius Fredericks, Hendrik Witbooi, Jakob Morenga, Simon Koper and Abraham Morris. He told him about Thilo von Trotha and how the Witboois and the Frederickses initially aided the Germans in fighting the Hereros but how they later turned against them. He told him about the cruelty of the Germans and of the rumours about Shark Island.

One day he gathered all his courage.

"Captain, I want to tell the world, but I don't know how. My mother started to write down an account of the atrocities and I also made some notes, but what should I do with all of it? Could you perhaps help me?"

"Mmm. Get your story together and then we can see," Tilley replied.

In the evenings they set up camp and drank wine from the Boland.

Ernst knew every inch of the hunting area. He succeeded in getting the captain to shoot and collect enough biltong, skins and horns to fully load an ox wagon. He taught the captain to hunt upwind, to track, to understand the signs of the veld and not to hunt ewes and cows in gestation. They walked for miles and experienced the beauty and silence of the Karas Mountains. Ernst enjoyed sharing his world with somebody else. He only wished it was Regina at his side. Captain Tilley kept an accurate record of all his hunting adventures in a large diary with a red leather cover. He illustrated the stories with beautiful watercolour sketches.

Six weeks later they were back at Keetmanshoop. The captain called Ernst into his office. "Young man, thank you very much for all your help and friendship. I learnt a lot from you. I enjoyed our time together tremendously and I am very satisfied."

He shook Ernst's hand and gave him a hundred pounds.

"Many thanks, Captain. This is very generous. This will get me on my feet again."

"Speaking of which, Ernst, what are your plans?"

"Captain, I will return to transport riding. That is my trade and what I love doing."

"Well then. We have many horses here. They never stop grazing. Would you be interested in a contract to supply grass?"

Ernst was delighted. For the next six months he and Andries roamed all over the veld again, as they had in previous times. They cut grass, loaded it, and delivered it to Keetmanshoop. All he did in Keetmanshoop was to ask about the war and the internees at Windhoek. They slept under the stars, lived off the veld and ate venison. Andries was good company, but Ernst's mind always returned to Regina.

One day, far into the veld, west of Keetmanshoop, they came upon a derelict camp. There was something strange about it. The place was deserted except for the remnants of a fire, an upside down black pot, a broken mule wagon with a drum of water and a number of empty bottles.

To one side they saw animal bones, a pick and a shovel, a weathered old suitcase and a withered heap on the ground under a blanket. The two men approached cautiously. At first it appeared as if there was nothing underneath the blanket, but then it moved. They were both shocked when they lifted the blanket and saw Joseph Luchtenstein lying underneath. Joseph was emaciated, and his eyes were sunk deep into their sockets. His long grey-black hair hung in strings across his face. He had only three teeth left in his mouth.

"Father!" Ernst called out, and shook his father's body.

Joseph's eyes fluttered open.

He wheezed. "Water…water…" Joseph whispered.

Andries jumped up and fetched a bowl of water from their wagon. Ernst held his father's head in his shaking hands while dripping water into his mouth. Joseph gulped the water but coughed so that he could not swallow properly.

For the rest of the day Ernst sat with his father, constantly giving him water. He did not know whether to feel guilt or joy. Who was this man? Was it his *Vater* Joseph? Father Joseph? *Vader* Joseph? *Pa* Josef? Or just Josef Luchtenstein? How did one spell his name? Was this the man who had begotten him or was it the man responsible for his mother's death?

Of one thing he was sure. He was no longer the son of a German immigrant. He had changed. He was a man and he spoke the language of the Namib and the Karas Mountains and the Kalahari.

Joseph's brain was muddled and his speech incoherent. Ernst heard him murmuring Therese's name a few times. In the late afternoon Ernst shot a springbok. He made a stew of the liver and the brains and fed it to Joseph spoonful by spoonful. He sat with him throughout the night.

In the middle of the night Joseph, in a fit of delirium, started screaming frantically.

"Go away, go away, you horrible snake! *Voertsek, voertsek*[131]!" Ernst held him, but the wild look in Joseph's eyes frightened him. Eventually he calmed down and fell asleep. Ernst also dozed off.

Early the next morning Ernst was with his father when he awoke.

"What's going on here? Who are you? Where am I?" Joseph demanded as he struggled to get up.

"Calm down, Father. Be still. It's me, Ernst. Your son."

Joseph's head jerked up. He stared at Ernst. Then he sank back slowly.

---

131 *Voertsek*: Exclamation used for chasing away an animal, usually a dog.

"My son," he whispered softly.

They fed him soft meat and water at intervals. The demented visions returned twice and his flailing arms had to be restrained but gradually he calmed down. Ernst could clearly see that he was in a lot of pain. He also noticed the swollen ankles and realised his kidneys were failing. He knew that his father was seriously ill and he had to get him to a hospital. But the nearest clinic was at Keetmanshoop, sixty miles away and the doctor only visited there once a week. He stayed with Joseph and tried to make him as comfortable as possible.

That evening Joseph became calm. His breathing was slow and even and he slept well. Ernst hoped his condition had improved. Late in the night he heard his father talk.

"Ernst. Ernst. Please come here."

Ernst bent over his father. "Here I am Father. What is it?"

"I want to talk to you, my son. So many things have gone wrong in our lives. I know tonight is my last chance to put them right, my son."

Ernst felt the tears and the lump in his throat. He realised they had reached the end of the road. That nothing Joseph once considered so important, mattered any more. Not money or a farm or all the cattle in Namaland. He knew he did not want to travel the same road.

"It's all right Father, don't worry," was all he could say.

"No, Ernst. Listen. Listen to me. You need to know. I want to tell you why I am here. Sit here with me." Joseph Luchtenstein started telling Ernst the tale of his wanderings.

"One day, at Lüderitz, there was a black beggar lying on the pavement. I sort of kicked him aside, but then felt ashamed of myself. So I turned around and bought him half a loaf of bread. He was very grateful. His name was Zacharias. He asked me my name. When I said the word Luchtenstein, he jerked his head around, looked up at me and said that God had sent me. He said that he had heard my name in jail and had a message for me. I didn't believe him, but when I turned around to walk away he called after me: 'Ernst Luchtenstein, come here!' I immediately knew his message was actually for you. I walked back to him.

'Yes, what is it?' I asked him.

'Cornelius Fredericks said I should give you some papers,' Zacharias said. Then he produced a bundle of papers. They are there in my suitcase. There! Go and fetch them. Now!"

Ernst obeyed. He groped around in the jumbled contents of the suitcase. At the bottom he found the bundle of papers, tied together with a piece of string.

"Here they are, Father."

"Take them. They are yours, not mine."

"Thank you, Father. Everything is all right, Father."

"Go and read them. There are stories about that island, the concentration camp on Shark Island at Lüderitz, where you nearly drowned. But on the last two pages you will find the reason why I am here: Great Snake and the diamond on his head."

Ernst stared incredulously at the bundle of papers and undid the knot. He sat next to the fire and started reading. Now and then he looked up at his father, but he was breathing comfortably. On the first page Cornelius Fredericks began:

"Dear Ernst, my young friend. When you read this, I will be in the home of my Father. This I have known for some time, but your visit to me in jail yesterday, here on the island, gave me hope that someone would one day know the truth about the war against my people. Your mother started to write the story and you told me that you also added to her writings. This gives me great joy. At the time I smuggled letters to my wife Magdalena, there in jail in Keetmanshoop, and I must believe that those will also find their way to you, like these I am writing to you now."

Ernst was shocked to read about the inhumane experiments, the forced labour, the executions and the abuse perpetrated by the German authorities. Then he arrived at the last page.

"Dear Mr Ernst, my friend. The Nama people owe you much gratitude and honour because of the effort and interest shown by you in our cause, and we would like to reward you, but at this time our nation has been prostrated, never to rise again. This was prophesied by the great prophet Shepherd Stuurman. He said when Great Snake died, it would signal the end of the Nama nation. Now we know it has already occurred. The fall of the Nama nation has commenced and Great Snake has died, but on his head he wore a large shiny stone as large as a man's heart. That stone is worth more than all the land in Namaland, some say. The Nama nation bequeaths that stone to you. You must fetch it.

"I will draw a map for you of the cave where you will find the diamond.

Yours faithfully,

Cornelius Fredericks.

Captain of the !Aman.

28 February, 1907."

On the back was a detailed map showing Keetmanshoop, Aroab and the Bak River and in the centre of these three points was a cross marking a cave.

Ernst folded up the papers, shoved them into his pocket and went to his father's side. "And so Father? Did you find the so-called diamond from the snake's head?" he asked bitterly.

Joseph's lips moved. His eyes fluttered. "No, only the head." He began to laugh uncontrollably.

"Slowly, slowly Father. Calm down now."

Joseph's breathing eased and he relaxed.

"Someone got there before me. As it has happened all my life, this mission also turned out to be a failure, but I have the head, I have the head right here with me," and he indicated the ground beneath his head.

At first Ernst thought his father was experiencing another hallucination, but Joseph insisted that Ernst must believe him.

"Dig here, just below the sand. I want to show you."

Ernst fetched the shovel and a lantern and helped his father to move to one side. He then worked the sand away. Then he hit something solid and used his hands to dig faster. He removed the oval-shaped object from the sand and removed the canvas cover. It was a skull with one half missing, broken off. Underneath were a few sharp teeth. At the top an eye socket was clearly visible in the dull light of the lantern. There was a large indentation right in the middle of the bone next to the eye socket, as if something was meant to fit in there. It was clearly the skull of an animal, reptile or fish.

Ernst tasted the sour bile of darkness welling up in his throat. He wanted to get away from this evil place. He cast the skull unceremoniously back into the hole and covered it up. Andries was still asleep.

When Ernst got up in the middle of the night, he found his father had stopped breathing. He felt ashamed that he had no tears.

The following morning they *trekked* back to Keetmanshoop with his father's body in the back of the wagon.

Ernst buried his father in the Jewish cemetery.

42

1917 A train trip, a wedding and a pile of papers

The railway bridge across the Fish River during construction.

Six months later, there were two thousand pounds in Ernst's post office account from his grass business: enough to look after his bride when she returned.

Captain Tilley indicated that he wanted to see him.

"Ah, morning Ernst. How are you my friend? Please sit down. I think I have good news for you."

"What is it, Captain? Is the war over?"

"No, the war isn't over, but things are moving in that direction. The Union government has decided that the internees may go home. I heard this morning that Mrs Göttiger and her children are on their way home. However, Mr Göttiger will have to remain in the camp until the war is over."

"What? That means Regina is on her way home! Thank you, Captain. Thank you, thank you, thank you! This is the best news I have ever received in my whole life."

Ernst jumped up and headed towards the door, but turned around again.

"Goodbye, Captain, sorry. Many thanks. Excuse me Captain, are they coming by train?"

"Yes. They will be here tomorrow morning, about half past ten." Tilley said, "I am almost as pleased as you are."

The young man's hands trembled. He did not know what to do first. He ran in to old Rischbieter.

"Please, *Oom* Kurt. Cut my hair please, I am getting married, to Regina Klube of *Haus* Streitdam near Aroab, the farm of *Hauptmann* Göttiger. They brought her up after the death of her parents."

"Oh yes, the Göttigers, yes. The policeman. But he is in the camp at Aus, not so?"

"Yes."

"But won't you need the *Hauptmann*'s blessing first?"

Ernst reflected for a moment.

"Mmm, yes. I will have to. *Frau* Göttiger and Regina will be arriving from Windhoek tomorrow. I will discuss it with *Frau* Göttiger then."

Ernst paid for the haircut and shave, and hastened to Hesselmann's shop in the main street.

"Good morning *Herr* Hesselmann. I want to buy a suit and a pair of shoes, please."

Hesselman regarded him with raised eyebrows.

"Marriage or funeral?"

"I am getting married. To Regina of Aroab."

"That wild girl who rides horses?"

"Yes, *Oom*, the most beautiful girl in South-West Africa."

That evening Ernst and Andries sat around the campfire until late.

"Now Ernst, tell me, what are your plans now? When you have done marrying this girl, what are you going to do then? Are you going to abandon the transport business? Are you going to start farming and have children? Are you going to open a shop here in town and become rich, or what?"

"Andries, I just want to do one thing, and that is to make my wife happy. I will work these two hands to the bone to care for her and make her happy. "

"Tell me Ernst, in what church are you two getting married, hey? You are a German Jew, or are you now a Scottish Nama? And the girl is a Lutheran who grew up in a Catholic home. Now which church will be interested in your muddled situation? Tell me. Who are you actually?"

"You are being difficult, Andries. And probably jealous because nobody wants to marry you."

"Gmf, rubbish. I know in which church I will get married, my own church, the Rhenish Mission church. I know who I am. And the ladies are queuing up, you hear. And, another thing. Tell me, what happens to a person when he dies, Ernst? Where does he go, or does he just lie there and rot in the grave or does he go to heaven, or what happens to him?"

"But I thought you were the one who knew everything. Don't they teach you anything in that Rhenish church of yours?" mocked Ernst.

"Yes man, you know what I mean. We all go to our churches like sheep and we believe what we must believe. We believe what they tell us to believe, but deep down it is different. There deep inside a little man lives with his own mind, who thinks what he wants and believes what he thinks. What does that man tell you, Ernst? That one there deep inside you?"

Ernst took a deep breath.

"Do you remember Johannes? My father's *touleier*?"

"That scared Topnaar? Yes, I remember him well. What about him?"

"He wasn't scared. He told me one evening about the fight between the little *hasie* and the moon. The little *hasie* said that people are just like hares. They live and die and then rot, just like a *hasie*."

"Yes, we all know the story of the *hasie* and the moon, Ernst. That's the story of the old Khoi people, but what do you say, white man? What does that little man inside you say?"

His Nama friend's angry tone took Ernst aback.

"Andries, you are right. There is such a man here inside me who talks to me. All the time there in the Karas Mountains I spoke to him, because there was nobody else to talk to. When you are alone, I mean really alone, you hear him clearly. Actually that is the only time you hear him. If there are other people or books or things around you, then you hear the voices of the other people and their books and the voice of their possessions. To hear the voice inside you, you must be alone. That is why I love the desert and the plains and the mountains of Namaland. This is the place where I know who I am and what I am doing here. What you are asking me is easy, but it is also difficult, because you have to hear your own voice as well. That you can only do when you are alone, as I was, but I will try to answer you. The voice here inside told me I have to look after, care for and love other people the way that Gertruida McKay cared for me and Charlotte. That is all. I only became a human being when I landed up at the McKays. I never knew my own mother well, because she was a quiet person who spoke little. I think my father made her that way, but I learnt two things from her: to be humble and that I am no better than other people."

Ernst became quiet, feeling the heartache and yearning stirred by Therese's memory.

"My mother looked after us and she loved us, but Gertruida set the example. It was she who taught me how to live my life. That was what the voice had said to me in the desert as well as in the Karas Mountains: live like Gertruida."

"Yes, but what then, Ernst? What then? What happens then? When you die? What does it help to live a good life, if you only die and rot like a *hasie*?"

Ernst raised his hands.

"No, no, Andries. You don't understand. You need to listen carefully. Go and live in the Karas Mountains for a year, man. Forget about yourself and what you are going to become. Live and think and work so that other people will be happy. Help other people. Serve them. Look after them. Then everything will go well with you too. It always works that way, always. *A i tarita-i hoa-e //î-i !gasab di !gā kai re!*"

It became quiet around the camp fire.

"I am going to bed," Andries said after a few minutes.

Ernst sat for a long time by the glow of the dying embers. He looked at the marks *hasie* had scratched on the moon's face and he thought of the scratch marks people leave on one another, because they did not live like Gertruida. Then he heard the whisper of the *spekvreter's* song in his head. Could he be so sure of what he had told Andries that night?

Keetmanshoop station was sweltering. Ernst was perspiring in his suit. He had been waiting for more than an hour for the train. His eyes were strained and dry from staring towards the north. In the distance he heard the train's whistle. He became short of breath and forgot about everything around him. Andries sat behind him on a bench. He had long given up on Ernst's impatience.

The train hissed and shuddered to a stop. Ernst strode up and down the platform, his eyes searching for Regina. Then he saw *Frau* Göttiger in her wide-brimmed hat stepping off the train. Then Regina came out of the carriage. His mouth became dry. He could not believe it. She was even lovelier than he remembered. She was dressed in a beautiful close-fitting dress with a broad frill at the hem and finished off with fine lace. Her thick hair framed her face like the clouds over the Karas Mountains and her face was radiant like the glow of the morning sun.

"Ernst, you came!"

"Regina, of course!"

"Are you two going to help me with the baggage, or must I do it myself? *Frau* Göttiger's words jerked the two lovers back to reality.

"Sorry, *Frau* sorry. Good morning *Frau*," Ernst greeted in confusion.

"Andries, please help here."

Ernst and Andries collected the four suitcases.

"*Frau* Göttiger, what should we do with all this stuff? My wagon is behind the station and we could take you to Aroab now, but ..."

"Yes, young man, we need to get back to the farm. *Hauptmann* Göttiger writes that he is worried about what is going on there."

"*Frau*, but there is one matter before we leave. May we first get married? Regina and I, I mean?"

Regina's face blushed furiously while Ernst twirled his hat round and round in his hands.

"It seems as if you are serious, young man! Regina, what do you say? Are you in agreement with this?"

"*Frau* Göttiger, yes! A thousand times yes. I do want to marry Ernst. Please!"

She went and stood next to Ernst.

"Well, well, well. This is a bit out of the ordinary. Mmm, let me think a while. No, it is in order, but I think we must also get Bruno's, *Hauptmann* Göttiger's, blessing. But as you know, he is in a concentration camp, Ernst."

"Thank you, *Frau*, thank you, thank you. I have thought about it for a long time. *Frau*, I propose that we take the train and go and see *Hauptmann* Göttiger at Aus. I will get a letter of introduction from

Captain Tilley to the commander of the camp and I am sure there won't be a problem."

The thought of seeing her husband for the first time in two years knocked *Frau* Göttiger sideways.

"Yes. Of course, of course. Why did I not think of it?"

"Andries, load everything back onto the train and also get my stuff. Regina, here's money. Please get us three tickets. I will be back in a few minutes."

Andries clicked his tongue and shook his head.

Ernst galloped down the street on a borrowed horse to the Union soldiers' camp. He ran in to Captain Tilley's office.

"May I please see the captain? It is urgent."

Ninety minutes later Ernst said goodbye to Andries. "Give us a week and then come back every day to see whether we are here. In the meanwhile, go to Paradys and tell the McKays that I am getting married. And look after Willie please. Keep well."

"Hey, Ernst, you have many plans. Your head is making a lot of noise," laughed Andries.

The two lovers sat close together on the hard leather benches in the train wagon, talking without stopping under the watchful eye of *Frau* Göttiger. In between they gazed into each other's eyes. Ernst told them the tales of his wanderings and dreams for the future. *Frau* Göttiger asked after his means to provide for Regina. Ernst announced the first thing he intended to do after their marriage was to purchase a farm, for cash. *Frau* Göttiger was impressed.

"Regina, I hope that you will not forget your poor foster parents?"

"Never, never, *Frau* Göttiger. I will never forget you. I love you too much."

At Seeheim the train diverted from the main line to stand overnight. It had no lights and it was too dangerous to continue the journey in the dark. The passengers settled down in their compartments. Ernst asked *Frau* Göttiger's permission to take his prospective bride for a walk in the moonlight.

"Please don't stay out late, Regina. Go and enjoy yourselves, children."

The couple strolled hand in hand across the bridge. He pointed to the Karas Mountains and Lord Hill, the highest point, showing her his home for eighteen months. Everything was beautiful that evening.

The train departed again the next morning, the two lovers on board. They arrived at Aus late in the afternoon. Ernst paid for two rooms at the Bahnhof Hotel, one for himself and the other for the two ladies. That evening, for the first time in their lives, the two young people dined with *Frau* Göttiger in a hotel's dining room.

After breakfast the following morning, they took the train on the special railway line that led to the camp and reported to the office.

"I am here to see my husband, please," announced *Frau* Göttiger.

The guard, a short, stocky grey-haired man in a khaki uniform with a white band and the letters PGR on his arm, looked up in surprise. He wasn't accustomed to requests of this nature.

"I am not sure about that. I will first have to ask the Commandant," he said and pushed his chair back wearily.

After a while he returned. "Please come with me."

He opened a door and ushered them inside. From behind a cluttered desk an officer in a creased uniform and with bags under his eyes stood up.

"Colonel Hawkins. Pleased to meet you."

"I am *Frau* Göttiger and this is my foster daughter, Regina Klube and her fiancé, Ernst Luchtenstein. We have come from Keetmanshoop, hoping to see my husband *Hauptmann* Göttiger, in order for him to give his blessing to the children's marriage."

Hawkins stepped backwards. "Well, well, well. Wonderful! This is the best thing that has happened in this awful place. Please sit down and excuse me for a few minutes."

He left the office and returned after a while.

"Tea for you, Madam?" he offered in a friendly way.

Ernst was somewhat perplexed. He remembered that he had come close to being a prisoner here himself, while now he was a guest and was being offered tea! He thought about Cornelius who sat in a cell not far from here, in the hands of the same people who were now being detained here. The same people who had imprisoned thousands on an island west of there and who used them as forced labour, wielding their crops all the while. The wheel had turned...or had it? He saw no sign of sjamboks, a gallows or forced labour. Was it not after all the British who had destroyed so many Boer women and children in the concentration camps? Who was this Hawkins? Englishman? Boer? South African?

"Captain Tilley of Keetmanshoop sent you this letter," Ernst said.

Hawkins opened the envelope and read the letter.

"It seems you are in a hurry, and serious. We will have to see what we can do."

There was a knock on the door. The sergeant opened the door.

"Prisoner Göttiger, Colonel."

Hauptmann Göttiger, dressed in khaki trousers and shirt and with shiny brown shoes entered the office. He saluted. "Colonel!" he greeted.

Only then did he recognize his wife who jumped up to embrace him.

"Frieda!" was all he could utter. The two stood like that for a minute, lost in their embrace. Göttiger kissed Regina.

Hawkins wiped something from his eye.

"What's going on here?" Göttiger asked when he had regained his composure.

"That's what I also would like to know," grinned Hawkins.

"Never before has the wife of a prisoner of war travelled so far, but there is always a first time. This war has been going on for too long, don't you agree, *Hauptmann*?"

"Definitely, Colonel."

"*Hauptmann* Göttiger, you say that tooth is still bothering you. Well, we can't fix that here. The only person who could help you is Doctor Schweitzer in Lüderitz. You have my permission to go to the dentist. Will three days be sufficient?"

Göttiger caught on immediately. "Oh yes, the tooth. Thank you, Colonel. I will see the dentist."

"Perhaps you want Breeza to take your wife and the children on a tour of the camp, *Hauptmann*? We all are proud of what the prisoners have accomplished here. The train only leaves in an hour or two."

Long after the family had left his office, Hawkins sat with arms outstretched on his desk, staring at nothing in particular. He hated this place and everything it represented. He hated what he did and who he was. He just wanted to get away from here, to flee. To hell with the Union, Botha, the war, to hell with them all. Life was worth more than this war.

It was only after they left Hawkins that Regina found the opportunity to introduce her foster father to Ernst.

"This is Ernst Luchtenstein, *Hauptmann*. Ernst, this is *Hauptmann* Göttiger."

The two shook hands.

"*Hauptmann* Göttiger, I er, I want, I mean…"

"Aha, now I understand what's going on here. Regina, don't tell me it's what I am thinking?"

Regina blushed red as a beetroot .

"*Hauptmann* Göttiger, I love Regina and she loves me and we have come to ask your blessing. We are asking your permission to marry. Please?" Ernst blurted out.

"Now let me see. Luchtenstein…You are Jewish, yes?"

Ernst nodded.

"So Regina, you want to marry a Jew? Do you think it can work? And young man, are you able to provide for her?"

"Yes!" exclaimed the two lovers with one voice.

"Well, nothing will give me greater joy than seeing the two of you happy together."

Bruno Göttiger gave them his blessing on their marriage.

He kissed Regina and shook Ernst's hand.

"This has to be celebrated. Hugo!"

His voice reverberated across the camp.

At that moment a petite lady with brown hair and dressed in red, came around the corner.

"Breeza, I would like to introduce you to my wife, Frieda, and my daughter and future son-in-law. Breeza is the wife of *Leutnant* Nelson, and a true angel. She nurses our sick soldiers. Oh, and Breeza, the camp commandant has given me permission to see the dentist."

Breeza took the group on a tour of the camp. She showed them the box-like houses the prisoners of war had built for themselves from mud bricks. The neatly-painted houses were huddled closely together. Some had gables and others had decorative plastering and even friezes on the walls. A few houses still had canvas roofs, but other roofs had been hammered together from empty bully beef tins and fish tins.

On one side the prisoners had erected a monument in honour of Kaiser Wilhelm II and in the middle of the camp was a clock tower, with a working clock made from paraffin cans.

"These prisoners of war are very skilled," Breeza explained. "They build houses and exercise, study and hold music concerts, gymnastic displays and even put on dramatic performances. Their brass band has already performed in Windhoek. That is how they spend their days."

When they got to the houses in the last row, Hugo appeared with a tray of glasses and an illegal bottle of schnapps.

"Aha friends!" he announced. "I am led to believe we have something to celebrate!"

"Hugo, you know that's against the rules," Breeza reprimanded with mock seriousness, but she also took a glass. Soon a group of prisoners gathered around them, sang and applauded spontaneously. The loving couple stood close together.

"It's time to go," Göttiger said after a while and went to fetch his bag in his room.

It was difficult to see who were more in love: Ernst and Regina or the Göttigers. The two couples sat opposite one another on the train that was slowly crawling westwards through the desert. Between them lay years of experiences to catch up with. At the same time Ernst gazed at the desert that he had crossed several times with wagon and oxen. He told Regina and the Göttigers of the days and weeks of scorching heat by day and freezing cold by night, sand that stung like wasps, the eternal howling wind, oxen that bellowed and died, and of the thirst and sunburn.

At Garub, thankfully, the train stopped to take on water, allowing the passengers an opportunity to alight. In front of them sprawled a vista of two hundred wild horses grazing on nothing but the dust of the rocky plain that surrounded the watering hole. Regina was elated.

"Ernst, look there. That little foal is only a couple of days old. Oh, and look at those two stallions. They are fighting over the mares! Where did all these horses come from?"

"Mixed up bunch of horses these, Regina. German, Nama, Boer and English."

"And yet they stay together in this harsh desert?"

"Regina, by living together and looking after each other, they survive. If only people could manage to do that as well."

The next stop was at Tschaukaib. Ernst and Regina walked off onto the desolate plain. In the distance a male ostrich and his mate were dancing in the mirage.

Ten miles before Lüderitz the train came to a halt. Everyone thought it was another stop, but the conductor came to tell them it was the sand.

"This track is forever under sand. It is the wind," he said. Some of the men got off the train and watched the railway workers struggling to free the line from sand.

They arrived at Lüderitz station just after dark. At the Kapps hotel Ernst paid for three rooms. It was a strange, yet delightful evening at a table laid with the finest silver, a white starched tablecloth, crystal glasses and German porcelain. They dined on crayfish cocktails, mutton and chocolate dessert and drank Cape wine. To Ernst this was all new. Regina showed him how to use all the different knives and forks.

"You two are getting married tomorrow, but tonight you are sleeping separately, do you hear!" ordered *Hauptmann* Göttiger in a stern voice.

When he and Frieda walked up the stairs, he burst out laughing. Frieda poked him with her elbow in his side.

"Bruno, you old devil! Was that necessary?" She winked at him.

"Woman, we were also young, or have you forgotten?"

"Come, show me, don't just brag about it," she teased.

The two young lovers walked outside and followed the warm glow of Lüderitz's new cast-iron streetlights down to the new quay. Ernst told his fiancée of his arrival in German South-West Africa. They walked along the causeway connecting Shark Island with the mainland. Ernst saw no sign of barbed wire or guard huts. The island was now simply a windswept rocky hill in the sea. They climbed to the highest point and saw the concrete platform where the Shark Island gallows once stood.

"Just there, behind that rock, is where I nearly drowned, Regina, but someone dragged me out of the water. The last I knew was a massive blow against my side and a great fin sticking out of the water. It must have been a shark, I think, but somehow I got out of the water. I woke up in a hospital. There was this weird doctor who was with us on the ship."

Ernst shuddered visibly but recovered himself after a while and carried on talking.

"After a while my parents came and fetched me. There was a camp here, where the Germans held the Hereros and the Namas. We saw some of them when they were building the railway line. Later I also visited my friend Cornelius here. He was thin, emaciated and sickly. I think they performed experiments on him. In fact, I have letters ... Never mind, let's not talk about that now. There are many stories and rumours about this place. That doctor's eyes and all sorts of other horrible images still haunt me. I really don't want to think about it now."

They walked back to the hotel, hand in hand, watched over by the Felsenkirche, the silent sentinel on the hill, a witness to the tides and the wind, and the lives, loves and deaths of the people of this land of thirst.

Ernst woke up early. Today was the day, their wedding day. From deep in his baggage he retrieved three gifts for his bride. Two of these he had been carrying with him for years, especially for this day. One of them was a tortoiseshell powder container with its precious body powder, *!uros*, like Ma Gertie always had – every Nama woman's treasured possession. The other was a broad necklace of beads, only for Nama women. The last gift was the ring with the pearl he had bought at Hesselman's shop.

He polished his shoes until he could almost see his face in the reflection. Then he put on his new suit and shirt.

Hauptmann Göttiger had breakfast with Ernst and then walked to the magistrate's office in Bismarck Street to confirm that the magistrate would be available later that morning.

Ernst was left to pass the time on his own. His nerves were on edge. He walked up and down along the quay, deep in thought.

A shadow in one of the side streets caught his attention. At first he thought it was a dog. Then he saw it was the hunched, withered figure of a man crawling on the pavement and holding out his hand with his face turned downwards.

He could not believe what he saw. The man's whole body had been contracted by some illness or other.

"Morning," he said to the pathetic bundle and dug around in his pocket for small change.

"Morning, my *baas*," he heard the whispering voice.

"Who are you?"

"Zacharias Zeraua from Otjimbingwe, my *baas*."

"Now what are you doing here, Zacharias? Here in Lüderitz? This isn't your place. Otjimbingwe is far from here." Ernst crouched down in front of the man.

The man lifted his head slightly and peered at Ernst.

"I am alive, my *baas*. I'm alive and I look at the sea. Each day I am alive."

Ernst saw and heard the resigned acceptance of many years of hardship and suffering.

"Zacharias, what is wrong? Are you ill, or were you injured??"

Zacharias looked down again.

"It's the poison, my *baas*, the German's poison of a long time ago. It made me crooked. Now I walk on four feet like a crippled dog."

Ernst's eyes narrowed.

"What poison, Zacharias? What are you talking about?"

"It's that doctor's poison, the doctor from *Haifisch*."

Ernst was shaken. He remembered his father talking about a Zacharias.

"Zacharias! Were you on Shark Island? *Haifisch*? Tell me?"

"I was there. Long time, I was there."

"Zacharias, tell me everything. Please."

Ernst sat flat on the ground in his wedding suit. He heard about the atrocities of 1906 to 1908, straight from the victim's mouth. As the tale unfolded, Ernst became more and more disturbed. Then he wept.

"You say you knew Cornelius Fredericks, Zacharias?"

"We were in the same cell, for a long time until the poison destroyed him, but I am alive my *baas*, I am alive."

"And Magdalena and the children?"

"I only heard later that she was also there, with her children. The women told how she had to scrape the flesh off her husband's head. One day she jumped into the sea and a large shark took her. In the beginning the Namas thought the sharks were their Great Snake, but later the number of sharks increased because of all the human flesh. The Namas learned then that they were man-eating sharks."

"And how did you manage to survive, Zacharias? When did you leave the camp and what became of the camp and everything else?"

"Just after Cornelius died, Von Estorff went away. He was the head of the camp and he went away. They closed the camp and moved it to a place where Boerekamp used to be. And when the railway line was completed, the war also ended, and one day the gate of the camp was open. The Germans chased us out and said we must *voertsek*. It was a great day. We cried a lot, but we had nothing. Some walked into the desert and died there, as free people. Others went to look for work at Kolmanskop and others at the diggings at Pomona, Elizabeth Bay and Charlottental. I could no longer walk. Someone carried me, and left me here at the harbour. I live here now."

Ernst stood up and dusted his trousers. "Zacharias, all I have is money." He took five hundred pounds from his pocket – what a labourer would earn in a year and a half – and gave it to Zacharias.

"If I get to Otjimbingwe one day, will I find you there?"

"If I am still alive, my *baas*. I am going home with this money. Thank you so much, my *baas*. What is the *baas's* name?"

"My name is Ernst Luchtenstein, old Zacharias."

The shrivelled old head jerked backwards and started trembling. Zacharias extended both hands to Ernst. The tears rolled down his face.

"It's true, it's true. You have returned. Cornelius believed that you would return again. He gave me lots of papers to give to you, but the other day another man came here and I thought it was you. So I gave them to him."

"Yes, I know, Zacharias. It was my father and I did get the papers. Thank you."

"But how did you know?"

"I did not know, old man. It just happened. The papers found me, I did not find them."

New life shone in the tired, bead-black eyes.

"You are Ernst Luchtenstein, the little general. You are the right one, the right one, Cornelius was right. There is still one paper I did not give to the other man. I forgot. But I gave it to Father Laaf. Go and look for him there at the Roman Catholic Church."

Ernst picked up the bundle of skin and bones. He helped him to the station in Bahnhof Road. There he bought him a ticket and asked a young boy to help the old man onto the train.

Ernst arrived at the Kapps Hotel, out of breath from his run from the station.

"Ernst, where have you been? We thought perhaps you had developed cold feet," *Hauptmann* Göttiger called out when he saw him.

"Sorry. I met up with somebody...."

"Come, son. Normally it's the bride who keeps the groom waiting."

They met the ladies on the veranda of Goerke House. Ernst drew his breath in sharply. Where did she find a wedding dress in this small harbour town? And in one morning? There was no time to ask questions. The picture of the lovely German bride in her beautiful long white wedding gown with the frills and lacework brought the whole town to a standstill.

There was a small crowd of curious people in front of Goerke House.

A veiled Regina carried a bouquet of *skerpioenvygies* and *kankerbos-sieblomme*[132] in her hand.

Ernst joined her. He blushed when the townspeople began to applaud. Someone opened the door from the inside. They entered, followed by the Göttiger couple. A guide led them to an office where a man with spectacles and a black gown awaited them.

"Good afternoon. Ernst Luchtenstein and Regina Wilhelmina Klube?"

The two nodded.

"Pleased to meet you. I am Magistrate Viljoen. You want to get married?"

"*Hauptmann* Göttiger? *Frau* Göttiger? Good, let us proceed."

The formality took a few minutes. Bruno Göttiger signed as witness.

"Do you have a ring, young man?"

"Yes, your Honour, I have."

---

132 *Skerpioenvygies* and *kankerbossieblomme*: Flowers of the Namib Desert

"Well, then I pronounce you husband and wife. I suggest you put the ring on her finger now, before the other young men from Luderitz hear of her!"

Ernst fiddled in his jacket pocket for the ring and slipped it over Regina's slim ring finger. Then they kissed.

The Göttigers congratulated the couple.

Outside Goerke House Ernst looked to the left. He saw the sun beating down on Shark Island.

"Regina, may we walk by the station, please?"

"Of course, why?"

But Ernst said nothing and took the hand of his newly-married young wife in his.

The group of four walked down Bismarck Street to the station. Ernst walked next to the train, his eyes searching for Zacharias.

The young boy who had helped Zacharias, came running toward Ernst.

"He is on the train, sir. He is already on." He showed Ernst where Zacharias was seated.

Ernst stood on his toes and looked through the train window. He saw the hunched figure in his rags on the bench.

"Zacharias, I came to show you my wife," he called.

The face looked at him in a quiet daze.

Then the boy who had earlier helped Zacharias jumped in and picked him up so that he could see Ernst and Regina.

Zacharias smiled – for the first time in thirteen years.

"You must go well, my little *baas*. God will keep his hand over you."

The train whistled and the steam pistons started pumping.

"Who was that Ernst?"

"It is a long story."

43

The treasure of Namaland

The pool in the Bak River below //Khauxa!nas

After the festivities in the Kapps Hotel dining room, Ernst carried his bride over the threshold of their room.

"I have two more gifts for you," he smiled and took out the *!uros* powder and the necklace.

"The Namas believe no woman can keep her husband happy without these. When I was alone in the mountains, they helped me to think about you."

"Oh, Ernst, that is so romantic!" said Regina, wrapping her arms around his neck.

The next morning, after breakfast, the two newlyweds strolled through the streets of Lüderitz. For once there was no wind. The sun's rays sparkled on the calm water. A few fishing boats bobbed alongside the quay. The scene looked exactly like a European painting. The two laughed and talked constantly as they walked along.

Ernst read the name on a board next to the green door of an old white building: Roman Catholic Mission Association.

"Wait, Regina. I have to pick up some mail."

"But this isn't the post office," she said.

Ernst knocked on the door. They waited a while. He knocked again. Later they heard someone fiddling with the lock and the door opened. A bald, pale head appeared.

"Yes, what do you want so early in the morning?"

Ernst smelled the sour odour of last night's gin and noticed the tired, bloodshot eyes.

"Are you Father Laaf?"

"Yes, I am. Who are you?"

"I am Ernst Luchtenstein. Father, I was told you have a letter for me. From Cornelius Fredericks. Zacharias Zeraua said he gave it to you."

The old man nodded his head.

"I think you should come in."

It seemed to Ernst that the old man was not fully aware of their presence.

Father Laaf shuffled through the rows of pews and led them into a room behind the pulpit. There were six chairs and a table.

"Please sit down."

The old man left the room. After a long time he returned with an envelope. He placed it on the table in front of Ernst.

"Thank you very much, Father," he said and started to get up.

"Wait," ordered the old man and sat down opposite them. "First tell me what is so important and why you are so interested in it? Why do you come looking for a piece of paper the first morning after your wedding?"

Ernst and Regina looked at each other.

"How did you know Father?" they both asked at once.

"Lüderitz is a small place, my children," said the old man. "So, what can be so important? Tell me please."

Ernst briefly told the story of Zacharias and Cornelius and their connection and his two visits to Shark Island. He also told him about his mother's notes.

"Now what do you want to do with all this information, young man?"

"Father, my mother said that the world should know. I don't know how, but someone has to complete her work. Someone must tell the world."

The old man sighed and his shoulders dropped. He turned his head. His weary eyes looked through the small high window.

"It was a horrible time. I tried, without success. I was there a few times, two, maybe three times, to talk to them. I wrote a number of letters, until the man from the newspaper came. Then I got scared. From then on I kept quiet. To my eternal shame."

Father Emil Laaf told the two the tale of Shark Island and all the rumours about what happened there.

"In the beginning I had my doubts. It just couldn't be. We, the German missionaries, came to this continent to bring the gospel and liberation. But in the end we only brought enslavement and death. That was all. And I was too frightened and too much of a coward to oppose them. Later on I found I couldn't live with myself. I still cannot."

When he had finished speaking, the broken old man remained silent for a long while, and the two young people just stared at him. The tears ran down his pale face. Regina could not help wiping a few tears from her eyes too.

At last Father Laaf looked up.

"Children," he said. "Promise me one thing. Promise that you will always remain loyal to the truth, because the truth will set you free. Thank you for listening to my confession this morning. It was the first time ever that I have told this story."

Then he got up. "Wait here, please."

He returned with an old brown envelope and a rusted soap tin in his hands.

"That man from the newspaper I told you about, this belonged to him. He gave it to me for safekeeping. I have done so ever since. Go, read it and tell the world. And now you must please leave."

When they stepped outside they were relieved to be free of the darkness of the past, but it took some time before they could speak again. Ernst placed the unopened papers in his suitcase. He did not want to read them just yet.

The infamous Lüderitz wind arrived as if from nowhere and howled around the corners as they boarded the train.

At Aus station Ernst and Regina said their goodbyes while *Frau* Göttiger went with her husband to the camp.

Their farewell on the platform at the concentration camp was difficult.

"I wish I could go with you, Frieda."

"Take courage, Bruno. One of these days it will be over, then it will be like the old days again."

While Ernst and Regina waited for Frieda to return from the concentration camp, they walked to the cemetery and searched through the rows of graves till they found the two greyish-white tombstones side by side:

Herbert Klube
Wilhelmina Klube

Regina stared at the two graves and then turned around.

"Let them rest. Come, let's go."

On the train Ernst looked through the papers in the soap tin and the brown envelope. Then he opened the envelope containing Cornelius's last letter and read it. The letters in Magdalena's soap tin and those in his father's suitcase, as well as the article by the reporter and the story related by the priest, turned and drifted in his mind like leaves in a whirlwind.

The train stopped at Keetmanshoop two days later. Andries and Willie were waiting for them.

"I thought you had run away, Ernst?" Then he removed his hat. "Afternoon Madam. Afternoon Regina. Did your wedding go well?"

Ernst accompanied the two ladies to Hesselman's shop. He introduced his bride proudly to everybody.

"Will the two of you manage without me for an hour or two?" he asked. "There is something I have to do quickly."

"But of course! Just leave your wallet behind. We women know what to do with money," replied Regina., Her face was as bright as the clear water in a Karas Mountain stream.

Ernst hurried to Captain Tilley's office.

"Aha, morning, morning Mr Bridegroom! Congratulations, man. Everything went off well?" asked the friendly Englishman.

"Morning, Captain. Yes, thank you. Many thanks."

"And what brings you here this morning? What can I do for you today?"

"Captain, do you remember the history of the Nama war I told you about in the Karas Mountains?"

"Of course I do, Ernst. What about it?"

"You remember my mother wrote down certain things and I also made some notes?"

"Yes, yes. I do remember."

Ernst took out his old exercise book, the brown envelope and the soap tin and placed them on the desk. He kept Cornelius's letter in his pocket.

"This is everything, Captain. All the information. I am giving it to you. Can you help me please? I am not a writer and I know no one at the newspapers or in the government. The world needs to know, Captain. Here are all the facts. You are an educated man and you can write. Will you help me, please?"

"I'll see what I can do, Ernst."

A while later the whip cracked. "Go, go! All together now!" Ernst called out.

The newlywed couple and the stepmother-in-law continued their long journey to *Haus* Streitdam at Aroab on Ernst's wagon. The trek took four days, in which time the two did not leave each other's company for a minute. They laughed and talked excitedly. *Frau* Göttiger sat on the wagon chest, silent.

Haus Streitdam looked the same as the day when the Union soldiers came. The doors were not locked. Old Lettie who had been waiting for her employers for more than two years was overjoyed when the wagon came to a halt and she recognized her people.

"Ai, ai, ai my *oumiesies*[133]. We so looked out for you. Each day we looked and looked, but no, you did not come. And where is the *oubaas*?"

Ernst had to help to get the farm going again. He oiled the windmill, mended the rickety fencing, helped to collect firewood and killed two snakes, but was keen to get back to his own work.

Regina was ecstatic to be with her horses again. Four new foals had been born during her absence. Her six riding horses still recognized her. Each day she rode and groomed them. She was impressed by Lettie's efforts at maintaining the farm.

"Just sometimes, *oumiesies*, when the hunger became too much, then we slaughtered one of the *oubaas's* sheep."

There were even beans and tomatoes in the vegetable garden.

Ernst was growing impatient. He wanted to get to Keetmanshoop, to his place of work, and also to Paradys, but there was a stronger urge driving him.

"There is a place I want to show you. Do you think we can leave *Frau* Göttiger alone here for a day or two?" he asked Regina one day.

---

133 *Oumiesies*: Common form of address to an older white lady by a person of colour, now considered archaic and politically incorrect.

"Ernst, she is a strong woman. We have to begin our own life some time. Where are we going?"

"You will see."

"Andries, we are going away for two or three days. You must stay here and look after the place."

"Ernst, when are we going to start to work again? My money is finished!"

Frau Göttiger said goodbye to them. She knew they needed time on their own. "Go and enjoy yourselves, my children. Don't worry about me."

Ernst and Regina rode in a south-westerly direction, their hearts brimming with excitement. They had with them sleeping bags, salt, cake flour and Ernst's rifle and slingshot. The horses, Keiser and Leeu, were excited and fat. Willie ran and barked alongside, looking up at his master in anticipation of the hunt. They rode through the quiet ravines and outstretched valleys, around mountainous outcrops and under cliffs. They talked happily about their new life and their dreams. Sometimes the starkness and dramatic beauty of the desolate landscape forced a silence on them. They stared wordlessly at the stunning beauty of the scenery. Now and then they saw herds of oryx and springbok or a lone steenbok, but it was too soon to think of food. There was no sign of people.

Late in the afternoon Ernst dismounted. He stood still and held Regina's horse, Keiser, by the bridle.

Then he started to whisper.

"*//Khauxa!nas, //Khauxa!nas.*"

He walked slowly, step by step, whispering all the while.

"Ernst, what are you doing?"

"Shh," he motioned.

"*//Khauxa!nas, //Khauxa!nas.*"

Out of nowhere a small bird fluttered before them.

"*Lek-ker, lek-ker, lek-ker!*" twittered the little bird.

They followed the honey guide through a ravine, over a hill, around a koppie and through another ravine to a place below a cliff. Ernst recognized it.

He looked for the thick bush and found it easily, but that was the end of the road for the horses. They unsaddled the horses and let them go. For the horse lady that was no problem, because she knew just one whistle would bring the faithful animals back to her. Keiser and Leeu whinnied and retraced their steps. Then they walked down the dry watercourse to the green Bak River, where it flowed on the eastern side under a series of cliffs.

Ernst and Regina clambered up the spiral cliff to the top, exactly as he remembered from his previous visit. Willie followed but at the steepest part Ernst had to carry him. The desolate ruins of the town lay before them. Ernst took Regina by the arm and led her to the ring wall. The bees had gone. The honey guide flitted around them to a single nest, the only one remaining from the dozens that used to be there.

//Khauxa!nas was deserted, with no people or animals, no friendly fires to visit, no roofs. Only stone walls, dilapidated in places, overgrown by creepers and grass. It was clear nobody had been there for a few years.

Ernst collected twigs and set them alight to smoulder. He then took some honey from the nest. He put the honey guide's share to one side. They sat down on the rocks and enjoyed their share of the sweet honey, with Willie waiting to lick their fingers clean.

"Regina, this is so sad, this place. Last time I was here, it was a thriving city with people and animals. They lived here, and it was clean and tidy. The houses had roofs and children, and chickens and dogs ran around. The people lived and laughed and wept here. Abraham Morris referred to it as their fortress. It was a living city with a contented soul. Now it is desolate, a forgotten cemetery. The Nama people have lost everything. Even the bees have deserted this tragic place."

They walked through //Khauxa!nas. They saw the remnants of the little dwellings, kraals, barns and the meeting place where Ernst and Andries had met the captains. Here and there a piece of faded cloth hung from a branch or a rusted buckle or tin lay on the ground between clumps of grass. Nothing survived here, only the smothered spirit of a conquered people.

He turned back to the meeting place.

"Come with me, Regina. There is something I have to do. Come help me, please."

"What is it Ernst?"

"You remember that envelope with Cornelius's last letter we got from Father Laaf?"

"Oh yes. I remember. What about it?"

"Come, I'll show you."

With a dried branch he started digging, right over the threshold of the meeting place. He dug and dug. Regina helped by moving the excavated earth away.

"What are you looking for Ernst?"

He did not reply. He just kept on digging. Then he felt something solid. He dug more and removed the stone. The gigantic diamond, as big as a man's heart, glittered brightly in the sun. Regina gasped.

"Ernst! What is this? How did you know?"

Ernst looked at the sparkling stone in the rays of the sun. He turned it around in his hands. On the one side there was a corrugated surface as if it had been attached to something. Regina was dumbfounded. She knew this stone was worth a fortune, but she also saw the frown and heartbroken expression on her husband's face.

"The legacy of the Namas, Regina. When this nation was at the pinnacle of its existence, something died in this tragic land. Now this is only a dead stone. Come with me."

They walked up to the ring wall. They looked over the abyss to the sun in the west. Far below lay the deep pool of the Bak River. At the river's edge Keiser and Leeu whinnied. Without a word Ernst threw the large diamond in a high arc and watched until it dropped into the pool. The horses skittered at the splash. The two young people turned around and walked away in silence.

Ernst saw something shiny in the last rays of the sun. A *dassie's* eye! He picked up his slingshot. Dinner.

He made a fire. They sat huddled together and stared at the friendly sparks dancing above the burning logs.

"Ernst, give me your knife, please."

He took the old Joseph Rogers from his pocket, opened the blade and handed it to her.

She looked for the thorn in her left thumb. Then she used the sharp point of the blade to retrieve the rough, brown fragment.

A drop of blood welled from the tiny wound, hung for a moment from her thumb and then fell to the ground. She raised her thumb to her mouth, but Ernst's face froze.

"Wait! Don't!"

He took her left thumb in his hand and stared in wonder at the copper-red blood in the light of the red and yellow flames. She looked at him.

He compressed her thumb on both sides from where the blood had come. Another drop and another appeared. He held her thumb downwards so that the drops fell to the ground, one next to the other. He let her hand go, took the Joseph Rogers, made a small cut in his left thumb and waited for the blood. When it welled up, he held his thumb above the drops from Regina's thumb, so that his blood dropped onto hers. Regina stared: amazed, quiet, happy. The drops of blood oozed into the ground, mixed, fused and coagulated after a while to a hard, solid crust. Little black ants appeared in search of this new source of protein. Ernst took his bride's left hand and pressed their two cut thumbs together.

"Regina, this country is a land of blood, anger and jealousy; it does not allow you to mess with it, but if you respect it, then it becomes a land of love and mercy. If you live gently and tread lightly, then this land will open its heart to you and hold you close. It is a land that provides for its people. The Namas understood this very well. The Topnaars get their harvest of !narras free every year and that is sufficient for them. Simon Koper's Fransman people got their tsammas every year and that was enough for them. Sometimes you even get a piece of honey cake.

"When I lived in the Karas Mountains, I always had food, even in the desert where it once was a scaly horingsman. This country has always provided for me because I love it. In the mountains it shielded me with its karos and in the desert with its white sheet.

"Other people don't understand this Regina. To them it is only a place to make money out of, to get rich and to consume. But when this country stands up to you, it will hang you the way a Kaiserbird hangs a lizard from a thorn to dry out in the sun. If you scratch its face with your greed, it will let you rot like a dead hasie in the veld. That is what happened to my father, Joseph Luchtenstein. And to Josef Fredericks. And to Adolph Lüderitz. And to the Wandering Jew, Moses Rosenstein. And to all those other fortune hunters who only wanted to enrich themselves, to grab and steal."

Ernst remained silent for a long time, staring at the blood on the ground. Like a dust storm on the plains the doctor's eyes, the glass bottles, the skulls and the words came rushing into his head again.

"Aber er ist doch nur ein Jude..."

Ernst shuddered. His gaze hardened. For the first time he understood. He knew what had actually happened on the island. All the pieces of the puzzle contained in Cornelius's papers fell into place. He understood that the experiments on the island were not only limited to the Khoi people or the Hereros. He himself had almost become the victim of an experiment, just because he was Jewish; "...just a Jew...". He was still alive because someone had spoken up, unlike what happened in the case of the Namas. Somebody, one of the soldiers in a black uniform and boots had stopped the doctor, had had the courage of his convictions to go against the doctor's intentions. Someone had done something, something that had saved his life. The doctor with the grey eyes still wanted to argue: "*Aber er ist doch nur ein Jude...*" but the soldier had resisted him.

Ernst recalled how his arms were loosened, how he wiped his eyes and saw the rows of bottles. He was alive because someone had intervened and spoken up.

Something exploded like a Mauser round in Ernst's spirit.

"I am a dune lark," he said.

"What? What did you say, Ernst?"

"A dune lark. I am like the dune lark, Regina. That's who I am, my wife. I am not a *spekvreter* or a *skaapwagter* or a Kaiserbird or a black eagle. I am a dune lark. This land is my land. Like the dune lark I have no other homeland. This is my only home, the land I love. Jakob Morenga named this place Namibia. It's a good name. Here we are in the heart of Namaland, the home, the fortress of the Namas and of you and me.

Regina prepared a place for them to sleep in one of the little derelict houses and Ernst cut branches to place in the doorway. They ate *dassie* meat and *stokbrood*[134] with honey. They gazed at the stars and the scratched face of the moon...and at each other.

"Regina, have I told you how much I love you?"

"No. Not in the past ten minutes, you haven't. Ernst, I love you. I cannot believe that we are now married."

"When I hid in the Karas Mountains, I sat like this many evenings wishing you were by my side. That was all I still wanted to have, only you. Now I have you, but I am your servant, your willing slave. I could stay here for the rest of my life and eat *dassie* meat if only you were at my side. We can stay here forever, but then we leave behind a world to become just like these ruins. With the money from that diamond we would never have had to work again. We could have gone to live on our own island, mountain or desert, forever, without any care or concern for other people, but that is not what I want or what I want to do.

"Let's go and build a world like the place I knew here: filled with life, joy, a world filled with love and people who laugh. Of people who care for one another, like you and me, of people who care about other people. If you and I don't do it, then it becomes a victory for all who exist to exploit others. You and I cannot live in our own concentration camp, even

---

134 *Stokbrood*: Bread from a dough of water, flour, salt, sugar and baked on a stick over an open fire.

though it might be as luxurious and comfortable as the Kapps Hotel. To cling to yourself and your own little world is to become a slave, a servant of your own greed. We have both learnt what it is to struggle, to be alone, but we have also learnt what it means to have a Gertruida or a Frieda in our lives. Let us go and become the Gertruidas and the Friedas of our world. The Namas say: *A; tarita-i hoa-e / /î gasab di !gā kai re!* That means everyone must become his brother's servant."

Regina took his face into her hands, looked into his eyes shining in the light of the fire.

"Ernst, I love you more than life itself."

"*Sats tita /nam hâs / /khâs khomi ta satsa /nam hâ,*"[135] he whispered.

The two slept in each other's arms, in total peace and harmony with the heartbeat of creation, and with Willie dozing at their feet.

The day's first light shone over the veld. For one last time they looked down from the cliff into the pool in the Bak River below them. Keiser and Leeu stood waiting on the sandy shore. They looked up and whinnied softly. A francolin shrieked its call from the thick shrubs. They could see very far, far into Bechuanaland.

"Come, let's go, Ernst," said Regina after a while.

They clambered down the rock crevice, picked up their saddles and bridles and followed the watercourse of the stream to the deep pool.

Regina whistled. Keiser and Leeu trotted towards her and followed them all the way to the small sandy beach of the Bak River.

"Close your eyes, Ernst. Go and sit there. Don't peek."

"Just promise that you won't run away," he grinned.

He sat on the sand and closed his eyes.

"Alright!" she called. "Open your eyes!" Regina stood at the water. On one side her clothing lay in a pile. All she had on was the Nama necklace Ernst had given her and a broad smile. "Come swim with me, Ernst!"

"Regina, beware. That is the home of Great Snake!"

"*Ach,* Ernst. The Nama snake is dead."

Ernst's frown disappeared. He took off his clothes, followed his wife into the water and held her against him. Then they swam deeper into the pool. Something bumped against him in the water, but he kept on swimming, while in the depths he saw thousands of shining eyes: the soul of Namaland.

---

135 "*Sats tita /nam hâs / /khâs khomi ta satsa /nam hâ*": As you love me, so I love you.

EPILOGUE

Ernst and Regina Luchtenstein, in later years

Ernst and Regina Luchtenstein lived a long and happy life together. He became the wealthiest man in South-West Africa and at one stage owned 500 000 hectares of land. He was never interested in minerals or diamonds. He donated vast amounts of money to individuals and organisations, amongst others the Roman Catholic Church, as well as the Protestant and, obviously, the Jewish churches. They had five children: Therese, Ilse, Bettie, Tudi (Herbert George) and Margaret. Ernst took care of the McKay children for the rest of their lives.

One day, in the autumn of his life, he was sitting in their home in Sea Point, Cape Town, staring at Johann Blatt's painting of Kraaikloof in the Karas Mountains, that he had specially commissioned.

"Regina, can't we just get on an aeroplane and go home?" he asked.
They went.

Ernst passed away in 1972 and Regina some years later.

The Germans could never apprehend Simon Koper. His descendants still live in Botswana. Until that country became independent the Kopers still received their money from the German government via the British.

Ernest Oppenheimer, Doctor Leander Starr Jameson's friend, obtained the diamond rights of the whole of South-West Africa, excluding Kolmanskop, in 1919. He moved Kolmanskop's labour force to Oranjemund. Kolmanskop became a ghost town.

The so-called "Bondelswarts Affair" of 1922 – the final uprising of Jakobus Christiaan and Abraham Morris and their people – was concluded by the Battle of Guruchas with a devastating air attack by the bombers of the South African Air Force the same year. Abraham died in the attack and Jakobus was imprisoned. The League of Nations, the forerunner of the United Nations Organisation, condemned South Africa's harsh actions and insisted on the independence of South-West Africa.

In an office somewhere in Pretoria, there is a thick file marked:
Highly Confidential, Censored
Classified Information: Not for Publication.
Reference: Capt. Tilley, SWA Force.

Cornelius Fredericks and the other victims of Shark Island remain largely forgotten.

References

To the River's End. Lawrence G Green. Howard B Symonds Cape Town: 4th Edition 1950

Lords of the Last Frontier. Lawrence G Green. Howard B Symonds Cape Town: 1952

The Lonely Grave in the Fish River Canyon. CNL van Huyssteen. CUM Books Roodepoort: 1981

Hard soos Kameeldoringhout. Dora Bolz. Protea Boekehuis Pretoria: 2006

Journey across the Thirstland. August Sycholt. John Meinert Pty Ltd Windhoek: 1986

Wars in German-South West. Gregor Woods. In: Man Magnum November: 2007

Die Verhaal van die Trekos. Daan Bosman. Promedia uitgewers Cape Town: 1988

Touleier to millionaire. Sam Davis. The Windhoek Observer p13.

Early days of a SWA pioneer. SWA Jaarboek. p68-69: 1962

"Touleier" on Trek. Ernst Luchtenstein. SWA Jaarboek pp 62-65: 1965

Chronology of Namibian History. Dr Klaus Dierks. www.klausdierks.com

Prisoner of War Camp Aus 1915-1919 Johann Bruwer Namibia Scientific Society Windhoek: 2003

Das hat man im Blut. Auf den Spuren der Nama. Lené Malan & Aneta Shaw Kuiseb-Verlag. Windhoek: 2011

Was hält Euch denn hier fest? Lisa Kuntze SWA Wissenschaftlichen Gesellschaft Windhoek: 1982

Gateway to Adventure. Pat Honeyborne Gamsberg Macmillan (Pty) Ltd Windhoek: 2003

Simon Koper and the Kalahari expedition of 1908. The forgotten story of the final battle of the Nama War and its results. WD Haacke. Journal of the Namibian Scientific Society, Windhoek. Volume 44: 1993/1994

Gouverneure-Administratoren-Präsidenten. Wer repräsentierte und regierte Südwestafrika/Namibia in den 125 Jahren von 1884 bis 2009? Journal of the Namibian Scientific Society, Volume 58 Windhoek: 2010

Auf den Spuren eines legendären Pioniers. Andreas Vogt & Peter Vogt. Journal of the Namibian Scientific Society, Volume 57: Windhoek 2009

Nama-grammatika, J Olpp, adapted by HJ Krüger. Native language bureau of the Department of Bantu Education, Windhoek: 1977.

Völkermord in Deutsch-Südwestafrika. Der Kolonialkrieg (1904-1908) in Namibia und seine Folgen. Jürgen Zimmerer. Joachim Zeller. Ch Links. Berlyn: 2003

The Kaiser's Holocaust. Germany's forgotten genocide and the colonial roots of Nazism. David Olusoga and Casper Erichsen. Faber and Faber, London: 2010

Herero heroes: a socio-political history of the Herero of Namibia, 1890-1923. Jan-Bart Gewald. James Curry publishers, Oxford: 1999

Koekemakranka. Khoi-Khoin-Kultuurgoed en kom-kuier-kos. Renata Coetzee en Volker Miros. LAPA Uitgewers. Pretoria: 2009.

Annerlike Afrikaans. Anton F Prinsloo. Protea Boekhuis. Pretoria: 2009.

Namibia: Genocide and the Second Reich: A film in six parts available on the internet:

http://topdocumentaryfilms.com/namibia-genocide-second-reich/ It documents the genocides in German South-West Africa and how these led to the tragedies of the Second World War.

Der Burenkrieg, W. Vallentin. Band 1, Leipzig: 1903.

ACKNOWLEDGEMENTS

The translation of this book from the original Afrikaans was the result of a combined effort by Leon Swart, Chris Stock, Bill Edmonds, Anita Dreyer, Felicity Horne and myself. Anita and Felicity deserve special thanks. They helped me to create a text that reflects the people, the culture, animals and landscape of Namaland in a true and accurate way.

Memoiree and the late Dickie Strauss of Kiriis-West, district Keetmanshoop. Dickie was the son of Charlotte Luchtenstein, and the first person to tell me about Ernst Luchtenstein.

Margaret and the late Dennis van Rooyen of Somerset-West. Margaret is the youngest daughter of Ernst and Regina Luchtenstein. I remember the many anecdotes she told me and her marvellous cooking.

The late Tudi and Annatjie Luchtenstein of Bethal. Thudi was Ernst's son and Annatjie another splendid cook.

Pastor Izak Fredericks of Windhoek, a direct descendant of the Fredericks family of Bethanien.

Gunter von Schuhmann of the Namibian Scientific Society, Windhoek.

Giel du Toit, photographer from Lüderitz, for loads of information and hours of pleasant conversation.

The Director and staff of the Sam Cohen Museum in Swakopmund.

The Director and staff of the Lüderitz Museum.

The Director and staff of the National Archive, Windhoek.

The Directorate of Survey and Mapping, Windhoek.

Douwleen Bredenhann and the late Hendrik Venter, who gave me a voice and believed in me.

Sarah Batley, Esmé van Zyl and Piet Botha, who read the manuscript, for their valuable input.

Prof. Fransjohan Pretorius, University of Pretoria, for photographs of the Anglo Boer War that were used to illustrate Chapter 12.

Piet Swiegers from Klein Aus Vista for information about the ox wagon routes and an unforgettable night spent in Leopardenschlucht.

And for Ingrid, my taras, for you, only for you, always.

AUTHOR'S NOTES

The late Dicky Strauss, son of Charlotte Luchtenstein, of the farm Kiriis-West, between Aroab and Keetmanshoop, told me in 2007 about the encounter between the Luchtensteins and the Nama commando in the Namib Desert. He erroneously believed that their leader was Simon Koper. Dicky did know though that their leader was captured afterwards and sentenced to death. In this respect he was more or less correct.

Marge (Margaret), the youngest daughter of Ernst and Regina, also knew about the incident but was under the impression that the leader was Hendrik Witbooi.

Later, while I was researching the Nama war, specifically the book *The Lonely Grave in the Fish River Canyon* by C.N.L. van Huyssteen, I realized that the leader was none other than Cornelius Fredericks. The fate of the other Nama leaders has been thoroughly documented.

In an interview Ernst Luchtenstein himself related Fredericks's instruction to Therese: "Madam, kneel before God alone! Not before me!" Pastor Izak Fredericks of Windhoek told me that Cornelius was poisoned on Shark Island. This information formed the spokes of the wheel of truth I put together and retold here.

Old place names are used to illustrate the development and vicissitudes of the characters and the country. Angra Pequena became Lüderitzbucht and eventually Lüderitz after the surrender to the Union forces, and Windhuk was renamed Windhoek.

The experience of solitude and peace when alone, particularly in places like a desert or the Karas Mountains, is given to few, but it has the capacity to enable one to acutely observe, both literally and figuratively, what really matters. This could be the reason Ernst became who he was.

The use of Nama phraseology is intended to remind us that these people were Khoi-Khoin, real people, human beings and not research material or "missing links". They were sheep farmers with a culture that had developed over hundreds of years. To this very day confusion and a misconception still exists among the general public over the difference between the Khoi-Khoin and the Khoi-San, the Bushmen.

The use of Nama-Afrikaans words and phrases was pared down in the English translation, but a few have been retained. Their use is intended to acknowledge the contribution these people have made to Afrikaans. The Namas of Namibia probably constitute the largest group of indigenous Afrikaans speakers in Africa outside the borders of South Africa. Linguists believe that the contribution of the Khoi-Khoin to the language could possibly be traced back to before the landing of Jan Van Riebeeck at Table Bay in 1652.

The focus on the Khoi-Khoin, and particularly the emphasis placed on the "first people," could also be regarded as a footnote on the land claims issue. Are there not in fact good reasons for them to lay claim to land of their own?

I used the German equivalent of certain military ranks in certain instances, especially in the dialogue, because that is the way some of the older folk in Namibia still speak and think.

Most of what happens in the book is historical fact although several incidents in the narrative are romanticized fiction. The actual Schützenhaus Hotel was only built a year after the events described in Chapter 30, but in the story it serves as an interesting point of departure.

There is some uncertainty whether Ernst's two older brothers arrived with him in Lüderitzbucht. For the purpose of the narrative their existence was ignored. One of Joseph Luchtenstein's brothers, Hugo, as well as his wife Hedwig died in the concentration camp Kulmhof at the hands of the Nazis.

Ernst purchased, and paid for, the farm Hariros from his father three times but Joseph conveniently "forgot" each transaction. The quarrelsome old Joseph Luchtenstein lived a considerably longer life than was granted him in the book.

The exact natural historical nature of the sharks of Shark Island is not clear. What we do know is that giant Great White sharks followed the whalers in large numbers. This happened in Durban harbour, then why not also in Lüderitzbucht? There is no certainty that they might acquire a taste for human flesh. One can only hope that such experiments will never be carried out. The name, Shark Island, and the history of this tragic place was too great a temptation for the author to resist.

Today honey guide birds (Family *Indicatoridae*) are not actually seen around Aroab but then in nature nothing is ever static. Distribution maps indicate the presence of small groups in southern Namibia, the Northern Cape and southern Botswana.

Michael Esterhuise, at the time still a young lad, was an eyewitness on 2 January and again on 13 January 1942 to a dragon-like snake with peculiar wings on either side of its head that attacked him on the farm Naute near Kiriis-West and then took flight by jumping from place to place. Sergeant Pat Honeyborne of Keetmanshoop and Mias Strauss, Charlotte Luchtenstein's husband, took photographs of the footprints left by the creature. Similar footprints were later observed in the Namib. The well-known Professor J.L.B. Smith of coelacanth fame also examined the tracks and declared that they could possibly belong to a giant-sized reptile. The water snake occurs fairly generally in Africa mythology.

//Khauxa!nas is a real place, exactly as it is described. The ruins can still be seen today and were "rediscovered" in 1987 by Klaus Dierks. During the Nama war and afterwards the *Schutztruppe* were never able to find the site. The pool in the Bak River does exist and is always filled with water.

The narratives about the journeys through the desert and Ernst's sojourn in the Karas Mountains are generally true, as is the killing of the leopard. The same applies to the story about Thilo von Trotha. Ernst was actually raised by Robert McKay and Gertruida, his Nama wife, at *Paradys* and could speak fluent Nama. The history of the horse girl, Regina, as well as that of her biological and foster parents is accurate. However, she and Ernst got married in Keetmanshoop and not Lüderitzbucht.

Regarding Therese and Cornelius's notes and the small tin with the scraps of paper as well as the thick file marked: *Top Secret – Censor – Classified Information – Not for publication – Ref: Capt. Tilley SWA Forces:* all these bits and pieces are the glue that holds this story and all its many historical facts together. Regrettably, these facts have never been written up and published. Had they been, it is possible that Auschwitz, Dachau and Buchenwald, as well as Fischer's and Hitler's other camps of hell, might never have come into being.

Windhoek's proud statue of the mounted soldier that commemorates the heroic acts of the Schutztruppe and which had stood in front of the Old Fort was removed from its place of honour and today stands on the ground inside the building and away from the public eye.

Glossary

Transportryer (singular) *transportryers* (plural): Generic term for the men involved with operating an ox wagon trek and transporting goods, including drivers and *touleiers*.

Schutztruppe: German. Literally "protecting troops."

Riempies diminutive form of *riem* (singular) or *rieme* (plural): Leather thongs used as binding or stitching material.

Kougoed: Edible plant with stimulating effects.

Klipbok: Nama-Afrikaans for *klipspringer*, a small rock-hopping antelope.

Koekemakranka, agorkies, snotterbelle, suuruitjie, taaibos, soutslaai, bergpruim, veldpatat, kambro, ghaap, borrelgom, slymstok: Edible plants eaten by the Namas.

Taras: Nama word for older women and mothers, used with respect.

!uros: Tortoise shell filled with a mixture of natural products, the Nama version of perfume. The word is also used as a synonym for the initiation school or kraal of young Nama maidens.

Baas: Boss, Afrikaans term for boss, loaded with racial overtones, now considered archaic, patriarchal and politically incorrect.

Riempiesbank: lounge couch made from wood and leather thongs.

Karmenaadjie: Nama-Afrikaans word for a gift of food for the road.

//hob: Nama word for a bag made from an animal skin by dissecting the carcass without major cuts.

Aslêers: Nama-Afrikaans word for bread baked directly on the ash from an open fire.

!narra: Edible desert fruit, also used to make bread.

Suurpap: Porridge with clover leaves added.

Karos: heavy blanket, sometimes made from animal skin.

Buchu: plant with multiple medicinal and some alleged magical purposes.

Bloudak, knietjiesgras and litjiesgras: Grass species of Namaland.

Oorlams: Afrikaans word for Nama people who had accepted the Dutch way of life, implying cleverness

!haru oms: Circular Nama dwellings made from reed mats fitted over wooden slats, suitable for taking down and erecting in another place.

!kom: Typical Nama dish of finely cooked venison or mutton.

Dassie: Afrikaans word for rock hyrax.

Smous: Travelling vendor.

!nabbas: Kalahari truffles, similar to European truffles.

Veldkool, surings, prei: edible plants.

Kaiserbird: literal translation of "*keiservoël*", colloquial Nama-Afrikaans term for the crimson-breasted shrike, a bird with the colours, red and black, of the then German flag. Synonym for "*keiservoël*" is "*Duitse vlag*," German flag.

Horingsman: Nama-Afrikaans word for sidewinder snake, literally meaning *man with horn*.

Spekvreter: Afrikaans term for the chat, *Cercomela* species of birds, literally translated as *eater of lard*.

Skaapwagter/skaapwagtertjie/skaapwagtervoëltjie: Afrikaans term for the wheatear, *Oenanthe* species of birds, literally translated to "shepherd or shepherd bird."

Sonkykergeitjie: sungazing gecko.

Khowesin: Nama clan of Gibeon, under the leadership of the Witbooi dynasty.

Penswater: Fluid from a slaughtered animal's rumen.

Geographic mile: One geographic mile as was used in Germany equals 4,6 English mile or 7,4 kilometer.

Aber er ist doch nur ein Jude: But he is only a Jew.

Wissenschaft ist Weisheit: Science is wisdom.

Hokmeisies: girls of pubescent age undergoing initiation rites.

Leiriem: Leather thong connecting the heads of the two front oxen in a team drawing an ox wagon. It is held by the *touleier*, usually a younger worker, leading in front.

Touleier: Worker with the responsibility of holding the *leiriem*, the thong connecting the leading pair of oxen's heads in the team drawing an ox wagon.

Pronking: peculiar trotting action of springbok showing streak of erect, white fur on its back.

Velskoen/s: Shoe/s made from kudu skin.

Kai tseb ge ne steba. Ne kuri ll aeb ge !gai llaeba. Hoagu !gai-ai ta ge satsa ra /nam. !Khu khoe ta a: Nama song meaning today is a festival. The season is beautiful. I love you above all. I am now rich.

Settees: Slow traditional dance music, possibly of German or English origin.

Totob ge khâi hâ: It is war now.

Nē //gâus !nâ du ra hō khoen ge toroba ‡ gao tama hâ: The people of this house do not want war.

Koekemakranka: Edible plant with a pleasant smell, also used as a term of endearment.

Kleinbasie: diminutive form of *baas*.

Condensors: Desalination plants for fresh water from sea water.

Jukskei or skei: Wooden shaft fitted into the yoke on either side of the ox's neck.

Disselboom (singular) disselbome (plural): Central towing bar, thick and strong, attached to the front of the wagon, can steer to left or right, and affords a traction point to the team of oxen.

Strops, ronge, dwarsboom, langwa: Parts of an ox wagon.

Nē kuri //aeb ge !gâi //aeba: It is a good time.

Trapmesiek: Nama-Afrikaans word for mechanical organ, operated by a separate foot pump for air.

Nama-stap: Folk dance of the Nama people.

Trektou: Afrikaans word for the heavy chain attached to the wagon's *disselboom*, leading between the two rows of oxen, and attached to each of the yokes. In earlier times it consisted of a thick, braided leather thong.

Hauptmann: Captain.

Boesmankers: Namib plant used as fire lighter and candle

Riempiestoel: small folding stool with a seat of riempies.

!Kharakhoen: The Fransman Nama tribe led by Simon Koper.

Tita ge satsa ra tawede: I greet you.

Titats ge ga hui: Help me

Kramme: Rectangular brackets on the underside of the yoke.

Teertrense: Strong leather thongs used to tie the *kramme* to the *trek-ketting*.

Feldwebel: Sergeant.

Die osse trek die wa deur die sand. Dit is warm in die woestyn. Ons trek Keetmanshoop toe. Ek is honger. Ek is dors. My suster is ses jaar oud: The oxen are pulling the wagon through the sand. It is hot in the desert. We are *trekking* to Keetmanshoop. I am hungry. I am thirsty. My sister is six years old.

A da /gore: Let us pray.

Hub, //îb aits mâb ge a !anu: The ground upon which you stand is holy ground.

/gôada: Young children.

!Gâi as ge //gû !hûba //ôbasa: It is good to die for the fatherland.

‡Aonin: The Topnaars, Namas of the Walvis Bay area.

!Gami-#nun: Bondelswarts/Bondels, Nama tribe of the far south.

//ôb hâ: He is dead.

Bankwasser: Literally bank water, a natural collection of rain water on hard ground in the desert.

Teerputs: Small barrel, usually hung below the ox wagon and filled with Stockholm tar, used for smearing working parts of the wagon. When Stockholm tar was unavailable animal fat (lard) was substituted. The *spekvreter* birds were partial to this lard and followed the wagons to scavenge some of it.

Skamel: Steering block attached to the *disselboom* of ox wagon.

Hasie (diminutive) or *haas*: hare or rabbit.

Lunsriem, plural *lunsrieme*: Small *riem* acting as cotter pin to secure wheel on axle.

Hotnot: From Hottentot, a derogatory term, politically incorrect.

Oberst: Colonel

Tsammas: a fruit of the desert.

Leutnant: Lieutenant.

Kort: Afrikaans term for the process of tightening the metal band on the external surface of the wagon wheel. Also meaning short, hence Hendrik Witbooi's nickname.

Karkoer: Afrikaans word for a fruit of the veld.

Wissenschaft ist Weisheit: Science is Wisdom

Tawede, tita ge Cornelius, taritsa?: Evening, I am Cornelius, who are you?

Hoada ge a //ore-gao: We are all sinners.

Die pad is lank en swaar en die mense wag al daar: Phrase from old Afrikaans folksong about life on the *trek* route literally meaning, the road is long and difficult and people are waiting for us.

Gao-aob, tawede: Nama greeting to a senior person.

‡*Au du niga ta ra mîba du*: I say this to you that you must know it (a form of emphasis).

Haaragteros: Right-hind ox, the last ox in the team on the right hand side.

Haarnaasagteros: Second last right-hind ox.

Haar-op-ses: The sixth ox from the front on the right side.

Haaros: right hand ox, as opposed to hotos, left hand side ox.

Vooros: Fore-ox, Voorosse: plural

Hotvooros: Left-fore ox.

//Khauxa!nas: Place name of the ancient fortress city of the Namas, southwest of Aroab.

Boetie: Afrikaans, diminutive form of the word 'brother' as a term of endearment.

Meid: Derogatory racist name for a female.

Strop, singular, *stroppe*, plural: Special leather thongs.

Haar. In the ox wagon context, right.

Hot: In the ox wagon context, left.

Haaragter: Right rearmost position.

Es tut mir leid, Mutter: I am sorry, Mother.

Inspan: Afrikaans order to tether and inspan a team of oxen to the wagon.

Nama-stap: Traditional folk dance of the Namas.

Riel: Another folk dance of the Khoi-Khoin people.

Oom: Afrikaans word for uncle, generally used as a term of respect for an older man.

Buchters: Nickname for the inhabitants of Lüderitzbucht.

Wabrieke: Afrikaans, literally the brake fitted to the rear of an ox wagon, implying grim, unyielding determination.

/Uru te tamats kom hâo: You have not forgotten me.

Skeibrekers: Literally breakers of *jukskeie*, the straight wooden slats fitted to both sides of an ox's head in the yoke. The term indicates a person or animal of wild, untamed disposition.

Cornelius sats ge? Toas go xawe: Hoara ti ûib ge rēba. Cornelius is this you? It is finished. This is my whole life.

Kabeljou: Fish of Namibian coast, erroneously named cob or salmon.

Kierieboud: Nama-Afrikaans for ostrich, literally: "haunch like a walking stick."

Lekker: Afrikaans adjective and adverb with multiple meanings, mainly indicating sweetness, pleasant taste, enjoyment and goodness.

Boertjie: Diminutive form of Boer, used with affection.

Vygie: *Mesembryanthemum* species.

Bittereinder: Afrikaans for soldier who refused to surrender, notably during the Second Anglo-Boer War, 1899-1902

Fransmanne: Equivalent term for *!Kharakoen*, literally meaning Frenchmen, yet with no reference to men of France.

Sakhom ge ra //khā //khā-aob tawede: We greet you, Teacher.

Arahoab: Present day Aranos.

Besembek: Literally "mouth like a broom." A rather rude name referring to an unshaven face.

Oubaas: term referring to master, boss, with the added meaning of an older man.

Knobkierie: Primitive weapon or arm in the form of a walking stick with a thick, blunt end, used for bludgeoning man or beast.

A i tarita-i hoa-e //î-i !gasab di !ga kai re!: May each of us become our brother's servant.

Tawede: Hallo

Sats ge: It is you

Orrabok: A goat ewe whose lamb has died.

Voertsek: Exclamation used for chasing away an animal, usually a dog.

Skerpioenvygies and kankerbossieblomme: Flowers of the Namib Desert

Oumiesies: Common form of address to a white lady by a person of colour, now considered archaic and politically incorrect.

Stokbrood: Bread from a dough of water, flour, salt, sugar and baked on a stick over an open fire.

Sats tita /nam hâs / /khâs khomi ta satsa /nam hâ: As you love me, so I love you.

www.ingramcontent.com/pod-product-compliance
Lightning Source LLC
Chambersburg PA
CBHW050659290626
47170CB00016B/2481